THE
OF DUTY

Siobhan Dunmoore Book 2

Eric Thomson

The Path of Duty
Copyright 2015 Eric Thomson
Third paperback printing February 2021

All rights reserved.
This book, or parts thereof, may not be reproduced in any form without permission.

This is a work of fiction. Names, characters, places and incidents either are the product of the author's imagination or are used fictitiously, and any resemblance to actual persons, living or dead, business establishments, events or locales is entirely coincidental.

Published in Canada
By Sanddiver Books
ISBN: 978-1-512195-27-9

— One —

The insistent thrum of the action stations siren wrenched Commander Siobhan Dunmoore from her slumber with a heart-stopping jolt. For a few panicked seconds, her brain dredged up the horror of the nightmares that still occasionally resurfaced to plague her.

Though the near destruction of the battleship *Victoria Regina* by the Shrehari Commander Brakal was a year in the past, she still felt a keen sense of loss for her captain and friend, as well as for so many of the crew. The urgent pulse of the call to battle on that fateful day endured as one of her darkest memories. She remained particularly vulnerable when her defenses were down, as they were now, her mind hovering between reality and the murky depths of sleep.

She instinctively took a few deep breaths and came to full consciousness, eyes darting around her darkened quarters aboard the missile frigate *Stingray*, the ship she had commanded all these long months mainly spent on the most boring patrol routes, far from the maelstrom of interstellar war.

Almost without thought, she sprang up and pulled on her battledress, not even pausing to do up the tunic as she headed for the bridge deep inside the frigate's hull, dodging crewmembers as they raced to their stations. Unless the first officer had decided to call a drill without informing her, this was the first real call to action in a long time, ever since the heavily damaged ship fled the Cimmeria system after destroying the better part of a Shrehari convoy and fatally damaging Brakal's cruiser.

Though it had been a satisfying revenge for his savaging of *Victoria Regina, Stingray* had suffered enough abuse under Brakal's guns to be relegated to a backwater of the Commonwealth, far from the front lines of the almost six-year-old war against the Shrehari Empire.

The memories of the past and the thoughts of the present crowded each other, fighting for space with the growing excitement at the prospect of action, any sort of action. The Shrehari were hundreds of light years away, and reivers, smugglers, and other unsavory elements were too canny to cross a Navy ship's wide sensor net. Moments later, she was through the door to the bridge.

"Status," Dunmoore demanded as she headed for the command chair.

The officer of the watch, Lieutenant Kowalski, stepped aside and made a signal to the petty officer at the gunnery console.

"We've intercepted a distress signal from the freighter *Nikko Maru*, Black Nova Shipping Line. She's being pursued by a pair of unidentified ships who've forced her out of hyperspace," Kowalski replied in a clipped, precise tone.

At that moment, a three-dimensional tactical schematic appeared on the main screen as 'Banger' Rownes brought up all of the available data. Commander Dunmoore glanced at the newly minted petty officer third class, glad to see that the former gun captain had settled nicely into her new role. Then she quickly scanned the information.

"For once, we're in interception range," a gruff voice commented behind Dunmoore.

She turned and winked at her first officer, who had just stepped onto the bridge, slightly out of breath.

"I think we can get this one, Mister Pushkin."

Dunmoore was not quite smiling, but her crew could feel the excitement of the chase oozing from her every pore. Weeks of futile patrols had redefined tedium as something you would not wish on your worst enemy.

Sub-Lieutenant Sanghvi, the junior navigation officer, piped up, "I have a minimum time jump solution, captain, with emergence one hundred thousand kilometers from projected position."

A jump plot appeared on the screen, and Dunmoore glanced at Pushkin. The first officer nodded in agreement.

"Very well." She pointed at the quartermaster, Petty Officer Takash. "Helm, engage."

The young woman touched her control panel and sent *Stingray* into hyperspace, a transition that triggered the usual jump nausea. When it passed, Siobhan rose from her chair.

"Set the conditions at 'weapons free' Mister Pushkin, and have the crew go to full battle stations when we're five minutes out. We're coming in ready for a fight."

*

Stingray collapsed her hyperspace bubble very close to the plotted position of the *Nikko Maru,* and as the transition nausea wore off, Dunmoore grinned at her sailing master.

"You've really got young Sanghvi doing well, Mister Tours."

Then she turned to Lieutenant Syten, who had joined the crew as the new gunnery officer several months earlier, and raised a questioning eyebrow. The young woman's fingers danced over her console, and a new tactical schematic appeared on the main screen.

"The *Nikko Maru* seems to be adrift. She's not showing any coherent engine emissions. The two ships near her have very high power emissions, but scan as relatively small vessels, no larger than sloops."

"Over-engined and probably over-gunned," the first officer commented, narrowing his hooded eyes at the data on the display. "Seems to me no honest ship goes around wasting that much power."

"Concur, sir," Syten replied. "I can't find a match in our database. I've therefore designated them as Tango One and Tango Two."

"They've spotted us," Petty Officer Rownes called out. "Their power emissions have spiked. We're being painted by targeting sensors."

"I see a shuttle leaving the *Nikko Maru,* heading for Tango Two," she added a moment later.

No sooner had those words left her mouth that the crew of *Stingray* watched in horror as the two tangos opened fire on the defenseless freighter with their plasma guns.

"I have a firing solution," Syten announced, her hand raised above her head.

"Four birds, two per tango," Dunmoore ordered. "Mister Guthren, maintain current acceleration."

"Aye, maintain current acceleration," he replied. Guthren was *Stingray*'s coxswain, the senior enlisted man and Chief of the Ship. Dunmoore trusted him at the helm of the frigate as she trusted no other. He had been her coxswain in the opening days of the war when she had taken command of the auxiliary scout *Don Quixote*.

Faint vibrations coursed through the warship's hull as four antiship missiles erupted from their launchers and sped off toward the targets.

"Sir, they've launched at us," Rownes calmly announced. "Two birds. I read them as Shrehari-built."

Dunmoore frowned as if puzzled.

"Do those ships look Shrehari to anyone?" she asked the bridge at large.

"Sir," Syten ventured, "the ships' emissions are too clean for Shrehari power systems. On the other hand, Shrehari ordnance is probably easier to obtain in the Coalsack badlands."

"Concur," Pushkin said.

"They've come about and are running." Rownes pushed new data on the screen.

"And the *Nikko Maru*?"

"Still there, captain," Syten replied. "Some extra damage to the drive sections, but she still looks relatively intact. Our jamming some birds up the tangos' skirts seems to have saved the freighter from getting wrecked."

The secondary screen showed bright flashes as the point defense guns fired but the action registered only briefly in Dunmoore's mind, as did the disappearance of the two icons representing the raiders' missiles when the plasma bursts vaporized them into atoms. Something bothered her about the weak salvo and the ease with which her gunners had destroyed the enemy birds. Shrehari missiles might not be quite as good as the newest human ones, but they were still very effective, as Dunmoore and the crew of *Stingray* knew only too well. Their last encounter with Shrehari weaponry at Cimmeria had almost spelled the end for the frigate. It had been nothing short of a miracle that they made it home with so few casualties.

"They've opened up on our missiles," Rownes stated. "No hits."

"Powering up jump drives, sir!"

Dunmoore leaned forward in her chair as if she could close the distance with the raiders through sheer force of will. She fought her urge to give orders in preparation for a stern chase. The *Nikko Maru* was now her first responsibility.

"Scan the freighter, Mister Syten."

She caught herself drumming her fingers on her thigh as she watched the distance between *Stingray* and the raiders increase. It would not do to look fidgety, she thought, scolding herself. Manic, unhinged, aggressive, no problems, but captains should never fidget.

"No life signs on board, sir. Engines are severely damaged. Looks like one of the raiders forced her out of hyperspace with a torpedo."

Dunmoore and Pushkin glanced at each other in astonishment. Torpedoes were notoriously hard to fire accurately, were very expensive, and took up way too much space on a ship. They were definitely not something an ordinary pirate carried, but they were the only weapon that could collapse a hyperspace bubble and force a ship back to sublight, where missiles could be used to burn out its shields before plasma guns punched through its hull.

"Either they've killed everyone on board, or they've taken them," Pushkin said, anger and disgust filling his eyes.

"They've jumped on a line straight into the badlands," Rownes reported.

"Very well. Mister Tours, plot a course to overtake them. Perhaps we can teach these pirates a lesson or two in torpedo sniping."

She heard Pushkin clear his throat very softly and turned to look at him, tilting her head.

"Standing Order Fifty-Three, captain."

"Also known as the Pirate Protection Act, Number One?" Her voice suddenly dripped with acid. Everyone hated Standing Order Fifty-Three since it forbade pursuit beyond the recognized limits of Commonwealth space without authorization from a flag officer.

Some maintained that it existed to keep reckless or overly aggressive captains from plunging headlong into parts of space where support would be non-existent and the risk of ambush high. Most, like Dunmoore, thought it was to protect the investments of the rich and well connected. Things could be done in places like the Coalsack badlands that one could never do in the Commonwealth, and the very wealthy tended to have the ear of senators and admirals. Less now, perhaps, after years of stalemated war, but still enough to make Dunmoore seethe when she let herself think about it.

"We'll just see where this goes for the moment, Gregor," she replied, her voice once more under control. No matter what she personally thought about orders from the Admiralty, she had to be careful in front of the crew. They took their cues from her, good or bad.

"The definition of where our recognized sovereignty ends and unclaimed space begins is a tad flexible in this sector. As long as we don't actually enter the Coalsack itself..." She knew she was stretching the point a bit too far. The nebula in question was so deep in unclaimed space that no one would consider it even close to the fringes of the Commonwealth.

"I have a jump solution, sir," the sailing master pointed at a side display.

Dunmoore and Pushkin studied it for a few seconds.

"Excellent. Cox'n, get us oriented and prepare to engage hyperdrives."

In moments, Guthren's deft use of *Stingray*'s attitudinal thrusters had shifted her course and pointed her toward their quarry. Then, jump nausea gripped them as they left normal space again.

"A stern chase is a long chase, Number One." Dunmoore rose from her chair and ran long, bony fingers through graying copper hair as she straightened her slender, almost rangy body. She wore thin black leather gloves, a souvenir from the injuries she sustained when the cruiser *Sala-Ad-Din*, in which she had been the second officer, was destroyed a few years earlier. Her left hand had sustained burns that had almost, but not quite crippled her.

"Shall we repair to my ready room? I have the urge for a cup of coffee."

Pushkin nodded, getting up from his station. He knew his captain well enough by now to understand she did not want to be seen fretting in public. That and her theory about the effects a relaxed and confident command team had on a crew under combat stress. It had been a hard learning experience for the first officer because they had not exactly started out well when Dunmoore took command of the frigate.

It could perhaps have been worse, but Pushkin could not quite see how. *Stingray* had been a disgrace to the Fleet the day Dunmoore had stepped on board, and while the previous captain bore most of the blame, he had his part in bringing the frigate to that state, small as it might have been, and Pushkin never let himself forget it. If he had shown more courage in standing up to Commander Forenza, he might not have lost the respect of the officers and crew. It was something he had fought hard to regain ever since.

"You have the bridge, Mister Kowalski." Dunmoore nodded at the signals officer before turning aft. Pushkin shook off his thoughts of what had been and followed her.

Lieutenant Kathryn Kowalski watched her captain's retreating back thoughtfully as she took the command chair. She had overheard her exchange with Pushkin concerning Standing Order Fifty-Three. Like most spacers, she considered the fetters on the Navy's freedom to pursue as nothing more than political corruption, but it was yet another opinion she kept to herself.

Life since Dunmoore had taken over had without a doubt become more entertaining. Where the late and unlamented Commander Forenza had worked hard to avoid battle, Dunmoore pursued it with relish. Their near-death experience in the Cimmeria system had not dulled her edge and neither, it seemed, had the boredom of patrolling a backwater. The morale of the crew had certainly changed so much for the better that they were not recognizable as the dispirited bunch they had once been.

*

Dunmoore dropped into her chair and put her booted feet up on the desk while Pushkin busied himself at the urn. Her part-time steward and bodyguard was at his primary duty station with the ship's security division under the second officer, Lieutenant Devall, who had been the frigate's gunnery officer until his predecessor suffered the finality of a plasma round, fired by that same steward. It had been a messy death, one that had covered Dunmoore with gore from head to toe, but that was preferable to what Lieutenant Drex had intended for her.

She gently shook her head at the memory of what had transpired during those tense weeks. No wonder the war was stalemated when even junior officers were co-opted by the rot that permeated the Commonwealth's centers of power. She managed to nip off one small part of it while saving *Stingray* and her crew from an ignominious end, but it just continued on elsewhere.

Pushkin drew two mugs of coffee and handed one over to his captain. She preferred it black and made a mock-disgusted face as he stirred in loads of cream and sweetener.

"You know, Gregor, if you wanted a candy bar, you could have asked. I'm sure Vincenzo has some stashed around here."

"I'm not convinced I'd want to raid any stockpile the man has set up for you. It might be more than my life is worth," Pushkin chuckled.

Leading Spacer Vincenzo's loyalty to the captain was almost legendary and had been since the day she extinguished the last vestiges of the bullying that had been all too pervasive under her predecessor. As one of the final victims of the callous brutality on the lower decks, she had taken his word over a petty officer who desperately needed to be stripped of his rank. The Dunmoore Magic, he heard Guthren say after the coxswain had indulged in one too many drinks during shore leave. The non-com in question had lost his stripes, and when the ship made port, his career in the Navy.

Pushkin studied her as he sipped his syrupy drink. She looked less driven than she had when they brought *Stingray* home on a combination of hope, good luck, and hard work, and by the sacrifice of two unlikely heroes. Brakal, the captain of *Tol Vakash*, had almost ended it for them. He was a tough, tenacious, and cunning foe, yet an honorable one as well, a puzzling combination that twisted his prejudices against the alien Shrehari into a mental pretzel.

"Have you put on some weight?" He asked mischievously, the hint of a smile playing on his lips.

"With Vincenzo's insistence on rich Italian food, how could I not. Even Viv Luttrell is happy that I've filled out a bit. She hounded me long enough to eat more."

Pushkin laughed at the mention of *Stingray*'s surgeon. A draftee doctor from a frontier colony, she had a uniquely direct bedside manner.

Dunmoore unconsciously touched her hair. Although she looked less gangly and tired than she had, the strands of gray had multiplied among her copper locks. At thirty-five, she had more lines around her eyes and mouth than any woman who had not spent her career on starships. If it were not for the intensity in her gray eyes and the quickness of her smile, she could have passed for someone much older. Getting a few ships shot out from under you by the Shrehari would do that.

"How long do we keep up the chase?" He finally asked.

"Until it either becomes apparent that we won't close the gap, or we lose them. They're smaller than we are, but their engines are damn near as big as ours, which gives them the edge. Those sloops seem to be very much like my old *Don Quixote* and in her, I could outrun anything short of an aviso delivering the latest secret dispatches from headquarters. If we keep sight of their wake by some miracle, but get too close to the Coalsack, I'd have to break it off anyway. That deep into the badlands, the admiral would have to take notice, and I haven't exactly endeared myself to our new battle group commander." She sighed.

"Rear Admiral Quintana would have turned a blind eye," Siobhan continued. "He preferred aggressive pursuit over regulation fetishism. I'm afraid Admiral Ryn isn't quite cut from the same cloth."

Pushkin grunted in assent. That she could obliquely criticize the new commander of the 39th Battle Group in front of her first officer was ample testament to the trust that had grown between them.

"I haven't made up my mind whether Admiral Ryn is a fetishist or more of a true believer," he replied, weighing his words, "but I have no doubt she'll be scrutinizing our logs the moment we report the pursuit." He grimaced. "And we'll certainly have to fill out all the requisite reports on the salvage of the *Nikko Maru*, lest there's a hint of criticism from the shipping line and from Lloyd's."

Dunmoore groaned theatrically.

"Damn. I hadn't thought of that. Just what I needed: more useless bureaucracy to fill my waking hours."

"It's not like we have much else to do outside of drills, drills, and more drills."

"At least we have this little bit of diversion."

Pushkin looked skeptical. "I don't hold much hope that we'll catch up with them, and there are many uncharted or uninhabited systems in the sector to provide convenient hiding places."

"Indeed. Well, let's see this one out as far as it goes. We're due for a return to port in a few weeks. Perhaps a more interesting tasking will turn up once we've finished our tour out here."

"From your lips to God's ear, captain. I never thought I'd hear myself say it, but I miss the Shrehari. At least they're predictable to a certain extent."

"Unlike our new admiral?" Dunmoore asked with a wicked gleam in her eye.

The first officer snorted as he shook his head in amusement.

"At least she's no Kaleri," he replied. Rear Admiral Kaleri, their battle group commander when they were part of the 31st, had been in large part responsible for *Stingray*'s descent into hell before Dunmoore took command and indirectly responsible for the assassination attempt on Siobhan afterward. Lieutenant Drex had been one of her creatures.

"Hopefully, there was only one of her in the Fleet," Dunmoore said, shaking her head. "Otherwise, this war will never end."

"Considering how prim and proper Ryn appears to be, I doubt she'd be able to breach the slightest regulation, let alone routinely sell naval supplies to the security spooks to top up the family bank accounts, so I think we're safe in our little corner of the Navy."

Pushkin's prediction was to be proven right. After six hours without spotting a wake, it was clear that *Stingray* was not making any headway. Dunmoore had the ship drop back into normal space to take a fix on their quarry and confirm their own position.

The two unidentified ships were no longer visible, be it as a disturbance in the fabric of normal space caused by their hyperspace bubbles, or as an emissions trail from their sublight engines.

Reluctantly, Siobhan ordered the frigate turned back toward her patrol route and the *Nikko Maru*. It was time to see if anything could be salvaged from the abandoned wreck.

She tried hard not to picture bodies torn apart by scatterguns but her imagination left her no peace. When *Stingray* emerged close to the last position of the derelict freighter, she ordered a boarding party made ready.

Lieutenant Devall, as the second officer, would have the dubious pleasure of finding out whether the crew of the freighter had been killed or abducted. She did not know what fate would be preferable. Most humans kidnapped by raiders were never seen again.

— Two —

"If we hadn't witnessed the tail end of the attack with our own eyes," Dunmoore commented softly as she watched the video feed from the boarding party, "I'd have said we have another *Mary Celeste* on our hands."

Pushkin glanced at her questioningly.

"Pre-spaceflight Earth sailing vessel. She was found adrift in the Atlantic Ocean looking for all the world like the crew had just vanished into thin air. The cargo was untouched, the crew's personal effects were still all in their places, it had food, and water for months, and the ship itself was still seaworthy, if showing some evidence of rough use. No one ever found out what happened to the people on board or why they had abandoned the ship."

"We do know what likely happened to the crew of the *Nikko Maru*," Syten offered, "but we don't know why or where they've gone."

"Indeed." Dunmoore nodded absently at the blonde gunnery officer. Earnest to a fault, she would have to break her habit of stating the obvious if she wanted to progress in the Navy. Perhaps Pushkin could have a quiet word again.

Devall and his boarding party had approached the freighter with the usual caution in the face of unknown circumstances, his shuttle making two complete circuits of the wreck's exterior before gingerly locking onto an undamaged docking port. Scans revealed nothing abnormal other than the absence of life and the presence of battle damage. The ship was still pressurized although a small cloud of frozen gasses was slowly forming alongside the worst of the plasma scars.

"Captain," he reported from the bridge compartment after going through the doomed vessel from stem to stern, "there are no dead bodies anywhere unless they've stashed them in the environmental sludge bins. We can't find traces of blood or other organics. That doesn't mean they're not here, but there's no evidence of a gross violation of the human body to be seen, be it by eyeball or scanner."

One of the suited spacers from his party raised her armored gauntlet to attract his attention. She sat at a worn and battered console.

"Sir," Chief Petty Officer Second Class Foste, *Stingray*'s boatswain and second highest ranking non-com after Guthren said, "the ship's data banks have been purged: no navigation charts, no bills of lading or crew manifests. Nothing."

"Had to have been done during the attack," Devall mused. "The cargo hold is full, and all cabins show signs of occupation."

Before he could voice any further thoughts, Petty Officer Rownes, the other non-com in the boarding party, called out with a distinct tone of alarm in her voice.

"Lieutenant, I'm getting a power surge in the weapon system."

"What?" Devall turned toward her.

"The gun capacitors are filling, probably from the batteries, since the reactor's pretty much gone."

"What would cause this?" Chief Foste asked

"More importantly," Devall interjected, "why and for what reason?"

As *Stingray*'s former gunnery officer, he knew more about starship armament than anyone else in his party did, and something was not right. His gut was giving him the subliminal alarm signals he learned to heed a long time ago.

"Okay, everyone," Devall ordered after a few seconds of thought, "back to the shuttle, at the double. What we've learned so far will have to do."

With a sharp wave of his arm, he directed his spacers out of the bridge and into the corridor heading back to the airlock. The last to leave, he had taken a single step out of the compartment when the freighter's gunnery control circuits overloaded with a whine and blew apart, sending shards of metal and plastic flying. Devall felt the impact of the debris on his suit and, after a moment's surprised pause, ran behind the others.

A louder whine filled the air as the forward gun capacitors overloaded. Without warning, they blew up, shaking the wreck. On the bridge of *Stingray,* Dunmoore could see the turrets ejected from their blisters by the force of the explosions as the *Nikko Maru* began to shake itself apart.

The boarding party barely made it to the shuttle when the keel gun turrets vaporized in a flash, breaking the ship's back. For a few tense moments, they struggled to release the docking clamps while the ship's batteries, overloaded in turn by the energy feedback, detonated with enough force to crack the aft hull wide open.

Under Devall's calm leadership, they managed to clear their moorings and accelerate away from the disintegrating freighter without incurring further damage.

"What in the name of the seven gods of Parsatut was *that?*" Foste cursed when the adrenaline rush ebbed, and she understood how close it had been.

She realized that her spacesuit's radio was switched to the open frequency when Dunmoore's voice came on.

"Either a very strange coincidence, chief or a cunning trap. What do you think, Mister Devall?"

The second officer looked lost in thought as his heart slowed back to a more normal tempo, now that the immediate danger had passed. After almost a minute of silence, during which the boxy shuttlecraft slowly approached *Stingray*'s hangar doors, he cleared his throat.

"Every weapon system produced in the Commonwealth has fail-safes to avoid overloading gun capacitors. For several separate capacitors to go critical and blow in very close succession defies belief. No one in his right mind disarms the fail-safes."

"The last explosion was from the engine compartment, likely the batteries themselves," Syten added.

"Aye, that would make sense," Devall nodded, "but only if the flow regulator diodes have been removed. Our chief engineer can confirm this, but all power conduits are protected from backwash by diodes, no matter what they're feeding."

"If it was a trap, what might have triggered it?" Dunmoore asked.

"Chief Foste digging in the data banks would be my guess," the second officer replied. "She's the only one who accessed the ship's systems."

"Could be we tripped a sensor somewhere," Rownes suggested. "Not hard to do."

"It's a possibility, but it takes a lot of forethought to set up a booby trap like that." Devall sounded skeptical.

"So does planting a software trigger," Foste replied. "We caught them on the run, sir. I'd say the chances that they went in with the trap already planned and either the code or the sensor primed, are pretty good."

"Which then begs the question," Dunmoore tapped her fingertips on her chin, lost in thought, "were they targeting us specifically, or did they booby trap the freighter on general principles."

"Even paranoids have enemies," Pushkin reminded her. "Our presence in this part of space isn't exactly a state secret."

"Indeed." She nodded. "Mister Devall, once your party's back on board we'll do a full debriefing in the conference room. I know HQ will want a comprehensive report because as sure as the universe is destined to end with a whimper, the Black Nova Line is going to be screaming mad we didn't rescue the *Nikko Maru*. Dunmoore, out."

She turned to Kowalski.

"Kathryn, run a deep analysis of the telemetry from the boarding party. Let's see if there's something they might have missed. Mister Guthren, take us out to one hundred kilometers. I'd rather not have to dodge wreckage until we get instructions for the disposal of the remains."

"Can't see anything other than being told to turn the large chunks into small chunks," the first officer said, shrugging.

"Perhaps, Gregor but the owners could just as well want to recover parts."

He snorted. "I can't see Black Nova being that hard up, captain. They have a reputation for getting some sweet contracts from various government agencies, including the Navy, and their owners are said to be very well connected."

"True. Nonetheless, until the *Nikko Maru* becomes a hazard to navigation, it's not our decision to make."

Dunmoore frowned as another thought occurred to her.

"Mister Syten, go through our database and see if there are any other reports of pirates, reivers, marauders or whatever, booby trapping a ship they captured and leaving it for some unfortunate salvager or naval crew."

"So you do think we might have been targeted?" Pushkin looked skeptical.

"I ask myself why," she replied, "if I knew a frigate was in the area, I'd take the time to set my prey up for self-destruct. If all I wanted were the people on board, then I'd take them and jump out as fast as possible."

"Perhaps for the same reasons I'd take the time to purge the databanks." The first officer remained unconvinced.

"Indeed, Number One. But what are those reasons?"

*

"Captain, it was eerie," the second officer recounted, "just like that ghost ship story."

He had changed out of his spacesuit and back into battledress before joining the others in the ship's small conference room. A few minor bruises from the explosion were the only physical mementos of his boarding party action.

"The *Mary Celeste*?"

"No, sir." He shook his head slowly. "I can't say I've heard of that one. I was thinking about the story of the abandoned passenger liner that was supposedly found drifting in interstellar space back, oh, a hundred years ago, I guess."

"The *Batavian Princess*," Pushkin said, slowly nodding while his memory dredged up the details. "As I recall that one was debunked as a story told to scare lazy navigators."

"Cargo?" Dunmoore asked, trying to forestall a lengthy debate between the first and second officers. Both were aficionados of historical accounts and would endlessly debate unresolved mysteries if left to their own devices.

"Outwardly, nothing unusual. The cargo hold doors were sealed, and when we entered, we didn't find a single container that looked out of place. I don't know what can be profitable enough to bring back from the Coalsack, but if it warrants the expense of the long haul, you'd think our friendly neighborhood pirates would like some of it."

"Lack of time, I'd say," Pushkin replied.

"Perhaps, sir, but they hadn't even looked at the cargo. If I were a reiver, my first order of business after securing a freighter's crew would be to see what I'd caught. As I said, no one entered the cargo holds. They had the shipper's seals from their last port of call still on them."

Dunmoore looked at her officers, eyes narrowing as she turned Devall's information over in her mind.

"Would it be fair to say, then," she asked, "that whatever the pirates were after was likely human or data?"

Devall nodded. "Or something that they knew wasn't stored in the holds. I can't see anything else being plausible."

"Did the analysis show anything, Kathryn?"

The signals officer shook her head.

"Our first pass showed nothing that we didn't already know. The computer is running additional recursive analyses, but I doubt we'll get any joy."

"So we have no idea how the freighter was set to self-destruct. It could have been on a timer for all we know, rather than triggered by the boarding party."

"Aye, captain," Devall shrugged. "I suppose we could dig through the debris by hand and see what we can find, but for my money, it was triggered via the computer by a given event. Whether it was us opening the airlock, Chief Foste digging in the data banks or PO Rownes looking at the gunnery console cross-eyed, we'll probably never know. All I can tell for sure is that someone took the time to disable the diodes and set the weapons capacitors to blow via feedback from the batteries. That takes engineering know-how and planning."

Dunmoore pursed her lips, eyes boring into the bulkhead as if the answers lay on the other side.

"Let's try this on for size." She looked at her chief engineer, Lieutenant Commander Kutora. "How long do you think it would take to rig the *Nikko Maru* as she was rigged, considering they're evacuating passengers, wiping the databanks and planting a trigger mechanism? Would they have enough time in the interval between when we received the distress call, assuming the reivers boarded soon after, and the time we saw them boost out?"

Kutora scratched his gray beard, eyes narrowed in thought. He had taken Tiner's place during *Stingray*'s refit and was competent enough or Dunmoore would not have kept him. But where the former chief engineer had been a nervous, self-effacing woman, Kutora was a brusque, opinionated, and abrasive man. Somehow, Dunmoore could not see him sacrificing his life for the ship in the way Tiner did, to let them escape the Shrehari assault force in the Cimmeria system. She tried to tell herself she was likely doing him an injustice, but Dunmoore just could not warm to the man as she had to most of the other officers and ratings.

"Well," he finally drawled, "I can't see it happening that fast. Not and be sure the beastie's going to blow. Rigging the capacitors to overload isn't just a matter of entering a few command strings into the computer. You need to send a tech to pull the diodes for each of them, and physically rig the feedback loops to the batteries."

As much as Devall seemed to want to disagree, having never warmed to Kutora either, he nodded.

"I concur, captain."

"Which means the distress signal was sent some time after the *Nikko Maru*'s capture."

"Aye, I can't see it happening any other way."

"Thank you, Mister Kutora. That helps, if only to deepen the mystery. We'll see if Lieutenant Syten finds any similar incidents, but I doubt it. I've never come across pirates, reivers or marauders deliberately setting a trap like that."

"Which, I suppose," Pushkin said, "brings us back to the question of whether we were specifically targeted or were just the first ones on the spot."

"If we were deliberately targeted," Devall replied, "then there's a leak somewhere. Our general patrol area isn't secret, but our daily position and course reports to HQ, are classified. If we'd been at the far end of our chunk of space, someone else might have been first on the spot." He shrugged.

"Or it could just have been addressed to 'any naval vessel, with love, signed Coalsack reiver clan' and not to us in particular." Pushkin sounded fatalistic. "We'll probably never know, but if they sent out the distress call after the capture, as the timings seem to indicate, they were trying to lure someone into a trap, even if it wasn't specifically *Stingray*."

When no one else ventured a new theory, Siobhan rose and nodded at her officers.

"Alright, folks, now I get to finalize the report to HQ. Thanks for the brainstorm."

*

It was four bells in the forenoon watch the next day when the intercom in Dunmoore's ready room chimed.

"Captain, incoming transmission from HQ. I've queued it to your console."

"Finally," she smiled wryly at Pushkin over the chessboard. "The blessed time lag can be just as annoying as it can be a good thing. I truly like having my tactical freedom, but I wish that when I really have to go back to the admiral for orders, it was a bit more instantaneous."

Pushkin snorted.

"You can't have it both ways, skipper. I would suggest that patience with the lag is better than having Admiral Ryn instruct you on what the galley is to serve for supper tonight." He moved his queen. "Check, I believe."

"Who knows? Perhaps those instructions are included in the transmission." She frowned at the board. "Damn. Gregor, am I right to assume that you'll have me mated in three moves?"

"At most, captain," Pushkin smiled. "You're still a bit too impatient."

"Rebuke noted, Number One." She shook her head. Her first officer had turned out to be a superb chess player and had taught her a lot during the long tedious hours patrolling the frontier. While he could not teach her patience, she was gradually making his victories less easily won. She tapped the screen on the edge of her desk and called up the message.

"We're to scuttle the *Nikko Maru*, or at least what's left of it. I think a full battle stations drill with live fire exercise would be appropriate. I'll not waste a missile, so gunnery practice is the order of the day – independent firing by turrets under Lieutenant Syten's control. Young Jeneva can use a bit of freedom to develop her self-confidence."

As she drained her coffee, another thought struck her.

"If I recall correctly, the *Mary Celeste* was also scuttled. Insurance fraud, I believe."

"Do you think...?" Pushkin shook his head. "Nah, it couldn't be."

"Why not? Look at it this way: we're going to atomize the wreck. No forensic investigation is ever going to find the truth after that."

The first officer put the chess pieces back into the velvet-lined box, lost in thought.

"It is just me," he said as he closed the lid, "or is this getting stranger and stranger?"

Dunmoore shrugged.

"It's a big universe. It could all be a simple, honest reiver attack, with no malice aforethought."

The look she gave Pushkin told him that she did not believe it either.

— Three —

"Secure from battle stations, Mister Pushkin, and resume patrol route." Siobhan Dunmoore ordered. "Mister Kowalski, report to HQ that the *Nikko Maru* has been comprehensively destroyed."

"Aye, aye, sir."

"The gunners thoroughly enjoyed it," Lieutenant Syten remarked after placing the ship's weapons back on standby.

"And I enjoyed watching them. You may pipe 'up spirits' for the best gun crew."

"Aye, sir. That would be Leading Spacer Demianova and her second."

"Excellent." Dunmoore watched the smile growing on Petty Officer Rownes' face. She had been Demianova's gun captain until her promotion, and the two of them had survived some harrowing hours locked in their turret during the pursuit at Cimmeria.

"You obviously taught her well, Rownes." The captain nodded, grinning back at the gunner's mate.

"Thank you, sir." The older woman's eyes shone with open pride. Her promotion to petty officer third class had been unexpected but her performance since then had more than justified Dunmoore's confidence. Rownes had been one of the few ratings willing to tell her new captain the truth and thereby help right the wrongs left by Commander Forenza.

Just then, the ship's bell rang eight times, marking the noon hour and Siobhan realized that she was famished. Breakfast, such as it had been, was already long gone.

"I believe you have the watch, Mister Syten."

"I do sir," she replied, rising to take the command chair from Dunmoore.

"I relieve you." Syten formally announced.

"I stand relieved."

Dunmoore quickly dropped her emergency gear off and headed aft toward the wardroom. Though her early days with her officers had been thorny at best, if not downright stormy, she had managed to gain enough of their trust and respect to earn a standing invitation to take her meals and her leisure in the officers' private preserve.

By custom, the captain of a warship could only enter the wardroom when invited. This afforded the officers a modicum of privacy and a place where they could discuss whatever issues they wished, within proper limits, without worrying that their captain would overhear. She limited herself to taking her meals in the wardroom and left them alone the rest of the time. If nothing else, it meant one of the stewards did not have to carry a tray to her quarters three times a day. There was enough work on a frigate already; she did not need to add private catering to the list.

The wardroom attendant was laying out cold food, in a 'make your own sandwich' line as she walked in. During battle stations, he and the cook had their damage control duties, and that meant no hot food for an hour or so until the kitchen was brought back online.

Lieutenant Viv Luttrell, the ship's surgeon, was already there, putting together a thick roast beef on a kaiser. For all that it was vat grown, the meat looked remarkably tasty. She dropped a large glob of horseradish on it before closing the sandwich with the other half of the bun. Then she turned around and smiled.

"Good morning, or rather good afternoon, captain. I gather the drill went well. No broken bones or bruises from incautious crew members to report from sickbay."

Dunmoore smiled back before turning to the buffet table.

"They're getting better at not tripping over themselves in a rush to beat the clock."

"Indeed. It keeps my life rather boring, but it beats the alternative."

Siobhan sat across from the older woman. Luttrell's dark hair had gained a further dusting of gray after Cimmeria, but the laugh lines around her green eyes and her thin-lipped mouth had deepened. She, like most on board, was finding life much more enjoyable of late. The exhilaration of battle rarely balances out the sheer terror of dying messily and quiet patrols suited them fine after years of war.

"Doc," she asked around a mouthful of corned beef on rye, "didn't you used to practice on this frontier?"

"That I did. The last place I lived before they drafted me into the Navy was Ariel Colony. I spent five years there. Before that, I was on Parth for a couple of years. Beautiful places if you like life with a techno-primitive edge, but they forced me to become a hands-on doctor instead of relying on fancy gadgetry to diagnose my patients."

The surgeon's reply was light, relaxed. They had not exactly started out on the right foot the day Siobhan had come aboard. She found her and two other officers gambling in the wardroom, in violation of Navy regulations, looking like they had been wearing the same uniforms for a week. But for all that Luttrell was a draftee, she knew her business and had saved many spacers at Cimmeria, who might otherwise have died from their injuries.

"Ariel is about six light years spinward from our current position, and Parth ten light years in the other direction, which means this is likely the closest to home you've been since you entered the Service."

Luttrell swallowed the last of her sandwich and took a sip of tea.

"Any reason you're skipping down my personal memory lane, sir?"

The captain sat back in her chair, slowly chewing her food and nodded. When she'd cleared her mouth, she said, "I'm trying to figure out why the *Nikko Maru* incident just keeps gnawing at me."

"You're not the only one. I'd say pretty much the entire crew is wondering what the universe is coming to when reivers take the time to booby trap captured ships."

"Glad to see *Stingray*s are wide awake, Doc. Let me ask you this. In all your years in this sector, did you ever get much piracy?"

Luttrell frowned in thought and then shook her head.

"Can't say that we did. Smuggling, absolutely. Pretty much a national sport on the frontier. Customs evasion, obviously. But never any raids on mining colonies in the asteroids or on the main colonies themselves. I don't remember hearing much about piracy."

"No incidents of slave taking then, I gather?"

"Nope, definitely not. Anything like that would have been reported by every news service in existence, and I would have remembered."

"That's what I figured. Slavery is mostly confined to the Shield Cluster, not the Coalsack."

Luttrell's nodded knowingly.

"And so you're wondering why the crew and passengers of the *Nikko Maru* were taken? They didn't struggle much if that's any help to you. I reviewed Devall's scans, and there were no blood traces. Whatever it was, they went quietly enough to avoid violence."

"A couple of scatter guns pointed in your direction have a very calming effect," Siobhan answered dryly.

"I guess they do."

The two finished their meal in companionable silence as the other officers straggled in and made their own sandwiches.

"I suppose I'd better go draft that statement for the shipping underwriters," Dunmoore finally said, rising from the table.

Luttrell laughed at her wry tone.

"Better you than me, skipper."

*

"Captain to the bridge. We have a contact."

Dunmoore put down the pad and rubbed her eyes with the thumb and index of her left hand. The Navy floated on a sea of reports and returns. If someone could find a way to weaponize the Fleet's bureaucracy, the war would end rather swiftly. She doubted her Shrehari counterparts had to deal with this much useless writing, though thankfully, they had their own problems, such as the *Tai Kan*, the governing council's secret police.

"On my way."

Life on patrol had become so ineffably tedious that she had left orders to be called whenever something, anything, happened to break the monotony. Even talk about the *Nikko Maru* incident had dwindled over the intervening days, though her officers had not forgotten it, least of all the second officer.

"Where?" She asked as she stepped onto the bridge.

Devall, who had the watch, touched the screen embedded in the command chair's arm and then stepped out of the way.

"Small vessel, on a direct course from the Coalsack. His hyperspace bubble tripped our sensors. We're only a few light minutes away." He pointed at the tactical schematic on the main screen. "Impossible to tell when he's due to emerge, but most ships try to get a clean fix once they're within our patrol sphere, so I'd venture at most within the next two hours."

Lieutenant Devall, for all that he looked and spoke like an Earth aristocrat, was a competent, knowledgeable officer, not a two-legged adornment for some admiral's salon. He had been an excellent gunnery officer and was doing very well as the second officer. Certainly Dunmoore did not have to worry about Devall trying to kill her, unlike his predecessor.

"What would be the most probable backtrack for this vessel?"

Devall leaned over the gunner's mate of the watch and tapped a few commands into the console. A dotted line appeared on the tactical schematic.

"Assuming he didn't tack any more than necessary, he could be coming from any half dozen systems along this path, right into the Coalsack itself. But I doubt he'd go that far."

"Why?" Dunmoore asked, her tone encouraging the second officer to continue. The remainder of the duty watch looked at Devall with equal interest.

"The vessel's jump bubble is tiny. That means range limitations, unless he carries highly valuable and very small cargo, using most of the space on board for fuel. Not very likely since the sector isn't known for its exports. Also, being small, he's a more tempting target for pirates, and the deeper into the badlands, the riskier. Pirates try to avoid coming near our sphere, and honest traders try to avoid going too deep into pirate territory."

At those words, Dunmoore and everyone else present, including Devall, thought back to the attack on the *Nikko Maru,* which had occurred very close to patrolled space.

"Most of the time they avoid coming near," he corrected himself, voicing the incongruity that had occurred to the others. "The deeper into the badlands, the less civilization per se, and less civilization means fewer markets. I'd say this ship probably didn't go much further than the Psi Caeli system. The one inhabited planet that supports our form of life, Psi Caeli IV, also known as Yotai, is pretty much at the outer edge of what constitutes civilization around here."

Dunmoore applauded gently, a pleased smile on her face. Devall nodded graciously as if it were his just due, at that moment every inch the aristocrat.

"Excellent analysis, lieutenant." She looked around the bridge at the rest of the watch. "Mister Devall will now take questions."

The comment earned her smiles from the crew. How much difference a victory and the better part of a year make, she thought, recalling the sullen silence that had surrounded her during her first weeks on board.

"Sir," the gunner's mate raised his hand, "the contact has emerged."

"Excellent." Dunmoore rubbed her hands in exaggerated anticipation. "Signals, stand by to transmit that we are intercepting for identification and customs inspection. They are to keep their current heading and speed. Navigation, I think a micro jump would get us into real-time communications range."

"Already plotted," Sub-Lieutenant Sanghvi replied, earning a pleased grin from his captain.

"Off we go then. Helm, engage!"

*

"Unidentified ship on my port bow, this is the Commonwealth Navy frigate *Stingray*. Maintain your present velocity and prepare for inspection." Kowalski, who had taken her station on the bridge during the short jump, as had every other member of the Alpha watch, Dunmoore's 'varsity team', repeated the order.

"*Stingray*, this is the trader *Alkris*, Captain Shizuko Reade commanding," a deep, yet feminine voice finally replied. "I acknowledge your orders and am ready to receive your boarding party. I assume you'll be matching my course and speed?"

"You assume correctly, Captain Reade. I note that your vessel is not broadcasting an identification beacon," Dunmoore said.

"Sorry about that, Navy. It's turned off when I pass the limits of your patrol routes. I should have turned it on the moment I dropped out of hyperspace, but I wanted to get a fix first and make sure this was home territory. Then you appeared on top of me, and I didn't know what to think."

Dunmoore and Pushkin exchanged glances. The first officer shrugged.

"Are you a crew of one, captain?"

"Yes. Things always take a little longer when you have to do everything yourself."

"Fair enough. My second officer, Lieutenant Devall, will come across with a boarding party for the customs inspection. Have your manifest, log, and cargo hold ready for examination."

"Will do, Navy. Keep your boarding party small. I don't have much room for visitors, especially if they're in pressure suits or armor."

"Very well. Stand by, then. *Stingray*, out." Dunmoore made a chopping motion and Kowalski cut the connection.

She touched the intercom.

"Second officer, this is the captain."

"Devall here," the answer came back seconds later. The slightly muffled tone indicated that he was already suited up and talking via his helmet radio.

"The target seems legit. Guns didn't get any anomalous readings and her IFF, now that it's been turned on, is registered with Lloyd's, but do take the usual precautions nonetheless. Try to see if you can get some intel from her, but keep it conversational."

"Will do, captain."

"Dunmoore, out. Helm, match velocity with the *Alkris* and position us a kilometer off her starboard side. Guns, keep her covered, but no active targeting for now."

*

Stingray's shuttle clamped onto the trader's airlock with a dull thump. When the light above the hatch turned green, indicating the airlock was pressurized, Devall nodded at Chief Foste. The bosun pulled the hatch open and stepped through. As she did so, the hatch on the freighter slid aside, revealing a small, dark-haired woman with a seamed face and bright black eyes. She wore a comfortable, well-used ship suit and calf-high boots.

"Welcome aboard, Navy," she said as Foste lifted her helmet visor to show her face. Shizuko Reade did not smile, but she seemed relaxed.

"Chief Petty Officer Foste, ma'am," the tall boatswain replied. She gestured behind her, "and that's Lieutenant Devall."

Reade nodded, her eyes taking in the young officer's handsome features.

"Shall we do this?" She asked.

"Ma'am," Devall sketched a salute, "if you could show me a copy of your manifest, bills of lading and show Chief Foste to your cargo hold, we can get you cleared through quickly."

"Of course, lieutenant."

The *Alkris* was a small ship compared to something like the *Nikko Maru*, and the inspection was quick.

"You get lots of shipping hazards out there?" Devall asked idly as he thumbed through the manifest on the pad she handed him.

"The odd ionic storm, I suppose. Navigation can get trickier closer to the nebula, but I don't go in that deep."

"Because of the two-legged hazards?"

She nodded. "Some of that beyond systems like Psi Caeli."

"Your last port of call?"

"Yes. There's no profit in venturing deeper and too many rumors of technobarb pirate nests."

"They sometimes venture closer, though," Devall replied. "We drove off a pair that caught and ultimately destroyed the *Nikko Maru* not long ago. Took everyone off and booby-trapped it."

Reade looked up at Devall with sudden interest in her eyes.

"I didn't know that. I last ran across her off Yotai as she was coming out of the badlands, headed for home. I had just arrived with my inbound cargo." She called up her ship's log and showed it to Devall.

The second officer glanced at the readout.

"You're probably one of the last to see her then, ma'am. By the time we got to her, it was too late."

The merchant captain shivered for a second or two.

"You can never tell when it's your turn, can you? I knew her master from the odd time we were in port together, both in the Commonwealth and out there. He always struck me as a smart, cautious man."

She stared at her log blindly for a few moments.

"If it weren't for the profits, I'd avoid the badlands altogether, but there's precious little for a small operator like me on the safe star lanes. The large shipping lines have the Commonwealth sewn up and did so even before the war. Now it's worse. I can't really afford to wait for convoys because every day at anchor is a drain on my narrow margin. So for me, it's here, away from the war or I might as well sell this old tub and take a third officer's slot on a liner."

"Your ship seems to have the engines to show any reiver a clean pair of heels." Devall tried to sound reassuring

"So long as he doesn't snipe me out of hyperspace."

Devall was about to note that torpedoes were not a pirate's weapon of choice but remembered the damage on the *Nikko Maru*. There was at least one torpedo-equipped pirate out there.

"Did you speak to the *Nikko Maru*'s captain the last time you saw him?"

"We exchanged hails. The usual: how are you, where are you bound, where did you come from?"

"Did he say where was coming from?"

She thought for a few seconds.

"You know, now that I think of it, he was pretty cagey when I asked. There aren't many good ports beyond Yotai, at least none that I know of." She rubbed her cheek as she recalled the encounter. "Another thing: he sounded like he was in a hurry. He didn't even land. Just had the local factor drop off a few containers via shuttle. I'd have thought a couple of hours on the surface of a reasonably safe planet was something the crew would have liked after spending time in the hind end of space."

She crossed her arms tightly and grimaced. "I can't really point at one single thing, but in retrospect everything put together makes the whole affair look pretty damned queer. I wonder whether he wasn't being pursued even then."

Devall looked at her for a few moments and then shrugged.

"I guess we'll never find out." *Or more accurately, Captain Reade will never find out,* he thought. *If I know our Siobhan, she'll gnaw at this even harder than before, and she won't stop until she is satisfied.*

"That'll be all then, ma'am." As he handed her the pad, he had an inspiration. "Say, you wouldn't perchance have some more accurate charts of the Coalsack sector than what the Navy issues? Perhaps something you picked up out there?"

"I can give you a copy of what I use, though how much more accurate than Admiralty charts those are, I couldn't say," she replied, surprised and a little doubtful.

"Foste," he called over his radio, "do we have any trading goods on the shuttle?"

"I think the purser keeps a case of Dordogne cognac stashed away just in case," she replied.

Devall looked questioningly at Reade.

"One bottle is more than enough, lieutenant. I'm alone here and don't drink much, though a splash in my coffee when I'm cruising at FTL would be nice."

"Done," he smiled broadly.

*

The ship's clock sitting alone on a shelf in Dunmoore's quarters softly chimed six bells. She saved the latest report and looked up at the antique timepiece with the silhouette of a gaunt knight on its face. A gift from the crew of her first command, the scout *Don Quixote*, it served as a reminder that she had the tendency to go tilting at windmills, something that did not always end well for her or those around her.

She knew that she should shower and climb into her bunk, now that it was eleven in the evening, but a certain restlessness still stirred within her. The nightmares she suffered after bringing the wrecked battleship *Victoria Regina* home no longer plagued her and her injuries from that fight had long since healed. What dreams she did get were all centered on their near-death experience escaping both Brakal and the Cimmeria Assault Force.

The intercom's chime broke her train of thought.

"Officer of the watch to the captain."

Siobhan reached over and touched the console.

"Dunmoore here, Mister Syten."

"Sir, we've received orders from battle group. We're to head back to base at best speed upon receipt of the transmission. The corvette *Brynjar* is on its way to relieve us."

"Transmit an acknowledgment and pass the word for the sailing master. I'd like us ready to jump within the hour."

Pushkin was already on the bridge when Dunmoore arrived to confirm their course back to Starbase 39 with Lieutenant Tours.

"Calling us home a bit early, aren't they, sir?"

His dark eyes, deeply set in a strong, square face showed healthy skepticism. It was better than the bitterness they had held in the first few weeks of her command. For all that Pushkin had been battered by the unfairness of her predecessor, he had grown into a superior first officer, and she hoped, a friend.

"A tad, yes. I was just reviewing the latest status reports, and by my calculations, we still have at least five to six weeks of fuel on board, on top of the reserve, and other than the brace of missiles expended on the pirates and the ammo on the freighter, the shot lockers are almost full."

"I suppose a few days ashore wouldn't come amiss."

"As long as no one gets into a scrap with the police again," Dunmoore commented with a sardonic grin. High-spirited spacers had a knack for finding trouble after a few drinks.

The coxswain grunted.

"After the last time, I think no one wants to see my face bailing them out. The defaulters are still working off extra duties on the environmental scrubbers. The stench of sludge will stay with them long enough they won't want a taste of ale."

"Captain," the somber, solemn sailing master interrupted, "I have a best time course computed."

"On screen."

She studied the schematic and figures for a few moments then looked at Pushkin.

"Concur, sir. The ionic storm reported between our current position and Beta Volans forces us around one way or the other, and that's all there is to it. It'll add three days to our travel time, but this type of ionic storm has a habit of disrupting hyperspace bubbles in a very nasty way."

The coxswain shuddered theatrically. "Story is the *Ragna* tried to shave a few days off her transit a few years back when they sent her to investigate a reiver attack on Coriolanus, and skirted a storm too closely. They found some debris and not much else."

"A better explanation than telling the universe she was destroyed by space scum," Pushkin replied, half in jest. "Wouldn't be good for the Navy's image."

"All's I know, sir," Guthren replied solemnly, "is that you won't get me to helm the ship into a storm. There's that small matter of liking life."

"Very well then, Mister Tours," Dunmoore cut through the banter. If she let them, Guthren and Pushkin could drag it beyond the sublime and into the ridiculous. Another change for the better, annoying as it could be to the captain at times. Guthren had felt nothing but contempt for the first officer in their early days aboard, but now, she suspected they conspired to tease her.

"Feed it to the helm and let's be heading home."

*

Starbase 39's spindle shape grew on the main viewer, its brilliant white hull contrasting the blues and greens of the planet below. Theta Cerberi III, also known as Isabella Colony, was a lush world and looked very inviting from space. Beneath the natural splendor, however, it resembled more closely the period on Earth known as the Cretaceous than anything else, but the high oxygen and carbon dioxide levels in its atmosphere meant that agriculture flourished, at least where the giant and deadly land creatures could be kept away.

Dunmoore's musings on the ethics of removing native species to feed invaders were interrupted by Kowalski's warning.

"Sir, incoming from the base."

"On speakers."

"*Stingray*, this is Theta Cerberi traffic control. You've been assigned external docking array twelve. You are authorized to approach under your own power. Come to a relative stop no closer than five hundred meters from the docking clamps. We will tractor you in from there."

"*Stingray* understands and acknowledges," Pushkin replied.

"Feel like taking her in, Number One?" Dunmoore rose from her seat and motioned toward it.

"Perhaps Mister Kowalski would like to try her hand at docking the ship," he suggested with a faint smile. "As I recall, last time she took her in, she played with the thrusters a bit more than I would have."

Dunmoore looked at her signals officer, a sardonic glint in her eyes.

"Feel like a little practice?"

Nodding, Kowalski got up from her console and gestured at her petty officer to take over as she took the command chair. If the young woman was nervous or in any way put out by Pushkin's comment, she gave no sign. That too was a change. There was a time where her dislike and contempt for the first officer would have been all too plain on her finely sculpted features.

"Mister Guthren?" The signals officer glanced in surprise at the coxswain as he got up from his helm seat and motioned over one of the quartermasters.

"Sir, I think it would only be right if Petty Officer Takash got a do over too," he answered with a mock-evil smile.

"Very well," she replied, resignation in her voice. Kowalski knew better than to argue with the Chief of the Ship, although she would rather have his deft fingers on the helm. PO Takash was not quite as good a helmsman, but if he did not think she could do it, Guthren would not have passed the controls to her.

Dunmoore and Pushkin watched the exchange from the rear of the bridge with amusement. The captain had taken a long time to get inside Kowalski's head. She was not only smart, she was also one of the most self-aware people Siobhan had ever met.

She had no doubt Kowalski would go far in this Navy, provided she survived the war. That would not be much of a problem if *Stingray* remained in one of the Commonwealth's more boring backwaters.

"Helm, we will do one orbit to shed velocity relative to the station, and approach on thrusters only." Kowalski turned to her signals PO. "Inform traffic control we require clearance for one revolution so we can match the station's orbital period."

"We have clearance," the sailing master announced shortly afterward, as data flowed on his screen. "Feeding to helm."

"I have the trajectory," Takash confirmed.

"Engage." Then, as the station passed by on the port side and receded, she said, "Fire braking and attitudinal thrusters for ten seconds to adjust course ten degrees to port, zee minus five degrees."

"Braking and attitudinal thrusters for ten seconds to adjust course ten degrees to port, zee minus five degrees, aye," Takash replied, fingers tapping her screen.

Dunmoore glanced at Pushkin and saw him study his console intently, forecasting their trajectory based on Kowalski's orders so that he could intervene if she made a mistake. When he felt his captain's eyes on him, he looked up and nodded minutely. So far, so good.

*

The mechanical moorings latched onto the frigate's hull with finality less than an hour later, their sound reverberating through the ship. She was now mated to a long latticework docking arm, one on the lowest of the three tiers of five arms radiating from the station.

"Systems to standby," Pushkin ordered. "Secure from approach stations and go to harbor watch."

"That was properly done, Mister Kowalski," he nodded at her as she got up from the command chair. "And you as well, petty officer," he added turning to the helm. "Any orders, captain?"

"Just the usual harbor watch, Number One. Off duty personnel are allowed the liberty of the station. Until we know how long we'll be here, no trips down to the planet."

"Sir, incoming from starbase control," the signals PO interrupted. "The admiral requests your presence in one hour."

"Acknowledge and advise that I shall be there." She glanced around the bridge. "Perhaps I'll find out why we were called home before we reached the usual turnover time. You have the ship, Number One."

She dropped her voice so only Pushkin could hear.

"I suppose the admiral will expect me in dress blues, so I'd better make sure they're properly pressed and dusted."

"Aye, and get your boots nicely shined," he replied, suppressing a grin. Then, once she had left, he turned to the hundred and one things a good first officer has to take care of when a starship docked.

— Four —

"The admiral will see you now, captain."

Dunmoore lifted her head to see the flag lieutenant pointing toward Ryn's office door. She had been waiting for well on twenty minutes past the appointed hour, sourly reflecting that some people liked to show their power by annoying others. The admiral's aide had treated her with exquisite courtesy, but she could not help feel an undercurrent of disdain in his manners. It was debatable whether he was reflecting the attitudes of the flag officer he served, or whether it was more personal, considering Dunmoore's reputation as the maverick captain of a clapped-out frigate. A shame that Admiral Quintana had taken his aide along to his new posting. She had been a much more pleasant person, who showed her superiors genuine respect.

"Thank you, lieutenant."

Siobhan rose, adjusted her tunic, making sure there were no flecks of lint on the dark fabric and squared her shoulders. Rear Admiral Ryn was not quite a martinet, but she had yet to meet anyone who actually enjoyed serving on ships she had captained.

"Commander Siobhan Dunmoore, captain of *Stingray*," he announced as the door slid open.

She marched into the large, synthwood-paneled office, stopping a regulation three paces in front of the large, ornate desk.

Rear Admiral Ryn, a compact, middle-aged woman who wore her gray hair in a brush cut, was staring out a large porthole at the planet below. After a few moments, she turned to acknowledge Siobhan.

"Commander Dunmoore reporting to the admiral as ordered, sir." Her right hand snapped up in a rigid salute.

Ryn dutifully came to attention and returned the compliment.

"At ease, captain." She motioned toward the unpadded chair in front of the desk. "Do sit and forgive me for the delay. As much as I might not wish to do so, I have to give the governor down below precedence when she calls. I've read your report on the *Nikko Maru* incident, as well as your logs, with keen interest."

Her voice was low, her tone hard, and her manner precise. If she did not present such a rigid persona, she would have been called pedantic, but Siobhan was sure that no one in his or her right mind would even dare express such an opinion.

"I know that I have no need to tell you your failure to intercept the pirates, coupled with your inability to detect the trap that destroyed the ship, has caused a certain amount of displeasure in some quarters, and you're hardly in a position to afford this kind of publicity."

Ryn held up her hand as she saw the furious glint in Dunmoore's eyes, to forestall the outburst that was sure to result from her words.

"Unfair? Perhaps." The admiral began pacing behind her desk, hands clasped in the small of her back. "The Black Nova Shipping Line has submitted a formal complaint to the Admiralty, accusing you of dereliction of duty causing the total loss of their ship, and the abduction of their employees and passengers."

"I trust," Dunmoore said through clenched teeth, "that the Admiralty told them to take a flying leap at a wormhole."

Ryn's laugh sounded more like a bark.

"The conglomerate that owns Black Nova Shipping has some powerful political allies, and the Admiralty would prefer not to have questions about the Navy's ability to protect civilian shipping raised on the Senate floor. What with all the other issues about the conduct of the war making daily fodder for the honorable representatives of the planets, the Navy doesn't need your failure added to them."

"My failure?" The blood drained from Siobhan's face as her features tautened in anger. "You did read my report and the ship's logs?"

"I did." Ryn leaned on her desk, arms rigid, fists clenched and looked carefully at Dunmoore. "It may surprise you, captain, but I once commanded a frigate at the outset of this war and have had my own unsatisfactory encounters with raiders. I hold no blame against you. That you were able to get there fast enough to see them, even shoot at them, is unusual enough these days. I also understand that a stern chase in hyperspace is a chancy thing if you haven't had the time to properly stalk your prey. I may even understand your boarding party missing the booby trap and destroying the freighter. After all, there have been few, if any reports of reivers doing anything more than the usual hit-and-run."

She straightened up again, holding Dunmoore's eyes and acknowledging the anger in them.

"However, that is all beside the point." She laughed humorlessly at Siobhan's expression. "Yes, I know that I'm considered a tyrant with an unnatural fetish for following regulations and using proper procedures. I can see that just by looking at your spotless uniform, more like a cadet's than a captain's."

Her hard smile widened at Dunmoore's surprise.

"I'm not the one lambasting you, captain. I have endorsed your actions in *my* report to the Admiralty. You'll not be surprised when I tell you that my support has had no effect. You may have quietly vanished from sight out here on the Coalsack frontier, but the moment your name came up, some folks demanded an investigation followed by a swift court-martial, presumably with a guilty finding at the end of it. Your part in Admiral Kaleri's downfall still resonates among our betters."

Ryn cocked her head to one side and examined Siobhan, gauging her reaction.

"Yes, captain. If it had been any other officer who had been in command of the ship that found the *Nikko Maru*, we would be talking about the weather or who will win this year's Antares Cup. But since it was you, I was asked to provide your head on a platter via the next available courier."

The admiral paused deliberately, noting how pale Dunmoore had become.

"Naturally, I refused. I told the Admiralty that they could relieve me as well if they intended to relieve you."

Ryn held Siobhan's astonished gaze for a few seconds before laughing with obvious delight.

"Oh dear. I believe I have one of the most outspoken frigate captains in the Fleet at a loss for words. Understand this: you acted entirely within the strictures of my standing orders and in accordance with accepted procedures and doctrine. If your actions are considered to be a failure warranting relief, then as your flag officer commanding, I share that failure. Once I'd communicated this to the Admiralty, it declined to act on the demands for your dismissal."

"Now do you see why I'm such a stickler for rules, Siobhan?" She asked, the softness of her tone surprising Dunmoore.

She nodded. "Yes Admiral, I do understand."

"Good." Ryn slapped the desk hard with her right hand, making a sound like a gunshot. "Finally one of my captains who gets why I'm such a prick. If you had not conformed to my standing orders or had violated procedure, I would have been forced to initiate a hearing into your conduct, and once we're down that road, it can quickly become expedient to transfer you to the worst backwater posting in the Navy to appease your enemies."

"And now, sir?" Dunmoore's voice had regained some of its confident tone. "I can't believe things will be left as they are, not if Black Nova Shipping is out for blood. Although I can't understand why they would want to hound a mere commander. Their loss had to have been insured."

Ryn shrugged.

"Perhaps you have a personal enemy on Black Nova's board of directors or in its executive suite. Be that as it may, I have been ordered to reprimand you."

"That's unfair!" Dunmoore protested.

"Indeed, it is. Please stand, commander, and come to attention."

Siobhan complied, her eyes showing anger as well as puzzlement.

"Commander Dunmoore, you are hereby reprimanded for your actions involving the loss of the freighter *Nikko Maru*. You may sit down."

The admiral reached over and touched her intercom.

"Russ, please get Captain Dunmoore and me a brace of coffees, black, no sugar."

Siobhan stared at Ryn, unable to come to grips with her superior's unexpected words. The flag lieutenant's appearance with two hot mugs stopped her confused thoughts in their tracks as Ryn motioned her over to the more comfortable arrangement around a low table and bade her sit in one of the easy chairs.

"I will record your reprimand in my log so that the Admiralty sees I've obeyed orders, but it won't be added to your personal file."

Dunmoore's eyes widened in shock.

"Isn't that against proper procedure, sir?" She immediately regretted her words, afraid they sounded sarcastic rather than inquisitive.

Ryn snorted.

"Captain, notwithstanding my reputation, I do believe in an officer using her judgment and discretion for the good of the Service where she has leeway. Placing a reprimand on your file would not be for the good of the Service, and I consider that I do have that leeway. But that doesn't mean you're getting off scot-free."

"I thought as much, sir."

"In the interests of demonstrating that you've been given penance, I will have to assign your ship to a task that few, if any captains enjoy."

Dunmoore almost groaned aloud, a look of dread replacing her earlier confusion.

"Yes, captain, you'll be escorting a convoy of merchant vessels to the outer colonies and beyond."

*

"*Yebat*," Pushkin swore in his mother tongue. "Fate's fickle finger has really done it this time."

"Eh," Guthren shrugged philosophically, "it could have been worse. We could have been assigned as picket ship in the Demon system."

"I think by the time we're done, we'll be thinking it'd have been the better alternative," the first officer replied sourly.

The coxswain shuddered theatrically, winking at Dunmoore.

"I can't see the Demon as the better alternative to anything, including getting my eyes gouged out with a butter knife."

Siobhan shook her head in amusement. The system in question, a mercilessly confused jumble of proto-planets, asteroids and assorted debris orbiting the binary star Algol, also known as the Demon Star from its ancient Arabic name, was a navigational nightmare, yet it had some of the richest rare elements deposits known to humanity.

"Be thankful *Stingray* isn't a monitor. Otherwise, I'm sure that thought would have occurred to the admiral," she said.

Siobhan was pacing her ready room, relaying what Rear Admiral Ryn had told her and giving them the gist of their orders.

"I think I would resign if they posted me to a monitor," Pushkin replied.

"Not much of a chance, Gregor, unless you get yourself demoted via the tender joys of a court-martial. Lieutenants command monitors. Over-age lieutenants at that. You don't qualify on either count."

"Thank God." The first officer shook his head ruefully. "So, Admiral Ryn's no ogre? She certainly hides it well."

"Indeed, and I can – we can – thank her for standing up to the nervous nellies at the Admiralty who wanted to throw us to the wolves."

"But convoy escort?"

"Wait until you hear the details before, as the cox'n put it, you gouge your eyes out."

"Very well, captain." He sounded resigned, gloomy even. A first officer's lot on a ship commanding a convoy escort was not a pleasant one, and Siobhan sympathized with Pushkin. But there was no escaping the task.

"We'll be forming the convoy in the Micarat system, with ships headed for Ariel, Parth, Mykonos, and Yotai."

Pushkin's head snapped up.

"Yotai?"

Guthren's amused chuckle sounded like the rumble of a volcano with indigestion, but the first officer's eyes narrowed in suspicion. He looked at his captain, cocking his head.

"It seems, Number One, that Admiral Ryn's response to the complaints from the Admiralty and Black Nova Shipping Line was to institute a convoy system along the Coalsack badlands."

"Ah," the first officer straightened, nodding. "Now I see the glimmer of a hint of logic. But convoy escort beyond our sphere?"

"Why not? Yotai is a common transshipment point for cargoes headed through the Coalsack, and this way, the Admiralty will insulate itself from further accusations of ineptitude on the frontier. Civilian ships that decline to join the convoy will be asked to sign a waiver indemnifying the Fleet."

"Cripes," Guthren was laughing openly, "the lawyers have finally taken over. A waiver! I'm sure Lloyd's will love that."

"Neither the judge-advocate general nor Lloyd's know about this yet."

"Another of Admiral Ryn's brainstorms?"

"Indeed," Dunmoore grinned. "I'd probably enjoy seeing the faces of the Black Nova directors when they hear about this."

"And I'd hate to see how they'll try to twist it back on us," Pushkin replied, his face still all doom and gloom. "Lloyd's aren't going to be pleased either. Underwriting is supposed to be about profit, not speculation."

"Do we know which ships we'll be escorting?" Guthren asked.

Dunmoore shook her head. "No. We get to find out when we make Micarat. The Admiralty has a bit of arm-twisting to do before we can form our convoy."

"We'll be the only escorting ship?"

"No, Gregor. I've been told that we'll have at least a corvette under our command."

"Heh," the coxswain grinned, "you'll be an acting commodore."

"Hardly an honor, Mister Guthren. Since there's no pay raise, no change in rank and no broad pennant, the honor is quite empty of anything other than headaches," Dunmoore replied with a touch of asperity.

"If I recall the procedures correctly," Pushkin frowned, "a two ship escort is pretty much the toughest configuration if you have more than two ships to protect."

"You recall correctly, Gregor. It'll mean the corvette in the lead and us in the rear as the only ship able to run down anyone trying to cut out a freighter."

"Considering the damage we did to that Shrehari convoy last year, just us against three escorts, I'm not feeling the warm and fuzzies." Guthren shook his head.

"I seriously doubt we'll encounter a *Tol* class cruiser or anything else Shrehari in the Coalsack, cox'n, and the reiver clans have yet to field anything larger than a very undersized corvette or attack in packs."

"How about those two that attacked the *Nikko Maru*?" Pushkin countered

"They wouldn't have stood a chance against us if they hadn't run. On the other hand, I hope that they're not discovering the joys of coordinated attacks all of a sudden," Dunmoore mused, abruptly feeling less sanguine about her mission. "Let's see if the admiral shakes more than a corvette loose for us. In the meantime, I think it would be prudent if all officers and chiefs familiarized themselves with convoy escort tactics, techniques, and procedures."

"Indeed," Pushkin nodded. "I'll so direct them. Once they've assimilated the protocols, I think the relevant department heads can come up with their sections of the convoy orders, especially signals."

Dunmoore stopped pacing and looked at her first officer.

"Make it so, Mister Pushkin."

At that moment, the intercom chimed.

"Bridge here, captain, HQ has transmitted our orders," Kowalski announced. "We're to depart for Micarat with all dispatch and once there, take the corvette *Erling* and the sloop *Cyane* under command to form convoy Thirty-Nine-dash-One."

"Thank you. Please have the department heads assemble in the conference room at six bells. Dunmoore, out."

She looked up at her first officer and coxswain.

"Evidently, the admiral isn't making this any harder for us than it has to be. That sloop is going to be very useful, even if she'd likely have the devil of a time standing against a brace of reivers. Now, if you'll excuse me, I need to parse our orders to make sure there are no surprises hidden in the fine print. Stop all leave and recall any crewmembers ashore. I'll see you at six bells."

*

"And there you have it." Dunmoore looked around the room at her assembled department heads. To their credit, none of them had shown any outward signs of annoyance at the unwelcome mission, but she could sense their vague unhappiness. Beyond superficial generalities, Siobhan had not shared much about her conversation with Admiral Ryn, and she realized that her officers probably thought they were being treated unfairly.

"If nothing else, it'll be a change from our routine of the last six months and if you think about it, Admiral Ryn's orders make eminent sense. If our friendly neighborhood reivers are adopting wolf pack tactics, convoying is the only sane alternative."

"Merchants could stay out of the Coalsack instead," the chief engineer muttered, annoyed at the thought that he would be spending many aggravating hours helping freighters tune their drives so they could jump in formation.

"They'll go wherever they can find profits," Devall pointed out. "If we weren't fighting the Shrehari, we'd have enough ships patrolling the sector to keep the reiver clans feeding off each other instead of raiding our commercial fleets."

"Wait until you've dealt with merchant captains, young man," Kutora replied. "We'll all have a lot more gray hairs by the time we're done."

"You have convoy experience?" Dunmoore sounded surprised.

"Nah," Kutora shook his head. "But I was station engineer at Marcastra and had the immense joy of conducting inspections on civilian ships wishing to use the orbital facilities. They can be pleasant enough, I grant you until they see their profit margin shrink even by as little as a cred. Running in convoy will increase transit time and they, or their owners, won't like that. Be prepared for a lot of complaining, captain."

"Noted," she replied dryly, wondering whether the engineer had ever met people he actually liked. It was just as well that they were leaving Cerberi almost immediately. If their last resupply at the station had been any indication, Kutora had the uncanny ability to rub just about anybody the wrong way. She had not enjoyed her conversation with the flag captain after his supply officer complained the last time they were in port.

"I trust we have the essentials on board. We'll be resupplied underway for the balance and a little extra to increase our autonomy. Our orders have us meeting the replenishment ship on the outskirts of the Micarat system. That way at least, we'll be freshly topped up when we corral our charges and chivvy them to their destinations. Are there any questions?"

She turned to Pushkin.

"Have the ship ready to sail at eight bells of the evening watch and arrange for refueling at the Cerberi Thetis station. We may still have enough in the tanks to get us all the way to Yotai, via Micarat and the rest, and back again, but I'd like a good margin for error. Whose turn is it to take us to the fuel pumps this time?"

"That would be Lieutenant Devall, sir," he replied, giving the second officer an ironic smile. "I think the folks there have recovered from our last visit."

Devall affected a wounded look that drew appreciative grins from the others.

"All right, folks. Let's get this show on the road, as it were. Admiral Ryn will appreciate our getting away without dawdling," Dunmoore said, rising from her chair at the head of the table. "She may not be the ogre we've all feared she was, but she still expects us to maintain the highest standards of efficiency, as do I."

— Five —

"Sir," the signals petty officer of the watch raised his hand, eyes fixed on his console.

Lieutenant Devall looked up from the command chair's small screen where he had been once again reviewing the convoy procedures he and the other officers had studiously attempted to memorize over the past week. At least he would be spared the next refueling maneuver, having finally been able to demonstrate his skills to Lieutenant Commander Pushkin's satisfaction, but as the second officer of the convoy 'flagship', he would be responsible for internal security within the entire flotilla and that meant vetting merchant vessel crews for potential reiver plants. He looked forward to the task even less than he had to the refueling exercise but as Pushkin's 'spare', the first officer was loading him with more and more responsibilities to ready him for the next step up the promotion ladder.

"What is it, Pine?"

"A distress signal just came up on the subspace emergency band."

"Put it on."

"It's data only, sir. No voice." He paused. "It just cycled through. Likely automated."

Devall turned his eyes to the main screen and read the words scrolling up. He touched the intercom.

"Bridge to the captain."

"Dunmoore," the reply came within seconds.

"Sir, we're picking up an automated distress beacon from the liner *Stellar Endeavour*, sailing the Micarat-Cerberi route. She's lost her jump drive due to a massive malfunction upon emergence and had to vent her antimatter fuel into space. Her engineering compartments have been breached and have lost pressure. Some crew members are unaccounted for. According to the position she's transmitting, we can be there in one jump," he looked significantly at the junior navigation officer, who held up nine fingers and then flashed all ten fingers once, "of about ninety minutes."

"Have navigation plot the course and pass it to the quartermaster so that we're ready to go," Dunmoore said. "I'm on my way." She paused. "Mister Devall, call up this *Stellar Endeavour* from the registry. Dunmoore out."

By the time she got to the bridge, the projected course was on screen. Devall stepped aside and took the first officer's console.

"The *Stellar Endeavour* is registered to Black Nova Shipping. She's a mixed transport, carrying both passengers and high-value cargo. She has space for two hundred passengers and thirty crewmembers."

Dunmoore frowned at the second officer.

"Black Nova Shipping? Again?"

Devall shrugged.

"They do have the most ships sailing in this sector, sir. Possibly up to half of all tonnage."

"Mister Sanghvi, how close to the position of the *Stellar Endeavour* does your course bring us?"

"Fifty-thousand kilometers, sir. I figured if she's in distress, I'd bring us in as near as was safe."

The captain shook her head once, chewing on her upper lip in thought.

"Let's triple that distance," she finally said.

The second officer glanced at her in surprise.

"Something wrong, sir?"

"A gut feel, Mister Devall. This is our second distress call from a Black Nova vessel within a few weeks, and we all know how the first one went."

"Aye," he replied thoughtfully. "Shall I call battle stations?"

"No." She thought again for a few seconds. "Mister Sanghvi, let's make that five-hundred thousand kilometers, shall we."

"Guns," she turned to Rownes, who had the watch, "when we emerge, bring shields up, and activate targeting sensors. If I don't like what I see when we get there, *then* we'll call battle stations. Alert the ship for jump stations, Mister Devall."

The klaxon sounded three times and then repeated. Dunmoore waited for a count of ten after it died down.

Then she ordered, "Helm, execute."

*

Ninety minutes later, the wrenching burst of emergence nausea passed just as quickly as it came on. Within seconds, the bridge was humming with activity again.

"Shields are up," Lieutenant Syten announced. She, like the rest of the Alpha watch, had taken her post whether they were on duty or not, on the off chance that they would be going into a fight. "Sensors probing."

"I'm getting the same beacon as before," Kowalski reported from her alcove.

"Do we have visual on the *Stellar Endeavour* yet?" Dunmoore asked.

"Zeroing in now, sir," Syten responded. "On screen."

The image of a large, yet sleek freighter appeared, its jump drive nacelles blackened and giving off sparks. A small cloud of frozen gasses hung above its engineering section, just forward of the sublight drive nozzles.

"The IFF checks out, and that's what she looks like in the registry."

"Thank you, Mister Kowalski. Try raising her on the emergency frequencies."

Dunmoore sat back in her chair and rubbed the scar on her cheek, eyes narrowed.

Pushkin cocked his head to one side in question, having recognized her unconscious gesture for what it was.

"Is something wrong, captain?"

"Why are we not getting any audio or video transmissions, Number One? They've seen us emerge right in front of them. There's no lag at this distance."

"No response, sir. Just the beacon repeating on both normal and subspace," Kowalski reported moments later.

Siobhan worked her jaw for a second or two before deciding what she would do.

"Guns, we're going to send a recon drone to take a look at this liner. There's something that bothers me, and I want to figure it out before I get the ship any closer."

"Aye, sir."

"Helm, fifteen degrees to port, then fire braking thrusters. I want to avoid getting any closer for now."

Less than a minute later, they saw the streak of the drone's ion drive as it accelerated away from *Stingray*. Telemetry results started scrolling up one of the side screens almost immediately. After a short burst, the drive shut down and the missile, equipped with a sensor package rather than an explosive warhead, coasted to its target.

"Take it around in a wide circle, Mister Syten," Dunmoore ordered.

The gunnery officer relayed the order to the missile chief.

"Strange," Syten frowned. "I'm picking up the right visual, but the power emissions aren't nearly high enough for a ship of this tonnage, dead hyperdrives notwithstanding. Mass readings are wonky too," she added, a hint of alarm in her voice. "It's almost as if..."

"Bring the drone in close," Dunmoore cut her off. "If that's a decoy, we'll see soon enough. Check for anything else lurking around. Decoys usually mean traps."

"Battle stations, sir?" Pushkin asked.

"Not yet, Number One. If someone wanted to ambush us, they'd either have done it by now, or we're not in their kill zone and at this rate likely won't be."

"Sir, drone telemetry is changing," Syten's voice had acquired a more urgent pitch.

The image of the liner flickered and for a moment, they saw a much smaller craft, almost a box. Then, the drone vanished in a bright flare of light as an antimatter device obliterated it, the decoy, and everything else within thousands of kilometers.

Pushkin was the first to react.

"Guns, all power to bow shields. Helm, keep her steady into the shock wave."

A fraction of a second later, the energy released by the antimatter explosion washed over *Stingray*, bathing her shields with vast amounts of radiation.

Dunmoore swore as the ship shook. Then, it was over.

"What the hell was *that*?" The first officer demanded incredulously.

"A trap, I'd say," Siobhan replied, sounding much calmer than she felt.

"Aimed at us?"

"We seem to have been the closest ship, Mister Pushkin."

"But why?"

Dunmoore smiled cruelly, "I can think of a few reasons off hand, Number One, but then, I have a very active imagination."

She turned to Syten.

"Replay the last few seconds of telemetry and freeze the moment before the explosion."

Kowalski whistled softly as the image appeared on the main screen. It showed a short-range bulk hauler, essentially a huge cargo container with a small sublight drive unit bolted on top.

"An automated ore carrier," Pushkin commented, his voice still a little shaky from the near miss. "A bit far out in interstellar space, isn't it?"

"Indeed. This thing shouldn't have been anywhere outside a star system. I'd venture to say that the cargo container held a magnetic bottle of antimatter fuel and a nuclear warhead for a detonator," Dunmoore replied.

"Thank God we didn't get too close then, captain. What was it that held you at a distance, if I may ask?"

"A feeling of unease in my gut, Number One. Any liner captain who loses his hyperdrives in deep space will be babbling all over the subspace emergency bands and scream at us the moment we emerge. Whoever set this trap thought *Stingray* would come in close enough before anyone figured it out, and we would have if I'd followed normal protocols."

"And you think they, whoever that is, were really after us?"

"Quite possibly. We're the closest Navy vessel, and our heading to Micarat wasn't kept secret, considering the Admiralty is mounting the convoy under our control. Guns, is there anything left for us to analyze, other than the telemetry?"

Syten scrutinized her readout then slowly shook her head.

"Destruction was total, sir. But there is one thing that may be of interest."

She enlarged the image of the hauler in the second before its cargo detonated and zoomed in on the sublight drive nacelle.

"A registration number."

"Excellent. Mister Kowalski, please check the database and see if that registration has a known owner."

"Sir." Her fingers danced over her console, and she nodded triumphantly less than a minute later.

"It's part of a block of numbers that belongs to Black Nova Shipping, but this particular one is listed as having been deactivated three years ago."

"Does the record say why?"

"Apparently it was sold to interests registered on Yotai, but we've got no further information on those interests."

"Shall I prepare a transmission to HQ to report this incident?" Kowalski asked after Dunmoore had digested the information.

"Not yet. I'll let you know when."

She pursed her lips in thought and turned to Pushkin.

"I think we'll delay reporting this for as long as we can. If someone's reading the battle group's mail, I'd rather they didn't find out we escaped this trap until we touch Micarat. Mister Tours, I'd like to find myself on our original course and heading soonest. We're scheduled to meet *Petrel* in a few hours, and it wouldn't do to keep her waiting."

*

"*Stingray*, this is your grocery run calling." The cheerful voice on the subspace radio announced. "Let us know where you sit, and we'll deliver to your doorstep."

Pushkin grinned at the lack of formality. The Fleet replenishment ship *Petrel* had a tedious job, and its crew was entitled to whatever amusement they could find.

"*Petrel*, stand by for our coordinates. I hope you've got fresh ale on board."

"Ale, lettuce and steak, among many other goodies, *Stingray*. Standing by."

The first officer turned to the signals alcove.

"Pine, as soon as navigation has fed you the data, encode it and transmit."

"Aye, sir." He nodded.

It would not do to send the frigate's position in clear, even if the subspace link was theoretically secure. More than just the Shrehari could intercept the Navy's signals. Knowing where a patrol ship was also showed where it was not, something smugglers and other assorted riff-raff would find absolutely fascinating, even if the frigate was a few light minutes short of the Micarat system's outer limit.

"Message away."

"Thanks, *Stingray*. Look for us two-hundred thousand kilometers off your starboard bow."

Pushkin noted with satisfaction that *Petrel* did not transmit a time on target in clear either, something that might allow an enterprising scofflaw enough data to deduce the frigate's approximate location.

"Guns, keep your eyes open for a ship in hyper."

"Sir," Pine said moments later, "encoded from *Petrel*: ninety minutes to arrival."

"There you have it then, guns. Mister Sanghvi, you have the bridge. Pass the word for Mister Rossum to meet me in the shuttle hangar."

Things always became interesting when the ship was preparing to replenish underway. Although the days of the jackstay, a physical connection between supply ship and receiving ship to send over provisions, were long gone, it remained a delicate operation.

*

"Mister Syten," Dunmoore asked, "how many underway replenishment maneuvers have you handled?"

"None, sir," she replied, a touch of nervousness in her tone.

"Then I think it's high time for you to have a go at one. I suggest you review the protocols." She rose from the command chair and indicated that the younger woman should take it. Syten had joined *Stingray* on promotion to her current rank, fresh off a tour as assistant gunnery officer on a cruiser. Quiet and unassuming, she nonetheless had proven steady and competent, even if she did not have Devall's flair.

"If you have any questions, or feel uncertain about any part of the operation, don't hesitate to ask," Dunmoore softly said, pitching her voice low so that only Syten could hear. "I'd rather you looked inexperienced but learning than have to take over myself mid-maneuver."

"Sir, I'm picking up a hyperspace track on the edge of our sensor range, closing with our position," Rownes reported from the gunnery station.

"Acknowledged." Syten raised her head. "Stand by shields and weapons, just in case someone's decided to interrupt our party."

"Aye." Then, "Emergence signature, just under two-hundred thousand kilometers."

"IFF?"

"It's *Petrel*."

"On screen. Signals, please hail them."

The tactical schematic dissolved to show a real-time view of the approaching supply vessel. Like all of its kind, it lacked the sleek lines of a frigate like *Stingray*, but what it lost in elegance, it made up through sheer bulk. From her boxy main hull to her massive hyperdrive nacelles, to her large ion drive nozzles, *Petrel* was not just built to haul, but to outrun what it could not outfight. It also carried three times more defensive weapon arrays than the frigate and could berth a half squadron of fighters in addition to its cargo shuttles.

"Hello, *Stingray*," the same cheerful voice boomed over the loudspeakers. "This is Captain Reed, your friendly neighborhood grocer."

"Dunmoore here, sir," Siobhan replied. *Petrel*'s commanding officer was a post captain, a four-ringer, and outranked her. "It's always a pleasure to meet you out here in the back of beyond."

"We aim to please, *Stingray*. Shall we put our first officers in touch to discuss the transfer operation?"

"By all means, sir." She nodded at Petty Officer Pine. "Open a line to *Petrel* from the shuttle bay." Then she turned her attention to Syten and smiled.

"You're up."

"Aye, sir. Signals, please provide me with a direct connection to *Petrel*'s ship handler."

"You've got it." Pine gave her a thumbs up.

"*Petrel*, this is *Stingray*. We're ready to conform to your maneuvering orders."

"Acknowledged, *Stingray*. Come to a course of three hundred by thirty-five and reduce speed to one-quarter."

"Come to three hundred by thirty-five, reduce speed to one-quarter," Syten confirmed, directing the quartermaster at the helm to implement the order.

Slowly, the frigate turned on a course to match that of the replenishment ship as the braking thrusters fired. Over the next few minutes, the two vessels neared at an unhurried pace, the frigate slowly catching up to *Petrel* until they were within a few kilometers of each other.

"*Stingray*, bear off five degrees to port and cut your speed to one-eighth, nice and gently."

"Five degrees to port and cut to one-eighth, aye," Syten replied, a small bead of sweat forming on her upper lip. "Helm, fire forward starboard maneuvering thrusters for five seconds."

"Forward starboard maneuvering thrusters five seconds, aye," the quartermaster replied, touching the controls.

"Helm, braking thrusters for fifteen seconds."

Dunmoore's mouth twitched as she suppressed a comment. Syten had to learn by herself, and the two ships were far enough apart that she still had room to correct. She saw the realization dawn on Syten's face, not a minute later, as the course projection on the tactical schematic showed she would not bring the ship parallel to *Petrel* at the correct speed. She had fired the braking thrusters too soon after correcting course.

Ears burning, Syten ran her fingers over the console, quickly calculating the correction required. The longer she waited, the closer the ships came to one another, and although *Stingray* was decelerating, it and *Petrel* still moved at a respectable speed.

"Helm, fire forward starboard maneuvering thrusters, three seconds."

This time, she allowed the slight course correction to settle.

"Fire aft thrusters, five seconds."

Dunmoore frowned again. Like any novice, she was overcorrecting her over-corrections. At least they were on the right course now as they approached *Petrel* from behind, but they had increased speed.

Before she could comment, Syten, now red from neckline to scalp in embarrassment, ordered, "Braking thrusters on for three seconds."

Slowly, almost painfully, *Stingray* shed velocity as she came alongside *Petrel*, a bare five hundred meters away. Dunmoore's eyes darted between the starboard view screen and the tactical display, almost holding her breath as the last difference in relative velocities disappeared and stayed at zero.

"Thank you *Stingray*, I confirm that you are in position. Prepare for tractor beams," *Petrel*'s ship handler transmitted.

"Standing by."

Dunmoore sensed, rather than felt the four energy beams tether her ship to *Petrel* in a solid embrace.

"We have positive connection," Syten confirmed, the redness leaving her face.

Dunmoore patted Syten on the shoulder. "Not too bad for a beginner."

"Thank you, sir," she replied, somewhat embarrassed. "I'll try to do better next time."

"I know you will. Overcorrecting is the bane of every ship handler's existence. The only cure is experience."

*

"Hangar deck is depressurized," Chief Foste announced.

"Open doors and extend booms," Pushkin ordered.

"Open doors, aye," the boatswain repeated.

The hangar bay was aft of *Stingray*'s upper superstructure, above her holds, and could carry six standard shuttles in addition to providing enough room for cargo handling. As the doors opened, Pushkin could see the main hull sweeping back toward the sublight drive nozzles, the entire vista framed by the hyperdrive nacelles on each side. Gun blisters broke through the smooth and elegant curvature, disrupting what would otherwise be a bland expanse of non-reflective metal.

Foste extended a thick retractable boom from the deck head of the hangar out through the doors while a matching boom extended from below the opening, just above the main hull. When they were fully extended, a brief flash of energy passed between them.

"The net is operational," she then announced.

Beyond the pressurized windows of the control room, six boatswain's mates in armored space suits were moving anti-grav sleds into place.

"*Petrel*, we're ready to receive."

"Acknowledged, *Stingray*. Firing number one."

A container appeared through *Petrel*'s open port side cargo doors, pushed by a finely tuned tractor beam. It crossed the void between the ships at what, in relative terms, was a snail's pace. When it touched the energy net deployed by *Stingray*, it had practically no momentum left.

Foste extended the manipulator arms from the deck head and pulled the container into the hangar bay while a pair of boatswain's mates positioned a sled beneath it. When it was secure, they threaded their way between the two rows of shuttles toward the portside lift.

In rapid succession, eleven more containers were shifted from *Petrel* to *Stingray* and stowed below, alternating between the port and starboard holds.

"*Stingray*, that was it for provisions. We owe you one missile packet. Unless things have changed since your last report, you don't have any other ammunition or parts requests, correct?"

"Correct, *Petrel*."

"Is your missile bay ready to receive?"

Pushkin looked down at his status board and saw that the gunnery chief was ready and waiting in his compartment on the underside of the ship

"Standing by."

Equally slowly, a missile packet containing four units floated out of *Petrel*'s forward cargo door, carefully guided by a tractor beam aimed at *Stingray*'s keel.

There, manipulator arms snaked through an open, elongated hatch to grasp the long, thick casing, pulling it into the missile bay in the lower superstructure.

"Packet secure," Penzara called, a few minutes later.

"Replenishment complete," *Petrel*'s first officer announced.

Pushkin nodded at Foste.

"Break it down and secure the hangar deck."

"Aye, aye, sir."

*

"Enjoy, *Stingray*. We'll no doubt see you again soon enough."

"No doubt, sir and thank you." Dunmoore motioned at Syten to remain in the command chair.

"All part of the service. Prepare for tractor beam release."

"Ready," the gunnery officer replied.

They felt a subtle change in the ship as the four energy tethers vanished.

"*Stingray*, maintain course and speed while we accelerate."

"Maintaining course and speed, aye."

With a flare of thrusters, the supply vessel pulled ahead of *Stingray*, and then gently arced to starboard, increasing the separation between the ships. Once her tail had cleared the frigate, her sublight drives lit up, and she accelerated away.

Dunmoore watched absently as *Petrel* vanished beyond visual range.

"*Petrel* has jumped," Syten reported, drawing her back to the present.

"And we're alone in our little corner of space again," Dunmoore commented as she got up to leave the bridge to the duty watch. "Resume course to Micarat. It's time to see what we're getting ourselves into."

— Six —

"Scan for traffic."

Dunmoore studied the planet growing on the main view screen. Micarat was one of the outermost member worlds, having barely scraped up to level 3 sustainability shortly before the war. It had no permanent military installation in orbit and only a few small civilian platforms used mostly for transshipment. What defenses Micarat possessed were limited to a few automated satellites and an occasional Navy ship passing through.

"Doesn't look terribly inviting," Pushkin commented as he walked onto the bridge. "I can imagine that all the ice down there didn't do much to help them develop."

"Probably not, Number One," Siobhan replied, "but you have to admire their determination to gain their independence while freezing their butts off year-round."

"If I were them, I'd save every cred I could to buy some terraforming stations and get a thaw going."

"That would quickly flood a lot of the settlements," Tours pointed out in his usual gloomy tone.

"Pack 'em up, move 'em to high ground and stop shivering," Pushkin said with finality, nodding at Syten, who waited for a break in the conversation to report.

"Sir, I read a dozen ships in orbit, including two naval vessels: *Erling* and *Cyane*."

"Ah," Guthren rubbed his hands, "our flotilla is here. Time to break out the broad pennant and let 'em know their commodore's arrived."

Dunmoore shook her head. "Not on this appointment, chief."

"Bah," he grinned, "who's to know?"

"I would."

"You would at that," the big man shook his head. "Shame, though. The pennant would give us a bit more gravitas."

"I doubt the civilian captains would care either way," Pushkin noted. "And the skippers of the two Navy ships wouldn't need one to know who the boss is."

Dunmoore put an end to the discussion before Pushkin and Guthren could launch into another lengthy debate.

"Signals, hail the local space control and get us an orbit assignment. The higher, the better. Then call *Erling* and *Cyane*, give their captains my compliments and invite them to join me on *Stingray* for supper at six bells in the dog watch."

"Face-to-face?" Pushkin looked surprised.

"We're going to be working together for several long weeks, and it's hard to gage a person over a comlink. I'll need to do the same with the civilian captains but that will be on the main station, such as it is, and won't involve a meal at my expense."

"Aye, captain." Pushkin nodded grimly.

*

Alone in her quarters, Siobhan watched the corvette decelerate to match velocities with *Stingray* a few kilometers off the port side. *Erling* was no youngster, her keel having been laid within a few years of the frigate's. She looked like nothing so much as a smaller version of Dunmoore's command: a similar tapered main hull, with a single tier superstructure top and bottom to *Stingray*'s two, and huge hyperdrive nacelles on either side.

As a class, the corvettes were on their way out, replaced by more versatile and better-armed frigates of the latest model. Useful for rear area duties and anti-piracy patrols, corvettes were too vulnerable to the Shrehari. It was fitting that the last of the Type 203 frigates would be sailing with another ship of an almost vanished breed.

A small shuttle broke free of *Erling* and arced toward her larger consort, intending to mate with the frigate at the main port airlock. She watched with interest as the boxy little craft came to a relative stop a hundred meters off, almost precisely level with the ship, and waited for *Stingray* to pull her in with tractor beams. It was a neat piece of boat handling. She nodded approvingly at a display of skill that spoke well of the corvette's captain.

Moments later, the shuttle became part of the frigate, airlock to airlock, and would remain so until the corvette's captain was ready to return to his ship. Dunmoore knew he would be well received by a polished and smartly turned out side party under the second officer's command.

She called up a view of *Stingray*'s starboard side, where a similar evolution was taking place, this time from the sloop *Cyane*.

Though of the same class as her first command, the *Don Quixote*, the sloop was a very different vessel. She had the sleek, dangerous lines of a reiver rather than the utilitarian appearance of the long gone scout ship. A narrow main hull with a single tier upper superstructure and oversized drives, she was clearly a ship that could brave a gravity well and land on planetary bodies. Siobhan knew, from looking her up in the registry, that *Cyane* was, in fact, a prize, captured in the Shield Cluster early in the war and bought into the Service after a refit that included naval systems and armament. In a head-to-head slugging match with another reiver, she would have a reasonable edge, but not so much as to be an effective pirate hunter unless her captain was exceptionally skilled. Some of the reiver clans in the Coalsack produced very dangerous starship commanders.

For all that, *Cyane* would be the fastest and nimblest ship in her little flotilla, able to jump circles around *Stingray*, let alone the merchantmen, and her piratical silhouette might come in handy.

Dunmoore watched the even smaller shuttle from the sloop head for her ship and, with a flourish, align itself to the starboard airlock, waiting for the tractor beams at the regulation one hundred meters distance. The lieutenant commanding the sloop would be given the same honors as the captain of *Erling*, with the side party under the orders of Sub-Lieutenant Sanghvi. No one would be able to accuse her of discourtesy.

Soon enough, the cabin door slid open, and a middle-aged officer in a well-worn battledress stepped in, coming to attention the moment he crossed the threshold.

"Lieutenant Commander Hayden Gulsvig, commanding *Erling*, sir." He saluted crisply, holding his hand to his brow until Siobhan had returned the gesture.

She extended her hand to Gulsvig after the man relaxed.

"Siobhan Dunmoore, captain. Pleased to meet you."

The two officers examined each other intensely, liking what they saw. Gulsvig was at least ten years older than Dunmoore and his craggy face bore the seams and scars to prove it. His iron gray hair was close-cropped, showing a scalp tanned by years of radiation in deep space. Siobhan especially liked the way his washed-out eyes held hers without embarrassment.

"I've heard a lot about you, sir."

"Then you'll have an idea of how I operate."

"Aye, that I do."

She waved him to the small table Vincenzo had set for supper.

"Have a seat, captain. The skipper of *Cyane* will be along shortly."

She noticed the merest tightening of Gulsvig's eyes at the name of the sloop and fought to repress her curiosity. This was not the time to ask personal questions.

"I gather from your file that you're not a career naval man."

"You gather right, sir. I spent twenty years working deep space liners, ten of them as captain. When the war broke out, I was called up from the reserve along with my ship. Thanks to the expansion of the Fleet, I quickly found myself transferred to command *Erling* after my liner was wrecked in the botched attempt at sending a relief force to Antae Carina. We were carrying part of the landing force." He shook his head at the memory. "The loss of life on that operation will stay with me until the day I die. I've had *Erling* for almost four years now."

"Going to go back the merchant service after the war?"

Before Gulsvig could reply, the door chime interrupted the conversation, and Dunmoore excused herself, turning to greet the next arrival.

The woman who stepped in and came to attention was a complete opposite to Lieutenant Commander Gulsvig. Where he was tall and thin, she was short and muscular, almost plump even; where the older man was seamed and gray, she had short platinum blonde hair framing a smooth, youthful face. Her dark blue eyes briefly met Siobhan's as she saluted, then darted around the room, taking everything in.

"Lieutenant Terica Stoyer, commanding the sloop *Cyane*, is reporting to the commodore as ordered." Her voice was surprisingly high for her compact size.

"At ease, lieutenant. Although we may be a flotilla, I've not hoisted the broad pennant, so I remain a captain."

Siobhan fought to restrain a smile at the young woman's all too evident eagerness to please. Her appearance, from the fashionable hairstyle to the well-tailored battledress that molded her shape admirably, was far removed from what Siobhan had expected of someone commanding a sloop that had started life raiding the human frontier.

Stoyer's handshake, when it came, was firm but she did not subject Siobhan to the kind of examination she got from the other captain. Try as she might, Dunmoore could not hold the lieutenant's eyes for more than a few seconds at a time. Whether this meant anything or was the result of youthful nerves was a question for another time.

Gulsvig politely greeted Stoyer, but their handshake was perfunctory. Neither seemed to be overjoyed at seeing the other, which was passing strange. Out on the edges of the Commonwealth, spending some time with Navy officers from other ships was always to be welcomed as a pleasant distraction from living with the same people in confined quarters for months at a time.

"Do you know each other?" She asked.

Gulsvig nodded curtly. "Aye, sir. Captain Stoyer and I have worked together before."

Dunmoore noticed that the older man had given Stoyer her title as commanding officer of a starship and nodded approvingly. Whatever dislike there was between them, it did not seem to extend to dropping the usual courtesies.

"Please sit. I think we'll take our supper first and then talk about the weeks ahead. All we're lacking is my first officer." She paused as the chime rang for the third time. "And here he is."

Dunmoore was not prepared for the reaction when Pushkin stepped in.

"Gregor!" Stoyer jumped up from her chair, a broad smile on her face.

Pushkin's disapproving frown materialized almost instantly, stopping her in her tracks. Before anything else could be said, Dunmoore took over.

"Gregor, this is Captain Hayden Gulsvig of *Erling*. Captain, my first officer, Gregor Pushkin."

The two men shook hands, testing each other.

"Pleased to meet you, captain."

"Likewise, commander."

"And this is Lieutenant Terica Stoyer, of *Cyane*. But then, you're clearly acquainted."

"Aye," Pushkin replied, turning toward Stoyer, a guarded look in his eyes. "We served together a few years ago. How are you, Terica?"

"I'm well, sir." Stoyer beamed.

Dunmoore met her first officer's eyes with a look that promised she would be questioning him later. He nodded minutely in understanding.

When they were seated at the small table, Siobhan reached over to the intercom console and signaled her steward.

As if he had been waiting in the corridor, Leading Spacer Vincenzo, boatswain's mate and part-time captain's steward appeared through the door, a white cloth draped over his left forearm and a green-tinted bottle of wine in his right hand.

"I've laid in some Dordogne burgundy for special occasions," Dunmoore said, smiling. "It's a surprisingly good vintage considering it didn't cost all that much."

"Huh," Gulsvig grunted approvingly, "there are a lot of underappreciated vineyards on Dordogne if you want my opinion, and that one," he squinted at the label as Vincenzo poured, "is one of the most underappreciated I can think of."

"You're a wine connoisseur, Captain?"

"One learns to become an expert, or at least fake it, on a deep space liner. Passengers, especially the ones in first-class cabins, love to eat at the captain's table and be entertained in high style. You could say wine snobbery is a professional skill."

Dunmoore smiled at his wry tone. She felt that she could learn to like the older man.

"Well then," she raised her glass, "this may not be the captain's table on a posh liner, but I think *Stingray* can do just as well. Your health."

"Your health," the others replied before taking an appreciative sip.

Gulsvig smacked his lips approvingly.

"An exceptional vintage, that. Pity it doesn't ship out here. We don't get many chances to head inwards for resupply."

"Perhaps I can bring you back a case, captain," Stoyer offered, though there was a faint but surprising undercurrent of malice in her tone. "*Cyane* gets more chances at returning to civilization than most patrol ships."

Gulsvig shrugged and replied in a carefully studied tone. "No need to put yourself out for me, captain."

Fearing the beginning of an open dispute, Dunmoore nodded at Vincenzo who stuck his head out the door and called on the wardroom stewards to bring in the first course.

"If you've been short of fresh food, I think you'll enjoy the meal even more. We've taken replenishment on our way here."

"I appreciate that, captain," Gulsvig nodded, "but we get fresh stuff from down there." He pointed his thumb over his shoulder toward the planet slowly rotating on the cabin's screen. "It's not bad for all that it's grown in the shadow of the glaciers."

"Ah," Dunmoore beamed as two stewards, each bearing a covered tray, filled what little space was left in her quarters. "That smells wonderful. What has the chef prepared, Vincenzo?"

The leading spacer grinned, revealing white teeth beneath his bushy black mustache.

"For an appetizer, bison carpaccio with parmesan cheese." He uncovered one of the trays with a flourish and placed a plate in front of each officer. "The main dish is chicken Napolitano, gnocchi, garlic green beans and a garden salad with Genji berry dressing. For dessert, tarte tatin flambéed."

Gulsvig nodded his approval as he savored the first slice of raw bison soaked in a delicate olive oil coulis.

"I suppose you dine like this every day," he commented in jest after washing down the meat with a healthy sip of wine.

"I wish," Dunmoore smiled. "I think the lower deck galley is serving the bison a bit more cooked and with a thick sauce. Leader Spacer Vincenzo is a bit of a kitchen artist, and he sometimes encourages the cooks to try some variations from the usual menu."

Throughout the meal, Siobhan kept the conversation on safe ground, avoiding talk of the mission and politics, which left the conduct of the war and the latest Fleet gossip. She caught Stoyer looking at Pushkin several times though the first officer remained detached almost to the point of ignoring her. An undercurrent of malice toward Gulsvig surfaced a few times, most notably in a rather unkind comment on the age of *Erling* and her captain. Dunmoore was intrigued at what it was that made Stoyer dislike the older man so much that she dared show it in front of her new commanding officer.

Gulsvig, for his part, let Stoyer's comments pass without seeming to pay much attention. His courteous manners remained unchanged.

When the last bite was eaten, and Vincenzo had removed the plates before serving coffee, Dunmoore judged it was time to discuss business.

"Do either of you have convoy experience?"

"No, captain," Gulsvig shook his head. "I've never had the pleasure. But I do know some of the villains we're about to escort, from my days in the merchant service."

"How about you, Terica?"

"None, sir. I've been used to sailing solo on my patrol routes, doing the occasional customs inspection. I've nowhere near the knowledge of traders that Lieutenant Commander Gulsvig has." She managed to make that last comment sound just dismissive enough to notice but not enough to call her on it.

"That makes three of us, then. I trust you've both reviewed the protocols. Otherwise, the next half hour isn't going to make much sense to you, and I'll have to go through it again tomorrow."

"Aye," Gulsvig nodded. "Read them front to back and vice-versa, twice."

She looked questioningly at Stoyer.

"I did." There was a note of discomfort in her voice as if she had skimmed the manual quickly just so it was not quite a lie.

"Very well."

Dunmoore launched into an animated discussion of how she proposed to organize and manage the convoy. Gulsvig and Pushkin contributed some good suggestions to account for some of the particularities they would encounter with the merchant captains in their charge, mostly based on the former's experience. Stoyer however, said little, confirming Dunmoore's suspicion that she had not given much attention to the matter.

"If we're all agreed, I'll be issuing my standing orders to the escorts by the end of the day tomorrow," she concluded. "That leads me to the next subject: our charges."

"If you'll allow me, sir," Pushkin said pulling a pad from his pocket, "I downloaded the latest list before supper. They're not all here yet, though."

"If the latecomers tarry too much," Gulsvig noted with a grimace, "you'll be hearing from those sitting in the orbital merry-go-round."

"Aye," the first officer nodded. "We've already had two complaints lodged with the signals officer."

"They're just testing you. I'll bet the first complaint came from Hoan Kiles of *Jade Delight*."

Pushkin chuckled. "How did you know?"

"He's been shouting at me since I arrived two days ago. It's a wonder he hasn't given himself a heart attack yet, what with him being constantly choleric." Gulsvig shook his head. "Bastard probably doesn't have a natural heart anymore."

"Aye. As Hayden said, we have the *Jade Delight*, bulk freighter from Jade Shipping and Commerce Company, under Hoan Kiles. We have the *Zebulon*, mixed passenger and freight, Xindu Transportation Limited, under Rego Minnau, the *Antares Loch*, freighter, Banff Shipping, under Lana Janrenk and the *Pride of Pallas*, passenger liner, Palladian Lines, under Garan Bane. Those are the ones in orbit. Two more are expected, and you'll love this, captain." Pushkin grinned mirthlessly.

"We're waiting for the *Fuso Maru* and the *Oko Maru*, freighters of Black Nova Shipping. The first is under Cadan Strazi, the other under Shao Lian."

"Black Nova Shipping," Dunmoore tapped her lips with her gloved index finger, lost in thought.

"You know them, captain?" Gulsvig asked.

"You might say that," she replied. "I'm sure you'll find this interesting." Siobhan recounted the incident with the *Nikko Maru* and the trap they narrowly escaped a few days earlier.

Stoyer seemed more stunned than Gulsvig, who contented himself with a soft whistle.

"I find it hard to believe that Black Nova would attempt an attack on a Navy ship, sir," she said hotly.

"Based on what?" Pushkin asked in a rather abrupt tone.

"My family's best friends own Black Nova. I can vouch for their honesty."

Ah-ha! Dunmoore smiled to herself. *Now we're getting somewhere.*

"You're from Pacifica, lieutenant?"

"I am, sir. Born and bred," she replied proudly.

"I do not doubt that the owners of the Black Nova Line are honest people. They may not always have honest people working for them, as is the case for virtually any organization, including our dear Navy."

"Yes, sir." Stoyer sounded contrite, even though it rang false.

"You've got it right, captain," Gulsvig was nodding. "I know Cadan Strazi from way back, and he's always got something going on to pad his pockets. I'm not saying he's a villain, but he'll not turn his nose on a chance to make money provided it doesn't come to the attention of his employers."

"Slippery customer?" Pushkin asked.

"Like an eel, Gregor. When you shake his hand, count your fingers afterward. Sir," he turned to Siobhan, "I hope you're not planning on inviting the merchant captains to dine here."

"No fears, Hayden. I'm as leery as you are of letting outsiders on board, honest or otherwise. I intend to call a meeting on the station once the laggards are in orbit."

Pushkin's pad beeped and he glanced down, frowning.

"We have a last minute addition: the trader *Alkris*, under Shizuko Reade."

"Well, well, the plot thickens." Dunmoore's finger traced her scar down to the jaw line.

"You're acquainted with her?"

"Aye." Pushkin nodded. "We intercepted her coming out of the Coalsack not long after we scuttled the remains of the *Nikko Maru*. Her captain was probably the last one to see them when the two ships passed each other in the Yotai system."

"Why would a small trader like that want to join a convoy?" Siobhan sounded dubious.

"Pressure from the Navy? Scared? Could be any number of reasons that weigh heavier than fast profits," Gulsvig replied. "Though I'll grant you that it's unusual for a single-hander like that to tie itself to the aprons strings of a flotilla."

"Seven merchants and three escorts," Siobhan mused, "ten ships. A nice round number."

"Seven wellsprings of trouble, if you ask me."

"I hope not, Hayden, I sincerely hope not."

Dunmoore felt less than reassured. First her chief engineer and now a fellow starship captain with experience in the merchant service. Somehow, the idea of a board of inquiry into the loss of the *Nikko Maru* as punishment instead of this mission was beginning to seem very appealing. She had survived the former before. The latter might just be more than she wanted to face.

*

Much later that night over a snifter of cognac, long after Gulsvig and Stoyer had left, piped off the ship by the same smartly turned out side parties, she finally asked Pushkin the question that had been sitting in the back of her mind all through supper.

"Gregor, what's your past relationship with Terica Stoyer? She seemed thrilled at seeing you. Your reaction, on the other hand, wasn't nearly as pleased."

He sighed deeply, eyes staring at the deck, glass held loosely in his hand.

"Terica was a mistake I made years ago."

"I somehow gathered that you might not have left each other on the best of terms."

"That would be an understatement. Which begs the question of why she seemed so happy to see me?"

Siobhan grimaced.

"I don't have a prurient interest in your relationship with Stoyer, but I am interested in anything that can affect this mission. Potential problems between the convoy flagship's first officer and one of the escort captains are my business."

"I understand that, sir." He sounded resigned. Shrugging off the old, deeply seated embarrassment of a failed relationship, he opened up to his captain. "Terica and I were on the operations staff at the headquarters of Fourth Fleet during the first year of the war. I was an over-aged lieutenant and she a freshly promoted sub-lieutenant just off her first tour aboard a ship. I thought I'd take her under my wing and teach her the ropes, seeing as how I'd been there for almost two years. She mistook my friendliness for romantic attraction, and I was dumb enough let myself get roped into a relationship."

He snorted in mock derision at himself. "I was flattered that a young, attractive woman from a wealthy family wanted me. It was rocky from the start. She wanted more than I was able or willing to give. I'd never before experienced someone who was that starved for affection. I guess it's true when they say that money can't buy you love. I finally broke it off after discovering that she'd been using the station's security systems to keep track of me when we weren't together."

"Really?" Siobhan's eyebrows shot up in astonishment. "She committed that gross a violation of privacy and yet here she is, a starship captain?"

"I never reported it."

"Why not?"

"I guess I felt sorry for her." Pushkin shook his head. "Another mistake, I suppose."

"What happened when you ended the relationship?"

"She went bonkers. Totally off the deep end: threatened to kill me, commit suicide, the works. I requested a transfer away from the station immediately, but that meant I also had to advise my superiors of the relationship. In the interests of keeping the problem from escalating, they had me on a transport the next day, headed for Third Fleet HQ with a notation on my file that I was being transferred as a result of demonstrating a lack of judgment. It delayed my promotion to lieutenant commander by at least two years."

"Do you think her family connections played a part in how it was handled?"

Pushkin laughed bitterly.

"No question about it. Had she not been a scion of the Pacifica Stoyers, she would have been the one shipped off, not me. Sure, I showed a lack of judgment by entering into a sexual relationship with an officer junior in rank to me, but that's hardly a court-martial offense seeing as how I wasn't her supervisor."

"And here she is, in command of a sloop, making moon-calf eyes at you."

"I'm not sure whether I should be glad that she's not carrying a grudge, or frightened. Perhaps she's matured."

"Or she's received some psychiatric treatment. Sane people don't violate the regulations so they can stalk their lovers, or threaten them with murder."

"Perhaps it wasn't so much a question of sanity, captain, as one of entitlement. I was probably the first man who pushed her away and she had no way of dealing with it. Growing up as she did, Terica could have anything she wanted."

"And when she couldn't have you..."

"Yeah, but that still doesn't explain how happy she was to see me five years later."

"No, it doesn't. Did you notice that Hayden seems to dislike her?"

"I got that sense, captain. It does show that he has good taste. I can only assume that she showed him up publicly, as she liked to do, to prove herself, back when I knew her. Or maybe, as an old space dog, he's merely annoyed at seeing a young puppy swanning about arrogantly in a fast warship."

"Now that didn't sound at all bitter."

"You didn't live through the drama that cost me a timely promotion, skipper. I might have been given *Erling* or one of her sister ships instead of landing in Helen Forenza's private nightmare."

"Well," Siobhan rose after glancing at the clock, "with any luck, you won't have to see her face-to-face again. I just hope that she got *Cyane* because she developed into an experienced, reliable officer, and not because of patronage."

"So do I, but I'm not going to hold my breath." Pushkin placed his empty glass carefully on the table and stood to take his leave. "She's smart alright, or she wouldn't have made it through the Academy, but I can't see her princess complex ever completely vanishing."

"As long as she does her duty." She gave him a gentle pat on the shoulder. "Good night, Gregor."

— Seven —

Siobhan felt uncharacteristically nervous as her shuttle approached the slowly spinning station. Bulky and inelegant, it showed its origins as empty 'instant colony' transport pods stitched together into a giant torus with a thin central axis. Considering Micarat had attained level 3 self-sufficiency, that station had been circling the planet in its current state for decades. Evidently the colonists had better use for their money than upgrading it, or they believed in the old engineer's motto that if it was not broken, you let it be.

The two missing ships had arrived twelve hours earlier, their captains not even bothering with so much as a 'hello' when they entered orbit under *Stingray*'s watchful sensors. Since there was no set time for the convoy's departure, Siobhan was in no position to ask for explanations or chide them for tardiness. She made a mental note to thank her signals officer for the deft way in which she had deflected the increasingly rude calls from ship captains impatient to get under way. The young signals officer showed great potential for flag rank, where politicking was the number one activity.

Behind *Stingray*'s shuttle, she could see several small dots sparkling under Micarat's sun as they leisurely approached the gaping hangar doors. For all their impatience at leaving, the merchant captains did not appear very eager to attend the conference. Gulsvig had warned her in a private exchange that she could expect a rough go of it. She had briefly wondered about the wisdom of having Stoyer at the conference along with the more experienced lieutenant commander, but if nothing else, it would allow her to see how the young woman handled herself in front of a potentially hostile group.

Lieutenant Kowalski landed the shuttle gently on the yellow spot in the middle of the expansive deck, shutting down her systems while the gantry's arm latched on. It bled off the static charge built up by the force field across the open hangar doors, while moving the small craft to a parking slot.

"Do you want me to accompany you to the meeting, captain?"

Dunmoore read the eagerness in her eyes, enthusiasm for the novel experience of witnessing a briefing a room full of civilian spacers impatient to break orbit and caring none too deeply about Navy protocol.

"Why not? You can tell me afterward what you thought of the merchantmen."

"Thank you!"

Gulsvig and Stoyer were waiting for her at the hangar deck's inner door, studiously avoiding any sort of conversation. If she did not know better, Dunmoore would have thought them complete strangers to each other.

They snapped to attention at her approach and saluted.

"Good morning, sir," Gulsvig tried an encouraging smile. It did not quite work.

"Good morning Hayden, Terica. This is Kathryn Kowalski, my signals officer, and shuttle pilot."

"You don't fly yourself?" Stoyer blurted out nodding at the pilot wings above Dunmoore's left breast pocket.

"Starship captains aren't supposed to."

"Oh." Stoyer suddenly looked embarrassed. "I didn't know that."

"No reason you should," Siobhan smiled. "Kathryn is going to join us in the briefing room."

"Taking notes?" Gulsvig seemed faintly amused.

"Something like that. Shall we?"

"I suggest we take the long way around, captain. It wouldn't do for you to show up before all of them are present."

"Very well then, Mister Gulsvig. Lead on."

*

The indistinct babble of a dozen humans speaking at once was loud enough to reach their ears the moment they stepped into the command pod where, courtesy of the station's management, they had secures a briefing room.

"That sounds like more than just seven ship captains."

Gulsvig grunted.

"Aye. They'll likely have brought some of their officers, possibly the navigator, and the ship handler."

"Strength in numbers?"

"Perhaps. Some of 'em will want to make sure they outnumber the Navy. We're not universally loved, you know. Something about ruinous taxes paying for our upkeep."

Siobhan smiled at his wry tone.

"An Earth author, back before spaceflight, wrote some exquisite lines to the effect that the military is despised until they're urgently needed."

"Kipling. Yes, he has a good take on that subject, as I recall. It goes: *It's Tommy this, and Tommy that, and chuck him out the brute, but it's 'Saviour of his Country,' when the guns begin to shoot!'*"

She stopped and looked at Gulsvig with gentle amusement. He shrugged.

"Lots of time to read on a merchant ship, Captain, and you eventually get down to the ancient classics. I recall another quote, of disputed origin but mostly attributed to one Francis Quarles."

"Do tell?"

"*For God and the soldier we adore, in time of danger, not before! The danger passed, and all things righted, God is forgotten, and the soldier slighted.*" He looked faintly embarrassed at declaiming poetry in an old orbital station hundreds of light years from the planet where those words were penned.

"Shall we go and get slighted then, Mister Gulsvig?" Siobhan laughed.

The noise of several competing conversations held at high decibels washed over her as she stepped through the door. At first, she was roundly ignored, but then, as the other three Navy officers filed in behind her, the assembled civilian spacers turned their heads toward them, their heated discussions dying off one by one.

When silence had descended on the bare, utilitarian room, Dunmoore smiled.

"Good morning, ladies and gentlemen. I'm Commander Siobhan Dunmoore, captain of *Stingray* and commanding officer of convoy Thirty-Nine-dash-One."

No one smiled back. Most had crossed their arms and were examining her with expressions varying from sardonic to openly hostile. She fought the temptation to take a deep breath, a sure sign of nervousness.

"If we can take our seats, we'll go through the round of introductions. With me, I have Lieutenant Commander Gulsvig, captain of *Erling*, Lieutenant Stoyer, captain of *Cyane* and Lieutenant Kowalski, flotilla signals officer. These three, and I, are the people you'll mostly be dealing with during our trip to your various destinations."

She looked at the swarthy, stout civilian to her left.

"And you are?"

He slowly removed the unlit cigar from the corner of his mouth and considered her, running his other hand through his greasy, graying hair.

"Hoan Kiles, *Jade Delight*," he replied in a gruff tone before sticking his cigar back in its place between his thick lips. Siobhan nodded politely and looked at the next spacer, realizing that only the captains had taken seats at the table. Their officers were all sitting or standing against the far bulkhead. That would keep the introductions to a minimum.

"Shizuko Reade, *Alkris*," the woman's tone was much friendlier than Kiles', but she appeared just as guarded.

"You've met my crew before, haven't you, Captain Reade?"

"Aye." With that, she sat back and crossed her arms.

The next spacer, a tall, muscular man with long white hair tied into a braid down his back was smiling at her, but it was the smile of a predator contemplating his next meal.

"Cadan Strazi, *Fuso Maru*. I trust you'll do a better job protecting us than you did our sister ship, the *Nikko Maru*." His tone was matter-of-fact but held a noticeable undercurrent of contempt. "I don't think any of us are interested in falling victim to a Coalsack reiver or two."

Everyone in the room now stared at Siobhan with renewed interest, waiting for her reply to the open insult.

"Keep with the convoy, obey all signals, and you'll be fine, Captain Strazi." She was pleased that her voice sounded calm, even a touch bored, as if she was used to abuse from uncouth civilians.

He let an amused smile cross his lips but remained silent. The man beside him uncrossed his arms and leaned forward.

"Shao Lian, *Oko Maru* – the other sister ship, and I echo Captain Strazi's comments."

Where Strazi could have passed for a reiver with his black leather clothing and the knife tucked into the top of his boot, Lian looked like he would be more at home in the headquarters of some interstellar conglomerate. Of all the officers in the room, he was the only one wearing a business suit.

Siobhan turned to the hard-faced woman beside Lian and nodded. The spacer met her eyes and held them for a few seconds before speaking in an affected drawl.

"Lana Janrenk, *Antares Loch*." She managed to cram a lot of arrogance in those few words. "And I'd like to get to my destination sooner rather than later. The Navy doesn't have to make a profit, seeing as it's paid off the sweat of our labor, but we do."

"What she said," the man next to her nodded. "Rego Minnau of the *Zebulon*. My passengers aren't overjoyed at the delay."

"They'd be even less overjoyed if your ship is hit by reivers, captain," Siobhan replied, smiling to soften her words.

The short, fat merchant spacer scowled back, dark eyes narrowed under thick gray brows as the last civilian captain, seated to Siobhan's left, introduced himself.

"Garan Bane, *Pride of Pallas*. I sympathize with my colleague for I also have impatient passengers, but your point is well taken, Captain Dunmoore. Better a short delay than a long captivity."

His green eyes twinkled as he spoke as if to assure her that he would not be the one making her life a misery during their passage.

"Thank you, captains. Lieutenant Kowalski transmitted the convoy instructions and signal orders yesterday. I trust you've all had a chance to read them."

Kiles snorted derisively.

"Who has time for Navy nonsense? I'd say your orders are simple, Captain Dunmoore: get us to our destinations quickly and keep marauders off our backs. The sooner we part company, the better."

Siobhan knew he was trying to bait her, but it was still an effort to keep the wrong words from escaping her lips.

"Those are indeed my orders, Captain Kiles," she replied, her voice dripping with syrupy sweetness. Only Kowalski, of all the spacers in the room, knew that the more honeyed Dunmoore's tone, the more danger lay ahead. "I was referring to your orders – the ones where if you disregard them, you'll make my job of keeping reivers away that much more challenging. I'm sure you know that Interstellar Lloyd's won't pony up insurance money if you're hit and I can prove you failed to follow my sailing directions."

Bane burst out laughing.

"She's got you there, Hoan."

"Go fuck yourself you floating brothel keeper."

"Hey, just because the *Pride of Pallas* is more nicely appointed than your tub doesn't make it a whorehouse."

"Gentlemen!" Siobhan's voice cracked over the escalating debate, momentarily silencing both men. "If I may continue so that we can wrap this up and break orbit?"

"Yes, please do." Janrenk's sour tone was directed more at her fellow captains than at Dunmoore. "It's one thing for the Navy to delay me. They have the big guns. It's another thing if your locker room garbage does. I'll gladly knock your heads together to make you stop."

Kiles sketched an obscene gesture in her direction but otherwise chose not to reply. Janrenk grunted and nodded at Siobhan to continue.

"Very well. I'll go through the convoy instructions and signals orders in detail for Captain Kiles' benefit." That statement earned her a few chuckles, proving what she suspected: the master of the *Jade Delight* was not particularly well liked by his fellows.

"No need, Captain Dunmoore," Kiles angrily replied. "I read your bloody orders. I just don't like my cooperation to be taken for granted."

"No danger of that," Siobhan replied with a tart smile, earning some outright guffaws from the room. It proved to be just enough to get them to pay attention.

Two hours later, she felt utterly drained by the questions and discussions but satisfied that they all understood what they had to do. Whether they would actually carry out her sailing instructions was a question whose answer lay in the future.

Of the seven, Kiles and Strazi remained the least cooperative, the one surly and the other sardonic. They did grudgingly participate in the debate however, Strazi going to the extent of requesting his ship be last in line, behind the *Oko Maru*, due to it being the fastest of the bunch, a suggestion that surprised Siobhan by its coherence.

"If there are no more points to discuss," she said rising from her chair, "I'll wish you a good day and good sailing. Barring any unforeseen problems, we'll break orbit at six bells in the morning watch tomorrow."

"And what time is that for civilized people?" Kiles demanded.

"Seven in the morning. I'll have Lieutenant Kowalski transmit our time signal so you can synchronize with us if you're not using universal time."

"Any well-run shipping line uses UTC," Bane commented, eyes on Kiles, waiting to see if he would take the bait, but the master of the *Jade Delight* was sufficiently bruised by his fellows' barbs for the time being.

"I have no doubt," Dunmoore replied, "but if a ship doesn't get the chance to synchronize frequently, its time will start to deviate from UTC. A pleasure to have met you all." She sketched a salute and left the room, trailed by the others.

"You made a few friends in there," Gulsvig commented when they were out of earshot. "Hoan Kiles is an ass, and plenty enjoy watching him get his comeuppance. That was nicely handled, captain."

"Thanks, I think. Kiles doesn't worry me so much as Strazi. The bugger knows more about convoy protocols than I'd give a civilian credit for, plus he carries off the reiver look like a natural."

Gulsvig nodded knowingly.

"Slimy bastard for sure, but he must do his job well for Black Nova to let him command a good, fast ship like the *Fuso Maru*. It and the *Oko Maru* are probably as fast as *Cyane* and as well maintained."

Stoyer voiced her agreement.

"Those two are probably the ones who can best outrun a reiver and need this convoy the least. As to being as well maintained as my *Cyane*, I'll hold my opinion on that, though their emissions are about as clean as any proper warship's."

"Really?" Siobhan was surprised that Stoyer had scanned the merchantmen on her own initiative. "Clean enough to go silent if needed?"

"I'd say so. None of the others is that good. The *Jade Delight*, in particular, needs a serious reactor tune-up. Even with all systems down, any reiver who's not dead drunk can find her within half a parsec. I'll have the emission signatures we took sent over to your gunnery officer."

"Nicely done, lieutenant." Although Siobhan would have liked to know about this earlier, she held her peace. One step at a time.

Stoyer beamed with pleasure at the compliment, more so than was warranted. Dunmoore thought about her discussion with Pushkin a few evenings ago and wondered again why the younger woman had been appointed to *Cyane* when there were plenty of officers without her history available. Trevane Devall or Kathryn Kowalski would certainly have been better choices, given the chance, though Siobhan admitted she was biased in their favor.

There had been a few times during the briefing where she feared an inappropriate outburst from Stoyer after a particularly pointed taunt from one of the civilians, but she had been able to hold her tongue. Only her bright red cheeks had betrayed her anger. It did speak of a barely suppressed streak of impulsiveness, however, which was not always a good trait for a warship commander, though ironically, Dunmoore recognized a bit of herself in that thought.

Kowalski commented as much when they were back in *Stingray*'s shuttle.

"I thought Terica Stoyer would burst when Strazi almost openly accused the Navy of being in the reivers' pay, and I think some of the others noticed it too, which didn't do our credibility any favors. She seems to have a pretty thin skin for a warship captain."

Dunmoore would not ordinarily entertain a discussion about another captain with anyone but Pushkin. However, Kowalski and Stoyer held the same rank, and she had promised herself to mentor a young officer who showed so much potential.

"It's not really a matter of having a thick or thin skin, Kathryn," she replied as they left the confines of the hangar and boosted away toward the frigate. "A captain needs to develop a good poker face and only let emotions show when they can convey a message; hopefully, the message that said captain wants to convey. Stoyer still has to learn that lesson."

Kowalski's ensuing silence made Siobhan wonder whether her real question was not 'why did she get a sloop command and not me?' If it was, then pursuing the conversation would be futile. Sometimes, it was merely a matter of right place, right time, under the eyes of an influential admiral, just as had been her fate when the scout ship *Don Quixote* became available to Admiral Nagira's Third Fleet.

"What was your impression of the civilian captains?" She asked instead.

— Eight —

"All ships have confirmed that they're ready to break orbit," Kowalski announced as Siobhan entered the bridge, "even the *Jade Delight*."

"They've fixed their reactor problem already?" She did not bother hiding her skepticism.

"It appears so, and without Mister Kutora's help."

"Probably didn't want our chief engineer to see the actual state of his engine room," Pushkin added with asperity. "After seeing the emissions scan *Cyane* took, I'm surprised he's still in space."

"Now, now, Number One," Siobhan chided him with an ironic grin on her face, "let's be tolerant of the diversity of starships out there."

"Diversity be damned, captain. We'll be towing the bugger into the next port, you mark my words."

"Noted," she replied dryly. They had spent the last twelve hours prodding the various captains along with their preparations and listening to endless complaints about the Navy, her sailing instructions, the signals instructions, and the lack of sympathy on her part. Pretty much what Gulsvig had warned her to expect.

"Is anyone still giving you a hard time, Mister Kowalski?"

"Not anymore, sir," she smiled, "not since I reminded the lot of them that idle chatter on an unsecured channel gave any halfway intelligent reiver enough information to cut them out of the convoy one by one."

"Let's hope that doesn't happen. No matter how difficult they are, we're still responsible for their safety."

"Aye," Pushkin sighed. "Remind me again what the alternative to convoy duty was."

"Your beloved captain getting the boot."

"Ah," he brightened artificially, "I knew there was a reason I hadn't yet lost my will to live."

"Cheer up, Gregor. This was the easy part. Now we get to make them sail in proper order. I understand that fighting a dozen Shrehari Marines single-handed is a less daunting task."

"Captain, we're at five bells," the sailing master reminded her.

"Indeed. I suppose we also need to quit bellyaching. Are our charges properly primed to break away in sequence?"

"I fed them the navigation data two hours ago. All have acknowledged."

"We'll see how far that takes us." Dunmoore shook her head as she settled in the command chair. "Guns, scan the convoy ships and advise whether they're spooling up to light their drives."

"Which ship do you think is going to cause us our first problems, Gregor?" She turned to the first officer.

"The *Jade Delight*, no question." He jerked his chin toward the port screen, where the sensor results where scrolling up. "Still leaking like a sieve. I don't know how the crew can keep sailing on her in that condition."

"Probably the type of spacer that can't afford to be choosy."

"Heh," Pushkin snorted, "that would make them the first to surrender to a pirate wolf pack and no big loss."

"I don't know," Chief Guthren said. "Scuttlebutt has it that reiver clans planted agents along the frontier, but I don't think they'd be as obvious as that. They didn't get to raid for decades without developing some smarts. The *Jade*'s crew might be folks no honest line wants as a first choice, but if there are spacers in league with pirates, they're like as not on another ship."

Dunmoore stared at the back of her coxswain's head, his words triggering a renewed cascade of doubt. What if some reiver clan had placed an agent in the convoy? Her sailing orders were clear and if they stuck to them, cutting a ship out in hyperspace was going to be next to impossible. In normal space, well, it would take a pretty bold pirate to try his hand under the guns of a frigate like *Stingray*, no matter her age.

But another part of her mind brought up the memories of her own raid on a Shrehari convoy and how she swatted aside the escorts to mow down transports filled with Imperial ground troops. The coxswain was right: reivers survived by being good at their craft. If they attacked the convoy, it would be because she had missed something or screwed up somehow.

The marauders did not have ships able to stand up to hers or even to Gulsvig's *Erling* and they knew it. Treachery was the only way they could get at them. She shook her head to chase away thoughts that threatened to swirl in ever tightening circles.

"Pirate agents might be successful on a single ship transiting far from patrolled routes," she said, as much to reassure herself than anything else. "They won't work terribly well in a convoy. The moment a wake disappears, we'll know."

"That's only if the following ship is paying attention," Pushkin countered, "and I don't trust these buggers to notice a torpedo coming up their rears."

Dunmoore snorted. "I'm counting on their sense of self-preservation, Number One. Perhaps I shouldn't. On the other hand, I can't see what else I can do. Until someone invents sensors that work between hyperspace bubbles, we'll just have to trust human instinct."

"Fifteen minutes," the sailing master announced. "I have active navigation links with all ships except the *Fuso Maru*."

Dunmoore's head snapped up.

"Any idea why?"

"No," Tours replied, shaking his head. "It's been intermittent all along. Their navigation computer doesn't seem to digest Navy signals as well as the others."

"Even the *Oko Maru*?"

"She's been solidly linked."

"Huh. If I had my choice of ships, I'd have said the *Jade*."

"Whatever she may have wrong in her engine room," Tours replied, "there's been nothing wrong with her navigation suite."

Dunmoore glanced at Kowalski. The signals officer grimaced.

"We have a reliable comm link. If I were paranoid, after seeing Captain Strazi in action at the briefing, I'd say he's screwing with us."

"Why?"

The lieutenant shrugged. "Maybe he enjoys being an all around asshole?"

"Guns," Siobhan turned to Syten, "keep a special eye on the *Fuso Maru*. I seem to trust the bugger less and less." She paused and stared briefly at the status readout. "Keep the same eye on the *Oko Maru*. We've had too much unwanted fun with Black Nova ships lately."

"Aye, sir."

Dunmoore glanced at the countdown on her console.

"Make to *Cyane*: proceed to the jump point."

She watched as the sloop gracefully broke orbit and headed out on a flare of ions from her sublight drive. Thin-skinned or not, Stoyer knew how to handle her ship. After a suitable interval, she spoke her next order.

"Make to *Jade Delight*: proceed in *Cyane*'s wake."

Much less gracefully, the ungainly bulk freighter tore herself free and lumbered off in the sloop's wake, her drives a sickly shade of yellow.

"She not only needs tuning in her reactor room," Pushkin commented. "I doubt her drive nozzles have seen maintenance since before the war."

"As long as she gets to Ariel, then we're shot of her."

"We might have to tow her there." The first officer sounded gloomier than usual. "There goes the *Antares Loch*. At least she's not spitting out bad ions."

Guthren, at the helm, grunted. "Not much prettier than the one ahead, though."

"No," Dunmoore agreed. "Is *Erling* in place?"

"Aye, captain," Kowalski replied. "Ready to assume the flanking position when the center of the convoy passes the moon's orbit."

"We have what? Sixteen hours to get them in proper order, at matched velocities and proper separation? We need to be merciless. The buggers might understand why they have to see the wake of the ship ahead when we're FTL, but that doesn't mean they'll make enough of an effort to keep formation before we jump." Dunmoore was aware she sounded irritable. If anything happened, she would get the blame, even if it was the fault of one of the merchant captains. Their shipping lines would make sure of that.

"*Zebulon* breaking orbit. He left it a bit late," Syten reported, "and he'll have to pour on the acceleration."

"Always one in every group," the coxswain grumbled, disgusted at the display of inefficient helmsmanship.

"At least the *Pride of Pallas* is moving out right smartly and not timing herself on the *Zebulon*," Pushkin noted.

"Passenger liners pay their crews better and therefore get better people, Gregor."

"Aye, captain. I'll be most interested to see how our Black Nova ships do."

"I'm sure they'll do very well."

"The *Alkris* is away."

"Funny about her," the first officer said, "a small trader like that can outrun reivers. Why'd she join the convoy?"

"Ours is not to question why," Dunmoore replied. "HQ approved her, and that's all we need to know. By the way, did someone check the charts she gave us? I completely forgot to follow up."

"Aye, I did," Tours replied. "They were no differences with ours."

"*Oko Maru* is moving out."

"On time and on target," the coxswain added.

"And there goes the *Fuso Maru*. Helm, light her up. Time to herd our flock."

*

"This extended line is going to kill us," Pushkin grumbled several hours later.

"With only three escorts, we don't have much choice," Dunmoore replied, sighing. "If we had one of *Erling*'s sister ships we could split the convoy into two columns, put the corvettes behind each and take the flanking position ourselves."

"I know," Pushkin replied, shaking his head. "But the buggers can't keep proper separation. Lose a wake or get up someone's stern and we lose half the convoy until we can round them up again. Do we still have time to report for a court-martial?"

"Don't sound so gloomy, Gregor. We're not the first tagged with convoy duty."

"But we're the first in this sector. They're used to it on the Shrehari frontier. This bunch? It's like teaching four-year-olds to calculate the square root of infinity."

"We can always sail further out at sublight before jumping."

"And have them scream at us for further delays, captain? I'd rather not."

Dunmoore smiled at her first officer. He was having a harder time of it than she was.

"That's pretty much unavoidable no matter what we do."

They were in Siobhan's ready room, staring at the tactical schematic on her screen. The line of starships strung out well beyond visual range looked ragged. The last three ships in the convoy held station cleanly and tightly, which was why she had placed them there and put the potential problems in the lead.

The icon for the *Jade Delight* suddenly turned from green to amber as the intercom chimed.

"Sir," Syten, the officer of the watch, called through the open door to the bridge. "Captain Kiles just advised us that his hyperdrives are flickering to red status. He won't be able to jump until he's stabilized whatever problem he has."

"And now we have a reason to continue sailing at sublight," Pushkin slapped his thighs as he rose. "Wonderful."

"Tell Captain Kiles that if he doesn't have his problems sorted out in thirty minutes, I'll send over my chief engineer and his team and they'll deal with it."

The first officer snorted. "Kiles is going to love having the Navy dig through the mess he calls his engine room. Our Mister Kutora on the other hand is going to hate every minute of it."

"It's that or he can stay here for all I care."

"Understood, captain. Shall I rouse engineering?" Syten asked.

"Please do so, and have a shuttle readied. If Mister Kowalski's available, I'd like her to fly it."

"So you're betting on needing to send a team over?"

"Not exactly betting, but I'd like to be prepared if I'm wrong about this."

A few moments later, Syten got up from the command chair and poked her head through the door.

"Sir, Captain Kiles strenuously protests your sending, and I quote 'a bloody naval boarding party, pirates more like' to help him sort out his engine problems. He assures us that he will have things fixed any minute now."

"Put him on," she replied, waving to the screen beside Pushkin.

Kiles' sour face appeared, looking like he had swallowed a drop of reactor fuel.

"Captain Dunmoore, like I told your officer, we'll deal with our problems. I don't want any of you Navy people setting foot on my ship."

"If your drives don't come online in the next fifteen minutes, I'm launching my shuttle with a team, Captain Kiles. I'm sure your fellow ship masters aren't going to be pleased if you delay the convoy, and my superiors would frown on my leaving you here to make your own way to Ariel."

"I'll deny them docking rights."

"My crew is experienced with boarding hostile vessels, Captain Kiles, and they could probably use the practice." She turned to Pushkin. "Have the team armored and armed. They may have to cut through the hull if it becomes necessary."

The look on Kiles' face was priceless, and Siobhan struggled to maintain her serious composure.

"Now look here," he sputtered, "there's no need to be threatening an honest spacer. I'll be reporting you to your superiors and — ."

"You may do as you wish," she replied, interrupting him. "However, you will either jump with your own engineering team or with mine, but you will jump."

"The boarding party is armed and ready," Syten announced loud enough for Kiles to hear.

"I – ah," the man's face lost its choleric red as he blanched at the threat, "I'll get my lazy chief moving. No worries, Dunmoore."

"One would almost think you have something to hide," Siobhan replied with a small, cruel smile. "Contraband you'd rather the Navy didn't see?"

The merchantman lost all his bluster at the accusation and remained silent, staring at Siobhan with loathing in his eyes. A voice said something that was not clearly picked up by the transmitter and Kiles looked to the side. He nodded once and turned back to Dunmoore.

"We're back up. You can issue the jump order anytime you want. Kiles, out." He abruptly cut the transmission.

"Wasn't that fun," Siobhan commented acidly as she rose to head for the bridge. "I wonder if he has any friends."

"Or any family willing to acknowledge him?" Pushkin added.

"Mister Tours," she said, settling in the command chair, "start the jump countdown and confirm that all ships are still synchronized. I'd really hate to spend hours rounding up strays if we emerge all over the place."

"Aye, captain, though I wouldn't be too worried. This leg is short. If someone's poorly calibrated, we'll see it soon enough, and I can compensate for it on the subsequent tacks."

"You may be able to make up for astrogation discrepancies, Mister Tours, but no one can compensate for a lousy navigator or a lazy helmsman."

"True." The sailing master nodded, eyes intent on his console. "All ships have returned the correct signal, sir. We're synchronized."

"Even the *Jade Delight*?" Dunmoore asked with amused skepticism in her tone.

"She was the first to ping back."

Pushkin snorted. "I think you've finally managed to put the fear of God in him, captain."

"More like the fear of losing whatever undeclared cargo he's bet his life savings on," she replied, an amused smile twitching the corners of her mouth.

"Thirty seconds to jump."

The siren bleeped three times throughout the ship, warning the crew they were about to feel like tossing their last meal. Then, when the countdown reached zero, the seven merchant vessels and their three escorts winked out of existence as their FTL drives formed bubbles of hyperspace around them, propelling the ships toward interstellar space and leaving Micarat far behind.

"Status?" Siobhan asked after her stomach had settled.

"All systems functioning normally," the first officer reported.

"I'm picking up the *Fuso Maru*'s wake cleanly," Syten added.

"All, right then." Dunmoore rose from her seat, "you may place the ship at cruising stations. I believe you have the watch, Mister Kowalski."

"Aye, captain," the signals officer replied, locking her console and slaving it to the command chair. "I relieve you."

"I stand relieved," Siobhan replied. "If I recall correctly, Mister Rossum wants to discuss problems with some of the supplies we got from *Petrel*. Let him know I'll be in my quarters."

*

The first jump was scheduled to last twenty hours, and when the time came, Dunmoore resumed her seat on the bridge, watching the countdown clock intently. They would see soon enough if the merchant ships were well handled. Theoretically, any of them could have dropped back to sublight, and the only ship that would know would be the one immediately following. However, it was safe to say no one could have forced a ship out of hyperspace without *Stingray* finding out. Any attacker would have to come up behind the frigate and take her with a well-aimed torpedo before reaching the first freighter.

Then, almost as one, the ten starships winked back into the normal universe, their synchronized navigation systems cutting out the FTL drives at the same instant.

Dunmoore groaned as the tactical display began showing the other ships. Not unsurprisingly, *Cyane* and *Erling* were in their proper positions, one in the lead and the other to the flank, ready to run down any attacker. The merchantmen were sadly out of alignment.

"Well," Tours was the first to speak, "I suppose it could have been worse. At least they all made it, including the *Jade Delight*."

"What's your professional opinion?" Dunmoore asked. "Are they off because their drives aren't calibrated closely enough, or do they simply have lousy crews?"

The sailing master rubbed his chin in thought.

"I'd be more inclined to look for a mechanical rather than a human cause for now, captain. The last three ships are the soundest, mechanically speaking, and they were able to keep station the best."

"They also strike me as having the best crews, or in the case of the *Alkris*, the best pilot," Pushkin pointed out.

"How long is the next jump?"

"I've set it at thirty hours," Tours replied.

"So we can expect that they're going to be half again as dispersed as they are now."

"Aye. I know what you're thinking, sir. They get scattered enough and someone might be able to sneak up on one of them without us knowing, though that'd be an impressive feat." He nodded. "I'll recalculate the jump instructions for the four lead ships to account for hyperspace drift. If it's mostly a calibration problem, they'll be in a tighter formation after the next tack. If it's both a calibration and a helm problem, they won't be further out than they are now. If it's all a helm problem, we might as well resign ourselves to ten-hour jumps, which means days more tacking before we get to Ariel."

"Agreed," the first officer said. "Let's stick to the sailing master's plan and see where we are on the next tack."

"Make it so, Mister Tours."

*

"Better this time," Dunmoore said, watching the tactical display as the convoy regrouped after emerging from the thirty-hour jump.

"Except for *Jade Delight*. She has both problems: poorly calibrated drives and a heavy hand at the helm. Thank God we're shot of her at Ariel and not the far end of our route." Pushkin shook his head.

"The *Alkris* and the two *Marus* could be mistaken for Navy vessels, their navigation is so precise." Tours pointed at the schematic. "They've kept the same separation and alignment since we left Micarat."

"Makes you wonder, doesn't it."

"Wonder, captain?"

"If Black Nova fields such good ships and crews, how did the *Nikko Maru* get picked off? I'm pretty sure the *Marus* could match *Cyane*'s top speed without problems. They're likely not even running at sixty percent with us."

"Bad luck." Pushkin shrugged. "It does happen. Or the bad guys had a mole on board. We'll never know."

"Right." Dunmoore stood up and stretched. "Let's get everyone re-synchronized and spooled up. I'd like to make Ariel before her sun burns out."

"Two tacks, captain, then the run on sublight to the planet. If the *Jade Delight* is the only one staying, I suggest we maintain our velocity and allow her to drop out of the convoy as we cross the outer system."

"Sadly, no. The *Antares Loch* has some drop offs and pickups. The convoy will have to decelerate enough so she can catch up with us."

"How long is she expected to stay?"

"Six hours, according to her captain."

"Shouldn't be a problem, then," Tours confirmed. "We'll start decelerating as we drop out of hyperspace after the last jump, while *Antares* and *Jade* maintain original velocity until they have to dump speed to make orbit."

"I think the next leg, to Parth, should go faster. The *Jade* was our biggest limiting factor."

"Aye, Gregor," Siobhan replied, "and we'll not be hearing a litany of complaints the moment we send fresh instructions."

"By the way, captain, how is the *Jade* getting home from Ariel," the first officer asked mischievously.

"I don't know, and at this point, I can't say I care either."

— Nine —

"And now the real fun begins." Dunmoore frowned, studying the navigation plot.

"Aye. At least we're shot of both the slowest and the most vulnerable ships." Pushkin did not bother to hide his relief at their flotilla's reduction in size. The *Pride of Pallas* was leaving the convoy at Mykonos, absolving them from protecting a starship that carried thousands of people. Anyone heading further out into the badlands would be transferring to smaller and faster ships there, but those were not Dunmoore's concern.

"I want to make the trip to Yotai with no more than three jumps. We know that reiver clans are active beyond our surveillance sphere and if they're in wolf packs, our three ship escort won't overly impress them."

"The latest intelligence report wasn't encouraging," the first officer replied. "Three more ships were attacked in the neighboring sector, and three more shipping lines are screaming in the Admiralty's ear."

"Just as long as it isn't mine."

"Do we know yet if we're escorting them back from Yotai?" Tours asked, looking up from the console.

"It depends on their orders. I would expect the *Zebulon* and the *Antares Loch* to want to stick close to our skirts. Their captains' reaction to the latest intel was rather strong." Dunmoore made a faint grimace.

"Why do they insist on trading in the Coalsack if it's that risky?"

"Profits, Mister Tours. The more hazardous the run, the more they can charge. A ship that can make it to Yotai and back in two or three jumps has a relatively small risk of interception. The reiver clans might be aggressive, but they're not over-endowed with decent sensor gear."

"Huh," Pushkin grunted, "we should just annex the whole sector and be done with it."

"Sure, but right now the Shrehari have a vote on our foreign policy and when we do decide to take the Coalsack, every reiver clan, marauder syndicate and planetary government will have its say. I'm not sure Earth is all that interested in expanding the Commonwealth."

"You'd think the commercial interests have enough senators in their pockets to force the issue."

"Cynic," Dunmoore smiled at her first officer. "The profits, legitimate and other, are probably good enough these days to leave the Coalsack its independence, such as it is. Yotai's the sector hub, and all the government needs to do is show it's keeping the lanes to Psi Caeli open and reasonably safe."

"No one will question our presence, captain?" Tours asked. "If I were the Yotai system government, I'd not be happy to see a Commonwealth Navy task force appear."

"They wouldn't have much of a choice." Dunmoore shook her head. "The planet has no unified leadership, let alone a unified system government. Half of the ships docking at Yotai are probably engaged in one criminal activity or another."

Pushkin nodded. "They'll love seeing our emergence signature. Watch for sudden departures."

"I'm pretty sure they know our rules of engagement don't allow us to open fire short of stumbling on piracy in progress or identifying them with complete confidence as being on the Navy's wanted list." She straightened her back and sighed.

"I think the proposed course is as good as we can manage. Get the convoy synchronized. We'll break orbit when the last cargo exchange is finished, which shouldn't be too long now."

*

The first tack had taken the convoy beyond the Commonwealth's sphere, past the very loose belt of patrol ships and automated buoy stations that defined the porous border. Dunmoore stared at the star chart, almost wishing the legend said 'Here be dragons.' At least the five remaining ships had kept station well enough to merit even Gregor Pushkin's grudging seal of approval. She had proposed switching the *Oko Maru* and the *Fuso Maru*, to spread out the pain of playing tail end charlie but Captain Strazi had insisted on keeping his position, claiming seniority within Black Nova Shipping. It sounded a bit strange to Siobhan's ears, but both Strazi and Lian had been playing it straight since they left Micarat so she gave him the benefit of the doubt.

"All ships report ready, captain."

"Begin the countdown, Mister Tours."

"Sir?" A female voice called out.

"What is it, Rownes?" Dunmoore turned to the petty officer at the sensor station.

"I've picked up a very faint reading two light minutes ahead of us. It was there for a few seconds then vanished again."

"Were you able to determine course and speed?"

"No," Rownes shook her head. "But the signal was athwart our planned course."

"Mister Kowalski, call *Cyane* and *Erling* and ask if either of them saw the contact."

"I'd be surprised," Chief Penzara commented, standing behind Rownes. "We've got better gear than either of them. *Cyane* wasn't fitted out as a scout."

Dunmoore caught her fingers drumming absently on her thigh, and a frown creased her forehead. Pushkin, glancing at his captain, gave voice to what most of them were thinking.

"Reiver lying doggo?"

"Paranoia's an ugly thing, Mister Pushkin, but it helps one stay alive in the badlands. Mister Tours, we'll be jumping a bit later than the rest of the convoy. I want to see if anything tries to get close once they think we're in hyperspace."

"Rig for silent running?"

"Yes. Once I'm happy there's no one wanting to follow us, we'll push the drives and catch up."

"Shall I let the convoy know?" Kowalski asked.

"Indeed."

*

They watched the five freighters and two warships vanish, taking the next leg as if they were a single entity. On the bridge, all was silent as they waited to see whether the convoy's jump flushed out an unseen hunter. *Stingray* herself was an electronic hole in space; her countermeasures effectively made her disappear against the background radiation.

The minutes ticked by, a countdown clock showing the maximum time remaining before the convoy got so far ahead that they would have problems catching up.

"Nothing," Penzara shook his head. "Whatever Rownes saw might just as well have been traveling away from us."

"Up systems, Mister Pushkin," Dunmoore ordered. "Spool the drives and call 'jump stations.' You can engage ten seconds after the third chime, cox'n."

*

"Ten minutes to emergence," the sailing master announced, sticking his head through the door to the captain's ready room.

Dunmoore looked up from the chessboard and nodded.

"I think we'll have to finish this game later, Gregor. It's time to call battle stations."

"Shame. I had you mated in three moves." Pushkin grinned evilly.

This jump had been scheduled to last forty hours, and they picked up the *Fuso Maru*'s wake three hours after jumping. With nothing else to do and caught up on paperwork, Dunmoore had continued her schooling in the fine art of chess at Pushkin's hands.

She had yet to win a game, but her mistakes kept getting fewer and fewer. Siobhan had decided she did not have the temperament for such a cerebral game, and the tactical instincts that served her so well in ship-to-ship action did not translate to the chessboard. The battle stations siren broke off any further conversation.

Ten minutes later, the all too familiar nausea gripped them as the weirdness of hyperspace was replaced by the normalcy of unblinking stars nestled in the velvety black of the cosmos. The darkness was further accentuated by the Coalsack nebula, now looming large enough to blot out a wide arc of the galaxy.

When humans and ship systems reconnected with the universe, the sounds of a well-drilled crew going through the emergence checklist filled the bridge. But not for long.

"Captain!" Penzara called out urgently from the sensor console. "We're a ship short."

"What?" Dunmoore sprang up and, in two strides, stood behind the gunnery chief.

"The *Fuso Maru*. She's not there."

The bridge crew looked at the screen in stunned silence. Guthren was the first to speak.

"We've been in her wake for the last thirty-seven hours, captain. There's no way we would have missed her dropping out."

"Aye, cox'n. And that can only mean we've been following the *Oko Maru* instead. They're almost identical and in hyperspace, we'd have no way of differentiating them."

"So where is the *Fuso Maru*?"

"That, Mister Pushkin, is the first question we'll get from the Admiralty. And they won't be too pleased when I tell them that I have no idea."

"Sir, incoming call from the *Oko Maru*. Captain Lian demands to know why his sister ship has vanished."

The burning sensation rising in Dunmoore's throat was no after-effect of dropping out of hyperspace. A ship under her charge had disappeared and the only time that could have happened was between when the convoy jumped and when *Stingray* caught up with it. In other words, it was as a result of her orders, orders that might have given pirates an opening.

"I do believe, this time, the Black Nova Shipping Line will want my head on a pike," she murmured to no one in particular.

*

"I intend to make a full report of this to my superiors, Captain Dunmoore." The master of the *Oko Maru* was seething with rage. "It was highly irresponsible of you to let the convoy jump without a chase ship. You would have done better to let one of your other two vessels sit back for that so-called contact no one else saw. If I were a paranoid man, I would consider that you might have a vendetta against my company."

Siobhan did not reply. There was nothing she could say to placate Lian. Yes, they could have left *Erling* behind to watch, but there was no violation of procedure in what she had done. Her sensors should have been able to pick up a ship trailing the convoy, either before she jumped or as she closed the distance. Dunmoore was still convinced that staying behind with the frigate had been the right decision, but Lian's rage was eating away at her confidence.

"I'm sure Black Nova will demand the Admiralty relieve you of command and beach you for good," he snarled. "Cadan Strazi was one of my best friends. He deserved better protection in this pirate-infested sector than what you gave him."

"Captain Lian," she finally said. "We have no idea whether or not the *Fuso Maru* was taken. She might have dropped out with drive problems. I've sent *Erling* to backtrack our course and find out what she can."

"Our ships are better maintained than the Navy's," he countered. "I'd be astonished if he had engine trouble. That contact you claim you saw was the more likely culprit."

"I would be equally astonished at a raider," she replied, her own anger beginning to bubble to the surface, "with enough skill to place himself between a Navy frigate and the convoy in the space of less than three hours. Your ships may be better maintained than ours, but I doubt that you and your officers have our appreciation of the difficulties inherent in FTL combat action."

She saw Lian's face tighten at the thinly veiled insult.

"We'll wait until *Erling* has returned before we make our next jump," she continued. "If there is a pirate stalking us, he'll not wish to attack a frigate in normal space."

"It's a wonder he didn't creep up on you in hyperspace and put you out of action," he countered.

Dunmoore laughed humorlessly.

"As I was saying, Captain Lian, your grasp of FTL mechanics is lacking. The disturbance caused by a torpedo exploding aft of a ship in hyperspace will, most of the time, collapse the firing ship's bubble as well. A pirate who tried that on us wouldn't have a chance to spool up his drives again and escape before I took him out. A brace of missiles tends to cause all sorts of problems for the intended target. They know that and won't try."

"All the more reason you shouldn't have stayed behind, Captain Dunmoore. You've condemned yourself out of your own mouth."

Siobhan felt her face redden at the accusation, and she bit down on choice words before they could form.

"We will wait until *Erling* returns. Dunmoore, out." She stabbed at her console with a stiff finger, cutting the communication.

"You know, sir," Pushkin softly said from the ready room door, "I think this time Admiral Ryn won't be quite as forgiving."

"Once is happenstance, twice is carelessness?" She raised a sardonic eyebrow.

"Something like that." He met her eyes and tried to gage her mood. Pushed hard and far enough, the recklessness she kept under tight control might surface, and if it did, they would all pay a price of some sort.

"Then we need to find out what happened to the *Fuso Maru* before the Admiralty decides that *Stingray* and her crew have outlived their usefulness." Siobhan's eyes glowed with repressed anger. "No, Gregor. There's more here than meets the eye and I intend to find out what that is."

"You think what we have here is a situation where once is happenstance and twice is enemy action?"

She nodded. "Yes, and if that's the case, we need to figure out who the enemy is. Cutting out a ship like the *Fuso Maru* is a feat even we'd have a hard time carrying off, and that worries me the most."

"What if Captain Strazi dropped out of the convoy deliberately?" Pushkin cocked his head in question, challenging her, happy that the recklessness was still well suppressed. Her ruthlessness might not be as tightly controlled, but it served its mistress much better, and he could live with that.

— Ten —

"Not a trace, captain." Lieutenant Commander Gulsvig's gloomy expression stared out at Siobhan from the screen in her ready room. "And by the time we got there, any ion trail would have long since dissipated."

"I know," she replied fighting the sinking feeling in her stomach. "I was hoping for a log buoy, debris, something. Gregor suggested that the *Fuso Maru* might have quit the convoy deliberately and without any evidence of what happened, it is a possibility."

"That would have been pretty nervy. Mind you, she has the legs to outrun your average reiver, so she's not nearly at risk alone as the *Zebulon* would be, for instance. But you don't do something like that on impulse."

"Maybe we were meant to drop back so she could vanish and that means the contact was deliberate." Dunmoore shrugged irritably. She held up her hand to stop Gulsvig. "I know, complicated schemes rarely work, and to arrange such a meet-up in interstellar space is far-fetched. Taking the chance that I'd be keeping *Stingray* behind instead of letting you play layback further complicates it, but otherwise, it's a chance event."

"Not all that chancy if you consider your sensors are the best in the convoy. It's not exactly a secret that corvettes aren't suitable for long-range detection, and *Cyane*'s not rigged as a scout. I wouldn't discount the notion." It was Gulsvig's turn to shrug. "The question is what do we do now?"

"Get the rest of the convoy to Yotai. I can't exactly ask HQ for orders. We're too far from a Navy subspace buoy for a secure transmission. I'm sure Captain Lian will find a way to contact his owners before I can report to Admiral Ryn, which means by the time we're in range, all hell will have broken loose back home."

"Aye." Gulsvig nodded sadly. "There's nothing to be done now. Are you thinking of reconfiguring the order for the last leg? I figure it may not be a bad idea if I take station between the *Alkris* and the *Oko Maru*. That way we box in the other Black Nova ship."

"It can't hurt, even though to our friend Lian, it might look like closing the barn door after the horse escaped."

"Bugger Lian," Gulsvig responded with feeling.

"No thanks. Let's get this convoy off on the last jump."

*

"Why do I get the feeling Yotai orbital control aren't overjoyed at seeing us?" Pushkin asked, looking up from his console.

"Eh," Kowalski shrugged. "I've heard surlier controllers in better systems. The registry says it's run by a consortium of 'trading' interests. Out here the Navy can put a dent in that kind of trade if it were so minded, meaning it's a given we're not their most favored guests. But pissing us off isn't going to help either, and you have to admit, giving us a high orbit works in our favor. We can hold pretty much anything around the planet under our guns."

"Too bad we can't go visit some of those over-engined and over-gunned vessels. I bet we'd find some fascinating cargo." The first officer allowed himself a small bloodthirsty smile.

"I'm not sure we could impose ourselves with only three warships, Mister Pushkin," Dunmoore noted. "If those over-gunned beauties figure out a way to work together, we'll run through our ammunition pretty quickly."

"Do we know what we have for the return trip?" He asked, dropping the subject. "I mean other than the *Antares Loch* and the *Zebulon*? I assume we'll not see a Black Nova ship, and Captain Reade seems to be too much of a loner to stick to our skirts."

"No idea. I'm assuming any Commonwealth-flagged ship that wishes to join us will make itself known."

"Captain," Chief Penzara raised his hand to attract her attention. "I've been taking scans of the ships in orbit, and I've found something that'll interest you."

She rose and went to stand behind him.

"Show me."

"See this emissions signature on the right," he pointed at his console, "and how it's almost identical to the one on the left?"

"Yes."

"The one on the right was from one of the ships we caught taking out the *Nikko Maru*. The one on the left matches a ship in low orbit."

"Degree of certainty?"

"Better than ninety percent."

"Now can we have some boarding party action?" Pushkin asked, only half facetiously.

"I've got a better idea," Siobhan replied, a wicked smile twisting her thin lips as she began pacing the small bridge. "Get the department heads together if you will, Number One."

*

"Why not send *Cyane*?" Lieutenant Devall asked the obvious question. "She has a much smaller signature than we do and can be spared from the convoy."

Siobhan looked around the table at her officers.

"She doesn't have the firepower to get out of a tight spot, for one, and I'm not well enough acquainted with her captain to know if she can handle this kind of hunt. At least we've done something like it before."

The fact that she did not trust Stoyer enough for this mission was not lost on any of them, even though she did not voice her thoughts on the subject.

"Point taken," the second officer nodded with a knowing look in his eyes. "And if there's any boarding action, we have a big enough crew and the shuttles to carry it off."

"Indeed," Siobhan smiled at him. Devall *was* quick on the uptake. "Are there any other questions, comments, or objections?

I'm taking a very liberal interpretation of my orders, and if this goes awry, we'll all be answering to a board of inquiry."

"Won't we answer to it anyway for losing the *Fuso Maru*?" Chief engineer Kutora sounded as miserable as she had ever heard him.

"It all depends on how loud Black Nova screams. The consequences of this operation, on the other hand, will hinge on our superiors' degree of forgiveness for failure."

"If there's nothing else, I suggest we be about it." Pushkin's tone held a note of finality, forestalling any further comments from the officers.

*

"I wish I could come with you," Lieutenant Stoyer said, her enthusiasm sounding almost artificial in its exuberance. "*Cyane* is a good ship to back you up in a tight spot."

"Sorry, Terica." Dunmoore shook her head. "For all the reasons I've just outlined, this is a one ship mission, and it has to be the one with the most firepower. Captain Gulsvig will need you if the two of you have to take the convoy back to Commonwealth space without me. A two ship escort isn't great, but a one ship escort is next to useless."

"We'll be fine," Gulsvig rumbled. "You just take care of yourself, captain. I'll try to delay sailing as long as I can, to give you a chance to rejoin us. If not, I'll have the navigation orders from your sailing master, and you can catch up along the way."

"That'll be all, then. If I could keep you on the transmission a few moments longer, Hayden? Some administrative points I need to pass along. Thank you, Terica." If Stoyer was put out at being excluded, she gave no sign as she ended her connection to the frigate.

"Hayden, I need you to be very clear about this. If you get back within range of a subspace buoy before I rejoin the convoy, you're to transmit the encoded report to HQ. It absolves you and Terica from any responsibility for the decisions I've made and the actions I've taken. Do not hang on to the report in the hopes that I can make it home before it hits Admiral Ryn's desk. I've included a second message, for the admiral's eyes only, detailing my suspicions and my intent. You're free to read it and add your own observations but make sure it goes only to the admiral. If you have to hand it to her personally, do so and don't worry about getting in trouble for it. I've learned that her bark is much worse than her bite."

"You make it sound as if you're not expecting to come back with us, captain. Is it a case of *with your shield or on it*?"

"Too many things stink in the Coalsack, and I'm not just talking about reiver nests. Finding one of the two mystery ships that destroyed the *Nikko Maru* sitting in orbit around Yotai, calmly as you please, has my bullshit detectors humming."

"Captain," Pushkin stuck his head through the door, "sorry to interrupt, but you'll be interested to know that the *Oko Maru* broke orbit just now."

"Really? She hasn't even had time to unload."

"Perhaps Yotai wasn't her final destination," Gulsvig suggested. "Or, like you, Lian saw something that impressed a sense of urgency on his actions."

"One more question mark, then. Are we clear on your orders, Hayden? This is all on me, so don't do anything that would get you into trouble as well."

"I'll be guided by my orders and my conscience, captain," he solemnly replied, the piratical twinkle in his eye promising more than just blind obedience. "And I'll handle our little sloop captain just fine. Have no worries on either count. Good luck."

"Thanks. Dunmoore, out."

She stretched, looking at her first officer.

"Am I doing the right thing, Gregor?" She asked softly

"Wasn't there an old Earth admiral or general who once said: in the absence of orders, go find something to kill?"

"Crude, but not inappropriate." She rose and tugged down her battledress tunic forcefully, feeling better than she had in days. Perhaps it was because she was finally doing instead of reacting and that suited her much better. "Place the ship at departure stations, if you please. I'll join you on the bridge momentarily."

*

"Yotai orbital wishes to know why we're leaving," Kowalski said the moment Siobhan had settled in the command chair.

"Tell them we have orders to conduct an astrographic survey of the region while the convoy forms. In a sense, that's not entirely inaccurate."

"Aye, sir." The younger woman grinned.

"Are we ready?"

"Yes, captain," Pushkin confirmed. "All systems are green; sublight drives are active and jump drives are on standby. By the way, the *Alkris* left not long after the *Oko Maru* and in the same general direction. Perhaps there's a lucrative market closer to the nebula we've never heard about."

"I'll not be surprised by anything today, Number One. Let's make a big show of sailing away. Cox'n, you may indulge yourself."

"Indulge myself, aye," he replied, amused at Dunmoore's choice of words.

Guthren steered *Stingray* out of orbit as slowly and with as much flourish as he could muster. All of her running lights were on, and she gave everyone within visual range a display of graceful ship handling. Dunmoore hoped that by leaving in a flamboyant fashion, their survey cover story would be more plausible than if they had snuck away quietly.

"We're on our planned heading," Tours announced. "Passing the outer moon's orbit in twenty minutes."

"Recon drone ready."

"Thank you, Mister Syten. I trust it'll be able to act with all due stealth?"

"Chief Penzara programmed it himself, captain."

"Then I have no doubt it'll lose itself against the background. Who'll be overseeing the feed?"

"Petty Officer Rownes."

"Excellent. She's becoming very adept with the sensor gear." Dunmoore glanced at the tactical screen. "You may launch at your leisure, Mister Syten."

Moments later, a smaller icon joined those of the other ships on the tactical screen. Programmed to watch the mystery raider, it would transmit basic telemetry to *Stingray* on a narrow laser communications beam. When the ship departed, it would register heading and speed, send them to Petty Officer Rownes and, if Siobhan so ordered, fire its sublight drive to follow the target at a distance. The chances of it being detected were slim to nil while it remained in very high orbit around Yotai.

"And now, we head off and make like we're interested in big space rocks," Siobhan quipped. "You have the bridge, Mister Devall."

*

"Captain, this is the officer of the watch." Dunmoore looked up from her book and reached for the intercom. The wait had not been long, barely enough time for her to finish a chapter.

"Dunmoore."

"The target has broken orbit and is headed out-system directly away from the primary."

"That was quick. Thank you, Mister Devall. I'm on my way."

"I'd hazard the guess that he was waiting for us to be looking elsewhere before he made his move," the second officer commented as he turned the command chair over to Siobhan.

"Most likely. What's the closest to the primary he can jump?"

"He'll be at his hyper limit in three hours. Shall I have the recon drone follow?"

Dunmoore stared at the tactical screen and shook her head.

"We're in decent enough position to keep track of him. The drone's sudden spurt of ions might make him suspicious."

"Shall we recover it?"

"No. Set it on observe and record. We'll pick it up when we're back."

"Self-destruct if someone tampers with it?"

"Definitely not. Have it slag its electronics only. I don't want to blow up some enterprising salvager whose only crime was to latch on to our hardware."

"Helm," she continued, "come very slowly to two-seventy-five, mark twenty. When he jumps, I want to be oriented as much as possible for a stern chance. Petty Officer Rownes, what's your estimate of the target's sensor range?"

The non-com frowned, fingers dancing over her console.

"Sir, if I use *Cyane* as a comparator, factoring in that a Navy ship will have more accurate gear, I'd say his sensor range is about two-thirds of ours."

"Concur." Chief Penzara nodded after looking at the readout. He gave Rownes a quick congratulatory thump on the shoulder.

"When we're beyond his range, plus a twenty percent buffer just in case, advise the officer of the watch." Dunmoore turned to Devall. "Maintain current velocity until you get the nod from Rownes. After that match course and accelerate but beware if he decelerates to check for a tail."

*

"He jumped," Penzara announced several hours later.

"Thank you, chief. What are the chances they saw us?"

"Slim, captain. We stayed at the limit of our sensors, so the last he should have seen was us making our merry way to the gas giant ninety degrees or so away from his course."

Dunmoore nodded and glanced at the sailing master.

"Mister Tours, if you were an outlaw and had seen three warships in orbit before you left, would you go on a long jump?"

"I would, knowing that I could outrun the one ship that actually sailed before I did."

"And yet..." She shook her head. "Make the next jump ten light minutes."

"Ready."

"Helm, engage."

*

"Scan." Siobhan breathed in deeply to dispel the emergence nausea as *Stingray* returned to normal space almost one hundred and eighty million kilometers away.

"Hyperdrive trace detected," Rownes replied. "But not on the same course."

"He dodged," she replied after examining the scan results. "Mister Tours, get us a new jump solution. Helm, come to three-twenty mark ten."

"Length of jump?"

"Fifteen light minutes this time," she replied, going with her gut.

"Expecting another dodge?" Pushkin sounded genuinely curious. He had seen an example of her hunter's instincts in action and the Shrehari in question had paid for it with their lives.

"If he did it once, he'll do it a few times." Her voice was low, almost husky as she stared at the tactical schematic.

For the next six hours, Dunmoore and the captain of the unidentified raider played a game of cat and mouse, with the target trying to confuse any pursuit and Siobhan trying to keep on him without being spotted.

"So far, his behavior has been consistent," she commented in an aside to Pushkin. "I don't sense that he's spotted us: he's not trying to run faster or lay in a more dizzying sequence of jumps."

"But all he has to do is wait just a little longer than necessary for a course change and to re-spool his drives and we'll come close enough for his sensors." Pushkin countered. "He may have decided not to let on that he's seen us. Or he's not sure he has the Navy on his tail, rather than someone less savory."

"True, but my gut tells me otherwise."

"You have to admit we cut it close on this one."

"We still emerged well out of his estimated sensor range, and he jumped before we came too close. I think the next jump after this is going to be the first long one. We may finally get an idea what system he's headed for. There are three likely destinations within a reasonable distance."

Dunmoore was proven right a few hours later. When they took a sighting on the target's hyperspace wake, his course was directly aimed at a system for which the navigational database had almost no information.

*

A few days later, after emerging on the edge of the system in question, Siobhan stared at the main screen, frowning.

"So, the star was not only mislabeled on the charts, but it appears to have a full set of planets."

"Indeed, captain," Gavin Tours replied. "No self-respecting navigator would let such a mistake get published. As you can see, there's at least one planet in the goldilocks zone, and it has an atmosphere. That alone should have made this system jump out on the charts."

She grunted. "Okay. I suppose we're still too far out to see any signs of civilization."

"Yes, sir," Syten responded. "If we get within about fifteen light hours, I think I can start to pick up any in-system traffic. Other than our target, that is."

"Anything on the normal and subspace frequencies, Mister Kowalski?"

"Nothing, sir."

"But that doesn't mean there's no one home." Dunmoore reflected. "We're still a tad too far out for anything more directed than radio."

"All right," she finally said, "let's do this a bit differently. I'd like us to come in on the system's planetary plane. Mister Tours, find me a spot that's shadowed from the goldilocks zone planet by one of the gas giants."

Pushkin looked at her questioningly.

"I'd like to go prowling a bit deeper into the system without anyone knowing we're there. If a reiver clan calls this home, it'll be best if we don't announce ourselves. We'll do a short jump to bring us to the outer edge of the planetary disk, say ten light hours out from the primary, then a micro jump into the system, just short of our hyper limit."

He nodded his understanding. "And when we emerge in the shadow of the gas giant, we go silent and head in-system on a ballistic trajectory."

"Indeed, Number One."

"I have the jump solutions, sir," the sailing master announced.

"On screen."

She studied them for a few moments. "I'd like to take another look at the system when we're at ten light hours, so you'll have to recalculate the next jump when we're done."

"Aye, sir."

"Helm, take us in."

*

"Other than our target headed for the habitable planet, I can't see any in-system traffic," Syten reported several minutes after the ship emerged ten light hours from the star, just shy of the outer planet's orbit. "No active sensor pinging either."

"And no communications on any frequency," Kowalski chimed in.

"Very well. Mister Tours, confirm the next jump. Mister Pushkin, prepare to go 'down systems' on my orders."

She waited until each of her officers signaled ready, then: "Helm, engage."

*

Stingray emerged close enough to the gas giant that the proximity alarms rang loudly before Pushkin shut them off.

"Guns, status?"

"Nothing on sensors, sir. We appear to be alone."

"Mister Tours, are we adequately masked?"

"For another five minutes or so, then we'll emerge from the planet's shadow."

"Confirm the ballistic trajectory and have the helm accelerate us in the right direction."

"Already done and fed in."

Dunmoore smiled. Tours might not be flashy, but he was a quick and accurate navigator.

"Let's do this. Mister Pushkin, down systems. Time to make like a dumb rock and see what's there. Helm fire attitudinal thrusters and prepare to engage sublight drive at maximum power for a twenty seconds burst."

With those orders, the frigate hurtled toward the inner system, giving off no more emissions than a slightly radioactive, iron-cored, five hundred meters long rock.

Dunmoore kept the ship at action stations through the long hours of waiting, knowing that the tedium could be shattered at any time and the frigate engaged in battle in the blink of an eye. It was hardly ideal, but the ship could go to full battle stations within ninety seconds, and the crew still got their rest, watch by watch.

The captain alternated between the bridge and her ready room, working hard at hiding her impatience. Sailing in on a ballistic trajectory was time-consuming, but at this distance from the primary, any use of the sublight drive could set off enemy sensors. Even braking thrusters could be detected by good gear. Only the maneuvering thrusters had a chance of losing their emissions against the background radiation of space, provided no one was watching too closely.

"Captain," Chief Penzara raised his hand. He had replaced Syten at the gunnery console an hour earlier. His voice was soft as if a loud sound could betray the ship. Dunmoore had often wondered at the human psyche's ability to ignore the laws of physics, such as the inability for sound to travel through a vacuum.

"What is it?"

"I'm picking up active emissions around the second planet, now that we're in range for the passive receptors. Looks like a starship just came out of its shadow."

"Bingo!" Dunmoore grinned widely. "Do we have a matching emissions fingerprint in our database?"

"I have one possible," Penzara said a few minutes later. The image of the other attacker responsible for wrecking the *Nikko Maru* appeared on the main screen.

"Well, well, well." Dunmoore frowned. "We have the both of them and now, like the dog that's cornered a squirrel, I need to figure out what the heck I do."

"Sir?" Penzara sounded alarmed.

"Just kidding, chief. This is a recon mission. Our trajectory will bring us close enough to the planet for a surface scan. Once we're past, we can go up systems and boost our way to the hyperlimit for the jump back to Yotai. They'll know we've been here, but that's about all."

"Um, captain," Petty Officer Rownes spoke up, an edge of worry tainting her otherwise steady voice. "The second ship broke orbit and is headed in our general direction."

"What's the distance?"

"Approximately three light minutes."

"We're within the hyper limit?"

"Aye, captain. He can only come at us on sublight," Sanghvi answered from the navigation console. "Depending on how much he intends to push his acceleration, we're looking at up to six hours before he passes us."

"If he's seen us or even suspects we're here, count on him accelerating as hard as he can," Dunmoore replied dryly. "Get the off-watch crew awake and at their stations at six bells."

*

The hours of boredom stretched out as they watched the unknown ship sail toward them. It had stopped accelerating after the first hour, but its course remained steady.

"Do you have a better fix on him, Mister Tours?" Dunmoore asked as she took the command chair from the officer of the watch.

"Somewhat, sir. If neither of us shifts, he'll pass within five to six hundred thousand kilometers," the sailing master, who had relieved Sanghvi at navigation, replied.

She winced. "If he's got Navy grade sensors and happens to look at us directly, he'll see the hole in space we're pretending to be."

"He'll notice any maneuvering thrusters at this point, sir," Syten said.

"Then I guess we're committed." Dunmoore's face took on a wry expression. "If not to an insane asylum, then to a course of action that some might deem crazy. What's the intercept time?"

"Another thirty minutes."

"All right. Get the crew to battle stations. We'll go 'up systems' only if he actively pings us."

Dunmoore was struck again by how much their current situation resembled that of a pre-spaceflight submarine playing hide and seek with a destroyer.

*

"He's entering visual range," Syten reported. "On this course, he'll be passing beneath our keel and to starboard at five-hundred fifty thousand kilometers."

"Murphy's Law of War," Pushkin commented, "if you can see the enemy, he can see you."

"We still have an advantage over him," Dunmoore replied. "We know he's there. At best, he may suspect something's here. If he knew about us, he would have us on active targeting by now. Provided we don't show a single light, the only way he can see us is by noticing that something is occluding the background stars."

"We can thank the engineering boffins for non-reflective hull coating."

"And many more things, Number One."

Dunmoore found herself holding her breath as the two ships closed at high speed.

"Sensor sweep just passed over us." Syten's voice was tense, more highly pitched.

"No active scan?" Siobhan sounded incredulous.

"No, sir. It felt like the navigation sensor, not weapons."

"Okay. He doesn't know we're here or even suspect we're here. At this velocity, he's just about reached the optimum engagement range. After that, it'll take him hours to decelerate and come about."

"He's not showing any signs of deceleration."

"Perhaps he intends to snipe with missiles," Pushkin offered.

"Always the optimist." Dunmoore flashed him a grin. "No point in wasting a bird if you can't follow up with guns once the shields are down."

"He's past optimum firing range, captain," Syten said moments later.

"What does his course look like from behind," Dunmoore asked the sailing master.

"He's heading for the hyper limit in open space. There are no planets on his direct track."

"Or maybe we're not the only infiltrator, just the one with better emissions control," she replied, eyes narrowed in thought.

They stared at the tactical screen in silence as the unidentified ship's icon receded to the edge of the viewer until Syten changed the scale.

"What's the other one doing?"

"Entering orbit around the planet."

"How far out are we going to pass it, Mister Tours?"

"Four hundred thousand kilometers."

"Hmm. A bit closer than I'd hoped, but there's no helping that now."

"Too far away and there wouldn't be enough gravity pull to slingshot us around and back toward the hyper limit without using our drives."

"Indeed. Mister Syten, are we starting to get some useful readings on the planet and the other ship?"

"We'll be in range for detailed sensing shortly."

Dunmoore bit back her impatience. They appeared to have found the lair of the ships that had attacked the *Nikko Maru,* and she wanted some answers.

"Sir, we've been sensor-swept again. It appears to be coming from the planet."

"An orbital installation, Mister Syten?"

"Possibly. I'm starting to pick up artificial satellites."

The tactical schematic of the planet's near orbit acquired orange icons representing suspected contacts.

"There's definitely a small station in geostationary orbit. Its mass appears to be slightly less than ours; possibly a manned communications and traffic control node."

"Or a weapon platform," Pushkin opined.

"Whatever it is, sir, that's where the sensor sweep appears to have come from. No active targeting yet."

Dunmoore's forehead creased with a worried frown. "If that orbital platform were one of ours, it would have more robust detection gear than a ship. What are our chances of passing the planet on the opposite side, Mister Tours?"

The sailing master put a three-dimensional diagram of their course on the screen and added the geostationary object's scanning field.

"We won't be in the planet's shadow long enough for it to matter."

Siobhan cursed softly.

"Sir," Syten's voice rose to a higher pitch in surprise. "We're being painted by a communications laser from the geostationary orbital."

Dunmoore stood up, face taut with surprise. "Narrow or broad beam?"

"It's tight enough that there's an almost one hundred percent chance it's deliberately aimed at *Stingray*, sir."

"How in the name of everything that's holy did they find us?" She whispered, turning to the signals alcove. "Is it a coherent signal, Mister Kowalski?"

"Yes, sir." The signals officer sounded only a fraction less shocked than her captain did.

"Put it on."

The bridge loudspeakers came to life with a perfectly cultured human voice.

"Commonwealth Navy vessel, you are ordered to cease silent running and identify yourself. Failure to comply will result in hostile action."

"It repeats on a loop, sir," Kowalski said.

"Captain," Syten raised her hand urgently. "A contact just appeared one million kilometers aft, accelerating toward us."

"A ship that's been running silently as well or our earlier contact?"

"A new one, sir. And we're now actively targeted by both the orbital and the newcomer," she added

Dunmoore cursed again.

"Up systems, Mister Pushkin. Shields up, weapons powered, begin targeting them back."

"Aye, sir." Syten and the first officer replied in unison.

The frigate came back to life quickly and entered full combat readiness as her drives, shields, guns and missile launchers powered up.

"Shall we reply?" Kowalski asked.

"No. I want to see what their next move is going to be."

She sat down again, fingers tapping her chair's console in a steady drumbeat. When she caught Pushkin staring at her significantly, she forced herself to stop.

"Incoming message on the regular channels."

"Put it on," she said with a tone of resignation.

"Thank you for cooperating, Commonwealth vessel. Please identify yourself."

"How about you identify yourself first? I've detected two ships in this system that were last seen committing an act of piracy against a Commonwealth-flagged freighter. I'd say I have ample grounds to arraign them."

The voice chuckled.

"You'd have a few problems with that." Pause. "Ah, our sometimes less than reliable sensors have provided us with identification. Now, why is the frigate *Stingray* so far from home, Commander Dunmoore?"

Siobhan's face began to turn a delicate shade of red as her ire mounted.

"Give me one good reason why I shouldn't come in hot and take you and your pirate's nest out."

"Perhaps because you wish to avoid blue on blue fire."

"What?"

"Captain Dunmoore, the fact that I was able to identify you and your vessel in the absence of a transponder might indicate that we're on the same side."

"Really? Type 203 frigates have a pretty distinctive hull shape, and there's only one left. Mine. Even the Shrehari can identify this ship and its captain on sight."

"Point taken, though, after your raid in the Cimmeria system, they have good reason to remember you above others." The voice remained infuriatingly calm and polite. "I wish to avoid an unfortunate incident, captain, while preserving the anonymity this station is afforded by its — shall we say — out of the way location."

"No dice. I'm looking to recover the passengers and crew of the *Nikko Maru* and bring the culprits to justice, said offenders presently visible in this system."

"I've heard about your headstrong temperament, Commander Dunmoore, and your propensity for reckless action. I suggest this is neither the time nor the place to play Doña Quixote."

All color drained from her face as her eyes widened.

The voice sighed.

"I can easily imagine the thoughts running through your mind, commander. Very well. If you give me your word as an officer that what you see and hear from us doesn't leave the system, I will break protocol and satisfy your curiosity. I'm afraid that the alternative might be to watch you indulge in your all too well-known tendency toward aggression, and I can't have that."

"What if I don't comply?"

"Pay attention to your sensors, commander. You will find that you are being targeted by two of my ships as well as the orbital platform. This far from any hope of recovery, I don't think you can afford to take the kind of damage I can inflict, let alone explain away the fact that you're operating without sanction."

When she glanced at Pushkin, he shrugged with a very eloquent 'he's got you there' expression.

Dunmoore took a deep, calming breath and squared her shoulders.

"Somehow, I think you can afford damage even less than we can, and if you know who we are, you probably know that I can get very nasty when someone's pissing me about. I can take out your vessel aft of us well before your ship in orbit, or your defense platforms can come into play. One ship down and I still have plenty of time to escape, circle back, and take out the next one. If you doubt my ability, ask the Shrehari what became of convoy Lhat One One."

There was a long pause before the voice replied.

"It seems that it's my misfortune to have become the target of your stubbornness, commander. However, in the interests of avoiding bloodshed, I will stand my defenses down and meet with you. I would rather not discuss matters over a comnet. You never know who might intercept and decode the transmission."

"In that case, I require your identity."

Kowalski broke the ensuing pause.

"Sir, the transmission now has a visual component."

"On screen."

The face of a middle-aged, olive-skinned human male appeared, his dark eyes staring intently at Dunmoore. He wore a nondescript battledress uniform without insignia. His close-cropped black hair was liberally sprinkled with silver.

"I'm Rear Admiral Lucius Corwin, senior naval officer in these parts, and I hope we can put an end to this nonsense now."

Siobhan stood and came to attention. "Sir."

Corwin's eyes slid to the side, and he smiled.

"Why hello, Kathryn. You seem to be keeping strange company these days."

Dunmoore swung toward Kowalski in astonishment.

"Good day, sir," the signals officer said, also coming to attention. "It's good to see you again."

At her captain's questioning look, Kowalski shrugged, feeling slightly embarrassed.

"I served as an ensign under Admiral Corwin when he commanded the *Valiant*. It was my first cruise."

"Do you accept my identification, Commander Dunmoore?" Corwin asked as he turned his piercing stare on her again.

"For now, sir," she replied, fighting to keep her tone neutral, if not respectful.

"Then I suggest you decelerate and swing around Arietis in the opposite direction from what you were no doubt planning. A little gravity assist to slow you down would be advisable."

"Yes, sir. Thank you, sir." Dunmoore bit back a more insolent retort. She did not need lessons in ship handling from a flag officer who looked for all the galaxy to have gone rogue.

"I will come up in my shuttle. Perhaps we can meet on my little orbital station."

"Sorry sir, but no. I don't intend to place myself that close to an unknown situation, let alone place my ship in such a position. I will decelerate enough to enter a very high orbit around the planet but my shields will remain up, and I will keep my targeting sensors on your ship and station. You are more than welcome to board *Stingray*."

Corwin studied her for a few moments. He clearly saw in her eyes the stubborn determination that was Dunmoore's hallmark. He made a slight grimace.

"Very well, commander, we shall do it your way. Make no mistake, however. If you initiate hostile action, I will reply in kind, even if it means firing on fellow Navy spacers. What I have here is too important for the Commonwealth to allow a rogue captain to jeopardize it. Corwin out."

Dunmoore felt anger war with embarrassment as she took her seat again.

"Mister Tours, adjust our course to place us around this planet — Arietis, I believe the admiral called it — at the best rate of deceleration we can manage. I want as high an orbit as you can plot and still remain within its gravity envelope. Guns, keep the ship at battle stations. The slightest hostile act and we will open fire. Keep a targeting solution on both ships and the orbital at all times."

The bite in her tone was hard enough that no one on the bridge other than Pushkin dared meet her eyes, but he held them long enough to satisfy himself that her temper was still under control – barely.

*

Dunmoore and her crew enjoyed several tense hours while the frigate decelerated. She had made a point of keeping both the ship and the station under constant active targeting. To her surprise, it was not returned.

"Sir, a shuttle has broken through the upper atmosphere and is boosting toward us."

"Type, chief?"

"It reads like a standard civilianized version of the Navy's utility craft."

"Somehow, I think it has a bit more than civvie gear inside that bland hull," Dunmoore replied dryly. "Please tell me you're getting life signs from it."

"Six, sir," Penzara replied.

"Any danger they could be spoofing?"

The gunnery chief turned toward her, a surprised look on his face. It was quickly replaced by understanding.

"You think they might try a bomb."

"Someone's tried before. I can't think of a better way to get rid of a pesky frigate without risking my own ships than sending a thermonuclear device into its hangar bay in the guise of a shuttle."

"Aye," he replied, soberly shaking his head at the thought. "You'll be wanting the admiral to dock externally, then."

"Oh yes. And after a solid scan from a stand-off distance."

"He might take offense, captain."

"He can take whatever he wants, chief. Until proven otherwise, the only claim to his rank and status is what he says he has. In the meantime, target the shuttle as well."

*

"*Stingray*, this is Admiral Corwin's shuttle. Please provide approach and docking instructions. I assume you'll wish to scan us."

Pushkin tilted his head in surprise as he turned to Dunmoore.

"It seems the admiral has anticipated your caution."

"Probably because he'd do the same in my place," she replied with a small, hard smile. "And you were afraid we'd be treated to a flag officer tantrum."

"If I may, sir," Kowalski interjected, "when he was captain of the *Valiant*, Admiral Corwin was well liked and respected by the officers and crew. He knew his business. That was before the war of course, so I never saw him command in battle. I never saw him throw a tantrum either," she added with a grin.

"All right. Make to the shuttle, she is to come to a halt relative to us, on the starboard side, at a distance of ten kilometers and wait while we run a thorough scan. If she has shielding, she's to drop it. We'll send further instructions once we've cleared her."

*

"She reads clear, sir," Lieutenant Syten reported a short while later. "No evidence of weapons beyond small arms, or signs of explosive devices. Six humans on board."

"Probability that we're being spoofed?"

"Negligible. *Stingray*'s frames may be old, but her sensors are as new and as good as they get, thanks to our recent refit."

"Mister Kowalski, make to the shuttle she's to approach the starboard docking ring, stopping at a distance of one hundred meters. We'll take her with our tractor beams and bring her in."

"They've acknowledged."

"Do you wish a side party, captain?" Pushkin asked.

"No. I did not see Admiral Corwin wearing any mark of rank, and his shuttle does not bear an admiral's flag. Therefore, he's not entitled to a formal piping aboard. Have Mister Devall and a few bosun's mates meet me at the airlock. They're to be armed, of course."

"Of course, sir." Pushkin nodded as he turned to carry out her orders, wondering whether she would be able to hold her temper in check. He had not seen her this tense and angry since her first few days aboard *Stingray* when the crew and ship had been a demoralized disaster.

To make her point, Dunmoore strapped on her personal weapon after making sure it was loaded and charged.

"Advise them that the admiral and his flag lieutenant are welcome to board. The remainder of his crew is to stay on the shuttle."

She definitely had a head of steam going, Pushkin thought as he watched her retreating back. Provided she could keep it focused, things would be okay, but he worried nonetheless.

*

"She's docked," Lieutenant Devall said, looking up from the airlock's console. "Equalizing pressure."

Four boatswain's mates, including Leading Spacer Vincenzo, were drawn up on either side of the hatch, slung scatter guns held at a low port.

"Opening the outside hatch."

Dunmoore watched on the small screen as the armored door unlatched and slid into the hull, exposing the shuttle's own airlock hatch. It swung inwards with a dull clang, and an armed spacer stepped through, carefully scanning the inside of the airlock. He wore an unmarked black battledress uniform but moved like someone with many boarding party actions under his belt. The man studied his hand-held sensor, nodded as if satisfied, and made a hand signal over his right shoulder.

At the signal, a tall, erect man with silver-shot black hair stepped over the coaming and gestured at the armed spacer to retreat into the shuttle.

Dunmoore nodded at Devall to open the inner hatch. The second officer complied after a last look at his security detail, to ensure they were ready. Then, the heavy door opened with a sigh, and Dunmoore was face-to-face with Rear Admiral Lucius Corwin.

— Eleven —

"Welcome aboard, sir," Dunmoore said in a guarded tone. She pointedly did not salute. Corwin took her less than warm welcome in stride, his eyes expressing amusement more than anything.

"Commander Dunmoore." He nodded. "I will be coming aboard alone as I don't have the luxury of a flag lieutenant on this assignment."

"You'll understand, sir, that I have to leave a guard detail at the airlock."

Corwin's amusement seemed to grow at Dunmoore's serious tone.

"I wouldn't expect anything less from a prudent captain. After all, we're not in uniform, and you don't know any of us from Adam."

He gestured toward the corridor.

"If you'll lead on, commander. I would prefer we discuss what I have to say in private."

"Of course. Please follow me."

Dunmoore led Corwin through the maze of corridors to the heart of the ship. She deliberately took him through the bridge to her ready room rather than use the private entrance from the passageway. When she glanced at him as they passed the door, she saw the hint of a smile tugging at the corner of his lips and for some reason, the sight infuriated her.

Lieutenant Commander Pushkin did not call the crew to attention, but rose from the command chair and nodded. "Welcome aboard, sir."

As Siobhan expected, Corwin saw Lieutenant Kowalski in her alcove.

"Kathryn," he beamed at her, "lovely to see you in person again."

Kowalski stood, if not quite to attention, very nearly so, and took Corwin's proffered hand.

"Admiral, it's good to see you again as well." Her tone was guarded, as was her smile. With a flicker of her eyes, she confirmed to Dunmoore that he was indeed Rear Admiral Lucius Corwin. Short of a DNA scan, this was as close to a positive identification as she was going to get.

"Mister Pushkin," she said, inviting Corwin to enter the ready room with a gesture of her hand, "pass the word for Vincenzo. Coffee and whatever sticky buns the wardroom has on offer."

"Aye, aye, sir."

Once inside the small office, Dunmoore invited him to sit. Corwin looked at her speculatively as she took her own chair, no doubt considering his next words carefully.

"Commander, your sudden appearance here causes me a bit of a problem," he finally said, his tone conversational as he crossed his legs and settled back in his seat.

"With all due respect, sir," she replied, her tone conveying the exact opposite, "I find it highly irregular that a ship we've identified as having committed an act of piracy under our very eyes several weeks ago and after that pursued to this system, is actually under Navy control. Has the Navy started a new sideline we weren't informed of? Has our budget been cut that badly?"

"You did not pursue a ship, commander," Corwin replied, his tone calm, tolerant even, in the face of Siobhan's insubordinate words. "You left your convoy to pursue a notion. These ships of mine do not indulge in piracy. Their mission is to protect this installation at all costs."

He was interrupted by the door chime and at Dunmoore's order, Leading Spacer Vincenzo, still equipped with his sidearm but bearing a serving of coffee and pastries, stepped in. He glanced at Corwin suspiciously before setting the tray down on the desk.

"Will there be anything else, sir?"

"Not for the moment, thank you."

The spacer came briefly to attention, then turned on his heel and left.

Corwin looked at her with a quizzical smile. "Your steward comes well armed."

Dunmoore tried to find a hint of mockery in his voice but failed. The man was infuriatingly calm and polite.

"Vincenzo is one of my bosun's mates. He picks up the odd catering duties since my former steward turned out to be a Special Security Bureau agent."

"Ah, that's right," Corwin nodded. "I recall hearing about your misfortunes. It's a sad statement on our Commonwealth that the security service sees fit to spy on the Navy in the midst of war. They would be better employed finding and eliminating the real traitors."

For the first time, Dunmoore heard some emotion in Corwin's voice. When he did not expand on his comment, Siobhan wondered whether only the story of the SSB mole in her crew had made the rounds and not the tale of the moneymaking scheme the mole was overseeing.

"Where were we?" Corwin continued. "Yes, I was mentioning how your appearance here is causing me a bit of embarrassment."

"In what way?" Dunmoore looked at him with unfeigned disbelief. "I mean other than my tracking down ships I've witnessed committing an act of piracy on a Commonwealth-flagged freighter."

Corwin sighed softly, communicating his growing exasperation with Dunmoore for the first time.

"Commander, I really did not wish to discuss my affairs with you, but I gather that your reputation for tilting at windmills is well deserved and that I shall find no peace until you've satisfied your self-righteous curiosity."

His harsh words, delivered in that same calm tone, hit Dunmoore harder than an all-out dressing down would have. She began to realize that Corwin was manipulating her and had been since the first radio contact.

"But you'll give me the 'need to know' speech anyway," she replied nastily.

"I probably should, commander. However, we are professional naval officers and fellow graduates of the Academy, meeting out here in the Coalsack badlands, far from home. I believe it might be appropriate that I put your mind at ease so you can act in the best interests of the Service."

When Dunmoore failed to reply, Corwin gave a small shrug and helped himself to some pastry. He chewed on the confection slowly as if savoring every mouthful, while he watched Siobhan. Once he had swallowed the last bite, he wiped his fingers on a napkin and sat back in the chair, elbows on the armrests and fingers steepled in front of him.

"My compliments to your cook. We don't get much good, fresh food out here. Arietis has subsistence agriculture of sorts, but what it produces is poor in flavor, even if it does provide adequate nutrition. Our supply runs are by necessity infrequent and not particularly generous, so pastry-making is not a luxury we can afford all too often."

"With the *Nikko Maru* destroyed, I suppose your supply runs have become even less frequent."

Corwin nodded, his amused expression returning, this time with a glimmer of respect in his eyes.

"Well deduced. Because of secrecy, we're obliged to use specially hired non-naval vessels."

"That would include your sloops."

"Indeed. Civilian vessels armed as privateers in covert service."

"Naval crews?"

"Private military contractors, though I have a few naval personnel with me." He smiled briefly.

"I find this highly irregular, Admiral."

"It is that, Commander Dunmoore. But it's part of the war effort against the Shrehari."

"So you admit to having your ships intercept the *Nikko Maru*, remove all persons on board, and set it to destroy itself. Your people's thoroughness almost cost me a boarding party." Though she tried to control it, her hostility shone through almost painfully.

"Unfortunate. My people were instructed to ensure no trace of our activities could be found and that the destruction of the freighter looked like an accident. Obviously, they weren't entirely successful. I must have a word with the senior captain."

"And the individuals your 'contractors' removed from the ship?"

"They're safe and sound, and comfortably housed within the confines of a base on the planet. We are a naval operation, and I am bound by the same laws as you, commander."

Dunmoore let her skepticism show without restraint.

"If you wish, you may accompany me down and confirm that fact for yourself," Corwin said, lips twitching as he read her mood. "However, until I can make the necessary arrangements to repatriate these individuals with all due concern for the security of my operation, they are de facto internees, as is permitted by our regulations in time of war."

"Admiral, if the *Nikko Maru* was one of your supply vessels, why the attack?"

Corwin tilted his head minutely as if evaluating his response.

"We discovered there was a mole in our operation, possibly working for the enemy, perhaps even working for the SSB. We didn't realize he was missing until the *Nikko Maru* had jumped out of this system on its way back home. My ships pursued but didn't catch up with it until it entered Commonwealth space. Unfortunately, it was in a spot close enough for your ship to respond to the distress call. If we'd had the time, we would have repaired the damage caused by the torpedo and sailed her somewhere safe, or failing that, scuttled her ourselves."

He paused to pick up his cup and take a sip of coffee.

"My people had to settle for removing the crew and rigging it to destruct. I just wish they hadn't been quite as inventive."

"Did you find the mole?"

"No." Corwin glanced away briefly. "He jumped ship at Yotai. But by the time we got that information from the captain of the *Nikko Maru*, he'd already taken another ship and headed deeper into the badlands. We tracked that one as well, only to find it had been taken and destroyed by pirates. There were no survivors."

Dunmoore's eyes narrowed over her coffee mug as she stared at Corwin.

"Very convenient, Admiral."

"Not particularly. We have no idea who the mole was working for and how he infiltrated my operation. That leaves us as vulnerable to hostile action as before."

"Which leads me to my next question," Dunmoore said. "Why does the Navy have a secret installation in a poorly charted system light years beyond our sphere?"

"And now we are approaching 'need to know' territory, commander." He placed his empty cup carefully on the tray. "The only thing I can share with you is that we are engaged in top secret research that will help speed the end of the war. It's so secret that the Navy couldn't take the chance of anyone accidentally stumbling across it."

"There are plenty of no-go systems closer to home."

"Indeed. But Arietis has a few particularities that commend it admirably for our purposes."

"Such as?"

Corwin shook his head slowly. "We've reached the point where I cannot share further information about our activities."

He reached into his tunic pocket and extracted a data wafer.

"Please familiarize yourself with these orders."

She made no movement to take it.

"Now please, commander."

Dunmoore could sense that Corwin's patience was coming to an end. She reached out and took the chip from his hands, dropping it on her console's reader. The screen came up with a login page demanding her identification. She tapped in the unique command code that identified her as captain of *Stingray*.

The login page disappeared, and the Navy insignia came up, with the words "These orders come under authorization AY63901TW."

"I suggest you consult your classified data banks to confirm the authenticity of the authorization code," Corwin said conversationally.

She glared briefly at him but called up the list of secret codes. Her eyes hardened as she matched letters and numbers.

"I confirm the authenticity of the authorization code, Admiral," she said, her voice as stony as her face.

"Then please study those orders."

Dunmoore tapped the screen and read. When she was done, she looked up at Corwin, confusion warring with anger on her face.

"I believe you're now clear on your position vis-à-vis my operation, commander?"

"Yes, sir." Her use of the honorific for the first time was not lost on the admiral.

"In that case, commander, I intend that you remain in this system for a while and assist me with a pesky problem I seem to be having of late."

"I do have a convoy to get back to, sir."

"Understood. Nonetheless, now that you're here and privy to our presence, I shall commandeer your assistance. The other vessels in the escort should suffice to organize the convoy, and if necessary, take your charges back."

"Yes, sir," she replied through clenched teeth.

"If that's all, I will return to base. My operations officer will be in touch within the hour to provide patrol instructions. You may have noticed that one of my ships has headed toward the outer system. An intruder tripped our surveillance perimeter. However, if it is what we believe it might be, we may need the greater weight of your broadside to successfully take care of this infestation."

He rose, as did Dunmoore a second or two later.

"Commander, you have my word as an officer that the work we're doing here will help end this war and save the lives of countless spacers. If you still have doubts upon your return home, Admiral Nagira can vouch for me."

She looked at him in astonishment. "He knows about this?"

"Not in detail, no, but Hoko Nagira and I go way back, and he's aware that I'm involved in highly classified work."

She nodded, unconvinced, but when Corwin stretched out his hand, she shook it, albeit reluctantly. Admiral Nagira was a patron of sorts for her. He had been the only flag officer to take an interest in a headstrong lieutenant at the onset of the war and had patiently guided her way up the promotion ladder and into increasingly larger commands as she gained experience and grew in professional stature.

Nagira had arranged for her to take *Stingray* when no one else wanted the old frigate, confident that she could rehabilitate her crew and name. If he and Corwin were close friends, then she had no choice but to submit gracefully. To do otherwise would show ingratitude to a man who had quite literally saved her career more than once.

"I'll see you to your shuttle, sir," she offered, trying to sound duly respectful.

"Thank you, commander. Your courtesy under these trying circumstances has been exemplary. I shall so note to Admiral Nagira when I next get the chance."

The smooth, gentle tone was back, and part of Dunmoore felt embarrassed at the way in which she treated Corwin, especially considering his forbearance in the face of her rebellious attitude.

*

After seeing Corwin over the coaming at the starboard airlock, Siobhan returned to the bridge and stood behind the officer of the watch, looking at the shuttle recede in the distance on the main screen. When she felt she had her emotions completely under control, she spoke.

"Guns, you may stand down targeting and return weapon state to standby. It appears that we have inadvertently stumbled upon a covert naval installation and those ships out there are under contract to the Navy for local protection."

"And the *Nikko Maru*?" Pushkin asked, doubt evident in his voice.

"Also under contract to the Navy. Admiral Corwin has had some security issues and we apparently, and quite unfortunately, witnessed the end result of those problems."

"You're convinced of this, sir?"

"Yes, Mister Pushkin, I am." She raised a hand, forestalling any further questions. "You'll have to take my word for it. In the meantime, we are at Admiral Corwin's disposal to help him deal with one or more unidentified ships lurking at the edge of the system, apparently intent on spying."

The first officer looked at his captain for a few seconds, one eye narrowed, and his expression conveying profound incredulity at the turn of events.

She sighed.

"Agreed, Number One, but that's the way it has to be. We should be receiving orders from the admiral's staff soon. You may secure the ship from battle stations." She patted him wearily on the arm. "I'll be in my quarters."

Dunmoore felt an irresistible urge to shower and change her uniform, and she could not quite figure out why.

The first officer stared at her receding back, unsure what had happened, but knowing that it had thrown his captain for a loop. He did not as yet know whether it presaged something unpleasant for the ship, but it was slightly unnerving to see her usual self-confidence wavering, be it ever so invisible to those who did not know her intimately.

"The captain doesn't look happy," Kowalski commented quietly as she looked up from the command chair.

"Your Admiral Corwin seems to have something to do with that," he replied.

"He's hardly mine, sir. I haven't seen him in more than six years." She shrugged. "He was a good captain back then, but I was just an ensign on my first cruise, so what did I know."

"Probably nothing, Kathryn," he replied, chuckling, "like every ensign ever birthed from the womb of our beloved Academy."

— Twelve —

"Mister Devall," the signals petty officer of the watch called out, frowning at his console. "The system's just picked up a tightly focused burst transmission."

"Point of origin?" Devall asked.

"From the planet, sir. Unless there's a ship hidden behind us that's on the same relative vector from Arietis, it could be meant for us."

"That would be some fancy transmitting if it were for our eyes only and a powerful burst too, considering the distance and our velocity," Devall commented. "Although it could have been for a ship between Arietis and us as well."

Stingray was a good five light minutes above the planetary plane and from Arietis itself, waiting and watching for the lurker to show himself.

"It could, sir. The only reason I picked it up was that Mister Syten also has the defensive sensors set to warn of any signal hitting the ship, no matter how feeble. When the burst painted the hull, the computer figured it was a message and routed it over to me."

"And what does it say?"

"Right now, all I've got is a really compressed load of gibberish."

"Coded?" Devall's aristocratic eyebrows rose in question.

"Yes sir, with an algorithm I can't match to anything we have in our records."

"Essentially unreadable by anyone other than the intended recipient?"

"Yes, sir."

"But if we're the intended recipient, why don't we have the means to read it?"

"Search me, sir. I'm not the crypto rating. Maybe Mister Kowalski can figure it out. She's not bad at cracking stuff like this." There was a hint of pride for his officer in his voice.

Devall checked the duty roster and saw that the captain was in her ready room, no doubt plowing through the day's allotment of reports. Perhaps she would like a small distraction, he thought and paged her on the intercom.

"Captain, this is the bridge."

"Dunmoore." She sounded tired.

"Sir, sensors picked up a focused burst transmission from Arietis, highly compressed."

"We're kind of far from the planet." She sounded less weary at the news. "Any of Admiral Corwin's little flotilla between us and the point of origin?"

Devall glanced at the gunnery chief who shook his head.

"Nothing we can see."

"Can we uncompress and decode it?"

"Negative, captain. Perhaps Kathryn can think up a way to do it."

"Understood. Push it to her work queue. She can tackle it when she comes on watch. Was there -"

"Captain," Devall's interrupted her, a tinge of excitement coloring his usually calm voice, "sensors just picked up an emergence less than two light minutes from our current position."

"One of the admiral's ships?"

"Doubtful. We have no sensor records of any leaving the system and a supply ship would emerge much closer to the hyper limit."

"Turn the ship on an intercept course." She quickly saved the ship's stores report and, with a sigh of relief, headed for the bridge.

*

"He's gone silent," Devall announced as he rose from the command chair and handed control over to Dunmoore.

"Last known vector on tactical." She glanced at the second officer. "If going silent's not an admission of guilt, I don't know what is."

"But is it because he's an intruder or because Admiral Corwin trusts us just enough to have us covertly watched?" Devall smiled tightly.

"Getting paranoid already, Trevane?"

He shook his head. "Just overly cautious for now. With your permission, captain, I'll be off to my station. I sense the call to battle in our near future."

She nodded, eyes on the screen, trying to divine the intentions of the other ship's commander.

"Thank you, Mister Devall."

Dunmoore was barely conscious of the primary bridge crew taking their seats around her, replacing the regular watch.

"Captain," Guthren broke through her concentration, "we're on a converging track to the last known vector of the other ship."

"Thanks, chief," she replied, eyes snapping back to the present. "Mister Syten, have we managed to crunch the sensor data enough for identification?"

"No, captain. It has no IFF, and all I can say with any certainty is that its size is somewhere between a sloop and a corvette. It seems to have excellent emissions control."

"Project his most probable course based on his velocity before we lost him."

A dotted line appeared on the tactical display.

"Could he be trying what we attempted?" Pushkin asked, standing behind her. "Get close enough to Arietis running silent on a ballistic course?"

"I doubt he'd have any more success than we had and Navy ships are pretty much the best at hiding among the background radiation."

"Perhaps we can intercept him before Admiral Corwin's mercenaries do. Show them how the Navy does it," the first officer suggested.

Dunmoore shrugged. "We have nothing better to do, and it's been quite some time since we last kicked butt."

"Mister Tours," she continued, "I'd like to cut across the target's hawse. Plot a jump that will put us about half a light minute short of his projected course. When we emerge, we'll decelerate to match his last known speed. With luck, he'll remain on passive sensors and won't pick us up until we're in range."

The sailing master nodded and began to feed the parameters into the navigation computer. Arranging to have two starships meet in an immense volume of space required very precise calculations and the cooperation of both captains. Fortunately, even if the lurker picked up *Stingray* as he sped toward Arietis, he could hardly decline the offer of surrender rather than battle, should they come within range. As far as the notion of cooperation went, that suited Dunmoore just fine.

*

"Decelerating, sir," Guthren reported from the helm a short time later, after the frigate re-emerged in normal space. "We should be able to tack in close succession within the hour."

"Anything at all on the sensors, chief?"

"Nothing, captain," Penzara replied.

"What's his projected position now?"

"Still a light minute away," the sailing master replied.

"Should we not report this incursion to Admiral Corwin?" Pushkin asked.

"Would it make a difference? His other ships can't be within range until hours after we've intercepted this bugger. They're scattered all over the place."

The first officer shrugged. "I suppose not, but he might take exception to your not informing him. You acknowledged his authority in this system, did you not?"

Dunmoore looked at him irritably. "Why is it that first officers always have to be a good angel sitting on a captain's shoulder and never a nasty little devil?"

"Union rules, captain," he replied with a straight face.

"Very well." She sighed. "Mister Kowalski, send an encrypted contact report to Admiral Corwin. Provide the contact's last recorded heading and speed, with a timestamp, our assessment of ship type, projected course and provide our own course and speed. Advise that I intend to intercept."

"Aye, sir."

"Sir," Petty Officer Rownes raised her hand, "I've got a faint trace on the approximate path predicted for the target."

"On screen."

Dunmoore smiled cruelly as she scanned the tactical schematic.

"Pretty close to where we thought he'd be. Cox'n come to one-one-three mark four-five. We're going to get ourselves in a nice position to shoot up his throat before he knows we're there."

"Come to one-one-three mark four-five, aye." Chief Guthren fired the maneuvering thrusters to nudge *Stingray* onto her new course. He knew Captain Dunmoore would be calling for more course corrections as they got closer, but he preferred tacking earlier and more often than a hard tack at the last moment. At the frigate's current velocity, course changes were best made long in advance, and they had hours to go before the two ships crossed paths.

*

"He's gone 'up systems,' sir," Syten announced excitedly, breaking the boredom of the long wait as the range between them decreased. "Still no IFF."

"Mister Pushkin, sound battle stations. What's the distance to the enemy?"

"One point one million kilometers," the gunnery officer replied.

"And we're on a converging course," Dunmoore smiled, "which means we'll be in missile range very quickly."

"He can still jump," the sailing master said. "We're outside the hyper limit."

Dunmoore watched the converging tracks on the tactical schematic, eyes narrowed in concentration.

"Captain," Syten sounded puzzled. "I've got a good read on his emissions now, and there's something strange with them."

"Does he look like anyone we know?"

"No, but I have a hard time figuring how a ship that's so leaky now that it's up systems could have been so well masked."

"Go to active targeting. Let him know we're not playing."

"Target acquired." Then, "He's jumped! One of Admiral Corwin's ships has emerged aft of the ship's last position."

"I suppose we could let the mercenary handle it from here on, but we should at least try to catch up." Dunmoore sounded irritated.

"Mercenary?" Pushkin softly asked over her shoulder. "Isn't that a bit rude?"

"I'm a tad tired of these games, Number One," she whispered back. Then, more loudly, "Cox'n, helm over; take us on a new tack to follow the target. Mister Tours, track the intruder and prepare a pursuit course."

"Aye, sir, but by the time we've turned, he'll be out of sensor range," the sailing master replied.

Dunmoore bit back a frustrated reply.

"Best estimate then. I don't think he'll be going far. He has to be as interested in this system as we are."

"The mercenary has jumped in pursuit," Syten said.

"Remind me to have a chat with everyone about not calling the mercenaries 'mercenaries,' Number One," she said to Pushkin in an aside, "at least not in public."

"I hope he has more luck than we did," Dunmoore continued, "although my guess is that he's just going to see what our unknown friend is doing. I don't think he's quite daft enough to try and intercept a ship potentially carrying a bigger broadside."

She tapped her chin with her gloved fingertips and pursed her lips.

"Since we probably won't be able to catch up to the target once we've completed our turn, perhaps it's best we leave it to him and return to our patrol station."

"Shall we report to the admiral and request orders?" Pushkin helpfully suggested.

"My conscience speaks again," she replied dryly. "By all means. Mister Kowalski, follow up on the initial contact report and summarize what little action has occurred. Specify that unless otherwise advised, we're returning to our patrol station."

The signals officer nodded and turned to her console.

"A thought just occurred to me, Mister Pushkin," Dunmoore said, contemplating the diverging ship courses on the tactical schematic. "Our mercenary friend didn't bother talking to us. He just jumped into a developing engagement and jumped out again, without as much as a by your leave."

"Not very sociable, is he? Come to think of it," the first officer eyes bored into Dunmoore's, "other than Admiral Corwin and his operations staff, no one else has bothered to speak with us. It's almost as if they've been ordered to stay quiet and stay away."

"Afraid of contamination? Or of letting out a secret or two?" Siobhan shrugged. Then she remembered a comment from the gunnery officer. "Mister Syten, you mentioned something about the intruder's emissions being strange?"

"Its emissions, when it went up systems, were pretty dirty. Not *Jade Delight* dirty, but more than they should have been for a ship that was practically invisible to sensors before. A ship with such poor emissions control can't run silent and hope to pass unnoticed."

"Perhaps they were distorting their emissions so we couldn't match it to anything in the registry," Kowalski suggested.

"That would imply it's a ship known to the Navy," Pushkin said. "Mister Syten, any chance you can clean up their signature enough to get a match?"

"I'll try." She sounded dubious. "But I wouldn't hold out much hope. I'll attempt to extract a useful visual from the sensor logs as well, but at that range, we'll have a hard time making out enough detail for identification."

"Just do your best," Siobhan softly replied. "Speaking of doing your best," she turned to Kowalski. "The signals watchkeeper pushed an encrypted transmission to your work queue."

"I saw that, captain. Focused burst from the planet. Fascinating and not just a little unusual. You'd only use that if you wanted to make sure no one could trace it back to the sender. But why us?"

"If we can break the encryption we should be able to answer that question," Siobhan smiled briefly. "In the meantime, let's turn back to our regularly scheduled course and speed."

*

"I think I may have something, chief," Petty Officer Rownes said, hours later, near the end of the afternoon watch.

Penzara got up from his station and went to look over her shoulder.

"See the sublight drive emissions curve from the target?" She pointed at the readout on her console. "What's wrong with it, chief?"

He frowned as he stared at the sensor data. After almost a minute, he nodded.

"The emissions are smeared across a wider spectrum than they should for a ship that can hide well enough to make it almost invisible."

"Right," Rownes grinned. "Since it's a lot harder to skew your emission signature, blurring it by opening the reactor dampers a bit wider is the next best thing."

Devall, who had noticed the interplay, joined them. Rownes repeated her comment, eliciting a knowing smile from the second officer.

"And what does that tell you?" He asked, pleased by her intelligent analysis.

"The folks on that ship don't want to detune their electronics and lose performance."

"And?" Devall cocked his head to the side.

"If they've gone to the trouble of smearing their emission signature even though we're deep in the Coalsack badlands, they know for sure that we have their fingerprint in our databanks."

"Well done, Rownes." He clapped her on the shoulder in praise. "How do you intend to clean it up?"

"That's a tough one, sir. I was thinking of running probability analyses over every peak and piece together the underlying real emissions curve; then I'll compare each result to the register until I have some close matches to work with."

"Concur." Chief Penzara nodded. "It'll be a bastard to work through, but there's no way to clean up the smear any more quickly."

"How long?"

"A day or so," Rownes shrugged. "I haven't exactly done this before."

"I'm sure you'll be fine," Devall replied. "I'll log this, so you can expect the captain and Mister Pushkin to show some interest after the next watch change."

Both Dunmoore and the first officer made a point of reading the log regularly throughout the day to catch up on events not momentous enough to merit an immediate advisory from the officer of the watch. Rownes' discovery, while interesting, had not reached that stage yet.

One deck below, where she shared a cabin with the surgeon, Lieutenant Kowalski was spending her off duty watch crunching through the encrypted transmission.

"Still at it, I see," Luttrell commented as she walked in. "You're going to go blind if you keep staring at the screen like that."

"Is that medical advice, Viv?" Kowalski sounded both tired and annoyed. "It looks suspiciously like my mother telling me I'd go insane if I kept playing with myself."

"Hmm," the surgeon perched on the corner of the shared desk, crossed her arms, and pretended to think hard. She turned her narrowed eyes on Kowalski, frowning.

"While there is possibly an element of truth to both, I'd be more concerned about your missing sleep, food, and," she added wrinkling her nose, "showers in your quest to prove your genius."

Kowalski snorted, slumping in her chair, a grin at Luttrell's sardonic tone spreading across her weary face.

"There's something that doesn't compute, Viv. If this message were intended for *Stingray,* you'd think there would be some hint to help us decrypt it, but none of the current and old codes match. The computer can't even find a string that might hint at a solution. That's some pretty heavy-duty encryption."

"Spook grade?"

"Could be, but if it were Intelligence or the SSB, I'd have found some hint of it. An electronic scent, if you like. Organizations have a tendency to leave traces of themselves in their communications. That's why really sensitive stuff is hand-carried and shipped by aviso, not sent through subspace radio."

"So why send us a love letter in gibberish?" Before Kowalski could answer a devilish smile spread across the surgeon's plain features. "Has it occurred to you fine bridge officers that the message may have been intended for the unknown ship that slipped through our grasp? Did you check if it was headed in the right direction when we ruined its day?"

"Viv," Kowalski sprang up and squeezed her cabin mate in a bear hug, "for a frontier sawbones, you're a bloody genius. If we can figure out who that ship was, we might have a hint at the encryption protocol."

"Sometimes, all you need is some common sense, young Kathryn," she chided her roommate. "Now wash, eat, and sleep, in that order."

"Not before I do one more thing." She stabbed the intercom. "Bridge, Kowalski here. I need to speak with the navigator."

"Sanghvi," a voice replied. "What can I do for you?"

"Our esteemed surgeon had the idea that the signal we intercepted might have been meant for the intruder we chased soon afterward. Is there any way we can reconstruct its original course to see if it could be a possibility?"

"Shouldn't be a big problem, lieutenant. Give me a couple of hours."

"Thanks!"

*

Dunmoore stared speculatively at her signals officer and junior navigator. Once Sanghvi had completed his analysis and relayed the results to Kowalski, she had immediately asked to see the captain.

"That puts an interesting wrinkle on the matter," Siobhan said, her eyes returning to the schematic on her ready room's screen. "How confident are you?"

"Better than an eighty-five percent probability," Sanghvi replied confidently.

"If we hadn't been there to chase the intruder away, the burst transmission would have crossed that path with a hundred percent probability," Kowalski added. "Provided it's a repeater signal, he'd have gotten the next burst not long after he emerged."

"We may never know for sure, but if it was a regularly scheduled transmission, they'd have done better to vary its direction," Dunmoore said, shaking her head. "I chose to patrol this area precisely because the intruders liked to show up here more frequently than anywhere else and it came to bite them. Do you think you'll be able to crack the code?"

"I don't know, captain. If we could figure out the target's identity, it might give me a thread to pull on. Different organizations have different ways of encrypting."

"With any luck, we should find out soon. Rownes has been working on the sensor data since early yesterday to strip off the masking emissions and get a clear fingerprint. If they felt they needed to hide it then we certainly have it in the registry, so you'll have your answer. If there's nothing else?"

"No sir," Kowalski replied. She and Sanghvi snapped to attention.

"Well done, the two of you. Dismissed."

Pushkin, leaning against the bulkhead, arms crossed, smiled at her knowingly.

"Why is it that I have the distinct impression you'll not be reporting this to the admiral, notwithstanding the fact that a clandestine, coded transmission seems to have come from the vicinity of his supposedly secure and secret research facility?"

"Because I'd rather present him with a full picture than feed it to him piecemeal. Once we figure out who the intruder was, then..."

"With all due respect, captain, that's a load of bull." Pushkin's smile broadened. "You don't trust Corwin any more than you have to. If you did, you'd have let him know by now he has a problem of some sort."

Siobhan felt her face flush as she recalled the ease with which Corwin had forced her out of silent running and into his service. She bit back the first thought that came to mind as being unworthy of her and her audience of one.

"You may have a point, Gregor," she finally admitted. "I do seem to carry some lingering resentment toward the admiral."

"Lingering?" Pushkin laughed amicably. "No, captain. You don't like Corwin, and I can see it in your eyes but," he continued, suddenly becoming serious, "your gut instinct is bothered by something about this whole setup. That's why you're cagey."

"So what do I do?"

"Continue to be cagey. If and when we figure out who the intruder was, we can kick it around some more."

The intercom beeped for attention.

"We may not have too much of a wait," she said sardonically as she accepted the communication. "Dunmoore."

"Chief Penzara, captain. Rownes has narrowed the fingerprint down to a couple of possibles. Nothing definitive, mind you."

"And?"

"Perhaps you'd like to see this on the main screen, sir."

Siobhan glanced at Pushkin in surprise. The stoic first officer shrugged as he pushed himself upright.

"On our way."

*

"This," Petty Officer Rownes pointed at the readout on the screen, "is the most probable 'clean' emission signature the computer came up with. As you can see, it's still a bit smeared. I don't think we'll get much closer, but it was enough to come up with possibles."

At her gesture, the readout vanished, to be replaced by several rows of starship images, with their signature curves beside them.

"These are all ships whose fingerprints are a ninety percent match, and they all share more than a few similarities."

Sensing that Pushkin was about to speak, Siobhan made a gentle stopping gesture. Rownes was entitled to have her moment in the spotlight.

"First, they're all either the same model or variations thereof and built to the same specs at the same shipyard. And second, they're all flagged to the Black Nova Line and all have *Maru* in their name."

"What are the chances our intruder was either the *Fuso* or the *Oko Maru*?"

"Considering we know they're in this sector. Or at least we know the *Oko Maru* is in the sector. The *Fuso Maru* might well be after her vanishing act, so the chances are pretty good," Lieutenant Syten replied, nodding at Rownes to amplify her statement.

"What the lieutenant said, sir. We can't really pin the signature on either in particular but they fit the profile we have, and they're nearest. The other *Marus* are either working known routes or in refit, based on the latest registry update."

"Which is from?"

"Two months ago, captain."

"Things could have changed in two months, but I agree, our old pals from the convoy are the most likely suspects. Of course," she shook her head, smiling sadly, "this just deepens the mystery. Why are legitimate, Commonwealth-registered freighters playing war games with private military contractors working for the Fleet?"

"They say that sailing too close to the Coalsack can make some people go nuts," Guthren commented. "Of course, they also say that even the most honest men can be tempted into piracy if there's enough money or power involved."

Dunmoore and Pushkin looked at each other, recalling their earlier conversation.

*

"You know how I said I'd wait until we knew who the intruder was before I reported to Admiral Corwin?" Dunmoore looked at Pushkin mischievously over the rim of her coffee mug. The restless night had not given her any answers, but it had made her feel like being more reckless.

"Let me guess: you've changed your mind. I should have proposed a wager. I'd be a few creds richer right now."

"I think I want to wait until Kathryn has cracked that message before I report."

"Hedging your bets?"

"Any problems with my course of action?" She asked instead of answering Pushkin's question.

"No, captain." He sighed softly. "Apparently, things are happening in this sector we aren't meant to discover. The less we let on that we're digging around, the better, I'd say. There's something about a naval operation using mercenaries that really irks me and I feel no obligation to share intelligence with them."

"You and the rest of the crew." Siobhan's tone made it a statement rather than a question.

"Aye. After the hell we suffered under your predecessor, everyone on board has developed finely tuned bullshit detectors and this place is nearing barnyard strength."

"Have you ever been on an actual farm, or are you just using an old cliché?" Dunmoore teased him.

"A little village not far from Sverdlovsk. We Pushkins had some distant family there, and when we visited Earth well before I joined the Fleet, we made the obligatory visit to the *Rodina*. A manure pile taller than a man, it was, and the stench! Traditional farming might seem fun for the tourists, but I couldn't see myself doing it."

"Was this an actual working farm, or a living museum?"

Pushkin snorted.

"I wasn't able to tell. If it was a museum, the curator had a mania for accuracy and a strange sense of history. You see, it was apparently modeled on a collective farm during the early communist era."

"Strange indeed." She shrugged. "History gets whitewashed all the time to accommodate the latest political fad. I wouldn't be surprised if, some day, the Migration Wars get turned into evil, reactionary revolts against a bunch of benevolent, progressive governments rather than the other way around."

"I hope I'm not alive to see that. Cognitive dissonance and I don't get along very well."

"Most spacers have that problem, Gregor. It comes from living where the slightest mistake can kill you and physics are facts, not someone's interpretation of what happens to be popular at the moment."

"So what are the facts telling us when it comes to Admiral Corwin and his secret operation?" He asked.

"I'm not sure. Perhaps I need to wangle an invitation to visit him dirtside." Siobhan grinned. "Beard the wolf in his lair, so to speak."

"Careful you don't get bitten."

*

"How's your latest effort going," Luttrell asked, peering over Kowalski's shoulder.

"I'd hoped that finding out who owned the putative recipient of the message might give me a clue but so far, nothing. The Black Nova folks have a pretty good crypto section if that's who it was addressed to."

"Better than a commercial operation should have?"

Kowalski laughed sharply.

"Some of the big corporations have a better communications setup than the Navy, including the ability to keep their mail secret, not only from each other but also from the various government agencies."

"You think it's the case here?"

"No other way about it, Viv. I'm afraid I'll be disappointing our captain this time."

Luttrell patted her on the shoulder.

"She's smart enough to know you've done your best."

"That's fine for her," Kowalski replied, "but it doesn't do much for my ego."

The surgeon laughed.

"Don't get too wrapped up in this. I'm sure our Siobhan is hatching some other plans to figure out what the hell is going on in this system."

"And our Gregor is doing his damnest to dissuade her from anything reckless."

"We each need a conscience. He's hers, and it's just as well."

"Yeah. Funny how that turned out, isn't it?"

She had a faint pang of guilt at her part in making the first officer look bad the day Dunmoore had taken command in what seemed an eternity ago.

"Maybe, but I'm not taking anything for granted anymore on this ship," Luttrell replied.

She sniffed the air around Kowalski half mockingly. "When's the last time you showered, bunkie?"

*

"Captain, we're getting a transmission from the planet. It's Admiral Corwin."

"Speak of the devil," Pushkin said. "Would you like your privacy?"

"No. Stay." She touched her console, and Admiral Corwin's patrician face appeared on the screen. "What's the time lag?"

"Five minutes each way," Kowalski replied.

"We're evidently not going to have a conversation."

"Captain Dunmoore," Corwin began, "belated thanks for helping chase that pesky pirate out of the system. Sadly my other ship was unable to catch up with it, but those wishing to interfere with our work are now on notice that the Navy isn't playing games anymore."

"Given the importance of my mission, I have asked the Admiralty to detach *Stingray* from its current mission and place her under my command. The response has been favorable. Welcome to the Arietis Squadron." He smiled genially. "I'm very pleased to have you. Your formal orders are attached to this transmission. Have no fears for your convoy as Lieutenant Commander Gulsvig has received orders to depart without you."

Siobhan looked at Pushkin in astonishment.

"Right now," Corwin continued, "you must be wondering how you'll be replenished so far from the nearest base or tender. I have arrangements for my sloops, and those should suffice for you. When the time comes, you'll be getting instructions. In the meantime, maintain your patrol route as per your original instructions. I'll be recalling you to Arietis orbit once my squadron is whole again, and we will discuss your future employment in person. Corwin, out."

The first officer whistled. "Now there's a turn of events. Weren't you saying just now that you'd like to wangle a visit dirtside? I guess your wish is about to be granted."

"How did he get orders from HQ so fast when we can't even reach back on subspace bands?"

"A booster station we don't know about? Or he has an aviso we haven't seen yet?"

"I get the feeling that if I ask, I'll be told it's classified," Dunmoore replied sourly. "Getting formally placed under Corwin's command isn't quite what I wanted."

"But it may give us the chance to figure out the story behind the *Nikko Maru* and why its sister ships are spying on this system."

"Let's see those orders," Dunmoore said, ignoring his comment. She read for a few minutes, grunting now and then.

"So?" Pushkin tried not to sound impatient.

"There's no copy of the orders from HQ assigning us here, merely a reference to such a directive, for one. We've been granted permission to open fire first and ask questions later the next time we spot an intruder who doesn't wish to heave to and be boarded. We're to remain within a third of a parsec from the system's primary. Any further out requires Corwin's permission, but I have the freedom to patrol as I see fit within those limits. He also provided his standing orders and signals instructions. Apparently, the ships we've been introduced to a few weeks ago near the *Nikko Maru* are *Carnatic* and *Coromandel*. His third sloop is *Malabar*. No mention of any further starships." She touched the console again. "I've posted the orders."

"And now?"

"Now we acknowledge receipt and carry on patrolling."

"Since Admiral Corwin is actually your commanding officer at this point, do you intend to share our identification of the latest intruder, as well as the fact that someone on the planet was trying to communicate with it surreptitiously?"

Siobhan considered her first officer for a few heartbeats.

"You know the answer to that, Gregor," she finally said.

Pushkin nodded unhappily and rose to see about implementing Admiral Corwin's standing orders. He hoped her stubbornness would not draw their new commander's ire. This far from home, he was the sole authority on all naval matters, especially if he controlled the only subspace link to HQ. Sometimes Dunmoore's fearlessness when it came to flag officers had serious drawbacks.

Kowalski noticed his worried frown as he sat at his station and correctly deduced that it had to do with the admiral's message. If the cautious first officer was apprehensive, it meant Dunmoore was planning to do things her own way again, and that could be terrifyingly entertaining. She settled back in the command chair and smiled.

— Thirteen —

"Doesn't look like much," Chief Guthren commented as he gently steered the frigate into orbit around Arietis.

"I wish I could tell what the charts say about the planet, but it's not listed anywhere," Tours replied. "From the looks of it, it's not far off Earth-norm, if somewhat dryer and colder, which doesn't surprise me, considering the small size of its oceans."

"Population?" Dunmoore asked.

"I make out some life signs," Syten said, "humanoid, but not necessarily human. At best guess there're about a million sentients down there, mostly concentrated in the one green rift valley near the equator and a few smaller oases spread across the main continent. The other concentration is on a plateau about two thousand kilometers north-east of the rift in what looks like a lifeless and desolate mountain chain."

"Corwin's base?"

"The power emissions are stronger than those coming from the main settlements, so I'd say it's likely."

"It feels like an old world, doesn't it?" Syten shivered slightly.

"Why do you say that?" Pushkin asked.

"I can't put my finger on it, sir, but I seem to recall seeing a projection of Earth's future a few hundred million years from now when I was a kid, and it had that same dry, empty, and unwelcoming feeling."

"From what I can tell, this sun is a lot older than our Sol," Tours said, "likely by several billion years, so Arietis could have been around for much longer than Earth, which would explain its ancient feel."

"*Stingray*, this is ground control," the radio came to life, "you can hold in your current orbit. There's no other traffic to be aware of, nor is any expected. Your shuttle's instructions to land at the main base will be coming shortly. Be advised that the station will keep a sensor lock on you for the duration."

"Acknowledged," Kowalski replied.

"Speaking of the station," Pushkin pointed at the side screen showing the boxy, inelegant structure, "isn't that a monitor with some bits added on?"

"Sure looks that way," Chief Penzara replied. "I wouldn't want to tangle with it at this range. It'll take the kind of punishment we can't hope to shrug off. Those monitors are nothing so much as heavily armored fusion plants studded with large bore plasma guns."

"With your permission, captain," Kowalski rose from her station, "I'll go prepare the shuttle."

Dunmoore waved the signals officer aft to the hangar deck, a thoughtful frown creasing her forehead.

"Misgivings?" Pushkin asked.

"Plenty, Number One. For example, I don't much like sitting under that monitor's constant observation. It could open fire on us at a moment's notice, and a three hundred millimeter round will hurt. We can't even tell if it has missile launchers tucked away in those pods hanging off the sides."

"Shall I keep our shields up?"

"As much as I'd like to say yes, showing that kind of mistrust won't be helpful. Just make sure you have someone locked onto the monitor at all times, with orders to raise shields the moment its sensors go to active targeting, or it looks like the guns are powering up."

"Aye." The first officer rubbed his chin. "I'd be a lot happier knowing the crew over yonder was one of ours, not a bunch of mercs who might be willing to open fire on a Navy ship if so ordered."

"So would I." Siobhan rose and repressed a yawn. She felt both irritable and nervous and hated the sensation. "You have the ship, Mister Pushkin."

"Aye, aye, sir." The first officer took the command chair, all too aware that he was fighting his own battle against the butterflies in his stomach. He was uncomfortable at seeing Dunmoore leave the ship, but they had no choice in the matter.

"Guns, keep the status of the monitor on the starboard tactical screen," he ordered. "If it powers anything up, I'd like to hear a really annoying alarm."

"Would a bit of Shrehari Opera do?" Penzara asked innocently. "T'krel's aria from Desa Dekai, perhaps?"

"Did I ever mention that you had a sadistic streak, chief?"

"Not recently, sir," he replied with a laugh. "But I do like to be reminded now and then."

*

The dusty plateau slowly turned from an indistinct mass into a jumble of rocks dotted with grayish, scrubby vegetation as the shuttle dropped through the thin atmosphere, riding hard on her thrusters to shed velocity. It looked arid and chilly, hardly a pleasant spot for a naval installation far from any support.

The base itself was more like a large hamlet made up of prefabricated buildings half buried in the mesa. It had no perimeter fencing and did not need any because the only way in was by air. A wide, gray, laser scraped area was marked in yellow and surrounded by flashing lights that outlined a landing strip large enough for a pair of sloops if their pilots felt confident.

A controller guided *Stingray*'s shuttle onto a big dot in front of the largest hangar and ordered them to shut down. A few moments later, a squad of armed mercenaries marched out in single file and surrounded the spacecraft. The leader made a 'come here' gesture toward the polarized windows, confident that he was being watched.

They were clad in the same unmarked black battledress uniform as Corwin, but their weapons were clearly of Commonwealth manufacture and matched those in *Stingray*'s arms locker. How private military contractors had managed to get their hands on service issue plasma carbines that were not to be sold to civilians was yet another question added to the growing list.

The six men were hard-faced and moved silently, with the ease and precision of professionals. Watching them, Dunmoore knew many, if not all of them, were veterans of one military service or another, but they lacked the mysterious aura that marked long-service Marines. Ex-colonials perhaps or national guardsmen.

She and Kowalski released their seat restraints and made their way aft, to the hatch. The signals officer released the locking mechanism and pulled the thick door open before hopping out into the cold, flinty air. The squad leader shook his head and pointed at Dunmoore, who joined her on the tarmac.

"Only the commander," he said curtly. "You stay with your shuttle."

Kowalski looked at her captain questioningly.

"You can work on your crossword puzzle, Kathryn. I'll be fine."

"Aye, aye, captain." She snapped to attention and saluted, giving the lead merc a dark look for his lack of military courtesy. The man did not react. He merely waited for her to re-board the shuttle and slam the hatch shut.

"If you'll follow me," he said to Dunmoore, gesturing toward a blocky, single-story building across the tarmac. "Admiral Corwin is waiting for you in his quarters."

The landing strip was hard and smooth, but dust devils stirred to life by the constant breeze whipping over the plateau broke the apparent evenness of the rock. To Siobhan's eyes, the view was depressingly monotonous and monochrome under a washed-out sky bare of clouds. The ambient temperature was a few degrees above freezing. It was not uncomfortably cold but after weeks in the controlled environment of a starship, the contrast was starker than she expected.

A short set of steps led down to a blank door flanked by polarized windows and Siobhan recognized the prefabricated structure as part of what the Marines liked to call an insta-base, a set of containers filled with everything needed to build an outpost and dropped from low orbit. It could be assembled by a small group of soldiers in a matter of days. What it lacked in comfort, it made up for by ease of deployment.

The mercenary opened the door to a small antechamber and motioned her inside. Then he and his men marched away, quickly disappearing around the corner.

Siobhan opened the inner door and immediately revised her estimate of the insta-base's comfort. The room in which she had stepped was well appointed, with luxurious furniture made from exotic woods harvested on dozens of distant worlds. Thick rugs covered the stone floor beneath soft lighting dispensed by intricate globes floating inside finely filigreed metal cages. A scent of age mixed with the bright tang of furniture polish filled her nostrils.

At the far end, Admiral Corwin rose from behind a large desk and strode toward her, hand stretched out, an avuncular smile on his lips.

"Welcome to my home, Commander Dunmoore. It's a delight to finally have you visit my little kingdom. How do you like my office?"

He waved around as he shook Siobhan's hand.

"Its, ah, unexpected," she replied, feeling slightly disoriented by his forceful geniality.

"It always has that effect on first-time visitors. You won't find another arrangement like it in the known galaxy." His smile became conspiratorial. "You'll understand soon enough and then you'll realize the importance of your new mission here in the Arietis system, to support our war against the Shrehari Empire."

Corwin led her to an intricately decorated wood cabinet and lifted the top to expose an array of decanters.

"Are you partial to scotch, Siobhan?"

Dunmoore barely repressed a flinch at his overly familiar use of her first name.

"I am, sir," she replied once she'd recovered.

He lifted up a bottle and showed her the label.

"Glen Arcturus. The finest single malt from Caledonia Colony. Smoky like an Islay and sweet like a Hibernian. I suggest a mere drop of water to release the esters."

Without waiting for her reply, he splashed generous measures in cut crystal tumblers and added a small amount of water from an antique soda siphon.

Handing one of the glasses to Dunmoore, he raised the other.

"To your health and to that of your crew, commander. Your ship will be doing a greater service to the Commonwealth with my squadron than patrolling the badlands or escorting cantankerous merchantmen." He took a sip and nodded appreciatively. "Without a doubt, the finest single malt anywhere."

When she did not reply, he studied her, letting the silence deepen.

"I can read the questions in your eyes, Siobhan," he finally said, smiling. "You're wondering how the old two-starred goat can live in such luxury in a temporary base on the hind end of nowhere. Don't deny it."

She cocked her head, letting a touch of the rebellious Dunmoore show. He laughed softly.

"All will be revealed."

At that moment, an older, painfully thin man in a severe suit appeared in a recessed doorway.

"The meal is ready, Admiral."

"Thank you." He turned to Dunmoore. "Henri has been with me for so long he's part of my family. Aren't you, Henri."

"If you say so, sir," the man replied dryly.

Corwin wrapped his left arm around Siobhan's shoulders and guided her toward the splendidly appointed dining room next door. Dunmoore tried hard not to squirm at the touch, but Corwin did not seem to notice her discomfort.

He settled her in an eerily carved chair whose proportions were strangely off kilter and sat down across the polished table. Henri quickly reappeared bearing the first course: a fragrant, thick soup whose aroma caused Siobhan's stomach to rumble loudly. She blushed at Corwin's amused smile, cursing her traitorous appetite.

The soup tasted even better than it smelled and Siobhan sipped with undisguised pleasure. While the food on *Stingray* was good and plentiful, it lacked this level of refinement, Vincenzo's forays into Italian delicacies notwithstanding.

An excellent conversationalist, Corwin made innocuous small talk, asking her about news from home, gossip from the Fleet and about life aboard her ship. He gave little away in return, and Siobhan was too busy eating between sentences to ask any questions of her own. The soup was followed by a crunchy salad that could only have come from a hydroponic garden, doused in a tangy dressing made from a fruit she had never encountered. The main dish was an exquisitely roasted fowl that Corwin explained came from the rift valley settlements south of the base.

When Henri had removed the remains of the main course and set down a platter of cheeses, fruits and nuts, and a bottle of port wine, Corwin finally dropped the small talk. After chewing on a round of cheese-smeared bread, he contemplated Siobhan.

"Have you ever heard of the L'Taung civilization?"

Siobhan frowned, dredging her memory for the vaguely familiar name.

"Isn't that sort of the Shrehari version of our Atlantis legend?" She asked, making the connection.

"Indeed," Corwin smiled, seeming pleased at her knowledge of the esoteric. "However, where Atlantis likely never existed other than in the minds of fabulists over the centuries, the L'Taung were very real."

"Admiral, as far as I can remember from my reading of their history, the Shrehari consider the L'Taung a myth. They don't believe that there was such a thing as an elder empire that existed over a hundred thousand years ago when our ancestors were still roaming the savannas of Earth and hunting game with stone weapons. The Shrehari have never found evidence of a prior high-tech civilization on their home world or on any of the worlds they've conquered or annexed."

"There's a reason they haven't found any evidence on Shrehari Prime." His smile was becoming positively vulpine. "Their present home world isn't their world of origin. What currently constitutes the Empire is, as far as we've discovered, descended from those who fled the downfall of the L'Taung a hundred thousand years ago."

At her incredulous look, he laughed.

"You think me mad. Don't deny it. You're too guileless to hide your thoughts from me."

He swept his arm around to take in the richly furnished room.

"None of the objects you see here were made by human hands, as you've no doubt figured out yourself. Look at your chair. Actually look at the carvings on it, and tell me what you notice."

Dunmoore stood and tilted the chair to better catch the glow globe's light.

"I suppose those could be proto-Shrehari figures, accounting for a hundred thousand years' worth of mutations, cultural shifts and the like," she said dubiously. "But if the runes under the images are supposed to be Shrehari writing, they bear no resemblance to any known form. No living Shrehari would be able to decipher them any more than we could."

"You're a hard woman to convince, Siobhan." He shook his head. "I can understand your skepticism, but these baubles are nothing compared to the artifacts we're uncovering under this plateau, and I don't doubt there are other sites on Arietis just as rich that we haven't yet found."

"Why is the Navy babysitting an archaeological dig so far beyond the Commonwealth's frontiers? And how was this first discovered?"

Corwin, unmoved by her overt skepticism, motioned her to sit down again.

"A long tale, Siobhan, one that requires a good cup of coffee and perhaps some brandy?"

Dunmoore shook her head. Between the Scotch, the wine during the meal and the port, she had already consumed more alcohol than she wanted.

"Only coffee for me."

Once Henri had left them again, Corwin led Siobhan back into the office and bade her sit in one of the strangely carved sofa chairs.

"Where to start," he mused, tapping the side of his leg as he began to pace the room. "Several years before the war, a human treasure hunter whose name is not important but who occasionally visited the main settlements on Arietis bought a trinket from a backcountry roamer. This vagabond had found it buried in some scree at the base of this plateau, no doubt the result of a collapse due to erosion. The hunter eventually sold it to a curiosities shop on Ariel, giving them what provenance he had. A visiting scholar saw the piece on display and thought there was some peculiarity to it. He bought the artifact and subjected it to extensive analysis, eventually determining its age."

"The notion of an unknown ancient civilization garnered a lot of interest within the archaeological community, and an expedition to this planet was organized. As they began to excavate the site, the war broke out, and the team was recalled, but not before discovering evidence of artifacts that would very much interest the Admiralty."

He stopped pacing and took a sip of coffee.

"Our betters were too busy stopping the Shrehari invasion to pay much attention at the time, but with the war grinding into a stalemate, an enterprising intelligence officer resurrected the Arietis file and convinced the Admiralty that it deserved another look."

Corwin was all too obviously enjoying his tale, and Siobhan felt irrationally irked.

"And did it?" She asked with a hint of asperity in her voice.

"Oh, it did, Siobhan, it did." Corwin drained his coffee and set the cup down.

"I was sent here eighteen months ago to resume the excavations and in that time, we've found the articles you see all around you, perfectly preserved in hermetically sealed rooms and boxes that were flooded with inert gasses. Yes, Siobhan, you're sitting on a hundred thousand-year-old sofa that's as new as the day it was placed into stasis."

"And ancient furniture will help us win the war?" That insubordinate quip earned her a quick frown of displeasure.

"No. When the L'Taung evacuated this sector, for reasons we've yet to establish, they left behind everything they needed to rebuild their civilization, carefully packed and stored underground, in what is the least seismically active place on this planet. They thought long-term. Perhaps they knew they were headed for several millennia of darkness, and they wanted to leave something to kick-start the climb back to the stars."

"But they never came back."

"No. Whatever the L'Taung fled from, be it another species, civil war or biological collapse, it drove them too far away and too far down the technological ladder. The remains of their era have been undisturbed for ages."

"Until we came along." Siobhan felt her thoughts beginning to spin out of control as she fought to grasp all the ramifications of Corwin's incredible story.

"Well, technically, until the archaeological expedition came along. And to answer your question: we've found technology, including what we believe are weapons so advanced that we're only now beginning to unravel their secrets. Think about it. If we can make a sudden leap up the ladder, we can end the war in the space of months and the irony of using technology developed by the Shrehari's distant ancestors is delicious."

Siobhan could only stare at Corwin, wondering whether he was telling the truth, fantastic as it was, or whether he was touched in the head. He certainly seemed to believe what he was saying and was not showing any overt signs of insanity. Instead of pursuing the thought, she asked another of her many questions.

"Why the private military contractors? Why not Navy sloops and a battalion of Marine infantry?"

"Political reasons, Commander Dunmoore," he replied, brushing her question aside. His return to her rank and last name did not escape her attention.

A hard glint appeared in Corwin's eyes.

"Now you see why security in this system has to be absolute. If this technology falls into the hands of people inimical to the Commonwealth, there's no saying the damage it could cause to our interests."

"And that's why you requested *Stingray* remain here."

"Exactly. Chance brought you here, but since you'd already found my operation, it just made sense to keep you with me. Admiral Ryn can certainly spare an old frigate whereas I can put it to much better use."

For the first time, she noticed a slight tic in the corner of Corwin's right eye.

"If added firepower was your intent, Admiral, may I ask why my standing orders keep me leashed to the general vicinity of this system? I get that at top speed, your sloops are faster, yet if the latest intruder was anything to go by, he'd sooner surrender to me than to your ships if caught and cornered."

"Those are my orders, commander." His tone was unexpectedly stern, and she understood that she had crossed some sort of line. "I expect you to abide by them. I cannot risk having you too far away if the foe enters in force. My orbital station is all well and good, but a frigate will command me more respect from the riff-raff of the Coalsack."

Corwin's earlier geniality had evaporated, leaving behind an increasingly irritable and brusque man. Siobhan briefly debated poking the bear just a bit more, to see what would happen, but she felt Pushkin laying a ghostly hand on her arm to still her words, his influence still strong even though he was high up in orbit aboard the frigate. Instead, she shifted the conversation back to the L'Taung.

"Any chance of my seeing some of that ancient technology, sir?"

"Perhaps another time," he replied distractedly as he touched the computer console on his desk. "Tobias will fetch you at the door and walk you back to your shuttle. I trust you'll keep what you learned here to yourself. As far as your crew's concerned, this is still a naval research station involved in top secret work that must remain closely held."

"Of course, sir." She rose, put on her beret, and saluted.

A distracted Corwin absently returned the salute, but his attention had already shifted away from Siobhan, and she let herself out with no further ceremony.

The same squad of mercenaries walked her back to the shuttle, and she found that her mood had sunk as well, almost in tune with Corwin's. Brooding over what she had learned, she declined Kowalski's attempts at conversation during the flight back to the ship.

The signals officer, attuned to her captain, did not mention the interesting scan results she had picked up while waiting inside the spacecraft. There would be time for that later when they had left the negative aura of this place far behind.

*

Alone in his office, Admiral Corwin poured himself another glass of port and stared at the ancient star map hanging on the far wall.

Siobhan Dunmoore was as willful as Hoko Nagira had described her and apparently as resourceful if she had the gumption to turn her convoy over to another officer and pursue a mystery. It spoke of a strong woman, who did not fear her convictions and was sure of her duty. She could be very useful to the cause. Very useful indeed.

He drained the thick, sweet wine and gently deposited the glass on the sideboard for Henri to collect. When he had asked that *Stingray* be detached to his command, he had not quite formulated Dunmoore's place in his plans, but he was a good judge of character. One did not become an admiral without being able to decide quickly who to trust and who to discard.

Perhaps he should ask for permission to take her further into his confidence but that would mean bringing the subspace transmission array on line again, and he did not want to risk giving away the relay station's position on the edge of the system by using it too often. The trust Nagira placed in Dunmoore spoke for itself. He was well known for his ability to detect exceptional potential in his officers, and that would have to do.

Corwin resolved to observe her for a little while longer before making his decision but all of his instincts told him she could safely become a close confidant. And what an addition she would make to his team. The only Navy captain to defeat the Empire's fearsome Brakal twice and bring home not one but two ships others would have scuttled.

He smiled at his reflection in the polished wood of the desk, satisfied with his decision.

— Fourteen —

Siobhan went straight to her quarters, nodding absently at crewmembers along the way. She felt a growing anger gnawing at her gut and did not know whether it was resentment at Corwin's abrupt dismissal or his chaining her ship to this system, denying her leave to return to the convoy or even act as she saw fit.

She had hoped to spend the evening alone, in part to flush the alcohol from her system, in part to let herself stew in private, but a captain served her starship before anything else. Siobhan could not fault Pushkin's curiosity either.

"So how was it?" He asked, entering through the open door at Dunmoore's permission.

She shrugged, eyes staring at the display of the planet on her cabin's main screen.

"The word strange comes to mind."

"You too, eh," Pushkin replied. "We weren't idle during your visit dirtside and spent some time scanning the monitor and this planet's near orbit."

"You must have found something of interest or you wouldn't be here." Siobhan immediately regretted the bite in her tone.

Pushkin stared at her, surprised by the uncharacteristic asperity. She had not spoken to him in that way since her early days on *Stingray* when he deserved her ire.

"I'm sorry, Gregor," she said, seeing the hurt look in his eyes. He deserved better than that. As first officers went, he was comfortably among the best and most loyal. She waved him toward a chair "What is it you found?"

"More like what we didn't find," he said, taking the proffered seat. "That monitor turned orbital platform has everything a good if improvised military space station needs except for one thing. It doesn't appear to have a subspace transmitter, nor did we detect a booster relay for a ground-based unit."

"Could it be camouflaged?"

"Maybe on a station three times the size, but there just isn't enough room in a monitor to hide an array that can reach back to the closest naval relay, even one with a couple of cargo pods welded on. Did you perchance see anything on the ground?"

Dunmoore shook her head.

"But there could have been a large array transmitter inside one of the buildings," she said. "Are there any communication satellites in orbit we might have missed?"

"If there are, they're in stealth mode; otherwise, we'd have picked them up along with every other piece of debris circling this planet."

She reached over to the intercom.

"Captain to the signals officer."

"Kowalski here," she promptly replied.

"Am I correct in assuming you conducted a scan of Admiral Corwin's base?"

"You are." She sounded pleased with herself.

"Did you find anything that might indicate a subspace transmitter large enough to reach back home?"

"No, sir. The only communications equipment I detected was radio, but that doesn't mean they don't have one elsewhere on the surface."

"Do you think any of the sloops carries a subspace transmitter powerful enough to connect to the closest relay station in Commonwealth space?"

"Not a chance, sir," Kowalski replied, an edge of excitement in her voice. "And I had guns scan the system for a relay station we might have missed so far, but nothing. We would at least be able to pick up a relay's carrier wave."

"Then I'm puzzled as to how Admiral Corwin received orders from HQ so quickly." She frowned. "It irks me to think that there's a subspace link in this system, and we're not privy to its location."

"That's what struck us, captain," Pushkin said, a satisfied smile slowly spreading across his face, now that Dunmoore seemed to be reverting back to her usual self. "There was still a small chance they'd put the array on the ground with a repeater in geosynchronous orbit, one that's powered down between transmissions, but that wouldn't have made nearly as much sense as mounting it on the monitor."

"Do the settlements have one, perhaps?" Siobhan asked Kowalski.

"I've had them scanned as well, and we couldn't find a trace there either, not to mention that they would need a repeater in orbit if there was one. Whatever they have that can reach home is well hidden, so at best guess, it could be sitting above or below the planetary plane and powered down unless required. I did find other items of interest on the base, however."

Dunmoore sighed. She was not going to get the rest she wanted anytime soon.

"Meet us in the conference room with Mister Kutora, Lieutenant Syten, the sailing master, and the second officer."

*

"Alright, Kathryn," Dunmoore gestured at Kowalski when all were seated. "Enlighten us."

"Sir." She touched the screen, bringing up a schematic of the installation. "The base's setup is fairly standard on the surface: shuttle hangar, fusion reactor, commo shack, barracks, hydroponics farm, and what looks like labs. What surprised me was the extent of the base underground, and I'm not just talking about the half-buried buildings."

When she did not see surprise on the captain's face, Kowalski gave her a thoughtful look.

"I guess you already knew about the big underground complex, sir."

Dunmoore nodded.

"To a certain extent. Admiral Corwin did tell me some of his operations are beneath the surface but provided no detail."

"I didn't want to push the scanners, lest they detect me and get annoyed, so I only got to a depth of about twenty meters." At her touch, the three-dimensional schematic of an underground warren appeared.

Pushkin whistled softly.

"That's quite a lot of drilling and excavating."

"I also detected a lot of life signs beneath the surface. Many more than the above ground structures would indicate."

"Mercenaries?" Devall asked.

"Possibly," Kowalski shrugged, "but that means there could be up to two and a half companies' worth and I can't see the admiral needing that much ground pounding in a place with so many natural defenses. There could possibly be more, deeper down."

She touched the screen again and the image transformed into a schematic of the hangar.

"A squadron's worth of attack shuttles," Syten said after a few moments. "Typhoons, it looks like. I didn't know they were approved for civilian use."

"Technically, the 'civilians' are under naval contract," Pushkin replied. "Are the Typhoons any good beyond lunar orbit?"

"Some." Syten made a so-so gesture with her right hand. "They're mostly for ground support and don't carry much that can harm a shielded starship unless they've been fitted with external ship-to-ship missile racks."

"Curiouser and curiouser," Siobhan murmured.

Pushkin gave her a sardonic glance. "Getting that looking-glass feeling, captain?"

She snorted. "You have no idea. And if I find out the crew calls me the Red Queen behind my back, there'll be the devil to pay."

"And no pitch hot," the first officer smiled, pleased that her good humor had returned.

"Anything else, Kathryn."

"We were tracked, coming in and leaving, by a very good air defense sensor, which implies the base has some sort of ground-based weaponry. It wasn't positioned close to where I sat so I didn't get a good look, but I suspect this may cover guns or launchers, or both." She flipped the image to a picture of the base seen from a few hundred meters up and pointed at large boulders that were just a bit too regular in shape to be natural.

"Must be one hell of an important thing they're working on down there. I've seen Marine outposts in the war zone that weren't as fancy." Devall looked skeptical.

Dunmoore studied her officers as she debated with herself by how much she was willing to break Admiral Corwin's strictures on secrecy. There had never been any question in her mind that she would tell Pushkin everything. A first officer had to know as much as his captain to be effective.

"Is there any chance Corwin's men might have caught you snooping, Kathryn?"

"There's always a chance, sir. But if I was them, and they looked professional enough to me by the way, I'd assume that any visitor would look around. I didn't use active scanners beyond what a shuttle pilot would usually run when sitting on a new, to her, landing pad."

The captain nodded.

"I'm about to do something that I hope you'll take as a one-off event resulting from our somewhat strange circumstances, rather than as an example to follow in the future."

If she did not have their attention before, she had it now.

"Admiral Corwin has instructed me to keep what I learned from him to myself. I'm going to disobey that order in the next few minutes, because although we've been taught mission first, I've decided that in this instance my greater duty is to this ship and its crew, not the admiral. Yes, I know – sheer heresy, but what you, my department heads, don't know might just kill us, and I'd rather we make it home in one piece. I've never witnessed the orderly decommissioning of one of my commands and I'd like to see *Stingray* off with due ceremony, not shedding rescue pods and venting gasses."

They remained silent, staring at her intently.

"I'll now be a hypocrite and ask you to keep what you learn here to yourselves. The crew will find out when I think the time is right." She took a deep breath and began.

*

"I'm sorry, sir," Devall was the first to speak after she had fallen silent. "But a L'Taung archaeological treasure trove on a dying planet in the hind end of space? If our old buddy Brakal were listening to this, he'd be killing himself laughing."

"Probably killing us along with him," Kutora muttered in his usual grim tone.

"Sir, the L'Taung are supposed to be a fable," the second officer continued. "Everything I've read about the Shrehari indicates that they consider it akin to a creationist interpretation of their history, believed by a few fringe groups that take religious mythology too seriously."

"That interpretation does have their very distant ancestors settle on what is now the home world, after a long voyage across the heavens," Tours noted helpfully.

"It's no more or less mythical than any number of creation legends among the various human cultures," Kutora pointed out.

"True," Tours admitted, "but if what the captain saw down there were ancient Shrehari artifacts, then we've finally hit that one exception confirming the rule: a myth solidly grounded in fact."

"It's a shame you couldn't take images, sir."

"I know, Kathryn, but I doubt the admiral would have been happy if I'd whipped out a sensor and started recording everything I saw. Judging by his mood when I left, it didn't take much more than me questioning one of his orders to turn him sour."

"Do you believe the admiral?" Pushkin asked.

"I'm not sure. I think he believes what he told me and I think the artifacts I saw were genuine. They certainly didn't come from a known culture, and there was a superficial resemblance between the carved figures and the Shrehari we know. But the writing didn't look like anything used in the Empire nowadays."

"And there's supposed to be war-ending technology down there?" Devall's sudden vehemence surprised Siobhan. "I don't know, captain, but it strikes me as a good way to unleash a catastrophe. It bears more than a little resemblance to the numerous speculative fiction stories about civilizations who built weapons so advanced they end up wiping out their own creators.

If that's really a L'Taung site down there, why did they hike halfway across the galaxy, abandoning everything?"

"Look, I'm not going to put this to a vote, folks," she said in an attempt to stem the increasingly futile discussion. "Until proven otherwise, Admiral Corwin is our flag officer commanding, temporary as that may be, and we remain bound by his orders. Whether or not he's unearthing a L'Taung armory or the remains of a furniture store, he's here under orders from the Fleet. Nothing other than the Navy could have assembled so many assets and transported them to, in Mister Devall's words, the hind end of space."

"Could we at least do a deep scan of his base?" Syten asked.

"Not while we're under that monitor's guns," Dunmoore replied, immediately wondering why she used those words.

"Are you saying you don't trust Admiral Corwin?" Pushkin's voice was soft, but his words resonated like the ring of a battleship's bell.

"I'm saying," she replied after almost half a minute of contemplation, "there are enough things that rub me the wrong way to make me think caution is the order of the day." In her mind's eye, she relived some of the stranger moments she had spent with Corwin.

"While we're on the subject, did anyone see a transmitter large enough and powerful enough to send a focused burst out to where we were patrolling?" Kowalski asked in the ensuing silence.

Pushkin shook his head. "Nothing that popped up as active, though it could be orbiting disguised as debris between transmissions."

"Apropos of nothing at all," Dunmoore looked at her officers curiously, "have we scanned the settlement area yet? We seem to have more missing communications nodes than can be explained by mere carelessness on the admiral's part."

"Not in any great depth," Syten admitted.

Whatever she was about to say was interrupted by the intercom chime.

"Captain, bridge here," Sanghvi's youthful voice rang through the speaker. "We've received orders from Squadron HQ. We're to break orbit immediately and investigate a contact reported by a sensor buoy."

"Acknowledged." She rose and looked at Syten. "We'll do one last pass over the rift valley where the highest concentrations of settlers live. After that, it'll have to wait until we're recalled."

"Mister Pushkin," she continued as her officers streamed out of the room, "set the ship at departure stations. Let's go see what has our admiral worried this time."

"Another *Maru*?"

"If it is, I'd dearly like to get it under our guns so I can obtain some answers from them."

"Answers you aren't getting from Admiral Corwin?" Pushkin's ironic smile underscored his skepticism at the situation.

"Aye. Whatever he's up to has the Black Nova folks taking an interest that goes far beyond the commercial."

"Revenge for the destruction of the *Nikko Maru*?"

"If it were an honest interest, Gregor, they would have filed a complaint with the Navy. No. This is something else, likely related to the L'Taung treasure trove down there." She shook her head wearily. "And while we're at it, I'd dearly love to find out how many buoys, sensor or otherwise, are floating around in this system. I just hate going about half-blind because someone's playing silly bugger with operational security."

— Fifteen —

"Another sneaky customer," Penzara grumbled. "Why is it again that we can't work with the mercenary ships or get direct feeds from the sensor buoys?"

"Obviously because they have something to hide, chief," Petty Officer Rownes smirked. "Those sloops are built for privateering if you ask me. Not for honest business."

"If they're on the shady side, how much worse is our peeping intruder?" Devall asked from the command chair.

"Maybe he's one of the good guys, sir?" Penzara shrugged.

"Don't know if there are any out here, excepting us."

"You're a pessimist, Rownes," Lieutenant Devall commented with a smile.

"Realist, sir," she insisted. "I've seen a few shady things when I was in the merchant service before the war. Remember the freighter *Mykonos* that was smuggling naval supplies, the one we intercepted last year? Well, those sloops make me think of nothing so much as its evil twin brothers."

"Why do you say that?" Devall, now genuinely interested, got up and went to stand behind Rownes at the sensor console.

"I don't know, sir. Just a feeling I got. The few times I was able to scan them closely, their emissions control was up to naval standards and what did leak was really clean, like it was damn near new." She called up a scan readout on her screen for the second officer's benefit.

"Hmm." Devall nodded. "Where are they now?"

"One's on the other side of the system, one's in orbit, and the third isn't showing up anywhere, but the last contact we had was of him jumping out behind the suspected *Maru* the other day."

"You'd think he'd have come back by now." Devall pursed his lips in thought. "It's been long enough."

"Maybe he's doing what we did: follow the suspect ship to its destination," Penzara offered.

"Maybe." The second officer walked back to the command chair and sat down absently. He shook himself back to the present.

"Where was the last contact with our current target?"

"On screen, sir," Rownes replied, bringing up the readout.

"Estimate trajectory based on last known vector, assuming he went silent."

Devall stared at the screen as the computer calculated probabilities and plotted a line through the three-dimensional representation of the system. After a few moments, a smile appeared on his face. He punched some numbers into the chair's arm console.

"Helm, come about to two-forty mark sixteen, but do it casually."

The quartermaster looked around at him in surprise.

"You know," Devall waved his hand, "make it look like we're just out for a nice slow sail that might coincidentally take us near the sixth planet, but not anytime soon. Sail casual."

"Ah," Penzara grinned, "you think he's going to hide in the gas giant's orbit."

"Not the most efficient overwatch position, I suppose, but yes, it's a good place to sit and observe without being seen. The moons and the strong magnetic field would be pretty good camouflage for anything, and while the planet's not at its closest to Arietis, it's not that far off."

He consulted the duty roster and decided to let the captain sleep another hour. Settling into the command chair with his ever-present smile, he began to play mental what-ifs for cornering the target and getting him to surrender without a shot. Assuming, of course, that he was right.

*

"Good thinking, Mister Devall." Dunmoore clapped him on the shoulder as he rose to turn the command chair over to her.

"I seem to recall learning that trick from my captain, and it fooled the Shrehari well enough."

"But it won't deceive us." Siobhan sat, her eyes taking in the ever-changing tactical schematic. There was a lot of space to cover, but perhaps she could tilt the odds just a bit in her favor.

"The trick is to get in close enough so that when he tries to bolt, we can talk him down with the threat of a broadside. I'd rather not shoot to kill without knowing what the score is. We're at war with the Shrehari and it's almost a certainty that this unidentified ship isn't one of them. I trust you told the helm to make it look like we're out for a Sunday spin," she added with an amused gleam in her eyes.

"I did, captain," Devall replied with a grin. "We'll be nonchalantly passing by the planet in two hours."

"Excellent." She rubbed her hands together. "Anything on passive yet?"

"Negative," Chief Penzara replied. "But that's hardly surprising. That thing has a strong magnetic field." He nodded toward the planet's image on the main screen. "We'll need to go active at this range if we want to find our needle in the orbital stack."

"Not yet," Dunmoore cautioned. "If he picks up a ping, he'll bolt, and we won't be able to catch him without shooting his drives off."

"That's if he's there, sir," Rownes reminded them.

"I think Mister Devall called this one," Siobhan replied, eyes twinkling with anticipation. "It's the best hiding spot around for someone who's had no luck sailing through silently on a ballistic course. And if he's not there, we'll have had a good stalking exercise to break the monotony."

"Mister Sanghvi," she turned to the navigator, "plot a course that will take us on a leisurely slingshot trajectory around the planet, something that will look like we're saving fuel on our return leg to Arietis."

"Maximum coverage without looking like we're looking." The young man nodded, fingers dancing over his console. "Done. Feeding to helm."

"Quartermaster, engage. Try to make it look like we're in no hurry."

*

The Jovian planet was banded in various shades of brown and red, each wider than Arietis, their edges twisting and melding ceaselessly under the impulse of storms birthed by its rapid rotation. Surrounded by multiple debris rings and over thirty moons varying in size from almost as big as Mars to no more than a few kilometers across, the sixth planet offered a lot of potential for starships anxious to escape the sensors of hunting Navy and mercenary vessels. Some of the larger moons even had atmospheres, although mostly made of methane and other unbreathable gasses. It was a miniature system of its own within the Arietis system as if the gas giant was a star that had failed to ignite.

Stingray swung around the planet in a wide parabola, sailing between the outer moons, well away from the rings. Her sensors were searching through the entire spectrum for the merest hint of a man-made object lying quietly in the shadow of some orbiting rock, anxious to blend into the background radiation.

Dunmoore had not really put the frigate into a slingshot curve. The velocity required would have left them too little time to search. Instead, she had ordered the ship to decelerate and then use thrusters to supplement the planet's gravity so that she remained on a curving course.

Whether or not it fooled the intruder made no difference. If he tried to bolt now, *Stingray* would be upon him in short order, well before he was far enough to dare a hyperspace jump.

In the intervening hours, there had been no questions from either Admiral Corwin or the mercenary ships, even though they had to have seen the frigate's change of course and unexpected swing around the gas giant. On the other hand, the third of Corwin's sloops could be laying silent close enough to snatch Dunmoore's prey from under her guns, just as it tried to do earlier. It was something she wanted to avoid because she wanted answers, not a prize or a missile sniping run.

Holding her impatience in check, she stilled her drumming fingers for the tenth time in the past hour, biting back yet another question for the silent gunnery non-com concentrating on the sensors. Rownes would tell her if she found even the slightest trace of a trace. The petty officer had taken to targeting like a natural. She was even better at it than she had been as a gun captain and she had been splendid at that.

Heading off to her ready room to pace in private would have been an acceptable if annoying alternative to looming over the bridge like a frustrated lioness. Or rather like a frustrated she-wolf, as Brakal had dubbed her. The thrill of the hunt was strangely absent this time. She was not stalking a prey she could take in the heat of battle. It was more like a game of hide and seek than combat.

She snapped her head toward the gunnery station the moment she caught Rownes' hand rising up to attract her attention.

"Yes?"

"The sensors picked up a faint trace of refined metal on the large moon ahead, ten degrees to port, somewhere well above the surface." She pointed at the side view screen where she projected the readout.

"Hiding in the atmosphere? That'll take some piloting skills. Why not land?" Tours asked from the navigation console.

"It'd be harder to escape if he has to climb out of the gravity well from the bottom. I can't see that he's been there long if that what it is. Maybe he saw us and snuck into the clouds, hoping for some camouflage." Dunmoore stared at the screen.

"Mister Guthren, take us into low orbit. Rownes, feed the coordinates of your potential target to the helm. Chief, when you have it, bring us over whatever it is Rownes found. Then we'll see if it's an innocent prospector or someone we want to talk to."

Dunmoore had barely finished giving her orders when Chief Penzara spoke up.

"I read sublight engines coming online from whatever that is. He's going to try and run."

The captain pounded the arm of her chair.

"We've got him." She swiveled around to the signals alcove. "Mister Kowalski, hail them. They're ordered to heave to and prepare to be boarded."

Thousands of kilometers away, a blocky starship that nonetheless had clean, fast lines, broke free from the soupy clouds encircling the moon and accelerated up and away from *Stingray*, its drive nozzles glowing yellow.

"No response."

"Helm, engage pursuit. Guns, go to active targeting. Let them know we're locked on."

Her fingers drummed on her thigh once.

"Signals, I wish to speak with them. Give me the emergency frequency. If nothing else, they must be monitoring it."

"You have it, sir."

"Unidentified vessel, this is Captain Siobhan Dunmoore, commanding the Commonwealth Starship *Stingray*. Please don't force me to open fire. I wish to speak with your captain, that's all."

"Still no response."

"Mister Syten, prepare for one salvo from the main guns. Target as close as you dare without risking a hit."

"Laid in," she replied a few moments later.

"Unidentified vessel, this is Captain Siobhan Dunmoore, commanding the Commonwealth Starship *Stingray*. If you fail to respond to my hail, I will open fire. If you're paying attention, you'll note that we have active targeting on your hull."

Suddenly the speaker came to life.

"And take us down like your buddies did with the *Nikko Maru* and the *Fuso Maru*? No thanks. I'm not having a conversation with pirates, and I'm certainly not heaving to."

"Captain Lian?" She looked up in astonishment.

"Yeah, Dunmoore," he replied. "I thought you were a typical Navy pain in the ass when I first met you, but I wouldn't have figured you to be capable of throwing in with a murderous rogue like Corwin."

She glanced at Penzara, who was pointing at the side screen, where he put up the picture of the *Oko Maru*, surrounded by telemetry. When he caught her eye, he nodded, confirming the identity of the other ship.

"Murderous rogue, Captain Lian? Why?"

"Your precious Admiral Corwin destroyed the *Fuso Maru* and killed all hands less than half a parsec from here. She was a legitimate, Commonwealth-flagged freighter. As far as I'm concerned, that was a criminal act."

"You witnessed it?"

"Of course not, or they'd have done me in too. I found the debris two days ago. When Strazi was overdue, I backtracked. His ship's emergency beacon was still working. That's two of our ships Corwin's wrecked. If that isn't piracy, then I don't know what it is."

She glanced at the telemetry again. The *Oko Maru* was still accelerating, but *Stingray* was catching up fast.

"Are you sure Strazi and his crew were killed? Did you find bodies?"

There was no reply. Finally, the speaker came to life again.

"None that we could find, but that doesn't signify. They could have been vaporized in the attack. We're armed freighters, not damned privateer sloops." Deep-seated anger colored Lian's voice, and Siobhan frowned.

"Will you heave to and have a face-to-face conversation with me, captain?" She asked, forcing herself to sound as courteous as her frustration would allow.

He laughed bitterly.

"No. Not now, not ever."

"Then answer at least one question and I'll hold my fire."

There was a moment of hesitation.

"One question, Dunmoore. Make it quick. The moment I can jump without tearing my hull apart, I'm gone."

"What is the Black Nova Shipping Line's interest in Arietis and Admiral Corwin's operation?"

"You wasted your one question on that?" He asked mockingly. "You work for that pirate, and you can't figure it out for yourself? Dunmoore, you have the reputation of being smarter than the average Navy puke, which means your fellow officers are dim indeed."

She thought for a few heartbeats, debating how much to say.

"My ship was conscripted," she finally said. "I tracked one of his sloops here after identifying it from the attack on the *Nikko Maru*. When Admiral Corwin became cognizant of our presence in this system, he placed me under his orders. I have no idea what his mission here is."

"Nice try, but you're lying. I'm pretty sure you were down on the planet and met with Corwin. Now if you'll excuse me, I'm just about at my hyper limit."

"You didn't answer my question, Lian."

"That's because I'm not going to but thanks for giving me time to escape."

"He's spooling up his jump drives," Rownes warned.

"Mister Syten, fire that warning shot."

"You said you wouldn't shoot." Lian was openly sardonic.

"I lied."

"Then we're even."

Before Syten could shoot, the *Oko Maru* wavered and then disappeared as she warped space around her to form a bubble.

"Shall we follow, captain?" Tours asked.

"Oh yes. Calculate the pursuit vector and feed to the helm. Chief, the moment you have it, steer the ship on the new course and engage. Warn for jumps stations, Mister Kowalski."

"Are you sure that's a good idea, captain?" Pushkin, standing behind her right shoulder, pitched his voice so only Dunmoore could hear. "We have no reason to shoot him out of hyperspace and Admiral Corwin's orders constrain us. We'll be past the limits he set pretty quickly, in a stern chase."

"The doctrine of hot pursuit," she countered, half in jest. "I have no intention of torpedoing the *Oko Maru*, Number One. I do want to track him until he emerges again and is stuck in normal space while he recalibrates his drives for the next tack."

"And the admiral?"

"Did I ever tell you that it's easier to ask for forgiveness than it is to ask for permission?"

The first officer sighed.

"Several times, sir. That still doesn't mean it's a good idea."

"Don't tell me you have no interest in finding out what our friend Lian knows."

"I do. But it's my job to tell you when I think you're about to do something that could get us into trouble."

"Indeed, it is. Fear not, Gregor. I'd say that either way, I'll be getting chewed-out by Corwin. I'd rather have something to show for it."

"Agreed. Even if we don't report this little incident, his tame mercenaries will have picked up the fact that we never opened fire."

"Ready, sir," Chief Guthren reported.

"Engage."

*

An hour passed, then two. Dunmoore had given herself six hours to pick up the *Oko Maru*'s wake. If *Stingray* could not close within that timeframe, the freighter would have made its getaway scot-free. It was smaller than the frigate, even if not by all that much and given equally powerful drives, its FTL bubble would be transitioning just a tad faster than *Stingray*'s. But luck smiles on disobedient captains every so often.

"Got him," Penzara announced, sounding very satisfied with himself.

"Perfect," Siobhan beamed at her gunnery chief. "Feed to helm. Mister Guthren, match velocity. I'd hate to ram our bow up his stern."

From his station, Pushkin smirked and shook his head at her innuendo. When she got into the spirit of the hunt, her choice of words tended to become rather unorthodox.

"Why don't we have your torpedo gunners do a couple of practice runs, Mister Syten," she said, still smiling. "If I read the sensors correctly, we're just a little to port from the strongest part of the wake, so it should make targeting a bit more interesting."

"Aye, captain. Right away."

To pass the time, Dunmoore watched simulated torpedoes erupt from the frigate's tubes set deep in her blunt bow, creating their own hyperdrive fields as they left the ship and headed into the *Oko Maru*'s wake. The computer assessed their success rate at a hair over fifty percent, which was more than decent. The notion of 'where' in hyperspace was somewhat fluid, and torpedo gunnery operated on a 'good enough' basis. It was good enough if it collapsed the target's FTL bubble. Actually damaging the other ship was a rarely collected bonus and depended on chance more than skill.

Rownes, still faithfully manning the second sensor console was the first to detect the freighter's wake flickering.

"Captain, she's about to drop."

"Helm, stand by to cut out FTL. Sound the emergence warning." Dunmoore snapped out of her idle thoughts, adrenaline suddenly pumping through her veins.

Over the sound of the siren's warning, Rownes shouted out the disappearance of the *Oko Maru*.

"Cut FTL!"

With a wrench *Stingray* collapsed her hyperspace bubble and shot into normal space, leaving her crew to fight back momentary nausea.

"Where away?" She asked the moment her stomach was back under control.

"Aft five-hundred thousand kilometers."

"Helm, braking thrusters on maximum. We'll let him overtake us. Mister Pushkin, sound battle stations. He's not getting away so easily this time. Pray hail the *Oko Maru*, Mister Kowalski, and order them to heave to before I shoot their hyperdrive nacelles off. Captain Lian still owes me an answer." She turned back toward the gunnery station. "Mister Syten, active targeting on the freighter; make sure they hear us loud and clear. The first salvo to go along their port side at my order. Try not to hit them just yet."

"No reply, captain," the signals officer said. "He's maintaining velocity."

"Aft view on screen," Dunmoore ordered. "Mister Syten, if you're ready, one warning salvo on his port side."

Two blinding flashes momentarily bathed the screen in white light, then quickly decreased in size as the plasma rounds sped away, passing the *Oko Maru* close enough to singe her hull.

"Incoming from Captain Lian."

"Put him on."

"So you're as much of a pirate as Corwin," he snarled, his face twisted with scorn and anger. "Firing on a legitimate commercial vessel flagged to the Commonwealth; that's one more thing to add to my report. You'll soon find yourself facing a general court-martial, Dunmoore."

Siobhan smiled sweetly, a sure sign of danger for those who knew her.

"Captain Lian, before you throw more recriminations at me, let me note that I could have shot you out of hyperspace at any time since the moment we picked up your wake hours ago. That's something a pirate would have had no hesitation in doing, and please, believe me, my gunners *are* that good. Feel free to ask the Shrehari the next time you sail into the war zone."

He snorted contemptuously.

"A beautiful piece of shooting that would have been. No, you just didn't want to waste a warhead."

"You'll also note," she continued, ignoring his outburst, "that I could have fired a crippling shot at you just now, not to mention the brace of missiles that would surely have made your day that much more enjoyable. You refused to answer the hails of a Commonwealth Navy vessel in time of war. That alone allows me to legally fire a warning shot, and as you can see, it worked. You finally switched on your comms."

"What do you want, Dunmoore?"

"An answer to my question. Except this time, we will discuss matters face-to-face. Either you can come aboard *Stingray* by yourself, or I can come aboard the *Oko Maru* with a fully armed and armored boarding party. Your choice. But you will not be allowed to leave until I'm satisfied, by the power vested in me by the weight of my broadside."

"Screw you, Navy bitch." He visibly fought to contain more invective, realizing from Siobhan's smooth, expressionless face that he had been bested in the game of wills.

"No thank you, Captain Lian. I prefer to practice celibacy when I'm on board ship."

She ignored the strangled snorts behind her but showed a faint smile, clearly enjoying the sight of the merchantman fighting to keep his composure.

"Come over to the *Oko Maru* with your boarding party then and be damned."

"Thank you for the invitation, Captain Lian. Do bear in mind that General Order Eighty-One will be in force."

Lian's eyes narrowed.

"And that means what, exactly?"

"General Order Eighty-One means that if you should decide to take my boarding party hostage, *Stingray* would disregard our presence on board and deal with you in whatever manner my first officer deems appropriate. If that means blowing up the *Oko Maru* and thereby killing us, so be it. The Navy does not deal with hostage takers."

By Lian's stunned silence, Dunmoore suspected that he had intended to use the boarding party as a cover to make his escape. He had no intention of dealing honestly.

"Would you like to reconsider?" She asked, the sweetness returning to her voice. This time, Lian understood that the reasonable words overlaid a ruthless streak.

"I'll come to you, Dunmoore," he replied his face working as he swallowed a stillborn string of insults. "Getting my hyperdrive damaged out here is a death sentence. Reivers can smell a disabled freighter from several parsecs away, and mine is the last of the Black Nova ships this deep in the Coalsack sector."

"Very well," she replied. Then she let the steel show again. "If you were thinking of sending a shuttle rigged as an improvised explosive device, I will slice off your drives and leave you to the nearest pirate, after planting a very loud and very visible beacon on your hull."

Lian laughed humorlessly.

"I doubt I could figure out how to make it powerful enough to disable you." Before Dunmoore could say anything else, he continued. "I know the drill: stop one hundred meters from whatever airlock you care to designate, wait until I've been thoroughly scanned and then let you tractor me alongside to dock. Come aboard by myself, no weapons."

"Forewarned is forearmed." She nodded in approval. "Within the next half hour, if you please."

*

Lian glowered at Dunmoore as he was ushered into her ready room by a well armed and grim-faced Vincenzo. As advertised, he was alone and did not carry a sidearm. He did, however, sport a large curved dagger tucked into the green sash at his waist. Dunmoore found the display vaguely Shrehari-like and said so. Lian shrugged.

"When you deal with iffy shippers out here, you try to look like you'd slit their throats at the slightest hint of cheating. It keeps arguments from getting out of hand. But no matter what you may think, I'm a trader, not a fighter. If there's no profit in it, I'm not interested."

"And yet you seem to pursue a course of action that seems entirely profitless to me," Siobhan countered, as she waved him into a seat across from her. "Coffee?"

He nodded curtly and watched her with hooded eyes as she filled two mugs from a small urn on the sideboard. Lian waved away the offer of sugar and milk and Siobhan handed him one of the cups before taking her chair. Her eyes bored into his as she took a sip.

"I enjoy a good mystery as much as the next person," she began, "but like you, I'm well away from my regular route and beyond the far end of my supply chain. Admiral Corwin has pulled me off convoy duty, for which I suppose I should be thankful, but that has left me patrolling this system without knowing quite what we're meant to help protect and from who, thus I have a few questions that need answering if I'm to do my job."

"That job being piracy?" Lian asked, mocking her openly.

"Have I done anything to give you that idea?" Siobhan's voice remained cool, her features smooth and relaxed.

"You've stopped me in deep space and forced me to come over under the threat of violence. If that isn't piracy, I apparently don't understand the term, or perhaps you don't."

She ignored his gibe.

"So far, two Black Nova ships have been destroyed; one inadvertently by my boarding party after it triggered booby traps destined to shatter it. You reported having found the wreckage of the other not far from here in astronomical terms, and now a third lies under my guns, its captain uncooperative. We can add to this mystery that the second destroyed ship vanished from the convoy

I led. I get to Yotai and what do I find: one of the two ships responsible for the *Nikko Maru*'s demise in orbit. It flees shortly after my arrival, but I manage to follow it here, where I find the second of the two ships. Are you beginning to grasp why I'd like to find some answers?"

When he did not react, she resumed her story.

"I quickly find myself relieved of convoy duty and placed under Admiral Corwin's command. And before you say anything about his legitimacy, I can assure you that he had the proper, up to date command codes. His presence here is under Admiralty orders."

Lian snorted, wholly unimpressed by her words.

"So the Navy legitimizes piracy. Who knew?"

"The Arietis system is a restricted military zone..."

"Bullshit!" Lian sneered. "We're not in the Commonwealth. You military types can't just declare an entire star system to be your private property."

"...necessary to the war effort," she calmly continued. "What I would like to know is why you and your Black Nova colleagues have such an abiding interest in this system. I fail to grasp how it could be profitable."

Siobhan fell silent and sipped her coffee as she watched conflicting thoughts chase each other across Lian's eyes. When the silence had extended to almost a full minute, the merchant captain seemed to come to a decision.

"Arietis has been on Black Nova's destination list for some time now," he began. "It's marginal as a planet, but there's profit to be made on 'untaxed' merchandise transiting through the system."

At the euphemism for smuggled goods, she smiled in amusement. The Navy knew much about the illicit trade in the sector, and as long as it did not involve drugs, military grade weapons, or any of the various forms of slavery, it was left alone. Space was too vast to enforce customs regulations with any sort of efficiency. She nodded her understanding.

"In the years before Corwin showed up and took over the place like he was a reiver lord, there had been a steady stream of alien artifacts showing up on Arietis. It may not look like much, but in those days, it was a bit of a hub for traders operating deep into the Coalsack and beyond the nebula itself. Corwin has put an end to that and no mistake. My owners saw real potential in selling off the artifacts to wealthy collectors back home, and we always stopped off to see what was on offer."

"Any idea of the provenance?"

He shook his head.

"No one has ever been able to link the objects back to any known civilization. The folks selling the stuff claim they find it on Arietis." He shrugged. "I have no idea whether that's true. All I've heard is that various analyses set the age of some of the items back around a hundred thousand years if you can imagine that. What lasts so long?"

When Siobhan shrugged in turn, he grimaced.

"Whatever they were, the supply dried up when Corwin arrived. I don't know how he got what passes for the government to cooperate, but all of a sudden, taking artifacts from Arietis became a criminal activity. We still stopped there on our way through and even offered to take on a contract to supply Corwin with consumables, which he accepted. For a while, it seemed to work well, though we never liked those unmarked sloops keeping us under their guns all the time."

"And then something happened to put the *Nikko Maru* in their sights."

"Aye, Captain Dunmoore." He nodded, not realizing that he had used her rank for the first time, a sure sign he was slowly bleeding off his anger. "I just wish I knew what. The first we heard was when your report made its way to our head office. We got orders to keep our ears and eyes open from then on, to do the job the Navy wasn't going to do. Strazi tracked back the *Nikko*'s course through Yotai all the way to Arietis. She didn't touch port at Yotai, and the harbormaster said she seemed in a hurry."

Dunmoore nodded. It matched Captain Reade's report.

"Strazi figured the *Nikko* must have fallen foul of someone before Yotai, and that left Arietis as the prime suspect." Lian stared at her with hard eyes. "And who says Arietis, says Navy."

"Why did Strazi drop out of the convoy?"

Lian smiled coldly. "If the Navy was involved in the *Nikko*'s destruction, it was best if Strazi disappeared without a trace. That way he could investigate without word getting back to Corwin."

"Let me guess some of what happened next." Siobhan put her cup down. "We arrived at Yotai and like us, you saw the sloop that matched the description we reported on the *Nikko*'s attackers."

"Yes. Then we saw you break out of orbit heading for the outer system and figured you'd try to pick up the bastard's trail. While you were following Corwin's pirate, we were following you."

"Really?" She smiled skeptically. "They train you that well at Black Nova?"

"We," he hesitated for a moment, "provide services to corporations and governments that require more than the average merchant captain's skills."

"Such as?"

"That would be telling, captain." He shook his head.

"May I remind you that I hold the last of the *Marus* in this sector under my guns?"

"And here I was beginning to believe that you weren't one of Corwin's buccaneers." He chided her. "Very well. We transport high-value passengers and cargo, some of it deep in the gray zone when it comes to the finer points of legality. But we never cross the line into the black. Customers looking for those services will pay handsomely and if we fail to deliver…"

"They'll punish you just as handsomely."

"As you say." He inclined his head. "The *Nikko* was carrying one of our high-value cargoes from deep within the Coalsack. You understand that we maintain regular routes to pass special passengers and consignments along with the greatest amount of anonymity. To placate our very upset client, Strazi and I were ordered to investigate."

"Why not ask the Navy?"

Lian contemplated her with such an expression of disappointed contempt that she felt the creeping red of embarrassment color her face.

"Point taken, captain," she replied contritely, inclining her head. "I suppose you'll refuse to tell me what was on the *Nikko* that has your owners upset."

"You assume correctly," his cold smile came back, "though you might wish to ask Admiral Corwin. If I understood your report correctly, all passengers and crew were removed by his pirates."

"But nothing was taken from the cargo holds," she countered, matching his smile. "So your particular transport was a someone."

Now it was Lian's face that turned red with embarrassment at being caught out.

"Touché." He inclined his head. "But I'll say no more, except that the person carried some items which would not have been stowed with the general freight. As I saw no mention of such articles in your report, I can only suppose they were removed as well."

"I can't say for certain." She shrugged. "My boarding party did a cursory inspection of each compartment, mainly looking for bodies, dead or alive, and could have missed things."

"They likely wouldn't have missed this."

Siobhan decided to change the subject since Lian clearly would not say more on the subject short of interrogation. She not only was not prepared to go that far, but the legal justifications she had for detaining his ship did not cover it by a long shot.

"You said you found the wreckage of the *Fuso*."

"Aye. Thoroughly destroyed. If it weren't for Corwin's pirates missing the beacon, we'd have never known."

"Perhaps they left the beacon on purpose."

"As a warning? Perhaps."

"Do you have sensor readouts of the wreckage?" Siobhan asked, her mind already racing toward a conclusion she did not like.

"I do, and I suppose you're going to ask me to hand a copy over to you."

"Captain Lian, I'm as much in the dark on a lot of this as you are and I'd dearly like to get answers. You call Admiral Corwin a pirate but he's my commanding officer, albeit temporary, and like as not, the truth is somewhere in between."

"If you'll let me speak to my chief officer, I'll get it over to you." He considered her in silence for a count of seconds. "You clearly have some idea. May I ask what?"

Siobhan smiled, warmly this time. "I prefer to see the sensor readout first."

With a sigh, Lian rose and cocked his head toward the door to the bridge. "Shall we?"

— Sixteen —

"There's no doubt whatsoever?" Dunmoore asked Chief Penzara, who was standing by the display with his analysis results.

"None, sir. Even the commercial grade sensors on the *Oko Maru* would have picked up the slightest bit of DNA among the wreckage." He looked at Lian suspiciously. "Especially since those commercial grade sensors seem to show better results than I would expect."

"Almost military grade?" Siobhan asked teasingly, giving Lian a sideways smile.

"Aye," Penzara replied with finality.

She glanced at the others in the small conference room, but they remained expressionless.

"Are you telling me," Lian said, "that whoever attacked the *Fuso* took everyone off before destroying her?"

"No other way to interpret the sensor data, sir," Penzara hooked a thumb at the main screen.

"Sounds a lot like what Admiral Corwin's mercenaries did with the *Nikko Maru*," Pushkin said.

"Mercenaries?" Lian asked incredulously. "Since when does the Navy hire mercenaries?"

"Private military contractors, more accurately, Captain Lian," Siobhan replied. "The Admiralty will hire PMCs for some non-combat tasks where it can't spare naval personnel."

"I'd hardly say this was non-combat," Lian protested.

"The way the Navy defines combat, it isn't." Pushkin shrugged. "They're employed as security guards for Admiral Corwin's

189

operation, and that will entail taking down threats. That's still a far cry from engaging the Shrehari."

"So my fellow merchantmen were threats, were they?" Lian's agitation was returning. "Honest spacers doing their jobs?"

Dunmoore held up her hand.

"Peace, Captain Lian. It was just an expression. My first officer meant nothing by it."

"Very well." He settled back, crossing his arms. "If they took Strazi and his crew off, where did they take them?"

Siobhan met Pushkin's eyes, and the first officer nodded minutely.

"I was informed by Admiral Corwin when I arrived in this system," she said, "that the people taken off the *Nikko Maru* have been interned on the planet until operational security permits their return home. I can only assume that the same holds true here."

Lian's bitter laugh echoed across the table.

"And he assured you they were well treated, almost like honored guests. No captain, I'm not feeling too sanguine about my comrades right now."

"Admiral Corwin is a Navy officer." Pushkin's tone was flat and unemotional. "He would treat detainees with all due respect for the law and naval tradition."

"Perhaps, but would his pirates — beg your pardon — his mercenaries?" Lian's voice dripped with sarcasm. "They aren't bound by your precious code of discipline, are they?"

"Enough," Dunmoore snapped, giving Pushkin a warning glance. Both men looked away. "PMCs are bound by as strict a code as the Navy, thanks to the Law Governing the Use of Military Forces, more commonly known as the Rules of War."

She relented and sat back in her chair, eyeing him speculatively. "I would say we have some common interests here. We both want answers and trading barbs won't get us anywhere."

Kowalski caught her eye and she saw her mouth the words 'burst signal.'

Siobhan nodded.

"Captain Lian, on the day the *Fuso Maru* was chased out of the system, we intercepted an encrypted directional burst signal that may have been aimed at Captain Strazi, based on our ships' relative positions at the time."

His head snapped up, and he looked at her with sudden interest. "You've decrypted it?"

"No. Does it matter?" When Lian seemed reluctant to answer, she continued. "If it's in Black Nova house code, my compliments to your cryptography section. Lieutenant Kowalski here is no slouch at it, and she was unable to get anywhere."

Lian looked relieved. "We have a factor on Arietis, who takes care of assembling or receiving our shipments. She's also part of the company's intelligence network." He smiled at the surprised looks. "Any business worth its salt working the frontiers needs its own spies since the Navy won't share. We're hardly alone in that. I'm shocked that you didn't know about the practice."

"Captain," Dunmoore's eyes took on an almost predatory cast, "I'll provide you with a copy of the signal if you'll share its contents, or at least those contents germane to our current situation. I won't pry into corporate secrets if they don't affect my ship."

"Sir," Pushkin's tone was matter-of-fact, "we have no way of knowing if whatever he tells us about the contents of the signal bears any relationship to the truth."

"Are you saying I'd lie to you?" Lian asked with a dangerous edge to his voice.

"I'm saying that we don't know you enough to trust you, captain," the first officer replied.

Lian conceded the point with a nod.

"Then it appears we have a stalemate. I cannot hand my decryption algorithm to the Navy."

"Do you carry it with you?" Kowalski asked. He stared at her suspiciously, and she quickly continued. "If you do, it'll probably be on a reader keyed only to your DNA. Perhaps you could decrypt it here with one of us watching as the clear text emerges. You do carry a company issued pad, yes?"

He stared balefully at the signals officer. She returned it measure for measure, but with a pleasant smile.

"I get the feeling that I'll be stuck on this tub until I've given you every last measure of satisfaction." Lian shook his head. "So be it."

"You," he jutted his chin at Kowalski, "will stay well away from me when I decipher the message."

She smiled as she rose at Dunmoore's silent order and headed to the bridge to get a data wafer with the transmission recorded on it.

"What did you intend to do when you crept back into the system?" Pushkin asked as they waited.

"Trying to get in touch with our factor," Lian replied sourly. "But it seems that Corwin's seeded the place with sensor buoys, judging by how fast Strazi and I got detected the moment we dropped out of hyperspace."

"Consider yourself lucky we're the ones who were sent to intercept you," Dunmoore said. "If it had been one of the mercenaries, you likely wouldn't have been given the chance at a civilized conversation."

"Oh, I'm grateful for the way you're treating me. I just wish I'd been able to avoid all this and get away clean."

"And where would you have gone? Back to Yotai?"

Lian grunted noncommittally. At that moment Kowalski reappeared, holding a small plas square. She handed the wafer to the civilian who examined it suspiciously.

"If you're worried there's a virus on it, feel free to scan," she said, still smiling. "You can keep it, in case you thought it might copy anything off your pad."

He thought for a while, jaw muscles clenched, trying to decide whether the risk was worth the reward. Curiosity finally won out, and he pulled a pad from his jacket's cargo pocket, laying it gently on the table. After a final moment of hesitation, he gingerly placed the chip over an osmotic reader and touched the screen.

"It's clean," he said, looking up at Kowalski after a minute or so. "Glad to see you're not trying to screw me over, but the day is young. Captain Dunmoore, I'm ready to decrypt the message, if you'd like to look over my shoulder."

The invitation was grudging, but Siobhan stood to place herself behind Lian where she could see the pad. He touched the screen again in a quick pattern and soon, words began to appear. Dunmoore's expression became grim, matched by Lian own scowl.

When it was done, she straightened up and ran her gloved right hand through her short, copper hair. Catching Pushkin's questioning look, she grimaced.

"If what the Black Nova factor reported is accurate, the Navy might have a slight problem."

*

Dunmoore walked Lian back to the airlock, both captains lost in their own thoughts, wondering what to do next. When they reached the hatch, she touched his arm and looked him squarely in the eyes.

"This is for the Navy to sort out. You've already lost two ships though hopefully your people are all right. I can't believe that Admiral Corwin would go so far beyond the pale as to kill them."

Lian snorted derisively.

"Men have killed in job lots to preserve secrets. If your admiral's off his rocker, there's no telling what he'll do."

"We have only your factor's word for that, and you did say something felt wrong about her message."

"Perhaps. If I can just get my subconscious to cooperate, I might figure out what it was that sounded off. But what she said fits with the rest."

"Disinformation isn't uncommon either, Captain Lian."

"Granted, but by who and why?"

"I hope to find out. You cannot risk returning to the Arietis system again. I, on the other hand, cannot leave it without orders."

"I'd say your orders are more than just a little suspect. The nearest subspace relay station is at Yotai, and I doubt the Navy would approve of its use."

"Would you do me a favor?" She asked, ignoring his comment.

"I suppose so if only to repay you not sending me to join the *Nikko* and *Fuso*."

"I imagine you're headed back to Yotai where Black Nova has a shore office." He nodded. "When you get there, and if the convoy still hasn't left, can you get in contact with Lieutenant Commander Gulsvig and tell him everything you've learned?"

"Sure, but why should he listen to me, let alone believe me? Wouldn't it be easier if you gave me a message chip?"

She shook her head.

"If you're caught and the message is found, we'll likely not enjoy the consequences. Just tell Gulsvig from me that I said the Chateau Altair is the most underappreciated wine in history. He'll understand."

Lian smirked. "It is for now, but the price will go up soon, mark my words. When we've reached the point where even Navy officers have discovered its secret..." He left the rest unsaid.

Dunmoore offered her hand. After a moment's hesitation, Lian took it and returned her firm shake.

"Good luck."

"Heh. All I need is a head start. You're the one who needs luck, Dunmoore."

"Captain," the intercom came to life with Devall's voice. "Our merchant friend had better make tracks quickly. We've picked up a hyperspace wake at maximum distance. If he decides to drop out in the next twenty minutes or so, he'll pick us up sure enough."

Dunmoore clapped Lian on the shoulder.

"Go. If someone shows up trying to get your scent, I'll do my best to stymie them."

He nodded once and disappeared into his tiny shuttle. Siobhan stood by the airlock watching it leave, her mind a maelstrom of speculation and worry. When it reached the freighter, she pushed her thoughts aside and headed for the bridge. They would have other visitors to deal with momentarily.

*

Dunmoore kept her eyes on the tactical display as the mercenary sloop sped toward *Stingray*. It had dropped out of hyperspace moments before the *Oko Maru* vanished and its sensors would have picked up the freighter's transition wave. Of course, by the time the wave hit the sloop's sensors, the *Oko Maru* would be long gone. It was one of the few times she blessed the time lag that distance imposed on all normal space events.

"Incoming from the sloop, audio only."

"Put it on."

"Why did you let the intruder go?" The voice was low, almost querulous, but female.

"And you are?"

"One of Admiral Corwin's captains. You can call me Bloggins if you like."

Chief Guthren began chuckling derisively. Bloggins was the name given to the Fleet's everyman or everywoman since time immemorial. It was the moniker used in jokes, stories, and lessons where the real culprits were best left unnamed. Everyone had tales about Able Spacer Bloggins of the Navy or Lance Corporal Bloggins of the Marines.

"Noted," Dunmoore replied dryly. "I shall try to refrain from remembering the latest joke making the rounds of the lower deck, Captain Bloggins."

Guthren's mirth threatened to become hysterical as the remainder of the bridge crew joined in one by one. It was a shame there was no video feed. Seeing the expression on the mercenary commander's face as she realized her flippant choice of alias might not have been such a great idea, would have been amusing.

"You've obviously never spent time in the Commonwealth armed services, have you, Bloggins?" Dunmoore asked when there was no reply from the mercenary, provoking further gales of laughter. "Even so, your name is well known."

When she saw that the coxswain likely would not survive the next assault on the mercenary captain's dignity, she relented.

"Now that we've taken care of introductions, might I ask why you feel the need to interrogate me in such an insubordinate manner?"

"My sensor readings give me no evidence that you attempted to stop the intruder. I require an explanation."

"What you need, Bloggins, is a lesson in courtesy. I'm sure you don't address Admiral Corwin in such a tone."

"You're not Admiral Corwin."

"How perceptive. I can see why you were hired for this job." Dunmoore let the sarcasm fairly drip from her voice.

"I still require an explanation for my report to the admiral."

"Perhaps I should be reporting to him directly," Dunmoore replied, that menacing sweetness creeping back into her voice. "After all, he is my commanding officer. You, on the other hand, are a contractor, a hireling."

"I require an explanation why you let the intruder escape."

"And here comes the lesson." She turned to the gunnery officer. "Active targeting on the sloop, if you please, Mister Syten, and make ready a brace of missiles."

"What kind of game are you playing, Dunmoore?" The mercenary managed to sound both aggrieved and alarmed.

"The one where a frigate takes a sloop. You can call it naval chess if you like."

Bloggins laughed harshly.

"One sloop, maybe, but not two at the same time."

"Would you and your colleague care to try? Where is he, by the way? You didn't stumble on me by yourself. The both of you had to have leap-frogged your way here."

"He'll be dropping out of hyperspace any moment now, Dunmoore, and then we can try playing naval chess our way," the mercenary sneered.

Siobhan made a cutting motion, ordering Kowalski to mute the transmission.

"Where is the *Oko Maru*?"

"Almost at the edge of our sensor range. A few more minutes and she'll be gone," Penzara replied, calling up the tactical schematic.

"Turn it back on, Kathryn."

"Bloggins, my job here is done. I chased the intruder out of the system, as per the admiral's orders. Consequently, I suggest we all return to our regular patrol routes. With the three of us in interstellar space, that leaves only one ship to cover Arietis."

She saw Penzara give her thumbs up.

"Mister Guthren, bring her about one hundred and ten degrees. Mister Tours, plot a course back to our assigned station."

"Shall I keep targeting the sloop, captain?"

"Aye, Mister Syten. And if her friend Captain Atkins shows up, you can target his sweet behind as well."

"Bloggins," she continued, addressing the mercenary, "your orders and those of your comrade are to return to Arietis immediately. Disobedience will have consequences."

"We'll see about consequences, Dunmoore. I'm sure the admiral will be less than thrilled about your dereliction of duty, but I congratulate you for having held us here long enough to let the intruder escape."

"I aim to please." She made the chopping gesture again, and Kowalski killed the link. "When ready, sound the jump warning, Mister Pushkin."

"Captain Atkins?" He asked

"Another everyman of the military services. Kipling, I believe. I thought it was a fitting companion for Bloggins."

"One does receive an education serving under you," he shot back, smiling. Then, as quickly as it had appeared, the smile vanished. "How do you think the admiral will react?"

Siobhan made a face.

"Probably not well. There's a dictatorial streak under the smooth facade that makes me a tad jumpy."

"Maybe we should just get the hell out and deal with any problems when we're back under Admiral Ryn's control."

"And abandon any chance at finding out what's going on, thereby coincidentally clearing our name? We're still in the doghouse over the *Nikko Maru* and likely her sister ship as well if we don't get some evidence we can show the Admiralty, Gregor. We haven't exactly made friends in high places when we shone a bright light on the dark doings of the Kaleri and Forenza clans, not to mention the Special Security Bureau."

He shook his head resignedly.

"I'll go see Viv for some pills. This situation is giving me a splitting headache. I don't know who or what we're working for anymore."

"Courage, Number One." She clapped his shoulder. "When things go strange, the strange, that being us, get going."

"Nothing from the admiral yet," Siobhan said, looking up from her pad as Pushkin walked into her ready room.

"Curious. We've been back on station for a day and your two Blogginses for not much less than that. Maybe he's experiencing some of that sweet cognitive dissonance as he compares your report to the mercenaries'."

"Perhaps." She smiled. "I can't quite remember the last time I used so many half-truths, weasel words, and outright almost-lies in a report to my superior. On the other hand, I'd like to get a chance to visit Corwin's lair again. The allegations made by Black Nova's factor are a bit too far on the side of incredible to swallow without corroboration."

"We need food."

"Oh? I haven't looked at this morning's report from Mister Rossum yet."

"No, sir. The excuse to spend some time in orbit: we need food."

"I'm not convinced the admiral will swallow that one, pun intended."

"One of the soy cultures spoiled."

"I hope you're joking. We don't have enough defaulters these days to ream out the vats, and I'd hate to assign the bosun's crew to the job."

Reaming out the vats and its companion, reaming out the environmental filters, was one of the dirtiest, smelliest pieces of work on board a starship. Usually reserved for ratings that fell afoul of their petty officers for one transgression or another that was not severe enough to merit the captain's attention, those duties generally made even the worst offenders repent.

"No fear, sir. All is fine. But it's a good excuse to spend some time dirtside."

"That it is. You're getting pretty devious for a first officer, Gregor. I thought you were supposed to be the good angel on my shoulder."

"It's all in service to a higher cause," he intoned sonorously, his index finger pointing upwards. "Shall I prepare a loss report?"

"Please do."

"Bastard's got active targeting on us," Rownes growled, "but the readings show his weapons are on standby."

"By all means, return the favor," Siobhan replied, smiling, as *Stingray* entered orbit around Arietis. "And bring our guns to a ready state, just to remind him that a frigate beats a sloop."

"Or two?" Penzara asked. "The second one just came out of the planet's shadow."

"Target him as well."

"And the monitor?" Pushkin asked mischievously.

"No. He hasn't annoyed me sufficiently yet."

"Captain," Kowalski interjected, "incoming from the planet. It's Admiral Corwin."

"I have a feeling the other shoe's about to drop." Siobhan rose and grimaced at Pushkin. "I'll take it in my ready room. No sense in sharing my upcoming flogging with the general public. It's bad for morale."

When the door closed behind her, she took a deep breath to compose herself, then sat down behind the desk and squared her shoulders. She touched her console.

"Sir, Dunmoore here."

Corwin's aristocratic face filled the screen. His lips were tight and his nostrils white with barely repressed anger.

"Siobhan, someone is lying to me, and I aim to sort out the guilty party."

"Sir?"

"My contractors reported that you let the intruder get away deliberately, going so far as to accuse you of colluding with him. This contradicts your story, needless to say."

She did not know what to reply and therefore remained silent.

"You're a Navy officer, Siobhan, and consequently your word is your honor. I couldn't begin to believe that you'd falsify a report to your commander. What I'd like to know is why Captain Marek and Captain Desai felt the need to slander your actions."

"I have no idea, sir. All I can tell you is that our conversation was less than cordial." She paused, wondering if Corwin actually believed what he just said or if he was laying a trap. "I don't know what your contractors think they saw, but I can assure you the intruder evaded my grasp. He had a slight edge speed-wise on *Stingray* and enough of a head start."

As she watched Corwin, she noticed the tic in the corner of his eye start up.

"Hmm," he nodded. "I'll ascribe it to jealousy, then."

She felt a sudden and unexpected gush of relief flood her veins.

"I should admonish you for heading out that far into interstellar space without my express permission, but I understand the doctrine of hot pursuit and at least you were able to confirm the identity of the intruder. Perhaps now they'll stop trying to probe where they have no business. Those Black Nova ships are half-pirate and good riddance to them."

"Thank you, sir."

"Bah," he waved her thanks away. "We're the senior Navy leadership out here by the Coalsack. We need to stick together, or the mission fails."

"As you say." She inclined her head.

"Take what time you need to gather victuals. The local chandlers have an arrangement with me, and as you're part of my squadron now, it covers you as well. Just make sure they don't try to pass off mutton as lamb. I'll expect you for another visit to my installation before you head back on patrol. Corwin, out."

"Well wasn't that special," Dunmoore said to the blank screen, mystified by Corwin's reaction. Where she had expected a chewing out, she got a declaration of solidarity. More importantly, he believed her when it came to the *Oko Maru*'s escape.

She tapped the intercom.

"Pass the word for Mister Rossum. It's time to sample the local farmers' market."

*

Corwin turned away from the console and studied the wall hangings recovered from a stasis chamber below. They predated the famous cave paintings on Earth by millennia and had an eerie quality to them. He could vaguely identify the scenes, but his brain had difficulty reconciling them to what was known of modern Shrehari.

Perhaps he should ask Siobhan the next time she visited. She had a reputation for understanding them better than most officers and more's the pity. Though the government and Admiralty bore a lot of the fault, the sheer ignorance of an officer caste raised to believe in human superiority and promoted on patronage instead of merit, had as much as anything else to do with the Navy's inability to force a conclusion to the war.

That she might be lying in her report did not occur to Corwin. Dunmoore was well known for being honest to a fault, irritatingly so if Fleet gossip was to be believed, and she had never shown any signs of currying favor with her seniors. Quite the contrary, in fact.

Still, something rang false in the competing reports, but he would trust a proper Navy officer over a private contractor any day. The Avalon Corporation people were in it for the money, though they would be better employed drafted into the armed services. Dunmoore, on the other hand, had proven over and over again that she was serving the Navy for the greater good, and if he had his way, he would give her, and others like her, greater scope to deploy their ruthlessness.

He did not enjoy his dependence on private contractors, but regular Navy and Marine forces would compromise security. At least the mercenaries could be counted to obey his orders to the letter without worrying about legal niceties, and since there was no question about the payment for services rendered drying up, he had no worries about their turning on him.

However, with an officer like Siobhan Dunmoore under his command, the scope for action became that much greater. Where the mercenaries might follow him because they were paid on time by the Fleet, the flame-haired starship commander could surely be convinced to follow him out of a sense of what was right for the Commonwealth and damn the consequences.

He smiled wanly at his reflection in the polished wood. It was a shame he could not recruit more of her kind, but he was still one almost obsolete frigate and one willful, capable commander ahead of the game.

— Seventeen —

"I still disagree, sir." Pushkin scowled at her. "If there's a risk, it fits within boarding party rules: no captains allowed."

"I fail to see how my visiting Cintrea counts as risky," Dunmoore replied irritably as she reassembled her sidearm. "Besides, I'm taking Vincenzo with me."

She slammed a power pack into the pistol's butt and stretched her arm out, aiming the weapon at the bulkhead. With a satisfied grunt, she holstered it and glared at her first officer.

"I'd feel better if you took the bosun with you as well," he said, glaring back at her, unwilling to back down. "As a matter of fact, if there were enough room in the shuttle, I'd send an entire platoon down with you."

"Stop being such an old fart, Gregor." Her unexpected grin took the sting out of the words. "We'll be okay. All I want to do is have a quiet chat with the Black Nova factor and find out firsthand what she knows about Admiral Corwin's doings, hopefully with more substantive proof than what she put in her message. Accusing a flag officer of acting like a tyrant is a serious matter, and I'd like to see some evidence."

"That's what concerns me, captain. She might have a target on her back."

"Maybe so, but there are things we need to find out, lest we get a big target on *our* collective back, and it's best I do it. If I let you or Trevane go, and things turn bad, you'll find yourselves in the line of fire. As it is, I'll be the only one to bear the blame, be it from Admiral Corwin or the Admiralty itself."

Pushkin shook his head in disapproval.

"Sometimes you take too much on yourself, captain."

"Comes with the job, Number One, as you'll find out yourself some day."

*

The Cintrea spaceport, a vast expanse of dusty tarmac ringed by warehouses and punctuated by a forlorn terminal, sprawled above the broad valley that held most of the settlements on Arietis. Perched on the lip of the chasm, it sat high above the chief city if that was not too grandiose a term for the loose collection of low-rise buildings dotting the banks of a slow, muddy river.

Under Lieutenant Kowalski's sure touch, *Stingray*'s shuttle had sped past the monitor close enough to stare down the barrels of its enormous plasma guns as they were tracked by the improvised battle station's targeting sensors. A surprisingly efficient controller had talked them down, even though traffic was light enough that they could spiral around the planet without concern. Only one other ship sat on the ground, its ramp extended, waiting for outbound cargo. The desolation made Arietis look like even less than the backwater it purported to be. No doubt Corwin's tightening control over all activities on the planet in the name of operational security had much to do with it.

Dust devils eddied over the cracked field as the small spacecraft gently settled down a short walk from the passenger gate. No one came out to greet them and, led by Dunmoore, the party made its way to what passed for the customs desk. A sad-faced humanoid glanced up at them with barely concealed disinterest and then, in an almost comical rendition of a double take, examined their uniforms with growing dismay.

"He doesn't look like he's too fond of the Commonwealth Navy," Chief Foste muttered to no one in particular.

"More like alarmed, I'd say," Vincenzo murmured back. "Maybe he got the shit kicked out of him by some of our spacers in the past."

Dunmoore briefly cleared her throat, more to warn her escort than anything else.

"Good day," she inclined her head politely to the official, whose eyes had now narrowed in what humans would interpret as suspicion. Though he looked bipedal and mammalian, his thick features and rough skin texture clearly marked him as a member of one of the many isolated species native to the sector.

"We are from the Commonwealth Starship *Stingray*, currently attached to Admiral Corwin's squadron, and are here to purchase supplies. Do you require identification?"

"No." The voice was rough, the Anglic heavily accented almost to the point of being indecipherable. "You may go about your business, officer of Admiral Corwin."

For a second or two, Dunmoore would have sworn she heard 'and be damned to you' appended to the official's curt reply. She glanced at Lieutenant Rossum with raised eyebrows. The purser, who had more experience dealing with non-human species in the course of his duties, merely shrugged.

"Our thanks." Siobhan inclined her head politely again, imitated by Rossum and Kowalski. The non-coms and ratings of her party briefly came to attention.

They exited the terminal into the pale, weak sunshine and headed for the large funicular system that connected the spaceport to the bottom of the valley. The air was not unpleasantly hot, even this close to the equator, but it was dry.

The compartment they chose was as empty as it was grimy, hinting at decades, if not centuries of hard use, and Dunmoore took the opportunity to review the plan as the primitive conveyance slowly descended the steep slope.

"Mister Rossum, you and your party will head for the chandlery recommended by the admiral's staff, to order some fresh meat for the galley as well as a batch of starter culture for the vats."

He nodded, mopping his head and neck with his ever-present white handkerchief.

"Indeed, and whatever else I find that might be of interest, seeing as it's not coming out of ship's coffers. Although I don't know that the quality here will be anything I would consider acceptable," Rossum frowned dubiously, "especially the vat culture."

"We don't actually have to use it," she replied with a faint grimace. "The whole point is to talk to people, get a feel for what's in the air, and not be too obvious about it."

"If that gray ghost up there is any indication," Foste interjected, "Uniforms make people nervous, and that's interesting intelligence right there."

"Let's try to be on our least intimidating behavior then." Dunmoore frowned dubiously. The tall, rangy boatswain and the compact, dark complexioned Vincenzo were anything but reassuring. Even the thickset purser and his people seemed the opposite of soft and cuddly.

"Chief Foste, Vincenzo, and I are going to track down the Black Nova factor and see if we can get some useful intelligence. We regroup at the shuttle in four hours. Keep the use of your communicators to a minimum. I get the feeling all frequencies are monitored from above." She nodded upwards.

"If you do need to call, try to use veiled language," Foste suggested. "And remember that if they can listen to you, they can pinpoint your location. There may be a naval base on this planet, but that doesn't mean it's safe for spacers."

Vincenzo snorted. "There's no world safe for spacers with a stack of cred chips and a raging thirst."

"Aye," Foste nodded, "and even less so in these parts. The databanks were pretty thin on information, so there's no telling if the law and order hereabouts are squeaky clean or dirtier than an old Shrehari reactor core."

"Pretend this is Caledonia on a Saturday night, and you'll be fine," Dunmoore said with a smile as the funicular car came to a juddering stop at the bottom of the valley.

The air, when they stepped out, was moist and rich with scents, in startling contrast to the plateau above. Trees covered in various shades of teal and other, equally sumptuous specimens of Arietis vegetation, carpeted the lower slopes and filled the empty spaces between the stone buildings. The spacers gaped at the radical change of scenery, enjoying the warmth and cheerful atmosphere so different from the rest of the planet's surface.

"The last oasis?" Rossum asked philosophically.

"Perhaps. This is an ancient world," Dunmoore mused. "It probably won't be all that long before even this dries out. Yonder star isn't going to get warmer until it gets too warm."

Alarmed at the reference, Vincenzo, and the purser's mate glanced up. Dunmoore grinned at their reaction.

"It isn't going to enter its red giant phase in our lifetimes. Perhaps not even humanity's lifetime, so you can relax."

"Aye, aye, sir." The two spacers, visibly relieved, examined the scenery again.

Rossum and Foste pulled out their pads and oriented themselves. With a nod to his mates, the purser headed across the small plaza at the foot of the funicular and turned right on a street paved with fused rock, disappearing around an ancient structure whose walls were pierced by tinted windows looking out blindly at the day.

"We'll be going in the opposite direction," Foste said, pointing to the left. "The factor's storefront is on the river's edge."

The streets were lightly populated this early in Cintrea's morning, but the beings they encountered spanned every known species in and around the Coalsack, including a healthy smattering of humans. Pretty much the only known races not represented were the Shrehari and their subjects. Whether they did not travel this far from their own space or were cleansed from Arietis as enemy aliens after Corwin took over, was yet another unanswered question.

Foste walked in the lead, keeping to one side of the street. She consulted her pad from time to time, her eyes never resting on one spot for more than a second. Sandwiched between the bosun and Vincenzo, Dunmoore took in her surroundings with interest.

The town felt as ancient as it seemed and she had no difficulties imagining that it had come into being before her own species had migrated out of the African continent tens of thousands of years ago. Stone buildings looked like they had been worn smooth by eons of rain and wind, but seemed so solid that they would probably still be standing when the Commonwealth inevitably collapsed into its long night of barbarism. Hopefully, after an equally long time as a dominant power in this arm of the galaxy — if it managed to win the current war.

The occasional ground-effect vehicle passed by on whistling fans, mostly laden with crates of mysterious cargo and headed for destinations she could not imagine. Although she had set foot on many worlds in her life, this was the first non-Commonwealth planet she had ever visited, and she could feel its alien heart, particularly as it held so many tantalizing non-human touches in the architecture, the smells, and the sounds.

"Three o'clock, in the alley," Vincenzo whispered. "Looks like the local plod."

Dunmoore and Foste glanced to their right in unison.

"Seems like a mercenary to me, sir," Foste immediately remarked. "Human-cut battledress, service issue carbine and stylish sunglasses."

Siobhan snorted at the asperity in her tone. Many professionals had little time for those who hired out as military contractors.

"Looks like he's having a 'chat' with one of the locals," Vincenzo said. "Just like the chief had a 'chat' with Spacer Frekar the other day."

Foste snorted. "I'll have a chat with you, young lad if you don't show more respect to your seniors. But he's right, captain. The merc looks like he's throwing his weight around."

"Not our business," Dunmoore replied, the words belying her interest. As she spoke, the man's head swiveled in their direction, and his blank stare followed them down the road. He appeared to make a point of fingering his carbine menacingly as he leaned forward, the local forgotten.

"I'd like to see him try," Vincenzo growled, hand going to his holstered blaster.

"Belay that," Foste ordered. "If he's the law, then we'll not gain anything by defending the Navy's honor on such a small point. We're almost there anyway."

"Go past, chief," Dunmoore said on impulse. "We'll swing back once he's gone. No point in being too obvious about our business."

"Understood, captain." She turned to glare back at the merc and something in her expression must have given him cause to reflect, because he turned on his heel and headed down the alley to the next cross street.

When they finally arrived at the address given by Captain Lian, they found a waterfront warehouse built of huge gray blocks, its few openings covered with thick metallic shutters buffed to a dull shine by age. A small sign with the image of an exploding star painted in black enamel was the only indication that they had found the right place.

Foste examined the person-sized door fronting the street for a call button or other means of alerting the factor to the arrival of visitors. When she found nothing obvious, she glanced at the captain and raised her fist. At Siobhan's nod, the boatswain pounded on the door, sending dull thuds echoing through the corridor beyond. After waiting for a minute or two, Foste thumped on the hard metal again, equally without success.

"Vincenzo," she turned to the young man, "take a quick jog around the place and see if there's another door, a call button or anything useful, and make sure you don't tumble into the river."

"Aye, chief. But just for your general fund of knowledge, I do know how to swim."

"Impudent bugger," she smiled as she waved him on his way. What if we draw a blank, sir?"

"Then we ask around to see if she's on a trip or laid up at home. Maybe she doesn't come to the factory every day."

"Wouldn't you think she'd live above the shop?" Foste nodded at the upper floor, where shuttered windows overlooked the loading area between street and river.

"Good point."

Before she could say anything else, Vincenzo reappeared, his easy jog belying the months he had spent cooped up aboard a starship.

"No joy, sir. Everything's shuttered." He glanced at the door Foste had tried and, without a word, went over to examine the lock. "That's what I thought."

"Let me guess," Foste replied, "you're going to tell me you can open it."

He grinned at her.

"I've yet to meet one that didn't succumb to the charms of a Vincenzo."

The chief looked at Dunmoore, her expression clearly asking whether or not she should let him try.

"Can he actually pick a lock?" Siobhan asked dubiously.

"Who knows? The one thing I've come to recognize about the lad is that he's had a terribly misspent youth learning all sorts of things that could get a spacer the undivided attention of the provost marshal." She met the captain's eyes, reading the conflict within her. "Sir, if it's important enough that you came down here yourself, maybe we should let Vince do his thing. Asking around might raise more questions than we want."

"What do you have, Vincenzo?" Dunmoore asked the spacer.

"It's a mechanical lock like they use back home, sir, not an alien one. I've worked on some like that back when I was a bad kid." He raised his sensor and scanned the area around the door. "Can't pick up an alarm system either."

"Stands to reason, captain. Human factory, human locks." Foste nodded. "Why mess around with stuff you don't understand when it comes to security?"

"Wouldn't it be just dandy if she walked up as we're opening her door without permission?"

"I'd say there isn't much chance of that." Foste drew Siobhan's gaze to the large warehouse doors. "Look at the garbage and dust piling up. There hasn't been a delivery or pick up by land in a while."

"Maybe she does all her business by water?"

"Watercraft won't get up to the spaceport, captain." The boatswain shook her head. "And her job is trade with off-worlders."

"Okay. I'm convinced." Siobhan nodded at Vincenzo. "Go ahead."

While he worked, Dunmoore and Foste stood guard, scanning the street and the river, eyes occasionally searching the rooftops of the neighboring warehouses. They kept a relaxed stance, but no one with military training would have mistaken their alertness, nor would they have missed the blasters loosened in their holsters. Passers-by, after taking in their black Navy uniforms, did not give them a second glance, preferring to scurry away as quickly as they could.

"Do you think we look like we're carrying the Halkan plague, chief?" Dunmoore asked in an idle tone as the latest pair of Cintreans abruptly turned around and vanished the moment they spied the three spacers.

"Done," Vincenzo announced to the accompaniment of a soft click, forestalling the boatswain's reply to Siobhan's question.

"Let me do the honors." Foste motioned him out of the way and cautiously pushed the door inwards. It swung easily on well-lubricated hinges, even if it felt as heavy as a battleship's main hatch under her hand. Soft glow globes came on as she entered, illuminating a stark, sterile corridor with stone walls and a polished floor. A stairway wound its way upward at the far end while two green doors on each side pierced the unrelieved, utilitarian gray.

"Hello?" She called out, her voice loud in the confined space. After listening intently for any sounds betraying a presence, Foste pulled out her hand-held sensor and slowly scanned each of the four doorways before aiming it up the stairs.

"Nothing, captain." She shook her head as she turned around and headed back to the exit. "Did you want to search the place?"

"I'd at least like to look upstairs. If the factor keeps her private quarters in this building, we might have some indication of where she went."

"Right." Foste gestured at Vincenzo. "Up you go lad and take it one step at a time, scan, move, scan, okay?"

"Will do, chief."

She stood aside to let him pass and then took up a position at the foot of the stairs to cover his back.

Vincenzo was halfway up when the sound of boots on pavement came through the open door. Dunmoore turned around, her right hand hovering over her blaster. Foste quickly ordered the spacer to stop and then joined her captain.

A squad of mercenaries, all dressed identically in black battledress, wearing dark eyeglasses and carrying carbines at the ready in patrol slings, marched into the yard. The leader, who wore a small gold device over his right breast pocket, ordered his men to stop when he saw Dunmoore staring out at them. He kept walking, coming to a halt three paces in front of Siobhan. To her surprise, he saluted her crisply, as if he were on parade.

"Captain Dunmoore?"

"Yes."

"Lieutenant Drash, of the Cintrea City security detachment. We're part of Admiral Corwin's garrison."

Siobhan nodded, keeping a wary eye on the man.

"The admiral has requested the pleasure of your company and asked that we arrange your transport to the base."

"Am I under arrest?"

Drash seemed startled by the matter-of-fact question.

"Of course not, sir."

"I suppose I have no option?"

"I have my orders, sir," he replied, trying to sound apologetic and failing.

Dunmoore was surprised that Drash made no mention of her somewhat irregular presence in the shuttered warehouse.

"Do you know the whereabouts of Black Nova's factor, lieutenant? I have business with her."

"No, sir." He shook his head. "Perhaps she went off-planet recently. A ship headed for Yotai and the Commonwealth passed through not long ago. I believe she hasn't transacted any business in that time so it may be possible she sailed in it."

"You seem well informed for a garrison officer." Siobhan injected a clear hint of skepticism in her tone.

"I'm responsible for policing, captain, and that means I need to know my part of the city and its notable inhabitants."

"So she was notable?"

"All off-world commercial representatives are, sir." Drash was obviously struggling to contain his growing impatience. "We have to be careful the relevant export-import regulations are respected."

"So that restricted artifacts don't grow hyperdrives and jump away?"

"May I advise the admiral that you're on your way?" He asked, after a moment's pause.

"And my people?" She waved over her shoulder toward the unhappily alert Foste and Vincenzo.

"My orders are to ensure you're conveyed to the admiral. Your people are free to return to your shuttle and wait for your purser's party to finish their business."

"And if I refuse?"

"I'd rather wish you didn't, captain. Admiral Corwin has no patience for officers who fail to carry out their orders."

Dunmoore felt Foste move behind her and raised a calming hand.

"Let's not escalate things, chief."

"Sir, I'm going to get spaced by Mister Pushkin if Vince and I let you out of our sight," Foste growled back, staring menacingly at Drash.

His men tensed up and made as if to raise their weapons in the face of the tall woman's open hostility.

"Chief, we're in the Navy and are expected to obey lawful orders. Advise Mister Pushkin when you're back at the shuttle." She looked at the mercenary officer again. "I assume the admiral will arrange for my transport back into orbit when we're done."

"I don't know, captain. All I have are my orders to transport you to the base. I have a skimmer about to land on the river."

As he spoke those words, a sleek, unmarked craft pulled up to the warehouse wharf and made fast with short grappling arms. A hatch opened on its side, and another mercenary stepped out, nodding at Drash.

"We ready?" He asked impatiently. "The boss doesn't like to wait."

Drash looked at Siobhan.

"Captain?"

"Sir, I really don't like this," Foste said. "I'd prefer we fly you to the base in our shuttle at the very least. If these rent-a-soldiers object, between Vince and me, they'll find out about the Navy's idea of pain."

"I wouldn't recommend it," Drash replied calmly. "The rules on Arietis aren't like they are at home. My men and I are the law and you Navy types get no special dispensation. Speaking of the law, you'll remove yourself from the private property you've entered without permission, and head back to the spaceport."

Dunmoore realized the mercenary was deliberately trying to provoke Foste and Vincenzo into some sort of rash action, the better to separate them from her. Or maybe he was just an arrogant ass. The armed services had plenty of those, so why would the private sector be any different?

"Back to the shuttle, chief. I'll get in touch with the ship when I'm with the admiral." Siobhan's tone held a harsh note of finality and Foste knew better than to argue with her. She and Vincenzo snapped to attention.

"Aye, aye, sir."

They stepped out of the warehouse and Vincenzo, after giving the mercenary officer a menacing leer, swiftly relocked the door.

"Take care of my captain, Mister Drash," he said, voice pitched low, "or I'll be feeding your guts to my pet targ, one millimeter at a time."

"That'll be enough, Vince," the unhappy boatswain snapped. "You'll not be speaking to officers in that way, even if they're rentals."

As Siobhan turned to climb aboard the skimmer, Foste saluted, and both spacers remained at attention while she vanished into the craft. They followed it with their eyes as it accelerated over the surface of the river and then lifted off, heading north and out of the rift valley. When it was lost from sight, the boatswain sighed, nudging Vincenzo in the ribs.

"C'mon, kid. Not for us to question an admiral's orders."

"Can I at least wipe the buggers' grins off their faces?"

"No, and it's too late anyway." She nodded toward the street where Drash's squad was wheeling around a corner and out of sight. "Let's find Mister Rossum and give him a hand. Might as well get something useful done this morning."

*

Dunmoore was alone in the passenger compartment of the skimmer. Although utilitarian in nature, the interior of the craft was clean and comfortable. She could see the back of the pilot's head through the opening to the cockpit but after giving her a curt nod as she climbed on board, he had studiously ignored her presence.

They flew over dun-colored, broken terrain, an arid wasteland dotted here and there by hidden oases tucked into narrow ravines, where there was enough moisture for life to flourish. A constant wind howled over the rocky plateaus, buffeting the skimmer and turning the flight into a roller coaster ride. They met no other craft and saw no living beings in the long stretch between the rift valley and Admiral Corwin's base, and if it were not for the faded blue sky, she could have been overflying some desolate moon on the far edge of the galaxy.

After what seemed like hours, the pilot cut through a narrow pass between two tall ridges and Dunmoore saw the familiar layout of the base ahead of them. As the skimmer banked in a wide circle, ant-like black figures spilled out of one of the buildings and assembled in a rectangular formation at the edge of the dusty runway. Whether that was the pilot's signal to land or not was unclear, but the moment the soldiers below stopped moving, he brought the skimmer down in a shallow glide, using his bow thrusters to shed all forward momentum. They landed in the same spot as *Stingray*'s shuttle on her previous visit, and as she stepped off the craft, the same flinty, dry smell stung her nostrils.

The platoon of mercenaries snapped to attention at the barked order of its leader, who raised his hand to his brow in a parade ground salute that would have done the SecGen's Guard proud. Dunmoore returned the gesture with a touch less formality, but she let the platoon leader read approval in her face. At least they were trying to provide the basic military courtesies this time.

When her hand had dropped back to her side, an older man appeared from the hangar and walked around the departing platoon toward her. He wore the same unrelieved black battledress as the remainder of the garrison, but a small badge with the oak leaf wreath and two four-pointed stars of a Marine lieutenant colonel shone on his right breast. His hair was close-cropped on the sides of his head and showed liberal streaks of silver. Shorter than Siobhan, he exuded a solid muscularity that made her think of a human tank.

"Captain Dunmoore," he stuck out his hand, smiling, "welcome back to Fury Station. Thank you for accepting the admiral's impromptu invitation. When he learned you were on the ground, he immediately changed his schedule and ordered us to fetch you from Cintrea. I'm Yan Rissard, his chief of staff."

"Fury Station?" She asked, returning the handshake. "I don't believe anyone's used that name in my presence before."

"We can be secretive," Rissard replied, his smile broadening. "It comes with the territory and the nature of our research."

He touched her right arm briefly as if to guide her out of the constant wind and into the hangar.

"The admiral has asked that I give you a quick tour of the base while he deals with some last minute issues. He's quite anxious to discuss how you and your ship can be of greater assistance in furthering our work."

"And help shorten the war?" She tried to hide her skepticism, but it must have crept through nonetheless.

"You doubt us?" He asked, stopping just inside the building to look her in the eyes. "Let me assure you, captain, that everything Admiral Corwin has told you is true. We're embarked on an extraordinary task here; one that history will call the turning point of the Shrehari War."

Dunmoore returned Rissard's stare, refraining from what might become a smart-ass answer that would not help matters. She saw that he had the eyes of a true believer and knew from bitter experience that one trifles with such ideals at one's peril. He must have been satisfied with what he saw and resumed walking toward the open staircase in the corner of the hangar.

"Admiral Corwin," he continued, "is a great man, a great leader. I believe you've never served with him before this so you wouldn't know, but he's a far-sighted man, with a much clearer vision than the Admiralty of how this war can be brought to an honorable end."

"That wouldn't be too difficult, colonel," she replied dryly. "The Admiralty has become mostly known for its uncanny ability to snatch defeat from the jaws of victory. Some days it seems like a fourth year Academy cadet could do better."

"Indeed," he nodded enthusiastically. "It's a shame Admiral Corwin wasn't given the opportunity to shake up the high command, but he can do so much more here, unfettered from the bureaucracy and those flag officers too timid to seize opportunities."

They stepped down a staircase carved out of the plateau's rock by something that left the surface smooth and even.

"You're a Marine, aren't you?" She asked, following his broad back down the stairs.

"Twenty-five years in the Corps this August," he replied proudly.

"What's a Marine doing here, if I may ask?"

"You may, captain. We're all comrades in arms here. The admiral wanted a ground pounder to oversee the Avalon PMC folks," he pronounced it pee-em-cee, "and since I had experience working with the private sector, I was the logical choice. It's a better assignment than what they had me slated for after I finished my tour as a regimental executive officer."

"What assignment was that?" She asked as they reached a wide corridor at the foot of the stairs.

"Divisional Staff, G-1," he laughed. "Me, a personnel officer? The Corps has a strange sense of humor."

He stopped and waved his hand toward the slick walls.

"We found an entire underground complex carved out of the living rock here, older than human civilization, almost as old as our species itself."

"Proto-Shrehari. The so-called L'Taung."

"Indeed. Note the smoothness and regularity. Whatever they used was immensely more accurate and powerful than our own mining and excavating tools. No human gear could achieve such precision and perfection drilling through hardened granite."

"Surely the light globes don't date back to the original inhabitants?"

"No," he replied, "but I wouldn't be surprised if we found their analog soon. We've only excavated a small part of the complex so far. The ancient Shrehari sealed their artifacts up very tightly. Come."

They resumed walking, their heels clicking on the bare rock.

"We took advantage of the first level of tunnels to connect all the structures on the base. As you may have noticed, it's always windy around here and sometimes those winds turn into punishing gales driving huge dust devils before them. It gets cold too, especially at night."

"How convenient." She immediately regretted the implied sarcasm of her words, but Rissard seemed oblivious.

"It is, isn't it?"

He led her through a big, square doorway and up another flight of stairs carved from the rock. They emerged in a large, airlock-style antechamber, with warning signs in Anglic proclaiming it to be a restricted zone. At Rissard's touch, a door opened smoothly, revealing a busy operations center.

Inside, a dozen people manned consoles and spoke softly into throat mics under the looming presence of a wall carpeted with large screens showing scenes not only of Fury Station but also of sites in the rift valley and the spaceport. To one side, a visual feed from the monitor in orbit showed the tiny shape of *Stingray* silhouetted against the larger of the two moons.

"From this room, we control Arietis, captain." Rissard sounded like a proud father. "With technology and two battalions of infantry, we've claimed the planet for the Commonwealth as jumping off point to our final victory."

Dunmoore stared at the screens, appalled. This was not so much an operations room as a surveillance center. Judging by the ever-changing images, no part of the settled area was without a panoramic camera, and if she understood what she saw on the consoles, no inhabitant remained unidentified, his or her affairs private. Small wonder then, that Lieutenant Drash and his men had found them so quickly.

"We can exercise complete control from this room, and we even have remote-controlled weapon stations to deal with criminality on the spot." He patted a nearby terminal. "Since Admiral Corwin decided to extend his authority over the remainder of the planet, lawlessness has sharply decreased."

"What's that?" She pointed at a side screen showing what looked like a military formation in front of buildings surrounded by lush vegetation.

Rissard's smile spread even further.

"Our training center. We've had so many people wishing to volunteer their services that we allowed Avalon Corporation to recruit on Arietis and establish a training camp."

Dunmoore felt momentarily dizzy. Black Nova's factor had not been exaggerating. Corwin *had* turned Arietis into his own, private police state. That reminded her: she needed to reassure Pushkin.

"Colonel, might I get a comm link with *Stingray*. My first officer must be wondering what became of me."

"But of course." He pointed at a station in the left corner. "Gershon will set it up for you."

Within moments, Pushkin's face appeared on the signals alcove screen, his eyes searching her face intently.

"Is everything alright, captain? Foste's report was rather, shall we say, animated."

"I'm all right, Gregor. The admiral wishes to confer with me on future operations. I'm being given the grand tour by his chief of staff, who's graciously letting me use the comms facility in his operations center."

Pushkin nodded his understanding that they were not on a secure link.

"Any idea when you'll need a ride, sir?"

Siobhan turned to Rissard who shrugged.

"No idea, captain. The admiral may wish to discuss his plans with you at length, and that can take time." His eyes suddenly lit up. "But I'm sure he'd be delighted to have one of our shuttles ferry you back to your command."

"Most gracious of him," Dunmoore murmured, watching Pushkin's eyes narrow.

"He is that," the first officer replied in the same tone.

"Anything going on I need to know about?"

"No, sir. Rossum and the victualling party are back. We've got the soy vat reamed out and restarted, and there will be fresh pseudo-chicken in the messes tonight."

"Pseudo-chicken?"

"That's what they call it on Arietis, apparently. It's supposed to taste just like real chicken."

"So does every other unknown meat in the galaxy. Save me a filet, Gregor. I'll call back later for an update." She gestured to the commo tech. "You can break it down. Thanks."

"Anything I can show you in here?" Rissard asked solicitously. "Any part of Arietis you'd like to see?"

Dunmoore smiled at his ever-growing eagerness to please her. There was no guile in his eyes, but they did shine with the fierce intensity of a zealot with a cause.

"Not at this time, colonel, thank you. Where to next?"

"We have enough time for you to see the rest of the surface buildings. Please follow me."

Dunmoore was shown an impressive set of facilities: barracks, mess hall, recreation complex, communication array, and well-sited and camouflaged defensive weapons. The missile launchers could easily send their birds beyond the planet's atmosphere and reach orbiting starships like *Stingray*, while the plasma guns could sweep the sky and ground clean with a few bursts of superheated matter.

"I guess the Navy spared no expense in setting this up," she commented as they walked through yet another underground corridor to Admiral Corwin's headquarters building.

"This project has the support of many at the Admiralty who could ensure that the proper funding and orders were issued. Most rear-echelon flag officers might not be visionaries and leaders like Admiral Corwin, but many share his goals. Ah! Here we are."

He pointed at a set of stairs going upwards.

"I have to attend to my duties. Simply go up and wait in the antechamber. Until later, captain." With that, he disappeared around a corner, the sound of his footsteps ebbing in the distance.

As with many of the other corridors, this one had doors set into the stone at irregular intervals. Rissard had failed to mention where they led, and she decided that someone, perhaps the admiral, would tell her when they wanted her to know.

For some reason, she had felt under a sort of secret probation since her first encounter with Corwin and wanted to see where it led her and her ship. With a shake of the head, she dismissed the temptation to explore and took the stairs as directed.

When she reached the top, a door opened, revealing the same luxurious office she had seen on her previous visit. Corwin motioned her to enter as he rose from his desk to greet her. When she got near, he stretched out his hands in greeting, taking hers between both of his.

"My dear Siobhan. You're well I trust." His deep eyes spoke of warmth and pleasure at seeing her, as did his open smile. "We have much to talk about."

"That's what Colonel Rissard said."

"I'll bet he also spoke of me in glowing terms as being a visionary." Corwin managed to sound just a tad embarrassed. "I'm afraid our resident Marine can sometimes be overly enthusiastic. It seems to be a common trait of the breed. But come, sit." He motioned her to the settee grouping around a table with the alien carvings. "We have much to talk about. Perhaps when we're done, you'll make your own judgment about my vision."

"Coffee?" Corwin asked as he walked over to the small urn sitting on another carved table. Without waiting for her reply, he filled two cups and, disdaining milk and sugar, brought them over to where Siobhan sat. She accepted the mug with a strained smile and watched him settle down on a hide-covered chair.

"You have an interesting reputation in the Fleet," the admiral said, after a sip of the black brew.

"Sir?" Dunmoore was puzzled by the unexpected statement.

"Your record is, by some lights, checkered, but many consider you a fearless, tactically superior starship captain; ruthless even. Yet you have many people in high places who hate you. The fallout from the Sigma Noctae Fleet Depot incident and the Kaleri affair still resonate deeply in certain quarters, and I expect your file will not be high up in the pile when the time comes to consider which commanders get their fourth stripe. The promotion boards at headquarters remain as heavily influenced by politics as ever. What clean up there's been of the Navy's officer corps has happened within the battle groups and fleets, not the bloated staffs distant from the everyday reality of war."

Siobhan nodded, unsure what to reply. She was well aware that other than a few flag officers like Admiral Nagira, or those who were equally on the out with the high and mighty, there was no one to act as her champion. Her unexpected command of *Stingray* had come in part because no one else wanted the ill-fated frigate. By the time she had turned an unhappy ship into a proud fighting machine, she had several better-connected families out for her blood.

"Hoko Nagira speaks well of you," Corwin continued. At the look of surprise on her face he smiled. "Nagira and I go back, way back. He was a senior at the Academy when I was a second-year cadet. I've served under his command a few times since. Judging by his appraisal of your abilities and what I've observed so far, you could be precious in helping me carry out my real mission."

He studied her in silence for a few moments.

"If we succeed and help bring this war to an end, your involvement could go far in safeguarding your career from those who would trample on it. I'll not blow the trumpet and try to stir your patriotic emotions. I'll only state that we can save many a spacer's life before it gets wasted needlessly by the donkeys in the Admiralty and the carrion-eaters in the Senate."

Dunmoore was startled by the sudden display of naked anger in that last sentence. She shared Corwin's opinion of their high command and its political masters, but she never expected a flag officer to state it so bluntly in front of a subordinate. His words stirred up emotions turned raw by years of war.

"Do you know what the real reason for our lack of victory is, Siobhan?" His tone was once more calm and urbane.

"Incompetent and corrupt leadership," she answered, aware that it was what he expected her to say.

"Indeed. The Shrehari are no bogeymen. Their ships are no better than ours. Case in point: you bested a *Tol* class cruiser captained by one of their finest with an old Type 203 frigate. Considering the quality of the Shrehari high command, we should have been able to roll over them by now. Men like Brakal are few in the Imperial Fleet and destined to vanish into the cellars of the *Tai Kan* in time. And yet, here we are, unable to liberate Cimmeria and the other occupied systems."

"But your finds here will help us tip the balance," she ventured, unsure of where Corwin was taking the conversation. It was the most candid assessment she had ever heard spoken by an admiral, but it was also unnerving, considering all the questions she had about him and what he was doing in the Arietis system.

"Not just my finds, as you call them." He carefully placed his cup on table and stood, gesturing at her to remain seated. With his hands clasped in the small of his back, he began to pace, looking up at the ceiling in thought, formulating his answer.

"Even though you haven't yet attended the Naval War College, I'm sure you've read enough about grand strategy to pinpoint the weaknesses in both the Commonwealth and the Empire."

He glanced at her expectantly and waited for an answer. She was smart enough to follow his thread of logic to its conclusion, of that he was sure.

"The role of grand strategy," she quoted, "is to co-ordinate and direct all the resources of a nation, or band of nations, toward the attainment of the political object of the war – the goal defined by fundamental policy."

"Basil Liddell Hart, word for word. Well done. He was one of the better military thinkers our species brought forth. Certainly much smarter than most of the theorists who've been scribbling about strategy since we discovered FTL travel."

Dunmoore suddenly realized that he was probing her, feeling her out, but for what reason, she could not tell. As a rear admiral, he could issue any lawful order, and she would be bound to obey it. He had no need to court her.

"Where is the Commonwealth's grand strategy falling down?" When he saw her hesitate, he added, "There's no need to be shy; it's Chatham House Rule between us. Just say what comes to mind."

"I suppose my smart-ass answer would be: everywhere, sir."

"From the cynical school, are you?" He chortled, enjoying her boldness. "One whose idealism has been ruined by experience? Elaborate, if you will."

"We should be in a total war, an existential war, even though the Empire's goal isn't and never was the subjugation of the entire Commonwealth. Total war means all necessary economic, financial, and political resources should be put to the war effort, and yet they haven't been. The member worlds far from the front lines haven't ceased their bickering and maneuvering for more power, money is wasted by expensive and futile schemes when it's even directed at ship building or weapon development."

"Yes," he nodded, pleased by the growing passion in her tone, "and those with the best connections are getting rich from untendered military and naval contracts. Isn't it almost as if there are interests who want the war to drag on, so they can extract the last cred of profit?"

"I wouldn't be surprised," she replied, astonished by her own emotions over the subject. "I've seen some of the aristo clans up close, and there's a depth to their selfishness that should sicken every sane person to the core."

"It would if our Fleet wasn't also heavily larded with members of those same families in the most senior ranks. Is it your assessment then, Commander Dunmoore, that our political and military leadership have failed to enact a viable grand strategy that would bring this war to an end?"

"Damn right it is, sir. There are a lot of people whose actions or lack thereof have caused many a good spacer to die."

"You experienced something like that personally in *Victoria Regina*, didn't you?" He stared at her, eyes narrowed as if gauging her feelings.

Siobhan was conscious that Corwin was pushing all of her buttons but the raw anger that had been driving her for so long was coming back to the fore, and she felt no desire to show restraint. Here was a senior officer who encouraged her to reveal her inner thoughts and who wanted her to feel the rage.

"Yes, Admiral, thievery to pad corrupt flag officers' bank accounts and underwrite the schemes of the Special Security Bureau, has caused many more of my crew to die than was made necessary by the demands of battle." Now the rage was there. She could feel her cheeks flush.

"Yours is but one story among many such in the last six years," he replied, voice soft and soothing. "But all point to the one thing that has prevented us from ejecting the Shrehari and reclaiming our space."

"Our own government," she whispered, as the direction of Corwin's questions became apparent.

"Not just our own government but our own military leadership as well." He sat down again, a pleased glint in his eyes. "If only we had more officers like you. Officers with fire in their gut and the courage to see reality as it is. Those of us who saw the true path of our duty to the Commonwealth and its people can no longer sit by idly and wait for someone with sufficient willpower to rise. Too many will die that could have been saved."

"When you were here last," the admiral continued, "I told you that we were sitting on a treasure trove of proto-Shrehari artifacts dating back a hundred millennia and that we were going to use the technology we're finding to break the stalemate and win the war for our side."

She nodded.

"When you were in the operations center, did you notice a feed showing soldiers training?"

"I did. Rissard said the PMC set up a sort of boot camp for new recruits."

"Trust Yan to be underwhelmingly vague," Corwin smiled again, sensing that he almost had her. "The ancient weaponry we're uncovering needs people to operate it, fighters we can trust."

"The Navy approves of this?" Siobhan inquired, her thoughts spinning wildly as she tried to divine where this was going.

"I've been given full authority to do what I must to help right the Commonwealth and give the Fleet tools with which it can achieve victory." If he was put out by her question, he gave no sign. His smile remained as friendly and as pleasant as before. He preferred that she ask all the awkward questions rather than simply accept what he said.

Challenging superiors was the hallmark of an intelligent commander, one who wanted to figure things out for herself and thus become personally invested in the outcome. What he had in mind required a commitment so far beyond the personal that few would be able to fill the role. He hoped that Dunmoore would be one of those very few.

"I was given to understand that the entire planet is now under your authority, sir."

Her statement snapped him out of his reverie, and he nodded.

"The magnitude of what we're doing makes that imperative." He waved away what he thought were her objections. "Oh, I let the existing governments do as they like. I've established more of a temporary protectorate than anything like a full Commonwealth takeover. The folks here will be left alone once we've achieved our objectives."

"And these objectives are?" The question came out as a whisper, hinting that her agile mind was making many of the right connections.

"Ensuring that those who have hobbled our efforts are removed from the equation." His smile became chillingly vulpine. "Getting the Kaleris, Forenzas, and other assorted trash as far away from the levers of power as possible, permanently."

"You're talking about a coup d'état!" Siobhan felt a frisson of fear mix with her desire to avenge the many deaths over the years.

"No, Siobhan." He gently shook his head. "A mere rearrangement of the lines of control so that the Fleet can be freed to prosecute the war as it should have been all along. We'll likely never be able to root out all the rot, but we need to excise as much as necessary to end this." His eyes became hard, uncompromising. "Your arrival here, while at first an inconvenience, has proven to be very useful to our cause."

"In what way?" Dunmoore was glad her voice remained steady because she understood she would not be allowed to refuse her help. Not if she wished to return back to the Commonwealth alive and in command of her ship.

"Useful as my Avalon Corporation troops are — their chief executive officer is one of ours by the way — a ship like yours, with someone like you in command, will allow us to strike more readily and with more decisive surprise."

He stood up with a sudden burst of energy and thrust out his hand.

"Are you one of ours, Siobhan?"

Shaking his hand, she replied, "I will do my duty to the Commonwealth and the Navy, sir."

At that moment, she could not have explained why she used those precise words, but they seemed to resonate with Corwin.

"Excellent. Welcome to Operation Valkyrie. Hoko Nagira would be proud of you."

"He's part of this?"

Corwin nodded.

"You'd be surprised how widespread and deeply felt this is among some of the finest senior officers alive and among some of the better known Outworld senators as well."

— Eighteen —

Siobhan fought valiantly to hide her dismay. She had little love for the politicians and senior officers who mismanaged the war, but to compel change by the force of arms struck her as repugnant. Her oath to the Constitution, while citing 'enemies domestic' did not allow her leeway to take up the sword against her superiors.

Or did it, if those superiors were themselves violating not just the spirit, but in some cases the letter of the fundamental laws that held human civilization together?

Corwin saw the internal struggle reflected in her eyes and relaxed. Having doubts was natural. He had his own when they approached him to take over Fury Station and play his part in the larger plan. In fact, he would have been worried to see Siobhan accept his proposal without reservations, for that would have indicated character flaws he found revolting, such as opportunism. Corwin would have been equally worried to see loathing, for that would have meant he could never trust her to preserve the secret until it was time to strike.

He held her hand a few moments longer until he saw the turmoil in her eyes abate, to be replaced by her more usual look of determination.

"Yours is the first warship to enter the ranks of Operation Valkyrie," he said. "I have no doubt that my colleagues are even now preparing their part of the Fleet for what we must do but you shall have the greater mission and thus the greater glory."

"May I inquire about specifics?"

"Not just yet, Siobhan." He smiled warmly. "Operational security. I may have to send you back into Commonwealth space before we're ready to move and we cannot afford the risk of you falling into security hands with detailed knowledge rattling around in your brain."

She was suddenly reminded of the message from the Black Nova factor and felt her heart sink. Captain Lian had enough information in his hands to make an alert analyst very nervous: details about the mercenary training camp; Corwin setting himself up as ruler of Arietis; rumors of super-weapons and more. Operation Valkyrie might already be compromised to some extent.

The urge to tell the admiral about her meeting with Lian to prove her loyalty was strong. It was a testament to the power of his charm, logic, and her visceral hatred of all that was wrong with the Commonwealth. Yet something kept her silent, some desire to keep her options open, even if Corwin believed she had pledged herself entirely to his cause. Remembering her own words, that she would do her duty, put her ambivalence in sharp contrast.

"Is something bothering you?" He asked, his face a mask of fatherly concern that was wholly unfeigned.

Well, at least it was fatherly and not motivated by an urge to get into my pants, I hope, Siobhan thought flippantly, suppressing her darker thoughts with a burst of inappropriate and irreverent humor,

"It's all just a bit much to process, sir. I'll be okay," she answered instead.

"I'm sure you will. You're a frigate captain, one of a rare breed whose distinguishing characteristic is adaptability."

"How much may I share with my crew?"

"Nothing, I'm afraid." He shook his head. "We cannot afford loose lips letting something out within hearing of the SecGen's creatures. You had one of such aboard, though now safely departed, I understand."

"You think the SSB may have planted another agent on *Stingray*? I don't really see why they'd bother."

He shrugged. "When it comes to those weasels, anything is possible. The depths of paranoia surrounding the SecGen and his minions are unfathomable by honorable officers such as you and me. No, Siobhan, not even your first officer. If there comes a time where he needs to be read into the operation, I will make that determination. Until then, the cover story remains."

"Sir, one question, if I may." When he nodded, she continued. "You've made several remarks that indicate you have access to subspace communications with home. This far out, you'd need a large installation, yet we haven't seen anything."

Corwin laughed softly.

"Well spotted, my dear. The monitor in orbit, formerly the Commonwealth Starship *Roberts* but now owned by Avalon Corporation, has an installation in one of the attached pods. We keep the array hidden when not transmitting."

"But that couldn't have the power to boost messages over such a distance," she protested.

"Indeed. There is a large relay buoy at the edge of the system. You'll not have spotted it because we keep it in hibernation most of the time."

"So you spoke with Admiral Nagira since I arrived here."

"I did." The warm smile broadened. "I decided to ask you to join Operation Valkyrie after he assured me you would be an exceptional addition to any team. Of course, it was all quite casual, you understand. It wouldn't do to discuss specifics over a naval comm link."

This time, Siobhan had to look away while she collected her thoughts. To her mind's eye, Nagira was the embodiment of the officer corps' honor. If he chose to participate or at least support this conspiracy — she forced herself to think the awful word — matters were much worse than she had imagined.

"What now, sir?"

"Now? I think you'll enjoy what I'll be asking you to do. Since the threat of intruders should abate, now that we've managed to rid ourselves of the Black Nova pests..."

"Sir?" She saw a flash of annoyance at her interruption in his eyes. "There's still one on the loose."

"The *Oko Maru*. Have no fear. He'll be dealt with promptly and won't be a bother to our plans."

"Yes, sir. Sorry, sir." She bit back the question of why Lian and his ship were no longer of any concern. If he had suffered the fate of his fellow captains, she probably did not want to know.

"As I was saying, since I no longer see the need to have my ships dispersed on patrol routes covering the entire system at all times, I want to begin exercising them to operate as a proper squadron."

He laughed with delight at the look of alarm on her face, Siobhan having been unable to check her reaction.

"I won't turn *Stingray* into my flagship and breathe down your neck, my dear. It wouldn't be efficient, and you don't have space for my staff, nor do you have a means to set up a flag bridge. For what we have to do, I can't afford to be tied down by squadron command. I intend to organize myself as many battle group commanders do, and have my second in command lead the vanguard. How would you like to be my acting commodore? It comes with a broad pennant this time."

Again, she felt his fatherly smile stir up a desire to show her loyalty. Here was one of the few flag officers willing to trust her and disregard the political baggage she dragged in her wake. And he was a friend of the man she respected the most.

Siobhan Dunmoore snapped to attention, letting a delighted grin transform her dark features.

"It would be my pleasure, sir."

He glanced at his timepiece.

"I see the sun is over the yardarm. I suggest we dine and celebrate your elevation over a glass of wine, Acting Commodore Dunmoore."

*

Sitting alone in the rear of the attack shuttle, Siobhan tried to bring some semblance of order to her confused thoughts. All through lunch, Corwin had been urbane, charming her with the strength of his convictions and his forthright views on ending the war.

He had controlled the conversation from start to finish, and she got no answers to the many questions plaguing her. She was sure he would have cited operational security to any probing of his activities, and Siobhan would have found it hard to blame him. The reprisals they would face if the operation was blown would be most severe. Treason in time of war still carried the death penalty, and those who could commute it to a prison sentence would have no appetite to spare their lives.

Part of her was furious that she and her crew had been dragged into the conspiracy, yet another part was glad at the chance to strike back and repay the rotten edifice of state for all the dead who still haunted her nightmares.

The pilot's voice broke through her thoughts.

"Commodore, I think it might be a good thing if you joined me on the call to your ship, just in case they don't like my looks and decide to keep us away."

She unfastened her restraints and made her way between the cramped seats to the cockpit. The pilot, a young man with a pleasant, open face, gestured toward the weapon controller's seat.

"*Stingray*, this is shuttle Avalon Bravo One Five. I have Commodore Dunmoore on board. Please advise."

"One Five, would you be so kind as to put the captain on the line." Kowalski's voice was not quite openly caustic, but it was a near-run thing.

Siobhan flicked on the video feed and had the satisfaction of seeing the signals officer's sardonic expression fill the screen.

"Mister Kowalski, my compliments to the first officer. I'd like to dock at the port airlock."

The other woman looked at her strangely, as if examining her face for some sign. Dunmoore quickly understood. The climate of mistrust compounded by her apparent kidnapping that morning probably made her loyal, yet cautious crew feel hesitant.

"Have Mister Pushkin wait for me in my ready room. He can help himself to as much sugar and cream as he wants."

Kowalski briefly glanced off-screen, then nodded, apparently satisfied.

"Approach our port side to a distance of one hundred meters and match velocities. We'll tractor you in."

*

As she stepped through the open hatch and into the airlock, she was greeted by the trill of the boatswain's whistle and a side party presenting arms with parade ground precision. She was surprised at the formality of the reception but then understood she was being piped aboard not as captain of the frigate, but acting commodore of the Arietis Squadron.

"Welcome back, commodore." Pushkin, hand raised in a stiff salute, stood at attention beside the inner hatch.

His eyes searched hers while she returned the gesture as if trying to find answers to this sudden change in fortunes.

"It's nice to be home, Gregor, especially to such a reception, and don't worry, everything is good."

"I hope so. The cox'n is over the moon at the thought of flying a broad pennant and being able to give the mercenaries heck."

"We'll have to stop calling them mercenaries, I'm afraid," she said, giving her first officer a wry grin as they headed for the bridge. "I've been appointed their commander so it behooves my flagship crew and me to treat them with standard naval courtesy. Henceforth, they shall be referred to as the Avalon Corporation ships *Carnatic, Coromandel,* and *Malabar.*"

"Have they shared with us which is which?" He raised his eyebrows with droll skepticism as he let her enter the ready room first.

"*Carnatic* is commanded by a woman named Marek. We know her as Bloggins."

"Aha! I knew that wasn't her real name." Pushkin snorted. "Can we still call her Bloggins behind her back?"

"No. If I'm commodore, be it ever so acting and temporary, it means you're the closest thing we have to a flag captain, and you need to play nice. *Coromandel* is the ship whose skipper we've nicknamed Atkins, real name Desai. We haven't had the pleasure of playing with *Malabar* yet, but its captain goes by the name of Thoran."

"What about that fusion reactor with plasma guns?"

"Ex-Navy ship, now Avalon Corporation, called *Roberts,* under a Lieutenant Kylan. The monitor isn't part of my command, though. It's answerable to the admiral through his chief of staff, a jolly Marine lieutenant colonel with the implausible name of Yan Rissard."

"So we're all one happy family then," Pushkin replied sarcastically as he offered Dunmoore a cup of black coffee before drawing his, heavily sugared and creamed.

"It appears that we are," she replied, feeling strangely irked by the first officer's attitude. "The powers back home have given us to Admiral Corwin in furtherance of his mission and he in turn has given us a squadron to lead. I'd say things aren't looking too bad for once."

"And when the time comes where we need to refuel the hyperdrives and re-arm, not to mention replace worn out parts? We're not exactly close enough for a quick run to a star base, and I doubt *Petrel* will venture out here."

"We left the Commonwealth with six months of autonomy."

"Assuming no pitched battles," he countered. "I'd rather not have to run home unbalanced due to damaged drives again. The Fleet engineers are still trying to figure out how we managed to do it without cracking the ship's frames."

Siobhan studied him, trying to find a meaning for his outburst.

"I get that as the first officer, your job is to make sure the ship is ready for action at my orders," she eventually said, locking his eyes with her own stare. "But I don't know if I understand your sudden vehemence."

Pushkin bit his lower lip and shook his head slowly.

"I don't know, captain. Nothing feels quite right around here, and now Corwin's made you acting commodore of the Arietis Squadron, which consists of one Navy ship and three mercenary — pardon me — Avalon Corporation sloops. I just can't wrap my head around it."

"Truth be told," she replied, gazing at the star field on the wall screen, "I'm not convinced I've wrapped my head around it yet either, but Admiral Nagira has recommended me to Admiral Corwin, and here we are."

His head whipped up.

"Admiral Nagira? How the heck did they get a message to Dordogne and back without a large subspace array?"

"It appears we haven't been looking in the right place for it."

"Bullshit. A subspace array or relay buoy, puts out enough emissions to light up like Founder's Day. We'd have noticed something by now."

"And yet, Admiral Corwin knows much more about us and what we've been up to than he could without talking to Admiral Nagira or others back home, such as our own Admiral Ryn."

"Truth be told, I really don't know what to think." His tone had lost its earlier intensity. "Did you at least learn something more about what Corwin's up to? Kind of hard to be at our most effective if we don't know what we're supposed to protect."

Siobhan glanced down into her cup, unwilling to look him in the eye as she lied. Ever since their rocky start, she had made sure to take him into her confidence at all times when it came to ship's business. He deserved no less.

"No. Admiral Corwin is quite strict concerning operational security. Getting back to your earlier question," she said, changing the subject, "it appears that we can receive limited replenishment without venturing too far from Arietis."

"Really? And how would that work."

"I suppose we'll find out when the time comes." She shrugged. "I expect that the admiral will transmit his orders by the end of the watch. Let me know as soon as they arrive."

Pushkin heard the implied dismissal and gently returned his coffee mug to the sideboard. His instincts told him there was more than what she had said, but he also sensed that probing would not be a good idea right now.

"I'll see about Kowalski rustling up the squadron signals instructions and I'll have some pro forma standing orders ready for you shortly," he said, keeping his tone matter-of-fact. "Is there anything else?"

"Not at this time. Thanks, Gregor."

When the door closed behind him, Dunmoore felt an unexpected surge of self-loathing. He was her right arm, her conscience, her best friend, and yet thanks to Corwin's orders, she could not tell him the truth.

*

"I get that you and your Avalon colleagues aren't used to squadron action, Captain Marek, but the admiral has ordered us to practice maneuvers as a formation."

Siobhan pinched the bridge of her nose, trying to forestall the headache she felt building behind her eyes. The three mercenary ship commanders had been reluctant, if not outright truculent at being placed under her command and had questioned every single order. In Marek's case, there was at least a hint of wanting to learn, but the other two made it repeatedly clear that they thought she was full of vat sludge.

Right now, she would give anything to have Gulsvig and Stoyer instead of those three. At the very least she clearly outranked her fellow Navy officers, and they had a solid grounding in multi-ship evolutions.

"Let's try this again."

She went through the entire process, step by step, for the third time. It was not that the Avalon people were stupid. Far from it, but they were not used to working under Navy tactical discipline and had no experience operating in consort with other ships in battle.

"I still have a hard time seeing what good this is supposed to do," Marek insisted. "A four-ship squadron like ours can't take control of a hostile planet's near space, not when it has an armed station in orbit."

The question was valid, and Siobhan shared her concern but absent a necklace of gun and missile platforms, there were always ways to avoid a station's ordnance. Then it struck her: Corwin was not expecting them to seize the high orbit against a prepared opposition. Quite the contrary. For a few seconds, she was paralyzed by indecision. How much could she share with the Avalonians? If her own first officer had to be kept in the dark, she was sure Corwin would not want hirelings read into the operation.

"This is why we need to practice," she finally said. "An orbiting platform like *Roberts* may look daunting, especially to a sloop, but it has one significant disadvantage."

"It can't change its position, at least not with any sort of speed," Marek said, nodding. "So the whole point is to keep its crew occupied while sneaking into the shadow of the planet, on the opposite side, and after that maintaining the same orbital period."

Siobhan wanted to applaud. One of them finally got the idea, but she was sure any praise would come across as sarcasm. The mistrust between her and the private spacers would probably never fully abate.

"Okay. Let's have some fun then. On the next run," she said, "I'll take *Coromandel* with me to harass the orbitals. Captain Marek, you and *Malabar* will move into Arietis' shadow and head for Cintrea at a low level to simulate a strafing run over the spaceport."

*

"I'm very pleased with the progress you've made over the last week, Siobhan," Corwin smiled warmly, and she could feel herself flush even though he was thousands of kilometers away, on the surface of the planet. Once the mercenaries had stopped fighting her and begun to think like members of a team, they had proven to be surprisingly good for private sector spacers. "The real test will be an actual operation."

Dunmoore started at his statement. While it was true that she mercilessly drilled the Avalon ships, she did not consider them to be quite ready for actual combat. Perhaps individually or in pairs for something easy like taking down the *Nikko Maru*, but a genuine raid on a planet?

"What's the target?" She asked, caution tainting her voice.

Corwin's smile turned into that disturbing vulpine grin.

"You'll enjoy this one. My intelligence people have pinpointed a reiver nest on a marginal planet in the Parvi system a few light years core-wards, on the edge of the nebula. They've been causing plenty of grief to the less fortunate colonies and outposts in the sector. I think we can marry training with pleasure by taking them out."

"Do we have information on the enemy dispositions, sir?"

"Indeed. Yan's folks are busy finishing their analysis. From what I've seen, it'll be a simple operation to blood our force. I'll let you draw up your own plan of attack. You can have two of the three sloops — your choice. I'd like to retain one for local security."

"The intel arrived on the ship that landed twelve hours ago?" She asked.

The vessel, a small free trader that looked remarkably like Captain Reade's *Alkris*, had not transmitted an active IFF signal as it flitted past the squadron and into orbit, but it had communicated with Fury Station.

"Just so. I'm fortunate to have a growing and quite active network in these parts. You'll be in overall command of the attack, but Major Ocano, one of the Avalon officers, will lead the landing force and be in command of the planetside part once his troops hit the ground."

"Of course." That was doctrine, as per the ancient quip that the Marine Corps was the bullet fired at the enemy by the Navy. Once it had left the barrel, the Navy no longer had control.

"You'll be getting the full information packet within the next two hours. Have your two ships chosen by then. I'd like you to depart no more than forty-eight hours from the time you receive Yan's analysis. I don't think the situation on Parvi VI will change dramatically if you should take longer to get there, but why take chances."

Dunmoore was as bloodthirsty about destroying reivers who plagued the frontiers as any Navy officer, but this seemed to her a bit hasty, not to mention unusual. Using mercenary troops under Fleet control in combat was not unheard of, but private contractors soldiered for profit, not glory, and dying for the flag just was not part of their business model.

An assault from space could quickly get bloody if the point was capturing the enemy rather than obliterating him. If it were simply the latter, *Stingray* could do it herself. A few kinetic strikes from orbit and all that would remain of the reiver nest would be a few craters.

"If I may ask, sir," she ventured, "was there any reason other than training to make this a landing op rather than a bombardment?"

He stared at her, the smile gone, and worked his jaw muscles for a few moments. She noticed the small tic in the corner of his eye starting up.

"They took something of mine, and I'd like to get it back. Now that I have the naval strength to seize Parvi's high orbit and more importantly, a squadron commander I trust, I can do so. It'll be your job to make sure our enemies understand they can't challenge me ever again."

— Nineteen —

"*Carnatic* and *Malabar* have emerged on the planned vectors and have gone silent, captain," Syten reported. "I can track them, but only because I know where they are. A random sweep is going to miss them unless they're almost within touching distance."

"Launch the recon drone. Mister Pushkin, once it's away, rig the ship for silent running."

"Drone away. Accelerating to maximum before burnout."

Her plan, had anyone cared to check, made sure none of her people or her ship would be in the place of greatest danger. She had no intention of taking damage that could spell too many problems this far from her supply chain.

The sloops carrying the ground troops would have the most hazardous role, swooping down on what was sure to be a fortified landing zone where they would have to neutralize the enemy defenses before they could offload troops.

Dunmoore discovered she was rather indifferent to the risk the mercenaries would be taking, an ambivalence that caused her some amount of second-guessing. As a conscientious commander, she felt responsible for the Avalon people, perhaps not as much as her own crew, but she rationalized the difference by telling herself the Navy folks had little choice in their assigned duties while the mercenaries were in this for money. It was not much of an intellectual fig leaf, but she did not have the appetite for more self-analysis.

"We have tight-link laser comms between all three ships," Kowalski said. "They report everything green." She held her hand up to her earpiece. "*Malabar* just advised that a jump drive went amber."

Pushkin swore under his breath.

"It's the damned *Jade Delight* story again and this time in bad guy territory."

"They have plenty of time to fix it," Siobhan replied, sounding calmer than she felt. "But just on the off chance, why don't we calculate how to spread out her crew and passengers between *Carnatic* and us for the return trip."

"You got a bad feeling about this, captain?" Pushkin looked up from his console.

"I just like to be ready, Number One." But in truth, she was nervous leading a raid deep in unclaimed space, with the full knowledge that there was no one to ride to the rescue if it went pear-shaped, not even for a salvage mission.

"But one thing at a time. First, we knock over the Kerell Clan. I can't say that I've ever heard of them raiding the Commonwealth, but I'm sure it'll be satisfying nonetheless."

"The intelligence packet from the admiral has them involved in the drug trade, as in growing and processing the stuff."

Siobhan snorted. "I really like the fact that the analysis shows they use 'legitimate' shippers to bring the drugs into the Commonwealth," she replied. "Next thing you know we'll find a Black Nova ship or two on the ground when we hit."

"That may explain a few things," Pushkin said, though he sounded dubious. "I could never figure out why Corwin has such a hate-on for them. Drug trafficking will do nicely for that, and if the Kerell managed to steal something that has military value, it wouldn't do to let them enjoy their pilfering in peace and quiet."

Dunmoore still could not shrug off the uneasy feeling she had about the operation. All was going fine, and this was not her first raid. It was not even her first multi-ship raid, and the last one had been against the Shrehari, not a petty alien warlord in a marginal system.

As the hours passed, the recon drone sent back routine telemetry. Space traffic ahead was non-existent, and Parvi VI itself gave off little in terms of artificial emissions, almost as if there was nothing on the surface other than the native flora and fauna.

"I suppose we can fill in the blanks in the database. That's something at least," the sailing master had said when Syten commented on the dearth of usable data. "The Survey Service didn't do much for planetologists when it swung through this system."

"When our government isn't interested in colonizing, the surveyors have little incentive to do a thorough job, Mister Tours," Siobhan said. "If the private sector is interested, as far as the Admiralty's concerned, they can have all they want."

"When you think about it, reiving is a private sector activity," Guthren replied from his helm station, scratching his short beard. "Not that it would meet guild certification back home, but out here?" He shrugged philosophically. "We have our own guild-certified private sector folks to take care of that, I suppose."

"Sir," Syten interrupted. "The drone just detected a liftoff from the target area. No ID yet."

This was the scenario she feared the most. They could intercept the ship in question, but not without blowing their surprise; if they kept silent and let the ship escape, they might find it carried Admiral Corwin's purloined possessions.

Twenty minutes later, the drone transmitted enough data for identification.

"The emissions and visual would make it one of the *Maru* sister ships," the gunnery officer said, pointing to the analysis results on the side screen. "No IFF, but that's not unusual."

Siobhan nodded, her index finger absently tracing the scar running down her jaw line. She had a decision to make. The *Maru* could carry many things, and Black Nova had shown an unhealthy interest in Corwin's operation. As she analyzed her options, she did not realize that she had already consigned Captain Lian and his warnings to her mental dustbin. All that mattered was the mission, this one and the wider crusade led by Admiral Corwin and his fellow flag officers.

"Make to *Malabar*," she finally said, "intercept and seize. Her captain is free to decide when to go up systems. We'll try to make it look like she's the only one. That way we can retain some of the surprise."

"What reasons do we have to seize what appears to be a Commonwealth-flagged ship in unclaimed space?" Pushkin asked in a soft voice, playing his role as her conscience. "Some would interpret it as piracy. Captain Lian comes to mind in this respect."

"Suspicion of consorting with known drug traffickers; suspicion of carrying contraband destined for the Commonwealth; our general powers of search and seizure in war time. I think those will do nicely."

Her tone was harsh, if only because the first officer's use of the word piracy had stung. It was a sign that she was not very happy with her new role, even if she was acting under lawful orders.

"*Malabar* acknowledges. She'll nudge herself on an intercept trajectory once the target's vector is clear and wait until the last minute to light up."

"What's the drone's time to orbit?"

"Three hours."

"Serendipity," Pushkin commented. "By the time the drone has to fire braking thrusters, the target will be too far to pick up the emissions."

"Just as long as no one else lifts off," Guthren replied, with a mock-somber tone.

"Always the optimist, aren't you, chief?"

"Aye, Mister Pushkin. They used to call me 'Smiley' when I was a kid."

"I find that hard to believe."

"That they called me Smiley?"

"No chief, that you were a kid. I thought cox'ns sprang from the ground fully formed and ready to chew antimatter."

The amused guffaws from the crew broke some of the tension on the bridge, and even Siobhan found her tight shoulder muscles relax just a bit.

"The target broke orbit. Vector appears to be," Syten hesitated as she refined the data, "toward us."

Siobhan made a grimace. It would be a shorter time to intercept, but *Malabar* would have to go 'up systems' now so she could change course to match the target's, thereby giving it plenty of warning and a good chance of accelerating away. Short of shooting a brace of missiles down its throat, there was not all that much they could do, and she was not about to destroy a civilian ship on a hunch.

"Make to *Malabar*, intercept orders are rescinded. We'll let the target go free. I'd rather not lose surprise on a less than optimal solution, and I'm not prepared to open fire without justification."

She expected the sloop's captain to protest, and he did, but Kowalski shut him up by indicating in not so subtle words that the commodore appeared to be in no mood to discuss her orders at the moment.

As the hours passed, they watched the freighter accelerate by and jump as soon as it reached its hyperlimit.

"At least we've got a name," Siobhan said to no one in particular. "I did think the admiral was a bit too optimistic about getting the *Oko Maru* out of the way."

The precise identification did cause her to re-examine all of her interactions with Captain Lian in light of his working with reivers. She had a moment of vertigo as she found herself adrift between two divergent narratives and no clear evidence, either way, to indicate which one was true. At that moment, she would have given much to be facing Brakal again.

*

The starships approached Parvi VI in the shadow of the largest of its three moons, having fired braking thrusters hours earlier. With no orbital station, the chances that their maneuvering would be picked up, even this close to the planet, remained slim.

"The sloops report ready."

"Okay." Siobhan squared her shoulders, struggling to suppress the butterflies swarming in her stomach. Going into battle never got easier and commanding a raid from a flagship put her at a further remove from the fighting, even though she retained full accountability for her force. She touched her console and brought up the faces of the other captains and the major in command of the ground force.

"After twelve hours in orbit, the recon drone has given us a pretty good picture of the place and the routine. We've detected a few ground-based launchers around the installation, and some guns by the airstrip, which I assume are mostly used to intimidate visitors or suppress anyone attempting a hostile landing, although the mounts indicate that they can probably cover up to ninety degrees on the vertical. A strike on the launchers from orbit should be sufficient. They're far enough from the built up areas to minimize collateral damage. The assault shuttles can take care of the guns and any other shorter range weaponry. There's only one ship on the pad right now so the intel that said the clan was off on a long-range raid was accurate. I would like to take the ship intact and bring it back to the admiral. Major Ocano, I trust your people have the necessary experience and training to board and seize ships on the ground."

"They do," he replied confidently.

"Captains Thoran and Marek, do either of you have the necessary people to sail the prize if the major can take her intact?"

"I can spare them for a short period but I'd rather not," Thoran replied. "If you can supply the prize crew, that would be better. I think my colleague would be in agreement."

"She is," Marek said. "You've got enough people that you can spare the bodies. We're not quite that fortunate."

"Noted." Siobhan felt a twinge of relief that neither of the mercenaries wanted to take the prize. With her own people on board, she would have two Navy-crewed ships, and that might just give her an edge, even if *Stingray* would be short-handed.

"Once *Malabar* has secured the landing zone," she continued, "*Carnatic* can head in with the remainder of the ground element. I'll send down the prize crew when the objective has been secured. One thing I'm adding to the mission is the destruction of the cultivated fields and any stored harvest, processed or unprocessed."

"That wasn't in the parameters," Ocano protested. "What if the Kerells come back unexpectedly or have allies on Parvi that could come to their aid? The more time we spend on the ground, the more risk we incur."

"That's why *Stingray* will be watching from orbit. Anything comes your way, we'll eliminate it."

"Couldn't you just take the fields out from orbit?" Ocano insisted.

"A frigate is a rather clumsy instrument for that kind of work, major. Better the assault shuttles take care of the fields. Your ground troops will have to destroy anything already warehoused."

He nodded curtly but did not protest any further.

"The place doesn't look as heavily defended as we thought it might be," Siobhan continued, "but what we don't see might be what bites us. The drone hasn't detected any underground installations; however it wouldn't take much to mask a few deep tunnels from the sensors. The nearest settlement is over two thousand kilometers away, so even at best speed, any relieving force will be in our sights long enough to regret leaving home. Should the reiver ships return while we're on the planet, we'll get several hours warning, more than sufficient to pack up and leave before they enter orbit. Any other questions or comments?"

*

"There's something curious about this, captain," the first officer said, staring at the tactical schematic on the main screen. The initial attack wave was speeding toward the ground, guns primed and ready.

"And that would be?" She asked absently, her attention entirely on the unfolding assault.

"Reivers are paranoid buggers. We should see something that looks a lot more like a kicked-over anthill down there instead of Parvi's tribute to Sleepy Hollow. We've been visible and detectable for over an hour now. Considering a couple of sentry satellites don't cost all that much, why is no one panicking? The sloops might look like ships from a friendly clan, but there's no mistaking *Stingray* for anything other than a Navy vessel."

"Are you saying we're heading into a trap?" Siobhan looked at Pushkin curiously, wondering what she might have missed. Her gut instinct did not tell her the Kerells were ready and waiting, well hidden and well armed. Reivers were not that subtle.

"No." He slowly shook his head. "I just can't put my finger on it, but a reiver clan that survives long enough for a permanent base didn't get there by being careless."

"I guess we'll find out in a few moments." The tactical display was showing *Malabar* almost in strike position. Lieutenant Syten switched over to a real-time feed of the target, as seen by the frigate's powerful optical sensors. Soundlessly, four energy blooms erupted from the ground, marking the destruction of the four launchers the recon drone had pinpointed.

"That takes care of step one. If they weren't awake before, they surely are now." Pushkin's tone was sober and unemotional as if he too was having difficulties with his role as a spectator while people were most assuredly about to die on the surface.

As they watched, small figures ran from the installation's buildings but instead of heading for undetected defensive positions, they came to a stop, no doubt staring uncomprehendingly at the rising columns of smoke. They would not have much time to reflect on the change in circumstances on what had started off as a beautiful, sunny morning. Avalon Corporation attack shuttles were screaming down to treetop height for a low-level strafing run, to take out the close-in gun positions and give the reivers the urge to duck and hide so that the ground troops could land unopposed.

"They're not quick on the uptake, are they," Chief Penzara muttered from his station, his eyes, like those of everyone else on the bridge riveted to the screen. The reivers seem frozen to the spot as long streams of plasma fire sterilized the area around the landing strip.

Siobhan felt a surge of distaste rise in her gorge. Reivers were heartily hated by all who wore the Navy's uniform, but this was a turkey shoot, a massacre. It was not war. She made a sudden decision.

"Mister Pushkin, I'm going down with the prize crew."

He stared at her in surprise, and then his features hardened.

"As much as I should object, captain, I see you've come to the conclusion that things are a bit off and that no amount of arguing will change your mind."

"I have, and you're right, no amount of arguing will." She nodded. "I want to see firsthand what we've raided."

"The breaching force has landed," Lieutenant Syten announced. "Reporting light resistance."

"Is there even a point in landing *Carnatic* I wonder?" Dunmoore studied the tactical readout with narrowed eyes. "Get me a line to Major Ocano."

"Ocano here," a slightly out of breath voice replied moments later. "What can I do for you, commodore?"

"Do you still need the rest of your battalion or will the force already on the ground suffice?"

"It should be enough," he replied after a few moments. "But for the purposes of the exercise, we should land them anyway."

"What's your overall status?"

"No casualties but the enemy has taken a lot. They're holed up in one or two buildings, still trying to resist. When I've found what I was sent to get, we'll bomb them flat, and that'll be that."

"What about the ship?"

"We've taken it without damage. There were only a few people on board, and they'd left the cargo ramp wide open for us."

"I'm sending down the prize crew now. Dunmoore, out."

When she ended the communication, she looked up and saw the question in Pushkin's eyes.

"I did indeed opt not to inform our good Major Ocano that I would be on the prize crew's shuttle." She sounded grim. "I don't want to distract him with the notion that I'll soon be breathing down his neck."

She caught Chief Guthren looking at her with a strange expression on his face when she rose from her seat.

"What is it?"

"Do you mind if I accompany you on that little jaunt, sir?"

Dunmoore nodded, understanding what the coxswain was really asking.

"We'll take Vincenzo too, chief."

As she turned to head for the shuttle deck, she saw Guthren and Pushkin exchange a significant look. The first officer nodded his approval and took the command chair while the coxswain handed the helm over to one of the quartermasters.

*

Stingray's shuttle landed on a tarmac sitting at the bottom of a broad valley between old, eroded mountains that loomed on either side like oversized burial mounds from some ancient race of giants. A sluggish, brown river meandered between fields covered with low shrubs whose leaves were a poisonously bright shade of green. The sky was a rare eggshell blue under the rays of its primary, and the two larger moons shone even in full daylight.

As Siobhan walked off the craft, clad in battle armor and carrying a carbine, her nose was assaulted by an acrid tang, similar to vegetation that had fermented as it rotted. It was underscored by the ozone bite of too many plasma rounds fired in too small an area.

Carnatic and *Malabar* loomed over the large landing strip though the captured reiver vessel held its own in the size department. A few shots echoed from the far end of the building complex but around the runway, armored mercenaries moved around openly and with clear intent. One of them approached *Stingray*'s party, nodding politely when he recognized the rank patch on Siobhan's chest. If he was surprised to see her, he gave no sign.

"Sir, I'm Sergeant Nix. The prize ship is all yours and Major Ocano says you can boost out any time you want. We've taken what was left of the crew off, but there's no gore to mop up, so you'll find it nice and clean."

"Thank you, sergeant. Lieutenant Devall is the prize captain." She pointed at the tall officer behind whom the boatswain and a dozen crewmembers had formed.

"Can I do something for you, commodore?" He asked, having decided she was not here to see the newest addition to her squadron take flight.

"You can point me at Major Ocano's location. I'd like to inspect the area and see the prisoners."

"Yes, sir. But you'll not get much in terms of captives. Those buggers won't give up, so we aren't taking any. Or at least we haven't yet."

A loud crump startled them for a second, then the sergeant nodded knowingly.

"Guess the major's found what we're here for. That was the mortar going off at the enemy's defenses." He shrugged. "If you'll follow me, commodore, I'll see you to the CO."

With a wave at Devall, she turned toward the base proper, Guthren, and Vincenzo forming a protective escort around her.

As soon as they got near the edge of the landing strip, she saw the first bodies. They all had charred holes where plasma had eaten through clothing and flesh. None was armored or even wearing simple protection, like a battledress tunic. Most of the bodies were clad in loose coveralls more suited to an industrial operation than a pirate's nest. There was a mixture of species, but humans were predominant among the dead. There were no weapons strewn about, but Siobhan figured the Avalon troops would have collected those already.

Sergeant Nix stopped her at the corner of a prefabricated hangar that looked like it had been there for a long time. Its plasticized coating was faded and dull, worn away by thousands of rainstorms and the harsh light of the bluish sun.

"Wait here. I've let the major know you're on the ground."

He left them standing there as he jogged away, keeping close to the building walls and pausing before turning a corner. Another mortar crump shattered the morning air, and they saw a platoon of mercenaries disperse among the low huts, headed for the last pockets of resistance.

"Did you notice anything strange so far, cox'n?"

"Aye, captain. The bodies weren't those of fighters, more like workers. Then there's the greenery. It stinks to high heaven, but it doesn't reek like any drug plants I've seen."

"That's pretty much what I figured."

"I can't actually prove it, sir, but I'd swear that some of the wounds on the dead were execution style like they were injured but alive and someone didn't want to bother with prisoners."

"That's a pretty serious accusation, chief."

Guthren shrugged.

"I've seen the like before, sir. If you can't treat 'em, you might as well put 'em out of their misery. It's kinder that way."

"Except that we have a full surgical theater on the ship," she replied through clenched teeth.

Vincenzo, who had been looking around the corner, raised his arm, and Siobhan bit back her next comment. It was just as well. Major Ocano, followed by one of his soldiers, jogged into view. He flipped his helmet's visor up to expose a scowling face.

"Commodore," he nodded, "I didn't expect you to come down here yourself. You should have warned me."

Though his tone was level and polite, his eyes showed annoyance at her unannounced presence. Siobhan found his reaction interesting. Although Ocano, as the ground forces commanding officer, was in charge planetside, she remained the overall mission commander and technically did not need his consent to move around the area of operations.

"Now that you're here, what can I do for you?"

"You found what Admiral Corwin sent us here to get?"

"We did. It's being loaded on *Malabar* as we speak."

"I'd like to see it."

"Sorry, commodore, it's already packed up. By the time we get to the ship, it'll be stowed in the hold. You'd do better to ask the admiral when we get back."

"What about prisoners?"

He shrugged.

"They weren't very good at surrendering."

"What does that mean?" Dunmoore's voice took on a dangerous edge.

"Reivers know what kind of treatment they'd get in Commonwealth hands. They're not interested in sampling the experience."

"So you shoot wounded?"

"My men have neither the equipment nor the time to treat criminals," he replied flatly.

"Funny, but the bodies I've seen don't look like hardened marauders to me."

Ocano's face tightened at the implied accusation and Guthren moved closer to his captain, carbine at the ready.

"It doesn't really matter what they are," he replied angrily. "They held an item stolen from us, and they opened fire on us when we landed. If they'd only run away, there wouldn't have been any dead."

"Major, the folks here had no way of knowing who we were when we first took out their launchers. We could just as well have been a rival syndicate." She took a deep breath to calm her rising anger. Getting into an argument with Ocano in public, in what was still an area where weapon fire rang freely, would be stupid.

"Please show me the warehousing and processing facilities. The size of the monoculture in this valley is big enough to warrant a complete production line."

He smirked nastily.

"The survivors are holed up in them. When my mortars are done, there won't be anything left to see, in accordance with your orders concerning the facilities." As if to underscore his words, the double crump of a salvo echoed over the installation. "I would respectfully suggest you return to the flagship and let us finish here."

Shouts suddenly rang out and they turned toward one of the cheap pre-fab huts, where a coverall-clad humanoid had erupted through a broken door and was running toward the fields. Before Siobhan could react, a mercenary with a plasma rifle took aim and shot the fleeing being in the back.

"As I said," Ocano spoke in the shocked silence, "they're not too keen on surrendering."

"Shooting an unarmed man in the back when he's running away just isn't right," Guthren growled. "That was butchery, no matter how much you dress it up, *major*."

The mercenary turned his hard eyes on the coxswain and considered him in the way an entomologist would look at a common species of cockroach.

"I respectfully suggest once again, commodore," he said, still staring at the chief, "that you head back to the antiseptic safety of your ship. Your people obviously don't have the stomach for ground combat."

Siobhan put a restraining hand on Guthren's massive upper arm.

"Major, Chief Petty Officer Guthren is a veteran of the special operations branch. He's seen more ground combat in the last few years than most people in uniform, be they Fleet or corporate."

"My apologies then, Mister Guthren," he replied after a moment's silence. His nod, while polite, did not in any way signal contrition. On the contrary. "My suggestion remains, commodore. Now if you'll excuse me, I have an operation to finish. I trust you can find your own way back to the landing strip."

Without waiting for an answer, he turned on his heel and left, followed by the silent, hulking presence of his wingman.

"Which building," Siobhan asked, her head swiveling on her armored shoulders as she looked around, "do you think might be the headquarters, or plant office or whatever you want to call it?"

"Recon?"

"I want to find out what this place is. It sure as hell isn't a reiver clan's base of operations, even if it had defensive weaponry. Anyone with brains tries to protect himself out here were interstellar law is pretty thin if it exists at all."

"Roger that, captain," Guthren nodded. "I've been in my share of pirate's nests and for one thing, this place is too clean. Or it was before Major Ocano and his bully-boys messed it up."

"Do you think those mercenaries would take pot-shots at us if we sniffed around a little?" Siobhan asked, heading for a two-story building that fronted the landing strip.

"If they do," Vincenzo replied, patting his carbine, "they'd better make sure they get first round hits."

"Whatever doesn't kill me has made a bad tactical mistake?" Guthren shook his head. "Don't be too sure these guys are bozos, Vincenzo. They can probably shoot the ravioli off your dingle at a hundred meters."

"I'd like to see them try, chief."

Siobhan shook her head in mild amusement.

"Keep in mind that the ship is tracking us, as is Lieutenant Kowalski in the shuttle. I'm sure our mercenary comrades understand that harming their commodore might make the voyage home that much more complicated."

Guthren grunted but did not otherwise comment. He merely raised his carbine and tucked the butt under his right shoulder, ready to fire at any threat.

As they rounded the corner, a pair of mercenaries guarding the entrance looked at them curiously before coming to attention.

Their posture and the way they held their weapons clearly indicated that they were not going to let them enter without an argument.

"Sir," the one on the right said, through a shut visor, "orders of the CO. No one is to go in."

"Isn't it convenient then, that as commodore of the attack force, I outrank Major Ocano," Dunmoore replied sweetly.

"I'm going to have to check with the major, sir."

"What you're going to do, son," Chief Guthren's voice was a low rumble, coming from deep within his barrel-shaped chest, "is get your ass out of my line of fire, and to accomplish that, you're going to do exactly what the commodore wants. Capiche?"

The blank visor swiveled between Dunmoore and her coxswain, and even if they could not see the man's face, they knew it would reflect uncertainty.

Without further discussion, she pushed the mercenaries' weapons aside and walked by. Guthren followed her in, signaling Vincenzo to guard their backs by remaining at the door.

The inside of the structure was marred by holes from the mercenaries' plasma. Guthren immediately voiced what both thought.

"No reiver clan has a front office that looks this normal, captain. I've seen shipping factors' offices exactly like this on a dozen worlds." He gestured at a long table with visibly damaged consoles. "Shame we can't see what they were transacting here."

"No joy with hard copies either," she replied, crouching over a mound of charred plastic. A mostly intact corner at the bottom of the pile attracted her eye, and she carefully worked it out of the mass of its burned and melted fellows.

"You ever get one of those days, chief," she said, rising up, "where you think you're fighting on the wrong side of history?"

"All the time, captain," he snorted. "Or at the very least, I think our government's on the wrong side, not so much us."

Siobhan held out the plas sheet.

"What does that logo in the corner look like to you?"

He considered it, eyes slowly widening in surprise as his brain processed what he saw.

"That wouldn't be a Black Nova Shipping Lines cargo manifest, now would it? Because if it is, then either Black Nova is consorting with criminals or..."

"Or this is a legitimate trading post, not a reiver nest."

"Which means the violently green plants out there could be pharmaceutical or food additives, or something that isn't necessarily frowned on by the law?" Guthren nodded. "I knew this smelled wrong the moment we saw how disorganized they looked when the first strike went in."

Dunmoore felt the blood drain from her face as bile rose in her gorge.

"If that's the case, chief," she whispered, "unless the Commonwealth is at war with the government of this planet, if it even has one, we've committed an act of piracy."

"Aye." He slowly nodded, anger filling his broad face. "And shooting that unarmed guy running away was murder. What do we do now? We can't arrest the entire merc battalion, not to mention the crews of those sloops."

"We'd have piss-poor standing in court anyway. We're just as guilty as they are."

"Captain," he lightly touched her shoulder, "*Stingray* didn't fire a shot, nor did any of our crew, and we acted on intelligence that made this a legitimate target."

She shook him off angrily.

"That doesn't matter. It was up to me to stop the assault the moment I had doubts about the legality of the operation."

"Look, sir, there's no sense in beating yourself up about it right now. The Navy will figure out a way to do it for you in good time. We need to decide what to do next, though. And for my money, we have no choice but to let this operation run its course. There's no telling what the mercs will do if we start pulling them up short. The two sloops might not be able to tackle *Stingray* on their own, but they can give us a lot of grief."

"You're a fount of good cheer, Mister Guthren." She punched him lightly on the arm. "And discretion being the better part of valor, I'd say we gather what evidence we can and very quietly make our way back to the ship."

A loud rumble interrupted the conversation, and Siobhan cocked her head to the side, listening.

"I'd say Mister Devall is taking the prize into orbit right now. I can't wait to see who we stole that ship from," she said dryly. "I'd also like to know what they're growing here. If it isn't illegal drugs, then it has to be something Black Nova carries legitimately."

"I get the idea that the Avalon folks are going to make sure nothing of the storage and processing facilities is left standing, so I'd say we pick a sample from the fields."

"Okay. Take a full sensor sweep of this building, chief. We can analyze it later. Then, we'll haul ourselves back to the shuttle. Major Ocano might just decide that my getting ambushed and killed by a reiver layback party would be an excellent idea."

"Especially if the mercs knew this raid wasn't legit," he replied, pulling out his hand-held unit. "Having us see the target up close makes it a bit harder to control the narrative."

While Guthren quickly worked his way from room to room, Siobhan tried opening various cabinets, in case something had been left undamaged. Most were warped, if not outright fried by gunfire. One of them finally ceded under her armor's augmented strength, and she found an intact box of record wafers. She quickly tucked it into her pack, hoping that the small slivers might contain the information she needed to figure out what this place had been. No sooner had she made the box disappear that a mercenary officer stuck his head into the room. His visor was raised, and she could see intelligent eyes taking in the ruined consoles, burned records, and the wrenched open cabinet.

"Commodore," he said, when his gaze had finally settled on her, "we're about to fall back. Major Ocano asks that you return to your shuttle and lift off ASAP. We can't pull out while you're still on the ground."

"The last resistance has been overcome, then?"

He nodded once, a sharp, almost hostile gesture.

"As per your orders, we're preparing to torch the fields. Unfortunately, the way things are, this installation will also be flattened at the same time. Fuel-air explosives are notoriously indiscriminate."

Guthren reappeared behind the merc and looked at her questioningly. She shook her head minutely and gestured toward the door.

"Time to mount up."

*

"Kind of convenient isn't it," Guthren said when the three spacers were out of earshot of the mercenaries.

"What is?"

"That your orders are going to result in all of the evidence getting destroyed."

Siobhan grunted, lost in thought. Around them, Avalon Corporation troops were falling back toward the landing strip in good order while columns of smoke were rising from the various buildings that made up what once had been, as she now suspected, a peaceful commercial operation. The mercenaries' success had come a little too cheaply.

When they got to the shuttle, they found that Kowalski had kept it spooled up and ready to lift at a moment's notice. Dunmoore also noticed that she had deployed the countermeasures pod. The lieutenant had a good head on her shoulders, and if she felt that they might become the victims of friendly fire, then this mess was more than just one captain and her coxswain taking their paranoia out for a stroll.

Quickly, they strapped themselves in while Kowalski linked up with *Stingray* to create a continuous telemetry and voice feed. Thankfully, there were no demands for information. Dunmoore felt in no mood to discuss the events of the morning. Even the shuttle's dramatic vertical takeoff, pushing the pilot and her passengers deeply into their seats, failed to distract her from the roiling in her stomach.

Sensing the captain's disposition, no one spoke during the tense flight out of Parvi VI's atmosphere and into high orbit, to rejoin the frigate.

By the time Kowalski lined the shuttle up with the hangar deck, their prize had taken station three kilometers to port and almost perfectly abeam of *Stingray*. The sight of the captured civilian vessel gave Siobhan's stomach fresh pangs of anger mixed with fear and guilt.

She now had no choice but to let her department heads in on the entirety of what Admiral Corwin was doing, including Operation Valkyrie, and she had no idea what their reaction would be. Pushkin could relieve her of command on the spot, if he so wished, provided the other officers sided with him.

Siobhan shook her head sadly as the shuttle slowly passed the energy barrier holding the ship's atmosphere in the hangar compartment. What a mess.

When the gantry had slotted the shuttle back in its spot and bled off the static electricity from the force field, she unfastened her restraints and crawled out of the co-pilot's seat, leaving Kowalski to shut down the craft's systems. The certainty Siobhan usually felt when it came time to act had left her entirely. Even Pushkin, waiting for her at the main hatch, noticed the somber, almost funereal expression on her face and whatever questions he may have had died before they escaped his lips.

"Status?" She snapped as they headed toward the bridge.

"All systems are green. We haven't fired a shot, so all of our ammo stocks remain as they were."

"And the prize?"

"I'm waiting for Devall's full report. He's already said that she's in good shape and looks well maintained."

"Do we know who owned her?"

He shook his head. "Not yet. It appears that most of her databanks were recently wiped."

"How recently?"

"Devall and Foste figure no earlier than this morning."

Dunmoore bit back a curse. She was convinced Ocano's men were the culprits, which was one more indication that they knew full well the task force was not raiding a reiver base.

"No other clues?"

"If you mean whether or not there was gear with a corporate logo or inventory number, none has been found so far. The IFF was wiped along with the databanks and we've found no listing in the registry for a ship that corresponds to the prize."

"So it could be a reiver ship?"

Pushkin shrugged.

"I suppose so. It seems to have a sufficient weight of ordnance and larger drives than the hull size would indicate as being necessary. But it could also be a fast trader, specialized in hauling high-value cargo or passengers."

"What's your take on all this, Gregor?"

The first officer stopped and turned to face his captain squarely.

"Shall I quote Shakespeare at you, sir? You've seen things up close while we've relied on what we could see from orbit and the feed from Kowalski's shuttle, and yet I think something's very rotten. Don't you?"

Remembering the box of data wafers in her pack, she pulled it out and handed it to Pushkin. "These might give us some answers. Have Kathryn and her team analyze them. I need to get out of this tin suit and take a shower." She grimaced.

"You'd better make it a long one, captain. I'd say whatever's eating you is going to be the devil to wash off." His tone remained unemotional, but there was a hint of accusation in it. "And then, I'd like to formally ask you to explain what we were doing here, sir. I'm concerned that we have engaged in an illegal raid and committed acts tantamount to piracy."

"Thinking of relieving me of command, Gregor?" She smirked. "Right now, I wouldn't blame you a bit. That, down there, really didn't look like a reiver base and I suspect the Avalon people have known all along, which makes me as guilty as they are. Something about the responsibilities of command."

She sighed. "I too need answers, and I don't want to risk getting into a firefight with the mercenaries to get them. Have the records analyzed and tell Devall he can rip the prize apart if he has to so he can determine its identity. If we did commit piracy, I'd at least like to return the ship to its rightful owners."

"If it was an independent, captain, then I'd say the rightful owners are smoking corpses." His tone was harsh, his words biting. He snapped to attention, saluted and turned on his heel without waiting for permission to dismiss.

She had not seen Gregor Pushkin this angry since her early days as captain of *Stingray*. He was going to be even unhappier when he found out about Corwin's true intentions.

— Twenty —

"Captain." Pushkin adopted the parade rest position in front of Dunmoore's desk, eyes boring into the bulkhead above her head.

"Stand easy, Number One," she replied irritably, "and sit down. We're not having the discussion this way."

She had shed her armor and taken a long, long shower before ensconcing herself in her ready room, leaving Pushkin to deal with the intricacies of breaking orbit in squadron formation and heading out toward the hyperlimit, leaving the smoking remains of their target behind. Without changing expression, the first officer sat stiffly in the chair and calmly met her angry gaze.

"Have Kathryn and her crew analyzed the data wafers yet?"

"Another hour or so. They were encrypted with a highly sophisticated algorithm."

"And the prize? By the way, what is its name?"

"From what Devall found so far, it appears to be called *Holgan*, with no known homeport or ownership. He does report that it's very well armed and has drives that would put ours to shame."

"Operating in the Coalsack sector mandates the ability to fight what you can't outrun and outrun what you can't outfight, don't you agree, Gregor."

"True," he replied, conceding the point. "It was definitely built in a Commonwealth shipyard, and within the last thirty years, according to Chief Foste."

"But was it engaged in illegal activities?"

Pushkin snorted bitterly. "Illegal appears to be a relative term around here, as you may have noticed earlier today."

She slowly nodded, ignoring the sarcasm. "Indeed, and I will demand answers from the admiral."

"I wouldn't hold my breath, captain. That being said, what are we doing, and I don't mean in the Parvi system, I mean working for Admiral Corwin?"

Dunmoore sighed softly. She would either have to disobey Corwin's orders or risk losing the confidence of the one officer she needed the most, shattering the relationship they had built from such a shaky start. With a resigned shrug, she began talking and over the next hour, she told him everything: the proto-Shrehari finds, Operation Valkyrie, the role she suspected they would have in it. When she was finished, Pushkin just sat there, his face pale and his expression pained.

"Sir, we're talking treason of the highest order." He finally said.

"Isn't what the government on Earth and some in our own Admiralty have done not treason?"

"Sorry, captain, that's pure sophistry, and you know it." He closed his eyes for a few moments as if looking for inner strength. "Please tell me you're not going along with this, that you're playing coy with Corwin because he could order his three sloops to take us out and they'd have a decent chance of leaving us a wreck."

"I don't know, Gregor." Her eyes wandered over to the star field displayed on the wall screen. "I've had too many die under my command because this war has been mismanaged from the outset."

"And you think whoever's going to take control once this Operation Valkyrie succeeds is going to do any better?" He sounded incredulous

"How could they do any worse?" She threw back, sounding defensive even to her own ears.

"You're willing to risk our lives and the lives of whoever participates in this madness, or who is unlucky enough to get caught in the crossfire, on the chance that we'll replace a bad batch of admirals and politicians with a better batch? What if this is the best the Commonwealth can do?" His voice was rising to a shout. "What if it makes matters worse? Did you ever think about that?"

Dunmoore let Pushkin's words and emotions flow over her without reacting. He suddenly seemed to realize that he was half out of his chair and almost yelling at his captain. Lips compressed into a thin line of disapproval, he sat down again.

"What now, Gregor?" She asked in a soft tone. "Are you going to relieve me for harboring treasonous intent?"

He glared at her for a good long count of seconds until he was satisfied that she saw his disgust at her question.

"And that would do what, exactly? If I relieve you, I put this ship on a collision course with Corwin and his cabal. I fail to see an upside for *Stingray* or the crew in such a course of action."

"So you'd follow my orders into executing whatever Corwin directs?"

Pushkin did not reply immediately. He looked down at his booted feet, marshaling his thoughts.

"That's not what I said," he finally replied. "I said I wouldn't relieve you at this time, because of the greater peril to *Stingray*. However, if we come to the point where you'll actually order this crew into committing a treasonous act, I will have you confined to the brig."

Siobhan felt a pang of anguish at his harsh tone. Gone was the easygoing relationship between captain and first officer. Whether it was for good remained to be seen.

"Very well," she said, "and what will you do if the crew decides to follow me?"

"What will you do if the crew refuses your orders?" He countered. "A crew refusing illegal orders is not in a state of mutiny."

They locked stares, each testing the other's resolve until Pushkin finally broke contact.

"Captain – Siobhan – I cannot believe that you would forfeit your oath. Yes, the government is corrupt, yes it's incompetent, as are many of our superiors, but the Commonwealth is still a representative republic, not a dictatorship. It's not up to the military to decide for the people how we change governments. Better admirals are coming up the ranks, pushing the old guard out to pasture. Perhaps we'll see Admiral Nagira and his like take their places at headquarters and chart a new course for the Navy soon enough."

At her pained look, his face fell.

"Not him as well?"

She nodded. "Admiral Corwin implied as much."

"And that's what influenced you into following his lead." He made it a statement, not a question. "Are you sure he's telling you the truth and not using your known allegiance to Nagira so he can manipulate you?"

She turned the question over in her mind and considered it from all angles.

"No, I'm not, but he's convinced me there are a number of high ranking officers and senators behind Operation Valkyrie."

"So what?" Pushkin shrugged. "The fact that something has the support of the brass doesn't make it right; otherwise, we'd have gotten rid of carriers a long time ago."

Dunmoore snorted at the unexpected observation on the usefulness of naval aviation. She had come to the conclusion that carriers were outdated the moment she joined an embarked squadron right out of flight school. Her assignment as a fighter pilot did not even last a year before she lobbied hard for a return to what she termed real warships. So far, their contribution to the war effort had been limited to acting as mobile battle stations orbiting planets far beyond Shrehari range.

"For what it's worth captain, asking the crew to choose sides will tear the ship apart and we can't afford that kind of turmoil this far from home," he said in a gentle voice. "Leading them into treasonous actions without their consent would be dishonorable, and you're not that kind of officer. If Operation Valkyrie fails, we could all face the firing squad; you wouldn't be allowed to shoulder the blame all by yourself. Politicians and admirals can act like violent, spiteful children if frightened badly enough, and a failed coup d'état is about as scary as it gets for them."

"I was going to make a snarky comment about your trying to be my conscience again," she said after reflecting on his words, "but in this case, you truly are."

"I have no doubt Admiral Corwin is a highly charismatic man, sir. Kathryn Kowalski said as much in the wardroom before we embarked on this raid, something to the effect of being able to charm a Shrehari into dancing the tango."

Without warning, Dunmoore burst into laughter at the image conjured by Pushkin's words and she felt the tension begin to drain from her body.

"I guess he managed to charm me into almost violating my oath," she said when her mirth had died down. "You have to admit his arguments are compelling."

Pushkin shook his head. "Not to me. You need to have a predisposition of some sort to consider such a step."

"You're not going to let me off easy, are you?" Siobhan asked soberly.

"No, I'm not. I want you to remember this moment and remember the danger you've called down upon a loyal, hard-working, and professional crew. There's ruthless, and there's reckless. We prefer the former to the latter and Operation Valkyrie sounds like one hundred percent reckless to me."

"Bastard," she said, half-heartedly.

"No sir. My parents were married." When he saw a faint smile appear on her lips, he continued. "I suggest we keep this strictly between ourselves. Word gets out, and there's no controlling where it will end."

Dunmoore nodded in agreement. "And now I have to find a way to get us out of the line of fire."

"Keep in mind that Corwin won't be happy if you rat on him. If he has as many highly placed co-conspirators as he says, we'll never be out of danger."

"Then we'll have to decide how much we want to do. Getting us out of whatever he plans is one thing. Denouncing him and his buddies to the Special Security Bureau is another altogether."

"If we're not with him, sir, then I can't see how we can morally stand by and watch Operation Valkyrie unfold. Inaction, in this case, is as culpable as the wrong kind of action."

"One thing at a time, Gregor." She shook her head. "First, we need to get away from the Coalsack to where we can't be roped into things we don't want to do. Then, I'll try and find a way to talk to Admiral Nagira."

"And if he's in on it?"

"Then I can at least shield the crew."

Whatever Pushkin was going to say in reply was stilled by the intercom chime.

"Dunmoore."

"Sir, incoming from *Holgan*." It took Siobhan a few seconds to connect the name to the prize ship. "It's Lieutenant Devall."

"I trust we're on a tight beam."

"Aye," Kowalski replied. "And no leakage. I made sure."

"Put him on." She flicked her console to repeat the transmission on the wall screen.

"Good day, captain, Mister Pushkin." Devall's aristocratic features filled the display.

"You've found something, then?"

"Yes, sir. And you're not going to like it." His voice was grim, devoid of the usual sardonic undertone. "I think we've found who might have owned this ship, or to be more precise, Chief Foste came to a conclusion on the matter. Remember the trader we intercepted on our way out to the front lines last year, the one that was running pilfered naval stores?"

"The *Mykonos*, I believe," Pushkin said. "Or at least that was its alias at the time."

"Right." Devall nodded. "Foste went through this tub with all the attention to detail only she can muster, and she thinks it's either the *Mykonos* itself or a ship very much like it. There are too many points of similarity. They've likely changed the outwards appearance, and I've no doubt the emission fingerprints are different, but if you'll recall, Foste was with you when you boarded the *Mykonos*. She swears this ship came from the same builder's yard and to the same design."

Dunmoore pinched the bridge of her nose with her left hand as she felt a headache come on again.

"Wonderful. That's all we needed: the bloody SSB spooks to show up for the party. Throw in a Shrehari *Tol* class cruiser and it'll be a proper reunion. Did you have Syten run the prize through the registry with these new parameters?"

"She's doing that right now, sir," Devall nodded. "It might take a bit of time, but hopefully, we can find at least enough of a possible match to know who we should avoid for the next while."

"Anything else, Trevane?" Dunmoore asked, letting her fingers tap on the desktop in an agitated dance.

"No sir. We'll keep digging. It's pretty hard to wipe databanks completely, especially if there are hidden backups."

"It'd be good to know why the SSB, if it is one of theirs, was playing silly bugger on Parvi VI and why they might have been playing silly bugger with a Black Nova ship if the *Oko Maru* did indeed take off from the place we raided."

"Indeed, it would," Devall agreed. "Other than that, it's a good ship, sir. We should have no problems with it, and if the Navy does buy it into Service, we should get a tidy sum."

"Not if Avalon makes a claim," Pushkin interjected. "They seized it. We're merely sailing it away."

"Bugger Avalon," Siobhan snarled. "They might not be around to try and make a claim at the rate at which they're pissing me off."

The second officer's eyes widened in surprise at his captain's unexpected and unusual crudeness, but Pushkin knew it came from her self-loathing at having started down the path of dishonor.

A small icon began flashing in the corner of the screen.

"Looks like the jump stations warning is about to go off," Siobhan said, swallowing any further imprecations against the mercenaries. "We'll talk again when we drop out of FTL after the first leg."

When the screen had faded to black, she grimaced.

"We have an admiral who's commanding a mercenary force, who has access to mythical proto-Shrehari weaponry and who's involved in a conspiracy to overthrow our admittedly corrupt government. Today we seized a ship that may or may not belong to the Special Security Bureau, which is waging its own war against the Navy. On top of that, we have a shipping line that lost two of its freighters to our admiral's mercenaries and whose remaining ships pop up across our hawse wherever we turn. Oh, and we have the possibility that the *Alkris*, whom we've encountered a few times too often for coincidence, is playing aviso for the admiral's conspiracy group. Is anything else going to drop into this toxic little stew?"

"A task force from the 39th Battle Group showing up to find out where we've vanished to?" Pushkin suggested. "By now Gulsvig should have sailed the convoy home and reported to Admiral Ryn."

"Perhaps." She shrugged. "Of course, if our friendly Captain Lian didn't bother passing on my message or missed the convoy, it might be a moot point: Gulsvig wouldn't have had much to report other than we left and never came back."

"If Admiral Ryn is part of Valkyrie..."

"Then we might as well go rogue and rent ourselves out to the highest bidding technobarb kingdom."

The jump siren sounded its warning, and they both braced for the uncomfortable transition between universes. It came and went as swiftly as usual, but the momentary discomfort had jolted Siobhan's brain.

"Captain to Lieutenant Kowalski," she said into the intercom.

"Kowalski here," the reply came back almost instantaneously.

"If you haven't cracked the encryption on the data wafers yet, you might try known or suspected SSB codes."

There was a moment of silence as the signals officer digested Siobhan's instructions.

"Aye, aye, captain. I suppose it's too early for me to ask what we might have gotten ourselves into."

"All in good time, Kathryn. Dunmoore, out."

"You know she's going to discover most of it on her own at some point," Pushkin said with a wry grin.

"I suppose. Having overly smart officers can be dangerous at times. Hopefully, she doesn't have the second sight and deduces Operation Valkyrie's existence. The proto-Shrehari digs, I don't really mind sharing, but the more people who know about the plot, the greater the danger to the ship."

"So what next?"

"I wish I knew, Gregor. I really wish I knew." Dunmoore sighed, slumping back in her chair as she laced her fingers together behind her head. "I don't think we'll be able to escape without expending some ordnance."

"Mutiny against Admiral Corwin?"

She saw the sardonic look in his eyes and briefly chuckled.

"Didn't you just tell me that refusing an illegal order can't be construed as mutiny?"

"I think the use of violence moots that excuse," he replied. "But if you do need to kick butt and take names, I don't think anyone on board would object, and that does help at a court-martial."

"I'm glad to hear that my crew giving character references will help me not get shot by a firing squad. Any other useful advice?"

"None at this time, captain," he replied, "other than I suggest you order me to re-align the watch keeping bill so we can permanently man two warships."

"Excellent idea. I'm sure Trevane will be delighted to keep his new toy for a while, and I'm equally sure that the admiral will like the idea of increasing the number of his naval hulls by one."

"I'll get Kutora to prepare an IFF module. We can transfer it while we tack between jumps, along with the additional crew Devall will need to run three watches. I just hope that the ammo stocks on the prize are reasonably high. Even if it's an SSB ship, she may not be able to accept our missiles in her launchers or our ammo in her guns."

"I wouldn't be too sure about that," Siobhan replied. "The SSB like stealing our stuff and if your logistics plan is based on pilfering, you're going to make sure you can use the ordnance you take."

The intercom chimed again.

"Captain, you were right," Kowalski announced, sounding excited. "The records were encrypted under an older SSB algorithm. I'll have them all done in a few minutes and then I can run the analysis."

"Excellent. Bless the boys in counter-intelligence. Without them, we'd have a hard time reading the spooks' mail."

She grinned at Pushkin.

"Perhaps now I might get some ideas."

*

"They're mostly accounting records," Kowalski said, flashing a decrypted readout on the conference room's main screen. "So much product in, so much product out, money transfers in creds, gold, platinum, and precious gems, and some Coalsack currencies no one's ever heard of."

Siobhan felt deflated but quickly chastised herself for having hoped that a random box of data wafers might contain high-grade intelligence. It was always more than probable that what she found were merely financial records.

"Any indication what merchandise they were shipping out?"

Kowalski flashed up a new readout that described an alien plant-based product.

"I have no idea what this stuff is supposed to be good for, but they were producing it in industrial quantity. The trade value is pretty decent, so it has to be something either very useful or very illegal, but I couldn't find any references in our databanks."

Dunmoore rubbed her scar as she thought. She stabbed at the intercom.

"Captain to Doctor Luttrell."

"Sickbay here, captain, what can I do for you?"

"Lieutenant Kowalski is going to send you some data on a product which seems to come from the cash crop that filled the valley around the raid target. Since you're the closest thing to an exobotanist we have, I'd like you to see if its chemical composition might be useful in something either high value or illegal."

"Got it," Luttrell replied. She hummed for a few seconds. "Let me run these sensor readings against the pharmaceutical library."

"What are you thinking?"

"It could be a precursor to something, perhaps a narcotic, perhaps an industrial chemical. I'll get back to you as soon as I have it. Luttrell out."

"Anything else in the records, Kathryn?" Dunmoore turned her attention back to Kowalski.

"Manifests that list quantities and ship names. The Black Nova ships feature predominantly, however, no mention of the name of our prize. She may not have been a transport or she may be recorded under another name."

"Anything about destinations?"

"Yes, but they're in code and not the kind that has an algorithm. I'd wager they assigned random names to protect the guilty. I could compare the frequency of a destination's occurrence with the *Maru* logs if we had them, but absent any secondary source, there's really no way of figuring it out."

The intercom beeped.

"Sickbay to captain."

"Dunmoore here, doctor. You have something?"

"I do. It may not be one hundred percent accurate, but the chemical composition described, based on the raw matter at the source, is indeed a precursor to a few high-value pharmaceuticals. I've searched the library and this chemical composition is not known to be naturally occurring or derived from plant matter."

"So it's new?"

"Looks that way. Someone found a plant on Parvi VI with the right composition, one that would only mature under the environmental conditions proper to the planet and decided to turn it into a cash crop."

"Could the precursor be used for narcotics?"

"Easily, though the higher value is in the pharmaceuticals, not in producing street drugs unless they make up for it in volume and low production cost."

"So this could have been a legitimate business operation." Siobhan sounded vaguely discouraged.

"If the SSB is involved, it'll be anything but legitimate," Pushkin pointed out. "The buggers are using it to generate funds at the very least, if not using the crop for more sinister purposes."

"Having the accounting records encrypted with a known SSB algorithm kind of makes it evident that it's a spook operation," Kowalski said. "They tend not to hand their codes out. I have no idea how counter-intelligence gets them for us, and I probably don't want to know."

"I hate to say this, but knowing that it was probably an SSB facility makes me feel a bit better about the raid." Dunmoore shook her head. "But not about shooting people in cold blood. That one remains on the ledger as a debt to be collected."

"Might I speculate, sir?"

"Yes, Kathryn, please go ahead."

"It may stretch the definition of coincidence, but suppose that the SSB business on Parvi VI and Admiral Corwin's operation on Arietis were set up in ignorance of each other. That is until a *Maru* happens to notice something funny on Arietis as it swings by on a regular run and reports it to its employer, who may in fact be deeply involved with the Bureau. Spooks snooping on the Navy is a time-honored game, and I'm sure they would dearly love to know what the admiral is up to, hence the pestering by the *Marus*. I'd be inclined to think our prize here was the next one to try an infiltration run, except either Admiral Corwin got some good intel, or we got very lucky."

"The mercenaries did have a recovery to make," Pushkin pointed out.

"Recovery of intel, then," Kowalski replied.

"All eminently plausible. Well done, Kathryn." Siobhan glanced at the first officer who gave her an 'I told you so' grin.

"With that being said," she continued, standing up and stretching, "we have things to do before we emerge, so it'll have to go on the backburner for now."

*

Dunmoore watched *Holgan* maneuver closer to *Stingray*'s port side. The helmsman, Petty Officer Takash, was showing a decent touch on the thrusters, keeping the over-corrections to a minimum. Devall was probably standing right behind her making sure nothing untoward happened. This was his first independent command, and he wanted to keep it for as long as he could.

She would have liked to speak with him in person and update him on the discussions that had occurred while the squadron was FTL, but there was no time. Even though no one would think of attacking a four-ship formation led by a Commonwealth frigate, Dunmoore was anxious to get to Arietis quickly, now that Pushkin had planted the idea in her head that the SSB might have gotten wind of Valkyrie somehow. She was afraid that the small window of opportunity she might have to extract them from a deadly trap was closing.

Over the tight beam transmission, Devall had looked unsurprised at the idea that Parvi VI was an SSB operation, moneymaking or otherwise, and that they had stumbled across Corwin's artifact recovery activities by accident via one of the *Marus*. But then, she had to remind herself that he was just as perceptive and intelligent as Kowalski.

She smiled when one of the frigate's shuttles came into view as it wafted toward the prize with additional crew and electronics. Since it was about to get a naval IFF, Siobhan had decided to classify it as a sloop and rename it *Fawkes* in an attempt at humor that remained obscure to most of her crew, although Pushkin had enjoyed the little joke once he had looked up the name in the historical records. She was curious to see what Corwin's reaction would be.

Devall would have a sufficiently large complement to man all vital stations in battle and take care of basic damage control, but it meant each of the frigate's departments would be working short-handed if *Stingray* started taking dangerous hits. By reducing the size of the watches and relying more on automation, Pushkin had been able to balance out the crews so that they could operate at high efficiency for several weeks before the extra work took its toll. Sanghvi had gone across to serve as both navigator and acting first officer, while Kutora had sent his junior engineering officer to take care of *Fawkes*' systems and drives. On balance, Devall had a young but solid team and one that was eager to prove itself.

She saw the shuttle land gingerly on the lowered cargo ramp and then vanish as it was raised into the hold. Siobhan did not want Devall, and his people to be without a means off *Fawkes* if things went sideways, and since a ship of that size only had a tiny hangar deck, they had come up with a decent alternative.

An hour later, Syten reported the IFF up and running. The prize was now identifying itself as a ship of the Commonwealth Navy, no matter how temporary that may end up being. If the mercenary captains had any objections to her unilateral decisions, they kept them quiet even though Siobhan now had enough reliable firepower to successfully take on all three Avalon Corporation sloops at the same time. If Gulsvig and Stoyer chose this moment to show up, she would not need an elaborate scheme either. As someone once said, quantity has a quality all of its own.

— Twenty-One —

"Now that we have two ships to their three, or four if you count the monitor, what are you planning?" Pushkin stirred another slug of sugar into his already sweet coffee.

"I have no idea, Gregor. I'm not even convinced Admiral Corwin's force is any kind of threat to the government. It might be enough to take a small colony or any of the primitive societies that infest the hind end of the galaxy, but raiding Earth might be a bit much."

"I'd not be too sure about that, captain. The guards are mostly ceremonial and haven't seen action as a unit since the last Migration War."

"They're still Marines," she countered.

"Perhaps, but if you ask any of the Marines serving out on the frontier, they'll tell you the 1st Regiment is about as useless as a colonial militia force if it's even that good. The front-line troops call them toy soldiers for a good reason, and their officers are appointed through political connections, not through merit. I think the Corps sends all its useless aristos to the 1st as a way of protecting the other regiments."

"To keep them far from the actual fighting units." Siobhan nodded. "Makes sense. Concentrate the rot away from the vitals. Assuming he does have proto-Shrehari wonder weapons and the Avalon mercs can flatten the palace guard, we'd still have to get this squadron to Earth and land the ground pounders."

"That should be the easy part." Pushkin sat across from Dunmoore and took a sip of his coffee, smacking his lips with satisfaction. "All it takes is the right people in the Admiralty to authorize an entirely legal flight plan — call it a training exercise if you like — and we're in. Once the strike is launched, confusion will do the rest of the work, though we still might face more missiles than our countermeasures can handle."

"One way mission?" She asked, an ugly idea worming its way out of her subconscious.

The first officer shrugged.

"Possibly, perhaps even probably. The 1st Battle Group might not listen to Admiralty orders telling them to stand down, much less provide support to Corwin's force. They may be just as rusty and filled with corrupt officers as the 1st Marines, but they'll still have a battleship, a handful of cruisers and escorts, not to mention the orbital platforms. Whoever's working Valkyrie at Fleet HQ had better be able to shut all of those off."

"Huh," Siobhan grunted unhappily. "Now that we're thinking it through some more, I can't see a good outcome for *Stingray* even if Valkyrie succeeds."

She suddenly sat up, a look of dismay creasing her features.

"Crap. How's this for a scenario. Corwin and his mercs, with us in tow make it through the defenses, raid the government precinct, gun down the palace guard, and shove the top tier of the leadership into cells or body bags. Then the conspirators at the Admiralty ride to the rescue, and announce the need for them to take the reins of power, temporarily of course, until a new civilian government can be elected or appointed. They become the reluctant heroes of a coup gone badly."

"And we end up being the treasonous patsies who get to meet a firing squad from the wrong side. Bloody brilliant, captain. We don't even need to do much damage for it to be plausible. Maybe even just showing up might be enough." Pushkin shook his head in disbelief. "I wonder if Corwin's figured that scenario out."

"Why not. He's probably well protected by his friends at the Admiralty. The only sacrificial lambs are mercenaries whom no one cares about and the crew of a frigate with a captain who has a patchy reputation and many enemies. Having us included in the raid makes the story of a disgruntled faction in the Navy even more believable and would allow the Valkyrie folks who 'rescue' what's left of the government to distance themselves from the obvious traitors, meaning us. I'll bet they already have a good cover story set up to direct the blame away from the real conspiracy."

"And what if we're overly paranoid?" He asked, grimacing. "Maybe Corwin's a fantasist who's going gaga running his own planet deep in the badlands. It's been known to happen. If we just open fire on the Avalon ships and either seize or destroy them, and there's no Valkyrie, we're done for. We may not end up in front of a firing squad, but twenty years in a penal battalion will make us wish we did."

"Not if we make sure we don't leave any evidence," Siobhan said, smiling darkly.

"Not even in jest, captain, please."

"Yes, Mister Conscience." She sighed. "You need to let your sense of humor out of whatever brig you condemned it to."

Pushkin snorted but did not protest.

"Then I'm afraid," Siobhan continued, "that I'll have to enter the mad dragon's den again and drill a little deeper."

"I thought you might come to that conclusion. May I suggest you ride *Fawkes* down to the ground? It has a better chance of absorbing hits from the defenses than a shuttle would if Corwin figures out you're no longer with him."

"I suppose that I could use the excuse of wanting to show the admiral our newest addition to the Arietis Squadron. I might also share our suspicions regarding the SSB. If he wasn't aware, then I'll have gained some points, and if he was, I'll have allayed suspicions. In any case, General Order Eighty-One will be in effect. That means you take *Stingray* out of the Coalsack and back home if I don't make it off the surface."

"Take Vincenzo with you."

"That goes without saying. I don't think he would let me off the ship by myself these days. Should I have Guthren helm *Fawkes*?"

"I'd rather you didn't. Petty Officer Takash is a good quartermaster and can do the job just as well. If you replace her with Guthren, it'll send the wrong message."

Pushkin was looking at her curiously, and it suddenly dawned on her that she was relying more heavily on him than she usually did. Her self-confidence seemed to have taken a hit, and even the usually stoic first officer was taking notice.

"I'll be fine, Gregor," she said, the reassurance sounding shaky to her own ears.

"We can all be blinded by our hatreds, Siobhan," he softly replied. "You're hardly the first to wrestle with your conscience on matters like these."

"Perhaps, but if the worst case scenario is right, then I likely put the lives of all those in *Stingray* at risk to get my revenge. I may still be putting them in unacceptable peril."

"We're not in the Navy to live a life devoid of danger, captain. It comes with the oath."

"Yes. That pesky oath," she murmured in what was almost a whisper, eyes staring at the star map on the wall. "It certainly complicates life."

"That it does."

They remained in companionable silence for a long time, each lost in thought until the ship's routine called them back to their duties.

*

"Incoming transmission from Admiral Corwin."

"I'll take it in my ready room, Mister Kowalski." Siobhan rose from the command chair and quickly isolated herself in the privacy of the captain's day office.

The squadron had entered the Arietis system the previous day, emerging at the very edge of the hyperlimit, to cut down on the sublight transit to orbit. They had been decelerating ever since and now were close enough to communicate via radio without much of a time lag.

"Siobhan," Corwin's smiling face materialized on her console, "I've read your report and must commend you on successfully leading the raid to destroy a nest of SSB vipers. That you bring back another sloop under Navy colors is an unexpected bonus. We cannot have too few ships if we're to do our duty."

Dunmoore felt a strange mixture of guilt and embarrassment at Corwin's effusive praise. She would have to suppress those emotions if she was to face him in person again. The admiral was much too observant to miss the doubt in her every word and gesture.

"It was a quick and clean operation, sir. Other than a few wounded among the Avalon soldiers, I'm glad to have escaped without serious casualties. The troops are splendid at what they do."

Which was shooting unarmed or badly armed opponents in the back, Siobhan thought savagely.

"If you'd like to see the new ship – I've named it *Fawkes* – I can fly it down to the base," she continued. "As you'll see, she can carry at least a company's worth of infantry for lengthy periods if necessary, such as a trip to the heart of the Commonwealth."

"Excellent, Siobhan." He beamed. "I knew I was right to bring you onto my team. By all means, bring *Fawkes* down. You and I are due for another long discussion. Now that you've begun to prove your mettle, I think it's time I gave you a better idea of what we're preparing."

"It would be my pleasure, sir. We'll be in orbit in eight hours. I'll shift over to *Fawkes* then and land right away."

"Yes, please do. By the way, I love the name you've given your prize. Very apt. Corwin, out."

Dunmoore slumped back in her chair once the screen had gone black. Fighting the admiral's all too palpable charisma would be bad enough, but this was going to be several orders of magnitude more difficult. She would, if she was honest, be looking for evidence to take out her own commanding officer and neutralize, if not destroy the three non-Navy ships under her command. And she had to get *Stingray*'s people home safely.

If she succeeded, she would not only have cemented the SSB's enmity, seeing as they probably already had her high on their list of least favored naval persons but also attracted the ire of all those senior officers involved in Operation Valkyrie, including Admiral Nagira, her sometimes mentor, and protector.

What a mess. She shook herself out of her growing funk and tried to inject some energy into her tired limbs when she rose to leave resume her place on the bridge. I'd rather face Brakal a dozen times over open gunsights than deal with this, she thought. At least he was honest.

"Anything?" Pushkin asked as she took the command chair.

"I'll be shifting my pennant to *Fawkes* when we arrive at Arietis and take her down to Fury Station."

She and the first officer locked eyes, sealing the deal they had tacitly made. Siobhan was reminded of a classic phrase that described her situation very nicely: the die was cast.

*

"Welcome aboard, commodore," Devall raised his hand in a stiff salute as Chief Foste piped her into *Fawkes*. The airlock was small, and the sloop's prize master and acting coxswain were the only ones to greet Dunmoore. By the time Vincenzo stepped off the shuttle, the compartment was getting distinctly cramped.

"How is she after the transit from Parvi?"

"Splendid." Devall's smile was positively radiant. "She handles like a purebred and can take on any of the mercenary sloops easily with a Navy crew. Say what you want about the SSB, they make sure their spy ships can get themselves out of any trouble they might encounter."

"Good. It might come to that, though I'll do my best to prevent it."

"Sir?" He looked at her with mild astonishment.

"I'll explain — in your quarters."

He nodded once and turned on his heels to head down the narrow passageway toward the heart of the ship. The captain's cabin was situated immediately behind the bridge and did double duty as the ready room. It was not much larger than the airlock, and its furnishings were spartan.

"Seems like your predecessor didn't make this much of a home," Siobhan commented, taking in the space.

"They may have been changing crews when we hit Parvi."

"Really?" Her eyebrows shot up. "Perhaps that would explain the *Oko Maru*'s presence."

"And the skeleton crew the mercenaries supposedly found."

"Do you get the feeling our Avalon Corporation friends sanitized this ship before they gave it to us?"

Devall shrugged.

"Maybe, but the SSB would make sure to keep it sterile at all times, wouldn't they, in case people like us decide to inspect them? They might have wiped all the databanks the moment the mercs dropped on the landing strip."

"True. Not that it really matters now that we've loaded a Navy baseline into your systems." She took the only chair and motioned for Devall to sit on the bunk. Siobhan studied his face for a few moments. Pushkin had convinced her that the second officer needed to know everything, for the sake of his ship and crew, but now, seeing him face-to-face, her apprehensions returned.

He came from a politically well connected family on one of the core worlds and was the closest thing to an aristocrat his planet produced. His extended clan included senators and admirals who might just as likely be involved in Valkyrie as be among the targets of the conspiracy.

Siobhan hoped he would react like Pushkin had, but even after more than a year, she knew little about the man behind the professional, efficient, and engaging mask. Then, she reminded herself that she had given Devall the prize for a reason other than his place in *Stingray*'s hierarchy. Devall was the best of her officers after Pushkin and distinguished himself from the highly competent Kowalski by a stronger aura of maturity.

"What I'm about to tell you, Trevane, I've only shared with Gregor, and once we've finished speaking, you will keep it to yourself, perhaps forever. You'll understand well before I'm done."

He nodded calmly, conveying in that one gesture both the assurance of his discretion and an invitation to go ahead. When she finished her tale, his typically detached expression had changed to one of disbelief mixed with righteous anger.

"How in the name of all that's sacred do they expect to get away with it?" He demanded.

"Gregor and I have been kicking around scenarios, and some of them would work, but none of them would work without *Stingray* and this ship getting the short end of the stick."

"The mercenaries as well?"

"They've been expendable all along, I think, which is why Corwin's force wasn't made up of Marines and Navy ships."

"But they're ready to sacrifice us?"

"We don't know that the intent is so crass, but what I do believe is that Corwin saw an opportunity when we showed up, sticking our nose where it had no business."

"Thank God we did," Devall replied with a heretofore-unheard depth of feeling. "We're the only ones who stand a chance of stopping that madman."

"And that's why I told you everything. Now for the hard part: I'm taking *Fawkes* down because if things go sideways, it has a better chance than a shuttle of surviving the ground defenses and, if necessary, taking them out."

"Why not simply drop a kinetic strike from orbit and be done with it?"

"Because I'm not convinced that I have enough evidence to relieve my commanding officer and detain him, nor do I have sufficient evidence to seize and if necessary destroy the mercenary ships and ground troops. And I certainly don't have sufficient evidence to destroy the proto-Shrehari archaeological dig, not if they're actually finding things that we could put to use against their distant descendants."

He considered her response for a good half minute and then nodded.

"Fair enough. Elements of the story seem so fantastic that it reminds me of an old, old tale about a man put in charge of an isolated outpost where he reigned over the natives like a king and slowly went mad from it. If there's a possibility Admiral Corwin might have lost touch with reality, then we owe it to everyone to tread carefully."

"The man in this story, what happened to him?"

"He died. In one version, he died as he was being brought back to civilization. In the other, he and his subjects were bombed off the face of the planet."

"Really?" Dunmoore almost smiled. "I suppose that those resemble the two options we have, seeing as how we're agreed that putting ourselves and our crews at the disposal of the Valkyrie folks is not an acceptable course of action."

There was a knock on the door, and Devall rose to slide it open, revealing Sub-Lieutenant Sanghvi eager face.

"Message from the planet. We're cleared to land at our convenience."

"Thank you, Number One," Devall replied. "Call the ship to landing stations and report when ready. You may take the time you need to consult the appropriate checklists since this is the first time we'll be performing the maneuver. It's a tad more complicated than takeoff stations, so don't rush things."

"Aye, aye, sir." The younger man's head bobbed nervously before he vanished.

"How's the lad working out?" Dunmoore asked.

"Quite well. He may still have that freshly graduated baby face, but he's not a lad anymore. And he's working his butt off. It'll stand him in good stead when he's eligible for his second stripe."

"Will he hold it together if it comes to shooting?"

Devall shrugged. "He did well enough at Cimmeria, I understand, after the sailing master got herself a touch of alcohol poisoning, so he's been blooded. And having you on board will help steady him as well."

"Why?" Siobhan looked at *Fawkes*' captain curiously.

"The lad, pardon me, the man has a case of hero worship where you're concerned, captain." His usual sardonic expression returned, and that was strangely reassuring. "I think he desperately wants to command a frigate just like you're doing when he's finished growing up."

"Then we'd better make sure we get him home in one piece."

"Aye." He sat again, looking fidgety.

"You're doing the right thing by not breathing down his neck, Trevane, hard as that may be. It'll give him self-confidence if you stay out of the way until he reports the ship ready."

He nodded. "Agreed. I seem to recall a captain who had to relearn that lesson rather quickly."

"Glad my example proved useful. If you have any coffee going somewhere on this spy tub, I will accept a cup."

"Black, no sugar, right?"

She smiled. "Just poke your head out into the passage and give the order to Vincenzo. If he hasn't yet figured out where the coffee is, he'll do so pretty quickly."

After Devall had complied, he remained silent, lost in thought, but it was a comfortable silence. He seemed entirely at ease with the situation and his captain's choices. Once the coffees were served, Devall spoke.

"Captain, I wouldn't worry too much about your going along with Corwin until the Parvi raid. Kathryn described how compelling he could be. Charm the last creds off a greedy senator, as my uncle would put it."

"Your uncle the senator or your uncle the admiral?"

Devall grinned. "No, my uncle the shipping magnate."

"How many uncles do you have?"

"Enough that I won't be allowed to live a life of idleness if I ever resign my commission." He became serious again. "I thoroughly understand your desire to sweep the corrupt bastards away so we can fight the war properly. My uncle, the senator, has often said it was a shame the code duello hadn't been resurrected; else there would be a wholesale cleanup of that noble house of assembly."

"But?"

"This isn't the way," he replied, shaking his head. "It can't be the way."

"Are you saying that because your uncles might get swept aside or worse?"

"No," he said, shaking his head. "Knowing some of them, they're probably at the heart of Valkyrie. I'm saying that an armed assault on the government precinct would likely have knock-on effects nobody's bothered to analyze. We might just as well end up making things worse for the Commonwealth. I don't deny that we need change. I'm just too pragmatic to see a coup as the way to go."

"Then we may have to contemplate an armed assault here, on Arietis."

A chime stilled whatever comment Devall was about to make.

"Now hear this: all hands to landing stations, I repeat, all hands to landing stations. Department heads report when ready."

"I guess Sanghvi's digested the checklist," Dunmoore said. "Shall we join him on the bridge?"

*

"All systems green, sir," *Fawkes*' acting first officer reported. "Engineering tested the antigravity modules individually, since we don't have a long enough runway to rely on thrusters alone."

"Excellent." Devall clasped the younger man's shoulder and gave him a quick congratulatory shake. "Nothing worse than overshooting into a deep ravine, eh."

He took the command chair while Dunmoore unfolded a jump seat behind him. Devall was conscious of her presence, but his calm voice betrayed no nervousness and helped steady his young crew.

The schematic on the side screen showed the presence of the monitor in geosynchronous orbit above Corwin's base and Siobhan wondered how she would deal with it if and when the time came.

Then, she saw the aspect of the planet shift on the main screen as the ship's orientation changed to break out of the stable orbit it had held until now and send it plunging into Arietis' atmosphere on a shallow glide path.

Soon, the force field sheathing the hull like a second skin began to glow under the friction of hot ionized gasses as they left the vacuum of space. With no traffic control other than that provided by Admiral Corwin's operations center, the radio was strangely silent where it would normally be crackling with advisories and instructions, had Arietis been a Commonwealth world, even a lowly level one colony.

"The monitor's tracking us," Petty Officer Rownes said from the small sensor console, "as are the ground-based defenses."

"How would you deal with the monitor, Mister Devall, assuming it were hostile to us?" Siobhan asked.

"Offer to saturate its defenses with missiles and then give its captain the opportunity to surrender," he immediately replied, proving he'd been thinking about the tactical problems even as his ship was moving. "Between *Fawkes* and *Stingray*, we can give him ample cause to choose discretion over glory."

"And the ground defenses?"

Devall grinned evilly. "Kinetic strikes from low orbit. We stay beyond the range of the guns and fire a couple of missiles without warheads. That ought to be surgical enough to avoid destroying the base itself. I'd say it would be a mission for this ship rather than *Stingray*."

"I see that you can take the gunnery officer away from his guns, but he remains as bloodthirsty as ever," Dunmoore replied.

"It's always good to have a plan."

The intense green of the rift valley appeared over the horizon, and Dunmoore had a flash of inspiration.

"Captain Devall, could we overfly the valley for its entire length and give your sensors a work-out? Without looking too obvious, I mean?"

He glanced at the small console in his chair's arm and nodded.

"Helm, adjust course three degrees to port. Make it look like we're just having a bit of fun."

"Adjusting course like we're having a good time, aye," Takash replied without missing a beat. Pushkin had been right about leaving Guthren on *Stingray*. She seemed to be handling the sloop just fine.

"Anything specific we're looking for, sir?" Rownes asked.

"There's supposed to be a training camp run by the Avalon Corporation people somewhere away from the settlements. I'm also wondering whether or not they've been holding internees or outright prisoners in the same vicinity. Admiral Corwin did mention that his forces had interned the crews of the Black Nova ships that interfered with his operations."

Devall turned to look at her.

"What are you thinking, commodore? A little search and rescue exercise?"

"Indeed." She smiled. "I think if things unfold the way we've discussed, it might be a fine thing to bring those internees home with us."

"And the Avalon troops?"

"Not my problem," she replied tartly. "I'm sure there are stipulations in their contract concerning repatriation, but since I have no orders in that respect, I don't really care."

"Coming up on the rift valley, sir," Rownes announced. "Scan results are on the side screen."

Dunmoore's smile became predatory as she read the data scrolling by. Whatever else the SSB might have done, they certainly had not skimped on the quality of *Fawkes*' sensors.

"Relay to *Stingray* on a tight beam."

She settled back and lost herself in possibilities, alternatives, and what-ifs as *Fawkes* shed altitude and speed.

*

"All hands make fast for the final approach. It might get bumpy."

Siobhan strapped herself into the jump seat, foolishly wishing she could take the helm as the sloop shed forward momentum to ride on its thrusters and antigrav modules. The landing strip looked unreasonably small on the main screen, almost too small for the ship, even though she knew from having checked the dimensions, that it had enough room for *Fawkes* and one of the slightly larger Avalon sloops, plus a safety margin. Perhaps not a healthy one, but a margin nonetheless.

The ship was too massive to be easily shoved around by the winds sweeping the top of the exposed plateau, but she could feel the vibrations of the thrusters trying to keep the keel even and stable nonetheless.

"Lower the landing gear."

With loud thunks that reverberated through the hull, squat, massive legs extruded, each easily capable of carrying thousands of tons.

Dust devils erupted from the tarmac as the thrusters swept across the hardened surface and Dunmoore could see beads of sweat rolling down Takash's face. The last fifty meters were the most dangerous, as the ship rested on a cushion part thrust, part antigravity, each conspiring to shove it to one side or the other while the distance to the ground decreased.

She forced herself to unclench her fists and relax her shoulder muscles. There was nothing she could do except watch the buildings change from toy blocks to substantial structures. She noted with approval that all the doors seemed to have been tightly shut against the pressure of violently displaced air. At least somebody had been thinking. Probably Lieutenant Colonel

Rissard. He seemed to have a good head on his shoulders, notwithstanding his hero worship for the admiral, which could harm or help, depending on how deeply he was involved in Corwin's plans. Not for the first time, she wondered how to handle the Marine.

That train of thought was cut short when she felt the pressure and vibration change as the ship touched down slowly, the shock absorbers in the massive legs transferring the weight to the granite of the plateau. Guthren would have been proud of Takash. It was a good landing, with barely any tilt to the side at the moment of touchdown.

"Secure from landing stations," Devall ordered, "but maintain a full sensor watch and keep gunnery up and manned."

"Aye, aye, Captain." Sanghvi nodded as he released his seat restraints. "I'll have the ramp down the moment we've finished our sensor sweep of the ground, just in case our landing damaged something."

"Incoming from the operations center," the signals petty officer called out, "from a Lieutenant Colonel Rissard for the commodore."

"Do you want to take it in my quarters?" Devall nodded at the door behind them.

She shook her head. "Put it on here."

The view of the hangars was replaced with Rissard's face. He nodded courteously and smiled.

"Welcome back, commodore. That was a beautiful landing if I may say so. I've seen too many that gave me heart palpitations. The admiral's on his way if you'd like to prepare to receive him. He's quite anxious to see our newest addition up close."

"We look forward to receiving him, colonel. Are you coming as well?"

"Not this time, sir. I have some rather urgent issues to deal with at the moment."

"Then I won't detain you any longer."

She turned to Devall as the screen went dark. He raised his hand to forestall her next words.

"Already in hand, sir. Chief Foste is organizing a side party, complete with bosun's whistle. Admiral Corwin will be received with all due naval honors."

"Lead on then, captain. You get to greet our flag officer commanding, not I."

*

"Outstanding," Corwin shook Devall's hand after he had returned the side party's salute to the tune of the boatswain's call. "That was a nice landing as well, captain. Our commodore chose well when she selected the prize crew."

He smiled at Dunmoore.

"You seem to be handling the broad pennant well, Siobhan. Admiral Nagira would be proud of you."

"Thank you, sir. Captain Devall would like to show you *Fawkes*. She's an elegant little sloop, probably better equipped and faster than the Avalon ships. The SSB seem to have spared nothing."

Siobhan could feel Corwin's magnetism again, that force of will he exuded in his natural smile, spare gestures, and patrician tone. But not this time boyo, she thought, forcing herself to look pleased and relaxed.

"I'd be happy to get the full tour, captain." He nodded at Devall. "You have no idea how useful your command is going to be for this squadron."

The younger man inclined his head slightly, his face a studied mask of calm and respect.

"If you'll follow me, sir." He turned toward Foste. "Cox'n, you as well."

*

"It's a shame the databanks were purged," Corwin said, as he settled into one of the few chairs adorning the tiny wardroom. "Establishing what our enemies were up to on Parvi VI would have been useful, but otherwise, what an excellent ship. Clean, well maintained with fresh spare parts in the lockers. I'm surprised your people were able to take it intact, commodore."

He looked at Siobhan questioningly as he took the proffered coffee mug.

"We've theorized that they were doing a crew change at the time of the raid and the few folks left on harbor watch were quickly overwhelmed by Major Ocano's men. It would explain the *Oko Maru*'s presence if one accepts that Black Nova is either a front for the SSB or under contract to them."

"Yes." Corwin nodded slowly. "Quite plausible. A shame that you couldn't intercept the *Maru*, but I wholeheartedly agree with your decision. The element of surprise had to be maintained. I shall have to have a serious discussion with Captain Thoran. *Malabar* was supposed to take care of the *Oko Maru* for us and evidently, he forgot to inform me of his failure to do so. This is why I prefer to have Navy crews, but unfortunately, the Admiralty decided on hiring private contractors for the Arietis operation."

He took a sip of the coffee and nodded.

"You can always tell a good ship by its brew. Well done." He smiled at Devall, who had the grace to look just a bit embarrassed at the unexpected praise. "I trust you're able to function for the long haul with a split crew, Siobhan?"

"We can manage. My only concern is damage control parties in battle. That might get a bit hairy if we take too many hits."

"Good. I don't know how long we've got until everything is in place, but in the meantime, we can continue training and planning. If we hear of more reiver nests in the vicinity, we can blood the troops some more."

"Speaking of planning," Siobhan ventured, "might I ask your indulgence in granting me a more in-depth discussion than what we've had so far? If I'm to lead a naval strike force, it would be prudent that I take part in preparing the plan, seeing as I know the capabilities of my ships best."

"A reasonable request," Corwin replied, nodding. "Unless you have pressing business in orbit, I suggest we head to my office and talk. *Fawkes* can remain here. If there is anything you need from supply stores, Captain Devall, just get in touch with Colonel Rissard, and he'll see if we have it or can get it."

He stood up in a fluid movement and gently deposited his mug on the table.

"Shall we, Siobhan? No need for a side party, Captain Devall. Thank you again for the tour and the coffee, and enjoy your command. It's a heady feeling that never quite goes away no matter how many ships you're given."

The flinty air tickled her nostrils as she strode down the ramp in Corwin's wake. Devall had given her a warning glance before he saw them over the side and she had no doubt he would fight his way through if the admiral and his mercenaries turned nasty.

"I shall take you into our catacombs," he said over his shoulder, "and show you what we're putting together. Now that you've passed the tests I set for you, I think I can let you in on most things. I've always needed a good deputy, a Navy deputy, and you're a godsend."

"Tests, sir?" She asked because she knew it was expected of her.

"Operation Valkyrie is the most important thing the Fleet is doing since the start of the war, and our part in it will be the most important of all. I had to make sure you had the ruthlessness and loyalty to your commander that others believe you have. I don't mistrust my fellow flag officers, but I do like to make sure of my closest subordinates myself. Who knows — when we've succeeded, you might be known as commodore by rank, not just by title." He winked at her, and she felt those manipulative tendrils playing with her wishes and desires again.

Corwin led her into the hangar and through the same warren of polished underground corridors she had traveled during her last visit, emerging in the antechamber to his office suite.

The same eerily carved, ancient furniture greeted her as he led her across the ornate formal room and through a side door to what was, for all intents and purposes a map room. Within, she saw charts of Earth's star system, its defenses, Earth itself, and detailed diagrams of the government precinct, including the Fleet HQ buildings.

She felt her stomach sink at the sight. Any lingering hopes that Corwin was a lone madman suffering from delusions of grandeur disappeared. Some of those maps could only have been obtained from Navy sources and highly placed sources at that. The Fleet did not exactly share such intimate details of the home world's defenses with just anyone, let alone someone whose marbles were not all present or accounted for.

It reawakened all of her fears that Operation Valkyrie would see her ships and the mercenaries used as disposable shock troops, something from which the conspirators would save the civilian, representative government after its current leaders had been neutralized or removed permanently.

Corwin's voice intruded with its soft tone.

"As you can see, we do not lack for intelligence. Planning is far from complete, so your request to be included is timely indeed. What plans I had begun to formulate have been discarded since your fortuitous arrival. The addition of *Stingray* and now *Fawkes* to the task force gives us that much more flexibility. Two Navy vessels can go much further into Earth's defensive rings than a couple of private sloops, even with naval IFF beacons."

He tapped a console and called up an intricate schematic of the home system.

"In essence, what I'm proposing is to infiltrate, under cover of orders from the Admiralty, two battalions of Avalon troops on board the ships of this squadron. These forces will seize the center of the capital and hold it until the members of Valkyrie can declare a national emergency and take the levers of power. With any luck, bloodshed will be minimal." The schematic came to life under his fingers as he spoke, shifting to the government precinct, with all its defenses clearly outlined.

"I'll let my colleagues figure out how to get your squadron to get past the orbitals, but I don't see it being a problem. The units stationed on and around Earth are nowhere near as battle-ready or battle-seasoned as your people."

His tone was so matter-of-fact, so normal that Siobhan felt cold shivers run down her spine. Corwin was discussing armed overthrow as if it were a tactical problem studied at the Naval War College. He kept talking for over half an hour, laying out ideas, concepts, calling up maps, charts, and diagrams.

"I'd be happy to hear any ideas you might have," he concluded, gently touching her shoulder and triggering an unexpected wave of revulsion within her. Pushkin's call to reality had permanently changed the way she reacted to Corwin, and she felt a slow rage building. But she had to play along, for all their sakes, until she found a way to extricate them from this death trap, for death it would be, even if Valkyrie succeeded. Having listened to him, not just to his words, but his tone and his body language, she had no doubt that the admiral considered her as expendable as he found her useful.

"Sir, if I may ask, it seems to me that a handful of ships and a few hundred ground troops are going to have a hard time getting the job done. You mentioned proto-Shrehari technology on my earlier visit. Might I ask what's been found? Any ideas or recommendations I can give you need to be informed by whatever force multipliers we're counting on."

Corwin considered her, head cocked to the side, his eyes searching hers. Siobhan struggled to maintain a neutral, if not an avidly curious expression.

"Fair enough," he finally said. "If I'm to ask you to take the Arietis Squadron into harm's way on behalf of Operation Valkyrie, I suppose I should allow you to learn all of the secrets. You've proven your loyalty, if not to me then very much to Admiral Nagira."

Again with the reference to the commander of Third Fleet, she thought irritably. It was as if Corwin was using Nagira as some sort of talisman to hypnotize her.

He reached over to a console and touched its surface briefly.

"Rissard here, sir," a voice announced almost immediately.

"I would like to take Commodore Dunmoore down into the labs and the digs. Please ensure all is in order."

"Will do, sir. Give me thirty minutes to clear everything."

Corwin looked up and nodded at Siobhan. "You'll soon see."

"Clear everything?" Dunmoore ventured.

"Our good Marine wants to make sure the folks are prepared to receive us so that we don't interrupt any sensitive experiments or surprise them to the extent that we don't get what we want from the visit."

They left the map room for the ornate office, her mind in a whirlwind. It was one thing to contemplate Valkyrie from a distance, but seeing actual maps and diagrams had made it frighteningly real.

"Tell me, Siobhan," he asked, "what are your views on how we should treat the enemies of the Commonwealth, and by that I don't mean the Shrehari?"

Momentarily put off balance by the question, she did not answer and tried to cover her confusion by serving herself a cup of coffee.

"I'm not sure what you mean, sir."

"Take for instance that blight on humanity called the Special Security Bureau. When we take control, I fully intend to purge it from top to bottom, perhaps eliminate it altogether in favor of a paramilitary constabulary actually devoted to policing."

"What happens to the SSB people?" She asked once she had digested the statement.

"The ones who've committed crimes will be tried and punished. Some might be useful and would get re-educated. The majority will likely be barred from any government work once the SSB is dissolved."

Corwin's matter-of-fact tone, the way he took it as a given that he would have the power to deal with those he perceived as enemies, chilled her to the core.

"I'm just a frigate captain," she said. "I'll leave those matters to my superiors."

It sounded lame even to her ears, and she expected Corwin to call her on it. But he did not.

"You're an acting commodore, Siobhan, and likely to achieve higher rank once we set the Commonwealth back on the proper path. You'll have a say on many things at my table." He reached over to touch her shoulder in what she assumed was meant to be a reassuring manner.

Liar, she thought. He planned to sacrifice her to the Valkyrie narrative. There would be no place for her at his table.

"Is something wrong?" He gazed at her quizzically, and she realized that she had let her mask slip.

"Sorry, sir. It's just that there's a lot for me to take in at once." She looked down at her scuffed boots.

He nodded. "You may have realized by now that I never ask idle questions. It used to keep my crews on their toes in the happier days when I sat in my own command chair. As I may have mentioned, I've interned some folks who were a threat to my operations, in large part those connected with Black Nova, but also Commonwealth government and military people who wormed their way into a position to imperil Valkyrie. In other words, enemies of the Commonwealth."

She looked up at him, wondering where his line of reasoning was headed. The sensor scans *Fawkes* had made, sailing over the rift valley, had shown two distinct concentrations of human or humanoid life signs set close together, but at some distance from the nearest settlement. One of them had shown emissions consistent with weapons and the visuals had shown ground troops engaged in training. The other had shown only prefabricated huts and a handful of people patrolling the perimeter.

"I've established an internment camp near the Avalon Corporation training facility," he continued, confirming their sightings, "and in this camp, I have intelligence specialists separating out those people who could be useful to us from those who need to be kept under constant guard due to their hostility. We're having some success in convincing the more enlightened among the detainees to join our cause. The remainder, once we've drained them of their knowledge, will be dealt with in time."

He sounded so reasonable, so calm that she struggled to repress a nervous twitch.

"Perhaps, I should bring you to visit the facility so you may judge for yourself. The Avalon people have some of the most unusual interrogation techniques I've ever seen, and as they're not limited in their freedom of action like our dear Navy, the results are often quite startling." He glanced at his timepiece. "Finish up your coffee. It's almost time to head down."

He took her back through the antechamber and down the stairs into the wide corridor running underneath the base, stopping at one of the closed doors. He placed his hand on a gray rectangle set to one side, and it slid open with a grating sound.

"Dust gets everywhere," Corwin commented. "That's why we've surrounded the labs with some safeguards."

They stepped into a large, boxy space that turned out to be an elevator and Corwin touched an identical gray rectangle on the inside wall.

"As extraordinary as it may seem, this lift is original to the site. All we had to do was figure out how to connect a power source. Imagine: a hundred-thousand-year old elevator." With a lurch, the bare metal box dropped. "They used frictionless materials both on the inside of the shaft and the outside of the cab, with a repulser module at the bottom to regulate the cab's position. Very slick, pun intended."

She forced herself to smile at what Corwin believed to be a witty remark. While its age made the contraption more interesting than it would otherwise have been, the technology was no different from what humans had developed some time ago. Siobhan decided it would not be politic to say so and tried to feign a believable expression of interest.

The cab came to a smooth stop, and the doors slid open, this time without the grating sound. Another long corridor, even better lit than the one they just left, opened up before them. The air seemed to hum with energy while the surfaces were cleaner and brighter. Several large doors opened on either side.

"We are one hundred meters below the surface of the plateau and only fifty meters above the valley floor. The first artifacts were found at this level. Or, to be more precise, the objects found by treasure hunters had fallen out of a chamber on this level when a cliff wall split and crumbled, likely due to repeated seismic shocks over the millennia."

He led her to a side door and repeated the same routine with the palm reader.

"We've removed everything from this level and either stored it or shipped it home. Most of it was art, furnishings and the like." The door opened onto a small space divided in two by a wall and guard station.

"This is the first layer of security." He motioned her to precede him. The guard, an Avalon trooper, snapped to attention and saluted. When Corwin had returned the gesture, he opened the airlock-like door and ushered them in.

"How are you doing, Baz?"

"Can't complain, Admiral. Got some leave coming up, so I'll be out of the catacombs in two shifts."

Corwin clapped the man on the shoulder. "Keep up the good work."

Then he led Siobhan through the second door into an entirely different world. The immediate feeling she had when she stepped through was that of entering a hospital: antiseptic, white and with a faint whiff of ozone.

"We've established the labs on this level. I have some highly talented scientists and engineers, Fleet, for the most part, working at deciphering the technological artifacts we're unearthing beneath the valley floor. They aren't part of our command team, you understand?"

She nodded. The people working here believed they were looking for technological means to tilt the war against the Shrehari. He quickly introduced her to some dour-faced men and women in lab outfits, and briefly explained what they were working on. One of the engineers, an older woman with dark hair, and a seamed face took a greater interest in Dunmoore than the rest.

"Commodore, I spent most of my career working in starships and have been out of touch with my fellow tinkerers since I came here. Might I ask who your chief engineer is?"

"Lieutenant Commander Kutora, Commander…?"

"Mathes, sir," she replied. "So you have the grumpy, bearded old bugger to haunt you. Give him my best when you get back to your ship. Tell him he still owes Wen Mathes from the last round of poker we played before I shipped out."

Conscious that Corwin was showing signs of impatience, Dunmoore smiled at Mathes and nodded.

"I'll certainly do that. Perhaps if standing orders permit, you could call him."

"I'm afraid that's out of the question," the admiral smoothly interjected, touching Siobhan's arm. "Commander Mathes needs to get back to her molecular disruptor. I believe we're close to a breakthrough."

"Is that what it is?" Dunmoore asked brightly. "I couldn't begin to tell by its appearance. It seems quite well preserved."

"Don't be fooled by looks," the engineer replied, giving Siobhan a significant glance and a very faint shake of the head. "Around here things are often not what they appear to be."

"Ah." Dunmoore shrugged. "Research can be as frustrating as it is fascinating. Thank you for your time, commander."

As they walked away, she caught Corwin giving Mathes a dirty look, which the older woman returned with surprising steadiness.

"She's a good engineer," he commented, "but a bit free with her opinions and like all those of her breed, prone to exaggerated pessimism when it comes to timelines."

"Aren't molecular disruptors on such a small scale an impossibility?" She asked. "The amount of energy required would be more than any portable power source could muster."

"That's the beauty of the items we're digging up. The proto-Shrehari were so much more advanced than we are and had solved many of the problems we still face." Corwin's answer was smooth and delivered with firm conviction.

The look that briefly flashed through the eyes of the passing scientist who overheard him told Siobhan a much different story.

Everywhere they went, she saw bits and pieces of technology that looked alien, but even to her own eyes, they seemed beyond repair. The people working on the items appeared more concerned with cataloging the finds than bringing them to life. More than one tried to subtly tell her Corwin was overly optimistic. If these were indeed the wonder weapons that were supposed to help propel her to victory, something was very wrong.

They left what the admiral characterized as the engineering complex and entered a biosciences research lab. Here, she saw complex-looking machines covered in alien markings, all showing signs of great age. It was impossible for her eye to tell what their use was or how anyone could have divined that this was ancient medical equipment. She said as much to Corwin.

"The boffins were able to decipher some of the hard copy documentation we found with these machines, by way of interpreting pictograms and approximating the script to present day Shrehari. I have high hopes that they will soon be able to put these devices to good use developing valuable weapons such as tailored pseudo-viruses, and I don't mean the nasty kind we've known for centuries. One of the leading theories of the L'Taung civilization's demise revolves around the use of biological warfare incorporating artificial viruses targeted at specific biomarkers. Imagine if we could tailor viruses to a specific DNA. We could get rid of our enemies without firing a shot." The way he emphasized enemies, Siobhan knew he was not talking about the Shrehari.

She caught the eye of one of the researchers who gave her the same brief look of skepticism she had seen from others as if he found Corwin's words to be more in the realm of fantasy than reality. What chilled her most, however, was his casual way of discussing what was in effect murder on a grand scale.

He did not give her time to dwell on matters as he led her to a large chamber filled with unsorted artifacts piled high on pallets, ready to be brought to the labs for analysis.

"The shaft to the lower levels is on the other side of the warehouse," he pointed to the far end. "We still have many months of work ahead of us. Extraction has to be very careful. Some of the chambers have collapsed over the millennia, and it wouldn't do to damage something that could potentially turn a single soldier into a weapon of mass destruction."

The sound of their footsteps echoed across the cavernous room as they headed toward the wide opening gaping in the smooth wall. To Dunmoore, the artifacts looked like old junk, objects only an archaeologist could love. She grimaced as the different things she saw and heard began to coalesce into a logical whole.

"Most of the excavating has to be done by hand," Corwin said as he led her onto what she assumed was a cargo hoist. "Fortunately, we've been able to accumulate a workforce using petty criminals expiating their sentence; don't be alarmed at the control collars you might see. They've been instructed not to speak with anyone, so please don't attempt to engage them in conversation."

When she nodded, he touched a control surface, and the floor fell away under her feet. Almost as soon as it had started dropping, the platform slowed its descent and came to a gentle stop, exposing a more roughly hewn chamber where groups of humanoids moved about with purpose.

"I can't take you too close to the digs. Some of them are still unstable and thus dangerous, but as you can see, we're making significant progress."

An Avalon officer approached them and saluted.

"Lieutenant," Corwin smiled warmly at him, "how is the coalface this afternoon?"

"We've had a bit of a cave-in in section Red Four. One of the workers was injured. He's being treated upstairs right now."

"Pity." Corwin grimaced. "We're not so flush with labor that we can afford losses. I'm showing Commodore Dunmoore the facilities, but if we have one instability, we'll have more so I think we won't go any further than this. Sorry, Siobhan."

She did not immediately reply, her attention drawn to one of the coverall-clad workers wearing a control collar. He had an uncanny resemblance to the officer sitting behind the captain of the *Fuso Maru* at the convoy conference. If it was indeed the same man, Corwin had a strange definition of petty criminal.

"No matter, sir," she replied, suddenly anxious to be gone. "Another time perhaps."

He nodded. "We should regain my office and discuss our next training raid. Maybe you'll stay for supper. I find the company of a fellow Navy officer quite refreshing after all this time on Arietis."

Without waiting for a reply, he led her back to the cargo platform and up to the lab level. As they made their way through the rocky warren, they passed Commander Mathes, who stumbled when Siobhan came near and grabbed her left arm. She righted herself with a mumbled apology and disappeared around the corner. Corwin shook his head irritably but kept walking.

"Some days I wonder whether she's worth keeping around," he commented. "She might be of better use in the excavations. If she wasn't a three-striper, I might just send her to run the engine room of our newest acquisition and put someone with more enthusiasm on the task of getting the disruptor working."

Siobhan felt something irritating the back of her hand inside the black glove she wore to hide the reactor coolant burns and briefly touched the spot with her right index finger while Corwin opened the elevator to the surface. She could have sworn that she had not tucked a small data wafer in there when she got dressed this morning. Now Dunmoore really wanted to get away, but escaping from Corwin's grasp without making him suspicious was going to be a challenge. She made sure the chip was firmly stuck inside the glove and tried to ignore its presence, albeit with limited success.

Discussing plans with Corwin was an ordeal she would remember for a long time. She was able to beg off from supper when Rissard reported some problem or other at the internment camp. Though she did not overhear what the Marine said, she could see, by the tightening of Corwin's face, that he was enraged. He rose from his desk and dipped his head briefly toward her.

"My apologies, Siobhan. A matter I have to deal with immediately, lest things get out of hand. Some people will never understand the dynamics of power and obedience, and I fear I shall have to provide an object lesson." The earlier contented charm had vanished, leaving behind a nervous tic and a transformed manner. "I think it would be best if you returned to orbit. We can discuss next steps over a secure link."

She came to attention, saluted, and followed the guard who had come in with Rissard back through the tunnels to the hangar. Devall was waiting for her at the foot of the ramp, hands clasped in the small of his back. He greeted her formally, eyes searching her face for answers.

"We need to lift off now, Trevane," she said by way of hello, "and make our course over the rift valley again." When she explained her reasons, he quickened his step and upon reaching the bridge, gave out rapid-fire orders.

Fawkes lifted off shortly after that and made a lazy ascent that took it within visual range of the internment camp at an altitude too high for the naked eye to see. Their equipment, however, could distinguish every pebble on the ground and what they recorded left them angry.

— Twenty-Two —

"I feel like we're in a bad dream, captain," Pushkin said slumping back in his chair as she finished telling him and Devall of her visit, the latter over a tight ship-to-ship link. "And we can't wake up."

"Nightmare, more like," Devall replied. "I guess Kathryn hasn't decrypted that wafer yet."

"No. Commander Mathes wouldn't have consigned whatever she wanted to pass on in clear, but it isn't any known algorithm, once again." She pictured the older woman speaking to her and sat up in her chair, stroking the intercom.

"Captain to Mister Kutora."

"Engineering," he replied a moment later. "What can I do for you?"

"Do you know a Commander Mathes, per chance?"

"Wen Mathes? She's down there?"

"That she is, working on Admiral Corwin's engineering team."

"Small universe, captain. She's a couple of years ahead of me, but we used to play cards when we were assigned to the Caledonia shipyards before the war."

"So I understand. She said something to the effect of telling you that you still owe her from the last poker game you played."

Kutora's laugh sounded more like a low rumble than an expression of mirth.

"I had a full house, aces over jacks and went all in on a night where no one got much in terms of decent cards. She called and laid down a straight flush. I had to borrow cash to get me to the next payday. Haven't touched poker since then, at least not for real money."

"Do you remember what suit it was?"

"I'll always remember the hand that cost me two thousand creds."

Pushkin almost choked at the amount while Devall burst out laughing.

"Is that young Trevane taking delight at my misfortune?" Kutora asked. "You just wait until the next time you need your plasma conduits reamed out."

"The suit, Mister Kutora," Siobhan impatiently reminded him.

"Spades it was, the trey to the seven. Any reason you're asking?"

"I'll let you know in due course. Dunmoore out." She stroked the intercom again. "Captain to Lieutenant Kowalski."

"Yes, captain?"

"That wafer I gave you to decrypt, would the notion of a poker hand, specifically a straight flush, spades, trey to seven help?"

"Perhaps." She fell silent, thinking it through. "Do you have an opposing hand? It seems to me a straight flush isn't random enough."

"Full house, aces over jacks."

"Any idea of the suits?"

"No, and after all this time, I doubt even Mister Kutora remembers."

"I'll give it a try."

"Why is it," Pushkin complained, "that everyone is talking in ciphers around here?"

"Secrets within secrets." Devall shrugged. "Captain, what you've described is pretty far-fetched. Is Corwin crazy or just cunning?"

"Why can't he be both?" She replied. "Why can't Corwin have gone insane out here in the back of beyond where he's the only law, but there really is an Operation Valkyrie he's supposed to be supporting, while at the same time the proto-Shrehari wonder weapons are a chimera?"

"Oh I hope they're a chimera," Pushkin said with deep feeling in his tone. "DNA-tailored artificial viruses? If that's not a war crime, I don't know what use the Aldebaran Convention has become."

"We have crimes no matter what," Devall reminded them. "What the mercs were doing to the internees down there was abuse, pure and simple. Clubbing prisoners with weapons while they're standing in ranks, just to teach them a lesson, is enough to get any of us sent to a penal battalion."

"Indeed." Siobhan sighed, feeling a nauseating migraine form behind her eyes. "Let's assume he was sent here to prepare an option for Valkyrie, with the mercs funded out of the black ops budget, under the cover of the archaeological digs. He sets himself up as a local despot since he's got the high orbit locked up and has the only organized military force for light years. What are the chances that it all goes to his head, and he cracks under the strain? It's not like he has any friends around here to keep an eye on him." As I do, she thought, glancing at her first officer.

"Where does he get the wonder weapons delusion?" Pushkin asked.

"Wishful thinking, nourished by ancient technology that may still look usable, but is utterly dead? Maybe they found a few innocuous items that still worked?" Dunmoore rubbed her forehead, wishing the growing pain would go away.

"Captain," Devall frowned, "a lot us hate the idiots running the Commonwealth, and you've got more reason than most of us, since they almost cost you your life, but isn't Admiral Corwin taking it a bit far?"

"Crazy is as crazy does?" Pushkin made a wide-eyed face to underline his comment.

"I've seen people eaten away by hate," Siobhan mused, "to the point where they begin to lose touch with reality."

"Folks who have three armed sloops, one monitor and who knows how many battalions of infantry at their disposal?" The first officer asked.

"Let's not forget a full squadron of assault shuttles," Devall added. "Out here, that's a big punch."

The intercom beeped. "Captain, Kowalski here. I have your message decrypted, and sir, I've had no choice but to read its contents."

"You might as well come to my ready room." Dunmoore cut the intercom. "How much do I tell her?"

"Kathryn's a smart cookie, sir," Devall replied. "She can handle it all and keep mum."

"Agreed," Pushkin said.

The door chimed, and Kowalski walked in at Dunmoore's call. She handed a pad to the captain and assumed the parade rest.

"Sit." Siobhan pointed at a chair while her eyes skimmed the screen.

"Commander Mathes seems to have given us an analysis of the weapons, plural, she's been working on. From what I can read, they're all one hundred thousand-year-old junk. Well preserved thanks to the stasis chambers, but junk nonetheless. She notes that the researchers are nowhere near understanding what they're finding, let alone figuring out how to replicate the technology." She glanced up at the three officers. "She indicates that Admiral Corwin has highly unrealistic expectations and has been behaving more and more erratically."

"Which dovetails with what we've just been discussing," Pushkin concluded.

Kowalski should have looked bewildered, but her narrowed eyes were flitting between her three superiors and Siobhan could almost see the gears turning in her head.

"This research station is unearthing non-human technology, and someone is hoping for wonder weapons to end the war," she said, "except that there aren't any, and the admiral's a nutter who's developed delusions."

Pushkin looked at Dunmoore with an ironic smile. "I told you she'd catch on quick."

"And demonstrate her lack of respect for senior officers," Devall added, laughing.

"People," Siobhan raised her voice, "funny as it may be to imagine flag officers losing their marbles, we do have a big problem. Kathryn, you're about to be made privy to information I shared reluctantly with the first officer and Mister Devall. Needless to say, what you're going to hear next remains strictly between the four of us for now."

She pinched the bridge of her nose again and sighed.

"I suppose the secret gets diluted every time I bring someone else in on it, but there seems to be no other way."

By the time she finished telling Kowalski what she told the other two, the signals officer had a distinctly strange look in her eyes.

Enough so that Siobhan examined her openly as if trying to read her thoughts.

"Comments, Mister Kowalski?"

"Operation Valkyrie has the right idea, sir, but the wrong approach."

"And what pray tell," Dunmoore asked, not bothering to hide the sarcasm born of her migraine, "is the right approach, leaving aside for the moment your insinuation that overthrowing the government would be an okay thing to do?"

She considered the question, then replied, "I'm not quite sure, but whatever the right answer is, it has to be more in the lines of divorcing control of military operations from pure politics. If this Valkyrie option is for real, all it'll do is replace one set of politicians with another set, even if those politicians either wear a uniform, or the uniforms have their hands up the politicians' rear ends."

It was a remarkably astute if crude analysis and Dunmoore's respect for Kowalski's ability to seize the nub of a problem grew. She might take second place to *Fawkes*' captain for now, but it would not last.

"What do we do?" Devall asked.

"Our duty," Dunmoore responded, almost automatically. She paused for a few seconds. "Which might be a bit more than we can chew off."

"I don't think I could live with myself if we turned tail and left Corwin to continue as is, Valkyrie or no Valkyrie. If the plot is for real, then even less so. What he's doing on Arietis is more than enough to relieve him of his command."

"I second Mister Pushkin's sentiments, sir," Devall said, joined by Kowalski's enthusiastic nod.

"You do realize we might end up getting the crappy end of a very short stick, even if we do everything right and for what we believe are the right reasons." Dunmoore looked grim.

"We do." The first officer spoke for all of them.

"Even if it means blue on blue fighting?"

"Are the mercenaries truly 'blue' as you put it, sir?"

"They're human and many of them are ex-Fleet, Gregor. Their company may have taken the contract, but those guys and gals are grunts, just like our people."

Dunmoore leaned forward and rested her elbows on the desk, steepling her gloved fingers as she pursed her lips.

"I seem to recall that a wise man once said words to the effect that removing a commanding officer for illegal orders or actions cannot be construed as mutiny."

Kowalski's head whipped over to stare at Pushkin.

"It was indeed our esteemed first officer," Siobhan nodded. "I think we have enough evidence that Admiral Corwin is either not playing with a full deck or is exhibiting a heretofore hidden streak of sociopathy. His treatment of detainees, for instance, is enough to trigger a board of inquiry which, I'll quickly add, isn't the answer seeing as we're very far from home. His planning the overthrow of the Commonwealth government, whether it's for real or a delusion is enough for his second in command to relieve him of duty and place him under arrest. What's less clear is the legality of using detainees as forced labor without a court condemning them. One of the control-collared workers I saw was a dead ringer for a *Fuso Maru* officer. But since we're not in Commonwealth space, I'm not sure if the lawyers would even touch that one."

"We do have Corwin ordering the attack on Parvi VI," Pushkin said. "Which might be okay if he had reasonable grounds to suspect a reiver nest, but his troops pressed the attack even after meeting weak resistance and finding out that it was a commercial outpost of sorts, not to mention shooting unarmed people. I'd say, captain — pardon me, commodore — that you have enough evidence to relieve Corwin of command."

"And how, pray tell would I do that?" Dunmoore asked, looking at her first officer with a twisted smile. "The mercs are under contract to obey Corwin. They don't give a damn about Navy regulations, and likely won't acknowledge my relieving the admiral short of actually having him locked away in the brig. Unless I take away Corwin's forces, there's nothing we can do."

"We could high-tail it back to the Commonwealth and report to Admiral Ryn."

"If Valkyrie is for real, Kathryn, we become a loose end. That won't be healthy for the crew," Pushkin pointed out.

"But is it?" Kowalski countered.

"It is," Dunmoore said, "I'd stake my life on it, and yours. Corwin might have taken his authority as despot of Arietis too far, and he might be hoping for too much out of the digs, but he's not crazy. He doesn't need wonder weapons to crack the government precinct. All he needs are some well-placed accomplices to divert the defense forces around and on Earth, not that they're very good to begin with. After that, we can wreak untold damage."

"And when we've wiped out half the Senate and most of the Cabinet, heroically loyal forces take us out to show this was a rogue operation and not a conspiracy," Pushkin concluded.

"So you see, Kathryn, running is not an option." Dunmoore grimaced. "We need to disarm Corwin and shut him down."

"We sail home having done that, won't his buddies want to shove us down the memory hole as well, sir?"

"I have an idea or two how to make sure, in as far as I can, that there won't be any overt retaliation. The Valkyrie folks will be anxious to ensure not a hint of what transpired here comes out, but to get to that point, we need to shut this down, and we need to do it now."

"I see by the gleam in your eye, captain, that you have a plan."

"Indeed, Mister Pushkin." She grinned, transforming her tired features into something that gave her officers renewed hope.

*

"Admiral," Dunmoore forced herself to look relaxed when Corwin's face materialized on the screen, "I trust you were able to resolve your little issue with the detainees to your satisfaction."

"That I was." He smiled openly, sending an ugly shiver down Siobhan's spine. She was about to betray him, and no matter how she felt about his actions, past and planned, Corwin was still her commanding officer and had treated her well. Very well, if she thought of how few flag officers had actually believed in her over the years.

"Some time in the digs will take care of the troublemakers who are still in a condition to work," he continued. "We'll have to resume our discussion at some point, but for now, I think I would like you to carry out more raiding exercises. I'm open to creative ideas, the more challenging, the better." His eyes twinkled with meaning. "We have a tough job ahead and as someone once said, the harder the training, the easier the actual fighting."

"Sir, short of another real target in the sector, I'd like to propose a simulated raid on Fury Station."

Corwin's eyes narrowed in surprise, but he simply said, "Go on."

"First of all, I'm thinking of force protection. With the research advancing so rapidly, the risk of taking most of the squadron out of the system is rising, especially now that we know for sure the SSB is lurking in the sector."

"An important point, yes."

"Second, the base is probably as good a proxy for the future target as we can find within a hundred light years and the garrison can play the part of the guard. Third, we know we'll be dealing with orbital platforms around the target and *Roberts* makes an excellent proxy for those. Finally, it'll give you the chance to observe the action personally and evaluate our state of readiness vis-à-vis the operational plans."

Corwin's eyes narrowed as he pondered her proposal. Siobhan struggled to meet his gaze and keep an enthusiastic demeanor. Whether he was crazy or not, he had been a leader for decades and could read others with ease. She, on the other hand, was no actress but was hoping that he would see what he wanted to see: a loyal subordinate ready to do her bit for the cause, whatever it might be. As she held that thought, she felt herself relax. She was, in fact, enthusiastic for the cause; it just was not Corwin's. With that in mind, she allowed herself a genuine smile.

"Very well, commodore. Draft up the plan for my review. Excellent piece of thinking; I like that in a squadron commander. You'll earn a permanent broad pennant yet. Corwin, out."

She touched her console and made sure the transmission was ended before turning to Pushkin, who was sitting in the far corner of the cabin, out of sight of the video pickup.

"That was easier than I thought."

"We should wait until he's approved the plan before celebrating, captain." He sounded glum. "Maybe my natural pessimism is playing me false again, or maybe it's because I know what we're up to, but he may still smell a dead rat."

"Cheer up, Gregor. For the first time in weeks, we're in control of our destiny. I find that strangely invigorating."

She rubbed her hands together gleefully, displaying the mercurial character that people either found very engaging or horribly irksome.

"And if it works out the way we want," she continued, "we stand a good chance of taking over without bloodshed. Or at least with a minimum of bloodshed. I don't mind blowing away Shrehari or reivers of whatever species, but I'd rather not decimate Avalon Corporation if I can convince them to surrender quietly. Even if their CEO is part of Valkyrie, the grunts have no bun in this fight."

— Twenty-Three —

"Piece of genius getting the admiral to observe the raid from *Roberts*," Pushkin commented as they watched the squadron's ships deploy to their attack positions.

"Flattery will get me everywhere, it seems. It isolates him from the base and effectively neutralizes him."

"If Kathryn's electronic countermeasures drones work."

"I see no reason why they shouldn't and since the plan calls for the attack force to communicate by laser, we won't be affected."

"Captain, all ships report ready," Kowalski announced via the intercom.

"Pass the signal to start our approach." She glanced at Pushkin. "Any last minute qualms? We're close to the point of no return. Once we launch the drones and Devall drops his little packages around *Roberts*, we'll be in a state of mutiny against Admiral Corwin."

"It isn't mutiny if we're trying to prevent a gross violation of the law," the first officer reminded her, sounding weary of the argument. "But no, I have no last minute qualms. I just wish we were somewhere else, like being chased by the Cimmeria Assault Force."

"Cheer up, Gregor. This is going to work, and it's not like we have any other options." She clapped him on the shoulder as they left the ready room to take their places on a bridge depleted of its primary crew.

Fawkes was carrying a large landing party as well as its regular complement, and since Guthren had the most ground combat experience, he was the party's senior non-com under Lieutenant

Syten. Siobhan had brought both of them into the fold and had been privately amused at the gunnery officer's indignation, but she and the coxswain had shown nothing other than a fierce determination to prevent a violation of their dearest oath. Chief Penzara now controlled the entirety of the ship's ordnance, with a junior petty officer at the sensors replacing Rownes.

Lieutenant Tours had been reassigned as the second officer in Devall's absence, and Kowalski had taken over the combined navigation and signals departments. If Dunmoore had more officers than the bare minimum she might have put one or two on each of the Avalon sloops, but that might have hindered her ability to neutralize them by force, whether or not General Order Eighty-One applied.

"I'm glad you reconsidered your plan of accompanying *Fawkes* down, captain."

Siobhan smiled tightly. "It would have been irresponsible of me, as you correctly pointed out."

"Glad to see some of my first officerness is rubbing off. Devall will be okay. He's as steady as they come."

"ECM drones away," Penzara announced. "Stealthing is working. I almost lost them after their thrusters shut down."

"And if *Roberts* detects them orbiting along with her, it's all part of the war games," Siobhan replied happily.

"The Avalon sloops have begun broadcasting Navy IFF signals," Kowalski reported.

"And this is where legality starts venting through the airlock," Pushkin said.

"Not necessarily. They're identified as auxiliaries, not warships. It's a very subtle distinction, but one that keeps them in the gray area, seeing as they're under Navy contract." Siobhan shrugged. If her plan worked, it was immaterial. If it did not, it would be immaterial in a different way.

"We're about to emerge from the shadow of the larger moon."

"Tell *Fawkes, Carnatic,* and *Coromandel* they may proceed on their landing paths, Mister Kowalski."

As the flotilla came within visual range of the monitor, they found themselves painted by its targeting sensors. However, there was no indication that it was charging its guns, or opening its launchers. By agreement, Corwin was to let the exercise proceed without intervention or radio contact. After all, he would not be there during the real raid.

"The drones are in position," Penzara finally announced, "and are ready to start scrambling all communications along the full spectrum."

"Laser optical links are operational," Kowalski added. "All ships are ready to switch over."

"Make to *Fawkes*: deliver the mail."

The three ships passed close by the monitor as if to show their complete legitimacy and confidence, playing the role of a task force under Admiralty orders. However, one of them was not playing.

They could not see it from *Stingray*, but Devall's crew were pumping mines out of *Fawkes'* rear missile tubes, seeding space behind the monitor with a deadly necklace of command-detonated ordnance. Dunmoore hoped she would not have to use them, but if she did, the mines, augmented by the frigate's own broadside, would turn *Roberts* into orbiting wreckage, hopefully before her captain could return the favor.

"*Fawkes* reports that the postman rang six times."

The prize sloop was sailing behind the two Avalon ships and masked its delivery with its own bulk and emissions. If *Roberts* detected the mines, they would become part of the war games as well, but some of the element of surprise would be lost.

"Entering the atmosphere. *Malabar* has taken up position ahead of *Roberts*. We can now cover both of them with the same broadside."

"Descent path divergence point reached," Penzara said, his tactical readout repeated on a side screen where one icon was peeling away from the other two. *Coromandel* was heading for Cintrea spaceport, while the others were descending on Fury Station, with *Carnatic* scheduled to land a few minutes before *Fawkes*.

The atmosphere on the bridge of *Stingray* was thickening with tension as the three sloops descended deeper into Arietis' atmosphere. The lower they were, the less they could do to counter Dunmoore, leaving her to deal only with *Roberts* and *Malabar*. A lot would depend on the survival instincts of the Avalon people in any case.

She caught her fingers dancing nervously on her thigh and forcibly stilled them, but a brief glance around the bridge showed that no one had noticed.

"Inert warhead strike has been loaded in the forward tubes and the mission parameters have been programmed."

"Launch," Siobhan ordered, feeling the tension drain from her body. She had crossed her Rubicon, and there would be no going back. "Activate the electronic countermeasures."

They watched the missiles drop into the atmosphere at high velocity. If the timing was right, they would take out the four defensive weapon arrays around Fury Station moments after *Carnatic* landed. Without warheads, she was counting on using the force of their impact rather than a nuclear explosion to wreak destruction. Kinetic strikes could be just as devastating, but they left no radiation for the follow-on force. Of course, if the timing was wrong, fun would be had by all as they attempted to land through a cloud of flying debris.

"I wish I could have seen Corwin's face when he lost touch with the outside universe."

"He's probably cheering me on." Siobhan chortled. "Any dirty trick to get the operation done and done well."

"He'll find out something's wrong when the strikes hit Fury. We can't scramble his visuals."

"By the time he figures out that things are not what he expected, we'll have seized control, Gregor."

"From your lips, captain..."

The minutes began to drag again while the ships shed speed as they descended deeper into Arietis' gravity well and Siobhan felt her earlier tension return. This was not the kind of action she enjoyed, especially since they were still very much under the monitor's guns. If Corwin had lost some of his marbles, he might act before she could convince the crew of *Roberts* that their lives depended on cooperation.

"*Coromandel* has landed at Cintrea."

"Thank you, chief. You may drop the packages."

Four mines with landing thrusters were ejected from the aft missile tubes and quickly fell away toward the spaceport. *Roberts* and *Malabar* remained silent spectators to the action, with the latter patiently waiting for the order to disgorge the squadron of assault shuttles, an order that would never come.

"*Carnatic* has initiated landing procedures."

"And the strike, chief?"

"Two minutes to target. *Fawkes* is four minutes to target."

Siobhan took a deep breath to steady herself. If Corwin had not smelled a rat yet, he would in less than one hundred seconds.

"Up shields, chief. You may arm all weapons."

"Shall I run up our true colors, commodore?" Pushkin joked, although the set of his jaw belied the confident tone.

"Captain?" Penzara sounded alarmed. "We've just picked up multiple emergence signatures at the outer hyperlimit."

"What?" Siobhan was up in a flash and standing behind the sensor console. "No IFF and the readings don't look like they're Navy. How long at this speed?"

"Six hours."

"Splash," the sensor technician announced. "All four missiles have hit the objective. On screen now."

The view of the planet was replaced with a close magnification of Fury Station. The tech replayed the moment of impact, and they saw a sudden eruption of debris and dust as the hypersonic missiles slammed through the camouflaged domes masking the base's defensive weapons.

"Right on target!" Dunmoore clapped Penzara on the shoulder. "Well done, chief. Tell me *Carnatic* was on the ground."

"It was," he replied after checking the sensor logs. "Mister Devall just overflew the landing strip and distributed his own packages."

"Well," Pushkin drawled as he joined them at the gunnery console, "the bloody things might as well be useful for something other than taking up space in the magazine."

"I'm sure Brakal found them annoyingly effective," Dunmoore replied, smiling. "What's the status on the spaceport drop?"

"A few more minutes. *Coromandel* is in the middle of disembarking the ground pounders, so it'll take it a while to button up again for a takeoff. We'll have her boxed in before that."

Dunmoore turned to her first officer and looked at him questioningly.

"I guess it's almost time, Mister Pushkin. Unless you have some very last minute qualms. Once we drop the ECM, it either ends up with a shoot-out or a court-martial."

"Or both," he replied. "But it's the path we've chosen."

"Mister Kowalski," she said, "prepare to silence the drones. Once the packages land at Cintrea, give me a simultaneous link to the two grounded Avalon sloops."

"*Fawkes* has landed."

"Any movement from *Carnatic*, chief?"

"Negative. I think they've figured out what the directional mines are meant to do."

A few more tense minutes passed by until Penzara announced the arrival of the mine package at the Cintrea spaceport.

"Drop the ECM coverage and open the comm links, Mister Kowalski," Siobhan ordered, "and make sure Captain Devall can listen in."

"Done," she replied almost instantly.

"*Stingray* to *Carnatic* and *Coromandel*. This is Dunmoore." She waited for what turned out to be angry sounding acknowledgments.

"As you may have noticed," she continued, "your ships have been surrounded by directional mines. We've specially adapted mines typically carried by a frigate for star lane interdiction missions to give you both an incentive to cooperate. If I have those mines triggered, they will damage your ships enough that they will not lift off from Arietis ever again. Do you understand me?"

"Marek here," the gruff voice of *Carnatic*'s captain came on. "Acknowledged. We figured out you were pulling some dumbass stunt when you blew up the defensive arrays around Fury Station. If you're crazy enough to destroy Navy property, I guess you'll have no problems doing the same to private contractor ships."

"Desai here," a second voice said, identifying itself as the captain of *Coromandel*. "Acknowledged. If you set your mines off, you'll be killing a lot of our people."

"Then I suggest you be cooperative, both of you," she replied, her tone hard and devoid of emotion. "Fury Station and the Arietis

Squadron are about to undergo a change of command, and I need to make sure you Avalon folks will play ball."

"The alternative being?" Marek asked.

"Death."

A silence descended on the open radio frequency as the two mercenary officers digested her one-word threat.

"I've heard that you were a crazy bitch, Dunmoore," Desai finally said, "and I'll take no chances with the lives of our people. What is it that you want?"

"I want your crews to stay put while we evacuate the Navy and civilian folks. I'm shutting the Arietis operation down."

"What about us? We have a good two battalions on the ground. Where are they supposed to go?"

"When I'm done here, you can go home for all I care."

"Dunmoore, I'm trying hard to understand why you're doing this, and I'm failing. Care to help?" Marek asked.

Siobhan saw Kowalski wave at her and made a cutting motion to silence the audio.

"Admiral Corwin calling, sir. He doesn't sound happy."

"Now there's a surprise," Dunmoore replied, her voice dripping with sarcasm. "Keep him on hold. Audio on."

"Apologies. I had a call on another frequency. You were asking why I'm acting like a lunatic, weren't you Captain Marek?"

"Lunatic is a good word for it, Dunmoore. Raving lunatic is even better."

"We have evidence that illegal activities have occurred under Admiral Corwin's command, some of them involving Avalon Corporation employees, such as mistreatment of Commonwealth citizens who were illegally detained."

Desai burst out laughing. "You've committed mutiny for some space rabble? You *are* insane."

"The raid on Parvi VI," she continued, ignoring the mercenary, "gave us further evidence that illegal activities were being committed by troops under Admiral Corwin's control."

"How the hell do you define 'illegal' in the shadow of the Coalsack nebula? The law you're quoting stopped applying about fifty light years back."

"Not for the Navy," Dunmoore replied, "and not for anyone under contract to the Navy." She let them digest that tidbit before speaking again.

"Furthermore, I have evidence that Admiral Corwin was planning one or more actions against the legitimate authority of the Commonwealth government, in other words, treason."

"Ridiculous!" Marek exclaimed. "Why would the Admiralty send a traitor to command a top secret excavation site, as well as give him full authority over Arietis and the Avalon Corporation employees here?"

"Perhaps Admiral Corwin has become a tad unhinged," Siobhan suggested in her most reasonable tone. "I've seen how he's been setting himself up as the sole authority on the planet. I've also seen that he believes the artifacts recovered will provide the Commonwealth with wonder weapons to end the war when the evidence suggests the contrary. Considering one of the wonder weapons he discussed with me concerns an artificial virus tailored to attack a specific DNA sequence, in violation of the laws relating to biological warfare, I'd say he has a few marbles missing."

Dunmoore could almost picture the expression on Marek's and Desai's face. Humanity's last foray into bio-warfare, two centuries earlier, during the Second Migration War, had resulted in a planet contaminated with an agent that created the closest thing ever seen to a living death. It had to be thoroughly sterilized, and the thousands infected had to be killed. There had been no cure. The planet had remained off-limits on pain of death for over a century before anyone was allowed to set foot on its surface again.

"Okay, Dunmoore. If what you've said is true, then I'll grant you your point. Maybe Corwin is insane, but you're not exactly known as the purest of the pure in the Navy."

"A Commander Mathes is working in the engineering lab on Fury Station. If we can get your fellow Avalonians to stand down while she shows you what's really going on deep under the base, you might get a better appreciation of the truth."

"What would be her motivation?" Marek demanded.

"You'll have to ask her that yourself. She alerted me to the fact that Corwin was delusional about the so-called wonder weapons. Mister Devall, please accompany Captain Marek."

"I will, sir," he replied, "as soon as those idiots massing behind the sheds with some heavy weaponry stand down. I'd rather not have to cut a path through them with my main guns."

"Good point. Mister Kowalski, please raise Lieutenant Colonel Rissard, who seems to be the chief of staff, base commander and whatever else needs doing down there."

"Yes, sir. The admiral's still demanding to speak with you and he's using words I didn't think flag officers even knew."

Siobhan snorted. "I can think of one way to calm him down while I deal with the situation dirtside. Chief Penzara, activate the mines we've seeded around *Roberts* and have them ping the monitor. That ought to keep their attention on more immediate things."

"I have the Fury Station operations center," Kowalski said, "and if the man on the other end is Rissard, he's appropriately furious."

"Commodore Dunmoore!" Rissard's outrage was almost comical. "What's the meaning of this? You've destroyed Navy property in an unconscionable attack on this installation. Admiral Corwin informs me that you're not responding to his hails. Is there a reason you're acting as if you were in a state of mutiny?"

"Plenty of reasons, colonel. However, you'll be surrendering Fury Station to Captain Devall of *Fawkes* in the immediate and directing all personnel to stand down."

"You have no authority to issue those orders."

"Work with me, colonel, or oppose me — it makes no difference except to the people who are going to die, you included."

"And I thought you were a kindred spirit, Dunmoore. Another one who recognized Admiral Corwin's genius as the one man who could help us end the war."

Pushkin barely restrained a guffaw and made the universal signal for 'he's insane' by circling his index finger at the side of his head. Siobhan was inclined to agree. No one could spend this much time close to Corwin and not figure out something was not right, unless they shared the same delusions.

"I'll not debate this with you, colonel. Might makes right, and I have the might. *Fawkes* can systematically raze Fury Station's above ground structures and vaporize everyone within. Or I can send another kinetic strike from orbit."

"Damn you to hell then, Dunmoore. I'll see that a court-martial hangs you for this. I surrender this base."

"Good choice, colonel. Dunmoore out." She smiled wearily at Kowalski. "Time to beard the bear in his den. Get me Admiral Corwin and pipe it to my ready room. You're with me, Mister Pushkin."

*

"What's the meaning of this, Dunmoore?" Corwin's patrician face was as hard as it was red, eyes seeming to threaten immediate execution. "I gave you my trust, and you dare betray me? I'll see that you face execution for your treason. In fact, I'll gladly shoot you myself."

Siobhan repressed a surge of fear as she came face-to-face with the victim of her disloyalty. Corwin's charisma and charm had turned into their opposites, and his venom touched something atavistic deep within her.

"It's really quite simple, Admiral. I'm relieving you of command for violating an extensive list of articles in the Code of Naval Discipline, chief among them being treason. I have enough evidence to justify my actions to any board of inquiry."

"You won't make it back alive, Dunmoore. There's too much invested in our plans to allow anyone, especially a nobody like you, to thwart them. With my weapons, we will be unstoppable." He paused to take a deep breath as if trying to regain a measure of self-control. "If you cease this madness now, I can still save you and your ship from the consequences of your folly."

"Sorry Admiral but no." She studied his face for a few moments, noticing the tic in the corner of his eye had returned. "It is my considered opinion that you've lost the ability to command, as evidenced by your delusion that Fury Station is anything more than an archaeological dig. There are no wonder weapons and there never were. All you have are one hundred thousand-year-old artifacts, none of which are in a working condition, and which will take years, if not decades to reverse engineer if it's even possible at all. In the meantime, you're subjecting detainees to what is in effect slave labor."

"Wrong, Dunmoore. You're so wrong." He shook his head, an expression of mild disappointment softening his features. "You're young and reckless. You can't see the big picture, the potential we have here. Let's call this a successful training exercise and discuss the matter over a cup of coffee."

His sudden transformation into a reasonable, if somewhat displeased flag officer was like a knife twisting in her guts. She steeled herself.

"No, Admiral. I can't allow someone who is actively plotting to launch a raid on the government precinct on Earth to continue in command of naval and military forces, even if they're private contractors. I certainly cannot continue to obey your orders."

"You will follow my orders," he suddenly shouted, "or I will relieve *you* of command this instant. Where's your first officer?"

"Here." Pushkin stepped into range of the video pickup.

"Congratulations, commander. You're now the captain of *Stingray*."

"With all due respect, sir, I decline. I agree with Captain Dunmoore's actions in all respects."

"Then you too will pay," Corwin snarled. "You leave me no choice. I will have my people take control of *Stingray*, for the greater good of the Fleet. Stand down and prepare to be boarded."

Pushkin gave Dunmoore a glance that asked whether Corwin was truly delusional enough to believe that a Navy officer would turn her ship over to mercenaries.

"And you intend to enforce your order by which means?" Dunmoore asked.

"With the guns of *Roberts* of course," he smiled.

"You'd open fire on a Navy ship?"

"If it's in full mutiny, I have no choice." Corwin managed to sound eerily rational, and that increased their uneasiness. He was beginning to exhibit such rapid mood swings that it was becoming more and more evident he had lost his grip on reality.

"You'll find, Admiral, that *Roberts* will not even get off one salvo. We've seeded mines around her, and they'll turn her into a wreck in a matter of seconds, the moment we detect her guns powering up. I'm sure the folks on board don't wish to die so messily."

"They will do as I order," Corwin snarled, his mood shifting again.

"Shall we test that?" Dunmoore, now convinced Corwin had become unglued, felt certainty set in. "Mister Kowalski, I know you've been monitoring this transmission. Get me a separate channel to *Roberts*. I want to talk to her commanding officer."

"How dare you..." Corwin started. Then, he stopped and swung around, angrily shouting at someone out of range of the video pickup. The transmission suddenly cut out.

"I have Lieutenant Kylan for you, sir."

"Kylan, this is Captain Dunmoore." Pushkin noticed she dropped the 'commodore' title and decided it was on purpose, to distance herself from Corwin. "You're aware that I can destroy your ship with a single order?"

"I am," an older, fair-haired man replied, eyes narrowed as he fought to concentrate on her and ignore Corwin's ranting behind him.

"I suggest you and your crew evacuate to *Malabar* now. You may leave Admiral Corwin aboard *Roberts*, but make sure you lock him out of all systems."

Kylan nodded once, his eyes darting down at then back up at Siobhan.

"I could also place the admiral in detention," he suggested, "and put myself under your orders. In fact, my men have already restrained him. He objected to my speaking with you directly and did so by assaulting a member of my crew. Apparently I'm accused of consorting with mutineers."

"Remaining on your ship would be in aid of what exactly? It isn't FTL-capable, and my intent is to evacuate everyone from this system."

"A couple of my crew are locals, and a lot of us have friends or lovers down below. It's not much of a planet, but it's still worth keeping *Roberts* aloft as its only defense once you leave."

Dunmoore was astonished by the answer but then reflected that mercenaries were, for the most part, rootless. Perhaps some of them had decided that roots laid down here were better than nothing. She held his eyes silently before deciding the man was sincere.

"Very well. I suppose if there are some among your crew who don't want to stay, they can shift to *Malabar*."

"There aren't, captain. Admiral Corwin deliberately transferred those who had developed attachments to Arietis into *Roberts*, to give himself a crew more highly motivated to protect the planet."

"Then you leave me with a problem. I cannot allow Corwin to remain aboard a vessel I do not absolutely control."

"Have no fear," Kylan replied, sounding tired. "I'll be glad to see him go. We've had to watch Corwin take over the settlements, and it's not been pretty. There's no love lost for him among my folks."

At that moment, Dunmoore realized that she had given no real thought about what to do with Corwin if her takeover succeeded. Bringing him back in irons would trigger a massively publicized board of inquiry, possibly revealing Operation Valkyrie — if it was not a figment of Corwin's fevered imagination and Siobhan did not think it was. Certainly, the SSB had been snooping around enough to jump at any hint of impropriety by the Navy, and that would not do the war effort a damn bit of good either.

Reckless, reckless, she chided herself. It was one thing to be a tactical genius but another to be an idiot when it came to the wider political ramifications. A glance at Pushkin confirmed that he had come to the same conclusions.

"We can leave Corwin in his own internment camp," the first officer suggested, "and report it to Admiral Ryn. Kick the problem upstairs so to speak."

"It's not something we can consign to the subspace transmitter."

"No. That would mean leaving him alone for however long it takes us to get the info to someone who cares and then for the rescue party to come along. I'd hate to think what might happen in the interval. Stuff like the locals taking their revenge for instance."

"We may have a bigger problem," Kylan interrupted them. "No doubt you've picked up the emergence signatures not long ago."

"Yes." Dunmoore nodded.

"I suggest you have your sensor tech take another look. We're starting to get some resolution from the scans."

Pushkin rose and headed out to the bridge, leaving the door open behind him. He came back looking grim.

"Six ships. We can't identify their signatures, which means they're either masking, or they're not in our registry."

"Type?"

"From what we can make out, they're all about sloop-sized with powerful drives and that typically means well armed."

"Reivers?" Dunmoore asked.

"More than likely," Kylan replied. "We've seen similar signatures before this. Intruders tried a hit-and-run ten months ago. They didn't get past the outer moon's orbit, but close enough for a few swipes from my guns."

"Six ships likely means a whole clan. That would be a tad unusual."

"They may have gotten wind of what's being dug up on Arietis, captain. Or they're related to the folks we raided on Parvi VI."

"Or both," Dunmoore said dryly. "That could mean our sneaky friends might be involved."

"Sneaky friends?" Kylan sounded puzzled.

"The Special Security Bureau seems to be involved in some more or less shady dealings in the Coalsack. Of course, their dealings are always shady," she added with a shrug. "*Fawkes* very closely resembles a ship we intercepted last year while it was operating undercover on behalf of the SSB."

"Ah." The mercenary's face lit up. "Strangely enough, that makes a lot of sense. It ties in with some of the other doings we've observed. Would the Black Nova *Maru* ships perchance be involved?"

"So it appears." Siobhan nodded. She was struck by a disturbing thought. "What puzzles me is why they've appeared now, just as we've got three of our ships on the ground, an admiral in irons and the high orbitals seeded with mines. If I were paranoid, I'd say this wasn't a coincidence."

"Mister Kowalski," she called out, "go back through the sensor logs and see if we picked up any stray messages coming from the vicinity of Arietis, directed toward the outer system."

Kylan had a sudden look of realization in eyes.

"Let me check our logs as well, captain. As you know, we also serve as retransmission station for the ground units."

Dunmoore waited impatiently as both her signals officer and the monitor's commander searched.

"You have a suspicion, sir?" Pushkin studied her intently as if trying to read her mind.

"Several, but only one of them really makes sense. If this isn't a coincidence, then our inbound friends knew about the raid on Fury Station ahead of time and waited until they got a trigger message to call them in."

"Captain," Kylan's face reappeared on the viewer, "our logs show the commo array retransmitted a coded message ten hours before Admiral Corwin arrived on *Roberts* to watch the exercise. A message with the same encoding signature was also sent six days ago."

"So the first one went out after Corwin approved the raid and the second one once he'd decided at what time he'd leave Fury Station." Pushkin nodded. "I think I see what you were getting at, captain. But it doesn't tally with the fact that we caught Parvi with its pants down."

Siobhan smiled. "We came into the Parvi system thirty-six hours ahead of the planned schedule, which is why we saw the *Oko Maru* skedaddle with whatever the spooks had her carry. Never underestimate the power of unpredictability."

"And now?" Kylan asked, puzzled by Siobhan's good humor.

"Was there any further message relayed from the ground since the one you reported?"

"No, and there won't be," the mercenary replied with finality.

"So whoever is bearing down on us doesn't know about the rather forcible change of command." She rubbed her hands.

"And this helps us how, sir?"

"The enemy is expecting Admiral Corwin to react. Obviously if the SSB have a spy on the ground, they'll have been briefed about his quirks and will be playing to those. They don't know that they're going to face my particular quirks."

"Got it." Kylan nodded. "What do you want me to do?"

"Speak with your fellow Avalon Corporation skippers and convince them that we need to face the oncoming raiders together. Then button up your ship and prepare to defend the high orbitals."

— Twenty-Four —

"Mister Devall, we have a problem and part of it is on your end."

"The folks on *Carnatic* are quiet, Captain," he responded, staring at Dunmoore with undisguised curiosity from the video screen, "So far Guthren has gotten no push-back from the mercs on the base."

"It's worse. There's an oncoming force of at least six ships headed this way, and I don't see it as a coincidence. Someone, let's say for argument's sake the SSB, wants to take over the operation here — the digs and supposed weapons, not the other thing we discussed. That someone has a plant on Fury Station and said plant tells his buddies that we're about to throw the Arietis defenses in turmoil via a heavy-duty training exercise."

"You intercepted a transmission?" Devall asked, sounding dubious.

"Not intercepted, no. Someone at the base used *Roberts'* automated relay to send a coded message out just after the plan was approved and then once we knew when Corwin would leave the ground."

"Were you able to decode it?"

"I've got Kathryn trying, but seeing as we're short-handed and need to get ready for action — real action — I can't spare much of her time."

"Any idea where I should look?"

"Divert Guthren to the operations center and arrest everyone there, including Colonel Rissard."

Devall's stared at her in surprise.

"Yes, including the Marine. They've been known to go bad as often as anyone. What I don't want is a spy sending messages detailing our activities. *Roberts* has shut down its relay, but as the raiders get closer, they'll be able to send directly from the ground."

"Will do. Was there anything else?"

"When the landing party's got Fury Station secured, have them assemble the folks who aren't part of the Avalon garrison somewhere close to the landing strip but under cover." She paused as another thought struck her. "Scratch that. Evacuate the base completely. Load everyone aboard *Fawkes* and *Carnatic*, garrison included and take them to the Cintrea spaceport."

"Fury's the target, then." Devall made it a statement.

"Yes, and I'm afraid that it might be a case of if I can't have it, nobody can."

"Got it. Will you be talking to the Avalon folks?"

"Right after this. Dunmoore, out." She turned to Kowalski. "Open a channel to all ships."

When five faces stared out at her from the main screen, she smiled harshly.

"As you all know by now, we're facing a situation that could determine whether we make it home in one piece or not. I've taken command of all naval and contracted forces in the Arietis system while Admiral Corwin is under arrest, pending serious and possibly capital charges."

None of the mercenaries reacted but their eyes did radiate a kind of sick interest.

"If any of you are not prepared to obey my orders, do tell me now. We already have one suspected mole on the base. My landing party is taking care of it as we speak but I don't need someone else ready to stab me in the back. At this point, I'm giving you an out, no harm, no foul, other than Avalon forfeits part or all of the bond deposited with the Adjudicating Authority for non-performance of the contract."

When she got no response, she continued.

"I have reason to believe that the ships headed for us are interested in what lies hidden beneath Fury Station. I also have reason to believe that they'll destroy it rather than leave it in our hands. On that basis, I am ordering that Fury be evacuated.

Captain Marek, you're to take all Avalon personnel aboard and transport them to Cintrea. Captain Devall, you'll do the same with Fleet personnel and internees. Once you've discharged your passengers, and that includes Major Ocano's troops, Captain Marek, you'll boost into orbit. I'll have a battle plan drawn up by then. Captain Desai, you can finish disembarking Major Terwan's troops and boost out immediately."

When she heard no objections, she said, "I think you're all experienced enough to know that the only way we're going to get out of this without suffering too many losses is by fighting as a squadron. Any ship that ends up with enough damage to keep it from going FTL isn't leaving this system. Let's make sure that doesn't happen. My goal is to wipe out the force approaching so that they don't get a second chance the moment we leave."

"Captain?"

"What is it Mister Devall?"

"I've just got word from Mister Guthren. He's got the operations center on lock-down and one furious Marine colonel threatening him with the mother of all courts-martial."

"Any indication who our mole might be?"

"Negative."

"Take the ops center personnel aboard *Fawkes*. I'd rather not take chances. Try and treat Colonel Rissard with the courtesy due to his rank, but never forget you're the sole master after God aboard your ship."

"Understood, sir," Devall grinned. "I might even put the good colonel to work on the guns. He should know something about them."

"Keep in mind that Rissard is Corwin's good buddy," Marek warned. "None of us had much time for him, and he knew it. If Corwin is as loony as you say, commodore, then Rissard is just as far around the bend."

Dunmoore lips twitched with amusement at Marek's use of the title 'commodore' for the first time since her private little coup d'état. It meant the other woman had acknowledged her authority, and that was all to the good since she appeared to be the straw boss among the mercenaries.

"What about the internees at the camp?" Marek asked.

"They should be all right for now. We'll pick them up with the rest of your troops when this is over."

"Then I'd suggest you commandeer the freighter sitting beside Desai at Cintrea. Otherwise, it'll be a long ride back crammed into our sloops."

Siobhan bit off a curse. One more thing she had forgotten.

"Captain Desai, please have Major Terwan secure the freighter as gently as possible." She paused. "Was there anything else I may have omitted?"

"Perhaps one more thing," Kylan suggested. "Can you do something about those mines you left around me? I'd rather not have us bump into any of them in the heat of battle, assuming the oncoming ships make it this far."

"No fear on that account," Dunmoore smiled. "Contrary to popular belief, those things are harmless when they're on remote command settings, but we'll spread them out a bit, just in case."

*

"*Carnatic* is lifting off, captain."

"Thank you, Mister Kowalski. I'm going to feel a lot better when we break away from Arietis and give ourselves some maneuvering room."

"At least, other than that unfortunate freighter, we've no vulnerable ships sitting on the ground."

"Thank the universe for small blessings, Number One. As long as we keep them far enough from the high orbitals, even it should be safe."

"At least until *Roberts* runs out of ammunition."

"That could apply to just about any of us," Siobhan shrugged. "Without resupply, we'll be pelting each other with rocks if we let it drag on."

"The approaching ships are decelerating," the sensor technician announced, "but I'm getting strange mass readings."

"On screen." Siobhan shot forward in her seat, an ugly thought gnawing at her.

"Crap," Pushkin swore as he interpreted the sensor data. "Part of the mass is decelerating while the rest is moving along at the same clip."

"How can that be?" Penzara asked, puzzled.

"The buggers have been using their tractor beams as mass drivers," Siobhan explained. "They've released whatever they were pushing or towing, and it's heading toward us at the original velocity while the ships have fired braking thrusters."

Dunmoore and Pushkin looked at each other.

"You were mentioning rocks a moment ago, captain."

"Rocks, cargo pods with an antimatter-filled magnetic bottle, missile packages. It could be anything." She rubbed her scar with her fingertips. "The primary goal is to screen their approach and force us to waste defensive ordnance."

"We've seen what an antimatter explosive device can do." Pushkin shook his head. "If that's a reiver clan, they've become way too inventive for comfort. What do you intend, captain?"

"Trying to swing around will take too long from our current course. They'll be within the inner moon's orbit by then and capable of bombarding anything they want. Whoever thought up this scheme timed it well. We were planning on a meeting engagement, trusting in the longer range and greater precision of our and the Avalon ships' weapons, and especially the greater weight of *Stingray*'s broadside. By throwing up a screen, they've effectively negated much of that advantage."

"It's almost as if they've been reading our game book."

"Almost, Mister Pushkin. Almost, but not quite. They obviously knew what ships we could put up against them, and it's no great feat to figure out how we'd react from what's almost a standstill." She rose to shake out the tension building in her shoulders.

"Chief, do we have any recon birds left?"

"Just the one. We converted the others into ECM drones."

"It'll be of no use to us sitting in the launcher if we get hit by whatever they have coming at us. We need to see what we're up against. Launch at the center of mass when ready."

"*Carnatic* has reached orbit," Kowalski advised a few minutes after the drone was away. "All ships are ready."

"Make to Arietis Squadron: break orbit in sequence and prepare to meet the enemy."

One after the other, the ships accelerated away from the planet, leaving only *Roberts* behind as the last line of defense. On Dunmoore's orders, the squadron adopted a diamond formation with *Stingray* in the middle and the sloops around her at the four cardinal points. The diamond was not ideal for pursuit, nor did it force the enemy to engage a dispersed target, but it did allow the ships to concentrate their fire and give each other maximum support.

Time seemed to flow ever more slowly as the two forces neared that point in space, beyond the outer moon's orbit, where their paths would intersect. Ahead of the flotilla, a small, stealthy drone sped toward the cloud of matter screening the advancing ships, its sensors reaching out to discover what devilry the enemy had prepared for the squadron.

Siobhan forced herself, with increasing difficulty, to project a calm, confident exterior. Inside, she was seething with anxiety. A ship-to-ship fight was something she understood intimately. Leading a multi-ship force into battle was new, however, and the added weight of responsibility for those other vessels and their crews was pressing down on her.

Part of her wished she could have tossed this problem back to Admiral Corwin, but she knew that it was not an option; it had not been an option from the moment she decided to relieve him. Now, she would have to assume all the consequences of her decision. She, and she alone commanded at Arietis.

Pushkin, from his console, kept an eye on her. He was all too conscious of her state of mind. After spending so much time in close quarters with Dunmoore, the first officer had learned to read the slightest signals that betrayed her state of mind and he could read them now, in the faint twitching of her jaw muscles, the repressed finger movements, the frequent rolling of her shoulders to alleviate stress. The enemy held the initiative, and it bothered her enormously. She was no doubt blaming herself for getting them into this situation.

"Sir, we're getting telemetry from the drone," Penzara said, raising his hand to gain her attention.

"Put it on, chief." Part of her flinched as she used the title, remembering again that Guthren was stuck on *Fawkes*. There had been no time to shift him and the landing party over, and *Stingray* was very short-handed for battle. Worse, she did not have the most experienced people, including the most experienced helmsman at the controls. Another failure for her debit column.

Pushkin whistled slowly. "Nasty. They've put everything in there but the wardroom table."

"Some of the asteroid fragments seem to have been seeded with improvised explosive devices." Penzara pointed at the readout. "And those things look exactly like the trap someone tried to spring on us weeks ago: there's no other explanation but that they're filled with antimatter."

"I've seen enough," Siobhan said. She caught herself tapping on the arm of her chair and forcefully withdrew her hand. "Send the drone into the nearest antimatter IED pod. Might as well end its life usefully."

Moments later, a tiny bloom appeared on the visual pickups, leaving the bridge crew mildly stunned.

"That was one hell of an explosion," Dunmoore finally said, "for us to have seen it at this distance. I'd expect it blew a fair sized hole in the screen."

"Maybe they overdid it," Pushkin replied, a hint of hope raising the timbre of his voice.

"It would appear so. Antimatter IEDs aren't the easiest things in the galaxy to build, but they're easy to over-fill. Chief, now that we have a couple of pods registered, fire a missile at each. Try to time them for simultaneous contact. The one that just blew got their attention. Maybe by popping off the rest all at once we can push them into doing something we can exploit. If nothing else, for the price of a half dozen birds we get a clear path to fire down their throats."

"Missiles away," Penzara announced, moments later.

They watched the orange glow of the drives wink out of sight as the warheads accelerated at a rate that went beyond what a starship's inertial dampeners could sustain. Missiles and IED pods converged at incredible speed and when the impact happened, it came as much of a surprise for *Stingray*'s crew as it must have been for the attackers. Six more blooms at ragged intervals erupted simultaneously.

"Now, all we have to do is dodge rocks," Siobhan said with an air of satisfaction.

"Rocks with mines," Pushkin reminded her.

"Those we can take with our guns. I doubt they'll have wasted magnetic bottles on smaller warheads." Dunmoore sat back, feeling more confident now that they had trumped one of the enemy's aces. "Any indication yet which one of them is the lead ship?"

"If they're communicating, it's by laser. No radio transmissions to be detected, captain," Pine replied from the signals station.

Siobhan's eyes narrowed as she studied the tactical schematic. Her fingers started drumming, but she swiftly moved her hand to her lap.

"They're in an inverted arrowhead formation," she mused, "pretty standard for raiders going after a single ship or maybe a pair in consort. Nine times out of ten, the clan leader is at the back of the formation."

"Able to run down any problems and protected from the front by the lesser ships." Pushkin nodded. "Also the best position to talk to all ships via laser."

"Any more resolution on their emissions?"

"Some," Penzara reported. "One of them isn't too far off from a class of ships we have in the registry."

"Let me guess," Dunmoore replied, sardonic amusement creasing the corners of her mouth. "A Black Nova *Maru*."

"Got it in one, sir," the chief nodded. "It's at the back of the formation."

"No." She shook her head after digesting Penzara's report. "It's not the lead ship. The *Maru*'s at the back so it can escape if things go wrong. No reiver clan, no matter how well paid, would let an outsider command a raid. Throw up the emissions curves of the other five ships side-by-side for comparison."

"Sir," Pine interrupted, "incoming from *Fawkes*. Mister Devall."

"Put him on."

"Commodore," Devall sounded excited, or at least what passed for excited in his case. "If you're looking for the lead ship, it isn't the one in the usual position at the back – that's a *Maru*. Our little *Fawkes* here has some nifty sensor gear we've only begun to appreciate. Did you put up an emissions comparison for the other five ships yet?"

"We just did," she replied, privately pleased at Devall's quick thinking and initiative.

"Look at the emissions of the one that's to our starboard, second in from the end."

"What are we seeing?" She asked.

"The fusion reactor emissions are just a little cleaner than the others, which means it's either newer or is getting more love."

"And a chieftain's ship will be more modern or get more love, or both." Siobhan nodded. "Chief?"

"Concur," Penzara nodded.

"Alright." Dunmoore clapped her hands. "Time to assign targets and commence saturation. We're going to get one pass, and if we don't stop them or slow them down enough, *Roberts* will have to deal with whatever gets through. It'll take us too long to turn back in time. Give me an open channel to the squadron."

Rapidly and in succession, the images of the four other captains appeared on the screen.

"Folks, herewith the target assignments. The enemy ships have been designated Tango One through Tango Six, as you'll now see on your own tactical schematics." She waited until they all nodded in acknowledgment.

"Tango Two has been tentatively identified as the lead ship, based on the quality of her emissions. Tango Six has been tentatively identified as a Black Nova Shipping unit, and I suspect she's in the tail position to enable a quick escape if the attack fails. This means she may well carry a controller from whatever Commonwealth interest is paying the reivers, such as the SSB. It makes her the second highest value target after Tango Two. You're all well aware that a reiver clan's cohesion is highly dependent on the chieftain, so taking him out early will help disorganize them. Tango Two will, therefore, be *Stingray*'s primary target. *Malabar*, you will take Tango One, the ship furthest to starboard; *Carnatic*, you'll take Tango Three, the lead ship on the port side of the arrowhead formation; *Coromandel*, Tango Four behind it and

Fawkes, Tango Five at the far end of the enemy's port side line. Tango Six will likely disengage if we manage to savage the others, so he remains a secondary target for the first salvo. Shoot to disable but don't bother trying to destroy — time is of the essence. Once we've sailed by each other, we're going to have to come around, and that's a stern chase we can't win by the time we're on the return tack. *Roberts* can maybe handle one, at best two enemy sloops for a short period of time, but that doesn't account for the damage the enemy can inflict on the ground. They may still be towing projectiles for kinetic strikes. We will fire missiles as a squadron salvo on my command, not before. You're allowed to expend up to two-thirds of your birds, but no more – it's guns after that."

"Do we wear ship on your command or once we're passed effective engagement range?" Marek asked.

"You can start veering the moment you pass optimal range. Once you're on the new course, accelerate as you see fit and engage on your own initiative if you get in range before we do. I may not be in a position to organize coordinated maneuvering. Any other questions?" When she saw nothing other than heads shaking, she said, "Thank you, captains. Please stand by for the order to begin engaging the enemy. Dunmoore, out."

*

Though the two formations hurtled toward each other, each second that elapsed until the inevitable clash became a little lesson in the exquisite agony of waiting patiently. Missiles had to be fired at just the right moment: too early, and the enemy had a better chance of knocking them out before they reached their targets; too late and the guns would not get enough time to pour through a weakened or punctured shield to eat through the hull.

In the dim battle lights, the bridge crew's faces were bathed in the glow of their consoles and had taken on a demonic cast as their eyes stared intently at the tactical schematic, waiting for the moment they would let loose the opening salvo.

"Optimal range in thirty seconds," Penzara reported.

"Signals, warn the others," Dunmoore said, her voice low and husky.

"Sir," Penzara sounded alarmed. "Tango Two just launched something, and it's accelerating like the devil. What the...?" He cursed. "Sensors say it looks like a torpedo with a couple of missile drives stuck up its back end instead of a jump drive."

A torpedo meant proper antimatter warhead, one powerful enough to ruin *Stingray*'s day if it exploded against the shields.

"Heading?"

"We're getting active pings from the thing, so I'd say it's coming for *Stingray*."

"Guns, open fire on that thing the moment it enters extreme range. Signals, transmit the data on the new target to all ships."

"They're nuts," Pushkin said. "Sloops aren't big enough for proper torpedo tubes, which means they had to have bodgered a feed to fuel the warhead."

"Or they carried an armed warhead from wherever they came."

"That still counts as nuts, captain, more in fact."

She ignored his comment, preferring to focus her full attention on the new threat.

"The tangos just fired missiles, twenty birds in the salvo," Penzara said. "We're getting painted like crazy."

"Signals, ask the other ships if they're being targeted by the oncoming missiles."

"You think we're being given special attention?" Penzara asked.

"Aye. Stands to reason: get big sister out of the fight and the others will be easier to sweep away. If they maul us with that torpedo, the missiles close behind it will hurt."

"Sir, the other ships confirm they're not being painted."

"Good. Divide the anti-missile assignments between the ships at five each and transmit. They're to open fire on their own when in range. This is where diamond formation will come in handy," Dunmoore smiled. "Where's the torpedo?"

"Ten thousand kilometers away."

"Fire all guns."

"Firing now." Streaks of light smeared the space ahead of the squadron as plasma rounds streaked out from all ships at Penzara's command.

Seconds later, a bright flash washed out the screen and *Stingray*'s shields lit up like a demented aurora borealis as competing energies fought for dominance, blinding the sensors and crippling target acquisition.

The frigate, as the torpedo's intended target, bore the brunt of the radiation wave, but the sloops did not go unscathed, though their shields were able to repel the onslaught. When the burst dissipated, the missiles had come close enough that *Stingray* on her own would have been overwhelmed. As it was, the five ships were able to swat them all down save for one, which exploded against the reinforced bow shield and buckled the energy sphere protecting the frigate's hull. Feedback howled through the ship as some systems overloaded, their protection circuits tripping them off.

"Damage report."

"Bow shield is down thirty percent, but no damage to the generator."

"To all ships, fire a full salvo at your assigned targets," Dunmoore ordered, nodding at Pushkin. Ten seconds later, she repeated the order, and the next salvo sped away, and then the next.

"If that doesn't saturate their defenses, I might as well retire on Arietis," she muttered between clenched teeth.

"*Fawkes* and *Malabar* report two-thirds expended."

"Let's hope we punch some serious holes, chief."

Far ahead, bright lights began to wink as the reiver ships engaged the oncoming missiles with their guns.

"Three birds down. Four." Penzara was counting off the enemy hits as missiles disintegrated under the plasma rounds. "Now eight.... First salvo depleted. Not bad shooting for a bunch of lunatic barbarians."

"Has the suspected *Maru* fired?"

"Negative, captain. Engaging the second salvo now."

"Make to all ships: prepare to open fire with your guns."

"Third salvo within enemy range. We have two missile detonations. Tango One and Five have received direct hits. Now Tango Two as well. Tango One, a second hit: shields are down.

Tango Three has three hits: two against the shields, one on the hull. She's leaking radiation badly."

Then they were within gunnery range, and blooms of plasma began sprouting on every hull. The dull vibration of the guns pumping out round after round permeated the ship in a syncopated beat that put Siobhan's nerves further on edge. With the melee joined, she no longer controlled the battle and did not enjoy that momentary helplessness one bit. It was gunner against gunner and the one with the fastest targeting sensor would win. Her turn would come again once they had fought their way through.

Energy struck the frigate's shields with metronomic regularity, but she gave back more than she received and Tango Two began streaming clouds of crystallized gasses through a black rent in her hull. Siobhan smiled grimly at the sight: the reiver chieftain would not survive unscathed, and if Penzara was lucky, he would not make it at all.

"Captain, we're being targeted by *Malabar*." The sensor tech sounded more outraged than alarmed as he shouted out the warning.

Dunmoore, mind immersed in the madness of battle, just nodded, adding *Malabar*'s treachery to the calculus of the Arietis problem and coming up with a logical answer.

"Return fire with everything that'll bear."

Fortunately, the range was too short for missiles. Even the slowest defensive array could pick them off while they were merely beginning to accelerate.

Then, with surprising suddenness, they were through the enemy formation, Dunmoore's ships already turning to port in a wide circle, shedding forward speed as their thrusters pushed them onto a new course. The frigate's guns kept hammering away at the rapidly accelerating *Malabar* in a last ditch attempt to prevent her from steering on the opposite tack and leaving the squadron formation.

"What in the name of all that's holy happened?" Pushkin asked.

"Evidently, the captain and at least part of the crew are in the SSB's pay. There can be no other answer," Siobhan replied. "It fits quite well. Thoran was privy to all tactical discussions, knew all dispositions, and probably originated the messages to the enemy, via the ground station."

"But why?"

"Think about it, Gregor. *Malabar* was the one sent to chase the *Oko Maru*. Perhaps they caught it and were offered a hell of a deal."

"Then why did they open fire on us? Even Thoran is smart enough to know he couldn't stand up to a frigate."

"I can only guess that when all their ploys to degrade us failed, he was ordered to carry out an abortive last ditch attempt. Our shields on that side were still at full power, so it was a foregone conclusion." She suppressed a yawn. "Guns, report."

"Tango Two is dead in space; Tango One is veering back to the hyper limit and streaming radiation from damaged fuel cells. Tango Three..."

Just then, a brilliant explosion aft stilled Penzara.

"Tango Three," he continued after a moment, "has been reduced to its constituent atoms. Tangos Four, Five, and Six are still headed for Arietis. Five has damaged shields. Four and Six have minor damage, with Six being virtually intact."

"Our side?" Dunmoore asked.

"*Malabar* is running toward the hyper limit with Tango One and good riddance to bad trash," Chief Penzara growled.

"Not necessarily, Chief," Pushkin countered. "That makes two who could sneak back while we're otherwise occupied."

"Sir, incoming from *Fawkes*."

She turned to the signals console. "Put it on."

"Captain, Devall here. The tangos got a pair of lucky hits on us. We have a lower hull breach and an electrical fire. Thank God Syten and Guthren were with us. They took the damage control party down immediately and got the fire under control. We won't be moving until we can reroute the power conduits, but mercifully they came nowhere near the antimatter fuel tanks."

"Any casualties?"

"Two. I had the detainees from the Fury operations center in one of the lower holds. Colonel Rissard is severely injured, as is one of the Avalon techs. It seems they were shaken around rather messily when we were hit. I expect they'll survive. One of the good things about running a sloop with a small crew: they're mostly deep within the hull and a lot harder to kill."

"When you're under power again, return to Arietis. We'll try to come up their skirts but by the time we finish changing course and accelerating again, I expect stopping the first strike will have been mostly *Roberts*' job."

"Acknowledged. *Fawkes*, out."

"*Carnatic* and *Coromandel* report minor damage but have finished tacking and are accelerating on the return course." Penzara said.

"How long before we catch up?"

"About ten minutes after the enemy reaches Arietis orbit, captain."

"Warn *Roberts* they'll have to entertain our guests for a while."

*

The hours that passed left Dunmoore suspended in a state of mild agony. She had to maintain the delicate balance between accelerating *Stingray* to catch up with the reivers and not pouring on so much delta-vee that decelerating at Arietis became a problem. The two remaining Avalon Corporation ships were decelerating already so that when the frigate caught up, they would pass the inner moon's orbit at the same time.

"A cred for your thoughts?" Pushkin asked, glancing at her over the rim of his coffee mug. She had taken refuge in her ready room and left the bridge to Kowalski, lest her frustration spread to a crew already on edge. The perceptive first officer had joined her if only to make sure she did not snarl at her own reflection to pass the time.

"Engagements in orbit can become messy very fast, Gregor," she replied, "especially if missiles fail to hit their target and do to the rift valley settlements what we did to Fury Station. This isn't their fight."

"A gun to gun battle, then." He nodded. "Pounding on each other at close range while enjoying the untold pleasures of orbital mechanics that make maneuvering starships so close to a gravity well a real art form. I think we'll do better at it than the reivers."

Dunmoore snorted. "I should hope so, as long as we hit them fast and hard. If they manage to play hide and seek, it'll be a different story. They can dip deeper into the atmosphere than we can."

"We can't dip into the atmosphere at all."

"Precisely."

The intercom chimed.

"Bridge to captain. Incoming from *Roberts*: we have engaged the enemy."

"Thank you," Dunmoore replied, fighting off a renewed surge of anxiety. It would not be long now before they were in range to support the monitor, but it still might be too late.

She stood up and tugged at her tunic. "Time, Gregor."

"Aye."

On the bridge, Kowalski made way for her and took the sailing master's console.

"Pine, make to the squadron," Dunmoore ordered as she sat in the command chair, "*Carnatic* to engage Tango Five and *Coromandel* to take Tango Four. *Stingray* will take Tango Six. We have some unfinished business with the *Maru*. We'll adopt echelon formation, with us in the lead and attempt to gain control of the higher orbitals."

"Both have acknowledged," the signals petty officer replied moments later. "*Carnatic* reminds us that they've expended two-thirds of their missile stocks."

"Then they'll have to make the remaining ones count," Siobhan replied somewhat tartly. "Don't transmit that," she hastily added.

"Too bad we don't have those assault shuttles *Malabar* carried," Pushkin said. "They're fully armed and ready."

"Armed for a ground attack. They wouldn't have lasted long enough against ships to make a difference with what they have."

"Right." He nodded. "I forgot you knew all about the usefulness, or should I say uselessness, of small craft in ship-to-ship engagements."

"Anything more from *Roberts*?" Dunmoore asked.

"Negative, sir. They've been off the net since they advised they were engaging the enemy."

Siobhan and Pushkin exchanged looks, but she shook her head. "Probably too busy fighting to send a stream of reports to a fidgety acting commodore."

"*Carnatic* and *Coromandel* coming up on visual," Penzara said, putting them on the side screen.

Both sloops bore black streaks where the enemy fire had punched through the shields but neither of them was streaming gasses or radiation, so they either had retained hull integrity or fixed any holes during the transit back to Arietis.

Up to now, Dunmoore had been impressed with the calm professionalism of the mercenary captains and their crews, and she idly wondered how good the pay was on the private side. Not that the Navy would release her from Service until the war was over or that she would seriously consider the private sector short of being dismissed, but the latter alternative might not be too far-fetched if the Admiralty took exception to her assuming command by force.

"Coming into visual range of *Roberts*."

"Put her on the main screen."

Plasma blooms were erupting from the monitor in a constant stream, but her hull bore more black streaks than the sloops, including a few visible punctures. Two of the reiver ships were bombarding her from a higher orbit, jockeying to keep within range while trying to dodge her guns.

"Where's the *Oko Maru*?" Siobhan asked. "She's not with her playmates. Scan the moons."

"No need, sir," the sensor tech said. "I have multiple missile signatures coming around the outer one. She's there all right."

"Target?"

"We are. All warheads are painting us."

"That makes no sense," Pushkin objected. "They'd have a better chance at taking down one of our sloops."

"No, it does make sense," Dunmoore pointed at the tactical schematic. "She's running. That brace of missiles is to keep us busy."

A small icon identified as Tango Six broke away from the moon on a vector to the hyperlimit.

"Abandoning their reiver friends?"

Dunmoore shrugged. "Never reinforce failure. They had hoped to catch us with three ships on the ground and the fourth a traitor. *Stingray* alone against five reivers would have worked just fine. The entire Arietis Squadron, even minus *Malabar*, not so much."

"Sir, *Roberts* just launched a shuttle."

"Abandoning ship?" Dunmoore asked

"Only if they've left their guns on automatic. She's still pouring out effective fire," Penzara replied.

The shuttle appeared to drop quickly toward the atmosphere but then broke out of the monitor's protective shadow, a victim of the same orbital mechanics that were causing the reivers so much trouble in subduing the makeshift station.

"Whoever's flying it doesn't seem to have much experience," Dunmoore commented. "They'll get hit the moment one of the bad guys notices."

But the reivers were too busy trading shots with the monitor to care and the shuttle quickly vanished.

"Time to put paid to the last two buggers," Dunmoore said. "Make to the other ships: fire one-half of your remaining missiles at your designated target at my signal. We'll split our salvo between them. Chief, as soon as they've acknowledged, you may fire at will."

Moments later, missiles erupted from launchers on three ships and sped toward their targets, drives glowing on the visual pickup.

Unbeknownst to any of them, an intruder was rushing toward Arietis at the same time, its drive off and its electronics, for all intents and purposes, dead. A sharp-eyed sensor tech would have picked it up if it were not for the many emission signatures filling an ever-decreasing volume of space as the squadron joined the slugfest with the reivers.

"Let's see how they like being caught between two fires," Pushkin noted with satisfaction.

"Why are they not running, now that we're almost on them?" Penzara asked.

"Who knows?" She shrugged. "Their clan leader's dead and their SSB control ran so there's no one to tell them to break off the attack. Reivers haven't always been known for using their brains more than their brawn."

"Maybe the SSB have a hold on them."

"Come back with your shield or on it, Mister Pushkin?" Kowalski asked.

"That's what I'm thinking. The SSB are scummy enough to be blackmailers or worse."

"Can't say I have much sympathy for reivers," Siobhan replied with a dismissive grimace.

"They're engaging the missiles," Penzara reported. "*Roberts* just got a hit on Tango Five's hull. She's venting gasses. Coming into gunnery range now."

"Open fire the moment all birds have either hit or been destroyed. Signals, send the same order to the others."

A massive flare filled the screen with unexpected brilliance.

"Tango Five just exploded. It must have been a catastrophic hit."

"Let's finish this, then. Open fire on Tango Four with all guns."

They watched the plasma punch a hole in shields already weakened by missiles that had reached their target and eat through the reiver's hull.

"Shall we offer them a chance to surrender?" Pushkin asked.

"Would there be a point?" She asked. "They know…"

Another bright flare filled the screen, and Tango Four joined its clan mates wherever it was dead reivers went. The bridge crew was about to whoop with the joy and relief of victory, especially one bought at so little cost when Penzara's voice cut through the animated babble.

"Sir, we've just picked up a massive explosion at the site of Fury Station."

"What?" Siobhan rose from her chair in astonishment.

"I'm reviewing the sensor logs," the chief replied. "It looks like a kinetic strike by something relatively large. There doesn't appear to be anything left of the surface buildings."

"How is that possible?" Pushkin demanded.

"Perhaps the *Oko Maru* left us a parting gift: if they couldn't seize the digs, they'd make sure the Navy couldn't continue exploiting them. Can we get a visual?"

"One moment, please. The sensors need to cut through the dust cloud."

Then, the ghostly image of a ruined landscape filled the screen. Whatever struck Fury had created a deep, wide crater and Siobhan knew without waiting for further scans that most of the tunnels in the plateau above the ravine floor had collapsed.

"What size of projectile could have made such a mess?" She asked.

"Larger than an anti-ship missile for sure, sir. Much larger. Probably something almost as big as a sublight tug, preferably one filled with the densest material they could find and assuredly at terminal velocity when it hit."

Pushkin grunted. "Do you think that thing might have had Black Nova markings on it?"

"At this point, does it matter?"

"I suppose not, captain."

She turned to the signals petty officer. "Pine, try and raise *Roberts*. I'd like a status report, and I'd like to know why a shuttle took off in the middle of the fight. Incidentally, have we picked up the shuttle's track again?"

Before Penzara could reply, the speaker crackled.

"*Roberts* here, commodore. You guys pulled up just in time. A couple more rounds of pounding and we'd be taking structural damage. As it is, we have a few weeks' worth of repairs already. I can't believe we poured so much fire at the bastards before they finally blew up; our ammo is over half gone."

"Any casualties?"

"Two dead, three wounded. Admiral Corwin escaped, so I don't know what might have happened to him."

"That was Corwin in the shuttle, then?"

"Yeah. The compartment he was in got a glancing hit, and it buckled the bulkhead enough to give him an opening. He had the override codes, which no one thought of changing when you relieved him of command, managed to steal one of my two shuttles and fly away before anyone noticed."

"I'll send my surgeon over to look at your wounded, lieutenant. And I think I know where Corwin went."

"Much appreciated, commodore."

She turned to Pushkin. "Pass the word for Doctor Luttrell and get a shuttle ready for me. I'm going down to the crater formerly known as Fury Station."

"Why?" The first officer looked at her suspiciously.

"That's where Corwin's headed. Chief Penzara should be able to confirm it any moment now. When he sees his dreams destroyed, there's no accounting for what he'll do."

"At least you had everyone evacuated from Fury, so no one died in the strike. Did you suspect the enemy would destroy it?"

"I don't know, Gregor. I had a gut feeling that the folks there might have a better chance of survival in the rift valley if the enemy came within range." She shrugged wearily, the adrenaline of battle dissipating and leaving her feeling drained.

"Before you object to my going," she continued, "hear me out. I removed him from command, and I'm in part responsible for the destruction of his facilities, whether there were wonder weapons or not. Therefore, I need to see this to the end."

Pushkin nodded solemnly, understanding the feelings behind her words. He knew that any objections would be met with a cold stare and if he were honest with himself, he would admit that he suspected her goal was not to cajole the admiral into surrendering and meekly follow her back to *Stingray* for an extended stay in the brig while she sailed home.

"As you wish, sir."

"I'll take Vincenzo and a couple of bosun's mates with me. Have the squadron assume standard orbit and sift through the wreckage for anything useful. I want the usual battle reports from *Carnatic* and *Coromandel* on my desk by the time I return. They should know how to fill them out, seeing as a lot of them were probably Navy personnel who got athwart a regulation or two and saw their careers terminated."

Pushkin nodded. "Aye, sir."

"You have the squadron. Make sure it's still there when I come back." She gave him a tight grin and a light punch on the shoulder. "And make sure we're ready to break orbit for home as soon as possible."

"Shall I fly?" Kowalski asked.

Siobhan stopped in her tracks and considered the question.

"It's probably just as well that you do, Mister Kowalski." A commissioned officer as a witness might come in handy, she thought.

"Vincenzo and his party will be waiting in the hangar," Pushkin said, settling in the command chair, "fully armed and armored."

"Overkill, no?"

"They were already suited up for battle stations. It's just quicker to leave them that way," he replied with a wry smile. "Make sure your sidearm is loaded, though, captain."

*

The immediate vicinity of *Roberts* was dense with debris and Kowalski picked her way through it carefully. She could have flown the long way around, but Dunmoore wanted to see the battered monitor up close. Men had died on it, and she owed them the courtesy of seeing for herself what mayhem her orders had wrought.

Black, gaping holes made a sobering counterpoint to the sheer relief of victory and spoke to the destruction within. She had a brief flashback to the last moments on *Victoria Regina,* before she started the wrecked battleship on the suicide run that had driven her Shrehari opponent away long enough to ensure the survival of what was left of the crew. With that flashback, pangs of anguish gripped her gut and she had to forcibly remind herself that she had bought this victory very cheaply, as space battles went. The reivers had paid in full, but they had chosen their violent lifestyle and were thus not to be pitied. As for Black Nova, they might never be given the full bill for their involvement.

— Twenty-Five —

Corwin's shuttle sat between the edge of the shattered plateau and a crater that gaped like a wide, suppurating wound on the skin of the planet. Debris, jumbled beyond all recognition, covered most of the area. The surface buildings had been vaporized by the impact yet here and there twisted metal glinted in the weak sun. A few eerily angular notches in the crater's flanks recalled the precisely cut corridors left by the L'Taung Shrehari long before humans established their first civilizations. To Dunmoore's tired eyes, the destruction of Fury Station was both vandalism and salvation, but it was the latter that concerned her more than anything else did. Ancient artifacts could not measure up to the lives of her people. The L'Taung were long gone.

Some spaces wide and clear enough to accommodate the small craft remained and Kowalski set down a few dozen meters away from Corwin, thrusters sending up a choking cloud of dust.

The admiral stood in front of his shuttle, hands clasped behind his back, chin up, watching them land. The expression on his face was unreadable, yet Siobhan could feel the rage radiating from his entire being. He did not even flinch when the debris raised by their landing stung his face and body.

When she rose to get off, Vincenzo held up a restraining hand and motioned one of his mates to climb through the open hatch. Siobhan met his eyes and read the warning in them: they would protect her whether she wanted to or not and if Corwin threatened any of them, he would not live long enough to carry out the threat. She nodded her understanding and Vincenzo snapped his visor down, sealing his armor before following his comrade.

The two men carefully secured the area under Corwin's contemptuous stare, and when Vincenzo was satisfied, he waved at Dunmoore.

She stepped out into the dry, cold air, her nostrils twitching madly at the flinty dust, and walked to a point halfway between the two shuttles.

"Returning to the scene of your crime, Dunmoore?" His voice was harsh, the tone dismissive, but his eyes burned with something that momentarily frightened her. "If you hadn't destroyed Fury's defenses when you mutinied, they could have shot whatever it was out of the sky while it was still a hundred kilometers up. But instead, you had to let your reckless streak take over. I should have ignored that old fool Nagira and listened to those who've seen through your camouflage and glimpsed the madwoman hiding under it. Your actions may have cost us the war. They will certainly cost you your life for I intend to see you shot."

Siobhan clamped an iron fist around her fluttering innards. Corwin's innate charisma and charm had turned into something equally intense but very dark. She forced herself to respond calmly.

"Admiral, there were no proto-Shrehari wonder weapons in there. Whatever your people found, whatever they would find, was one hundred millennia old. Technology doesn't survive that long, even in stasis chambers. Interesting artifacts for sure, but nothing usable."

"Liar," Corwin shouted. "I saw them. They were real. I suppose that ninny Mathes put those ideas in your head. Why the Admiralty saw fit to give me an engineer with so little competence and even less imagination, I cannot understand. I should have put her in the internment camp with the rest of my enemies."

"Even if they worked, Admiral, a means to fabricate cybernetic viruses keyed to specific DNA sequences is a violation of the Aldebaran Convention, a war crime for which the penalty *is* death."

"The Shrehari aren't signatories to the Convention," he spat out, "and they started this war. We'll end it by whatever means it takes."

"Sir, the ends do not always justify the means. Weapons such as those are never justified."

He looked her up and down, lips twisted in a sneer of disdain.

"You have a reputation for ruthlessness, though I fail to see why. If you're not willing to use whatever means are at your disposal to win, you're nothing. Less than nothing. You're a drag on the war effort."

"Whatever I am or am not is immaterial. You had no hope of using the weapons you found and little to no hope of reverse engineering them to build something that works. You've been deluding yourself. And while you've been doing so, you've violated at least five articles of the Code of Naval Discipline."

"Ends, means, Dunmoore." He shook his head. "You don't get it do you? To win this war, we have to violate whatever article we must."

"Even if it means high treason?"

He laughed. "You really don't understand. And to think I had such high hopes before you turned out to be a viper like the rest of the fools I had to intern. I don't know what Nagira sees in you." Corwin shrugged and began pacing. "Perhaps he always was weaker than he let on and that's a shame. Only the strong can save the Commonwealth."

He stopped pacing and stared at her.

"The true traitors sit in the government precinct on Earth," he said, sounding as reasonable as Gregor Pushkin proposing a new watch keeping bill. "Our duty is to remove them and cleanse ourselves of the weakness, corruption, and incompetence that has cost millions their lives. Valkyrie was the only way to carry out that duty and now you've removed the best chance it had for success. After this, your protector will not be able to save you from your enemies and those now include some of the finest and most honorable officers in the Fleet. Or at least they will be once we get back, and I have you brought up on charges."

Siobhan clenched her fists as she fought the rage that had begun to displace her fear.

"I dare say, sir, that your Valkyrie friends will not be pleased with you after you let the Arietis operation go so horribly wrong," she replied. "Perhaps you'll join me in front of the firing squad.

Perhaps it'll be a hovercar accident or a lonely mugging gone wrong. You may wish to bring me up on charges, but I have a crew and logs to testify against you. I have Commander Mathes to give evidence against you and reveal your delusions. I have the internees to make sure you are charged with piracy. No, Admiral, your Valkyrie friends will not shield you. You're an embarrassment to them, to your uniform and to the Fleet. You don't deserve those stars you're wearing nor do you deserve the respect they bring. You're a sick man with a sick mind."

She saw him flinch but persisted with her relentless attack.

"You might have been a principled officer at one time, but you threw away all pretense at honor, and for what? To assuage your demons? I too have demons, but I've kept them at bay by remembering my oath. Without our oath, we're nothing, unfit to lead the men and women who look to us."

Corwin's faced had turned an alarming shade of puce as she spoke while the rage burning in his eyes had slipped into the ferocity of madness.

"Admiral," Siobhan calmly continued rage and dread banished by the realization that she almost had him, "you've lost your grip on reality, and that's why I relieved you of command. No board of inquiry will fault my actions. I have all the evidence I need."

"I've lost my grip?" He screamed, spittle flying from his lips. "I'll show you a grip."

He sprang toward her arms reaching for her throat, but she just sidestepped and tripped him before Vincenzo and his mate could react. Corwin tumbled down into the dust and lay still. He remained there, face down, for a long time before Siobhan carefully approached. Her heart sank as she realized that the admiral was sobbing. Quietly to be sure, but the small shivers were there for her to see. It was a sad end to a career that had once been promising.

She had achieved what she had wanted and broken him. Now she had to face the wreckage of the man she pushed over the edge. Perhaps her actions had not been honorable, but they had been necessary to shield her crew and her ship from Corwin's co-conspirators. There was one last thing she had to do, the hardest part of her improvised plan and thinking of it, she almost backed out. Yet having robbed Corwin of his dignity, she had no choice but to restore what she could.

"Admiral," she murmured, "there is another way out for you."

Corwin turned his head, revealing a sunken cheek smudged by dust and tears.

"There's no way out, Siobhan," he replied between soft sobs. "You're right. I have to face the consequences of my actions."

For the first time since she met him, Corwin sounded like the officer he once was, before the madness had taken hold and driven him off the path of honor. Her heart almost broke at the thought that she had brought down a man with such an exceptional service record.

Dunmoore took a deep breath and pulled a small blaster out of her pocket. She placed it on the ground beside him.

"One round and enough of a charge for one shot, sir. The official log will show that you were killed in battle, leading the Arietis Squadron. A much better end than any alternative."

She straightened up and walked away, signaling to Vincenzo that they were to get back aboard the shuttle.

As she climbed through the hatch, she heard a soft cough behind her and stopped. She took several seconds to steady herself before turning back and facing the last of the many consequences of her mutiny.

Corwin had stuck the blaster barrel in his mouth and blown his brains all over the dun-colored rocks that marked the death of his dreams, hopes, and desires.

Suddenly Dunmoore felt sick, and she just had enough time to jump clear of the shuttle before she vomited until nothing but bile remained.

Vincenzo climbed out and handed her a water bulb as he tried to shield her from sight. When she had taken it, he keyed his helmet radio and ordered the landing party to prepare a grave for Admiral Corwin. It was somehow fitting that he would find his final rest among the wreckage of what he personally had believed to be his greatest achievement.

As a final gesture, Dunmoore had a smooth slab of stone put over the burial site and, using the shuttle's emergency tools, had it engraved with rank, name, and serial number. Then, in accordance with regulations, she registered the grave's position for the log before ordering Kowalski to fly them back to the ship as fast as the shuttle could manage. If she never set foot on Arietis again, she would die happy.

*

Pushkin met her in the shuttle hangar with a grim face. Dunmoore had ordered that no one watch events below but by her expression and Corwin's absence, he knew the admiral was dead.

"I need a shower," was all Siobhan said as she left the landing party behind and headed to her quarters with a determined step.

"The admiral?" Pushkin asked as he followed her into the cabin, worried at her mental state.

"He chose to die where all of his dreams died."

"Did you...?"

She laughed harshly. "Good God, do I look like a cold-blooded murderer, someone who'd appoint herself judge, jury, and executioner? Have you that little faith in me?" Upon seeing Pushkin take a step backward at her violent outburst, she shook her head, chastising herself of losing control. When she spoke again, her voice was low, if unsteady.

"No, I offered him a choice: come with us or avail himself of a blaster with a single round and enough charge for a single shot that I just happened to have handy."

"You planned for this outcome?" The first officer realized he sounded both appalled and admiring and felt distinctly odd about it.

"I planned for many possible outcomes, Gregor. But the required end-state has always been the same: get this ship and crew home, and do it in such a fashion that no blame is attached to them and that no one in league with Corwin will deem them a danger."

"So you think Operation Valkyrie is real, even if Corwin was nuts?"

She nodded wearily as she began to strip off her battledress.

"I think he was sent here in the hopes of finding something useful, and he began to believe so strongly in his mission and the coup that he deluded himself. From there it was but a small step to madness. Corwin probably always had a sociopathic streak in him. People with that kind of magnetism, that much charisma, are often unbalanced in some way. Being the sole master of an entire planet probably pushed him over into his dark side. If we look around, we'll probably find a lot of examples of egregious behavior that would have cost him any chance of remaining a flag officer."

"Will we look around?"

"No." She shook her head. "We'll take all of our people, the Fleet folks who worked on the dig, and offer to take anyone stuck on Arietis after the mercenaries seized their ships. There should be enough room between *Fawkes* and us. The mercenaries can take care of their own. They have the freighter down at Cintrea after all."

"You're just going to let the mercs go?" He sounded indignant at the idea.

"What else should I do with them?" She asked irritably. "They were contracted to defend the Navy's interests in the Arietis system. The Navy no longer has any interests in the Arietis system – I seem to have made sure of that. And anyway, their ships fought well enough under my command. The ground pounders are another story but at this point, I really don't give a tinker's damn. They can figure out how to be paid for their work when they're home. I daresay that they won't complain too much about me if they even feel it wise to contradict anything that will appear in my report."

"Are you going to sail in consort with them?"

Siobhan laughed bitterly. "Another convoy, Gregor? No. Look how that worked out for us last time. We'll break orbit as soon as we've loaded our people. The mercs have a lot more to pick up, and it'll take them longer. By the way, where are young Devall and his valiant little ship?"

"They entered orbit moments before you came back aboard. He reports all systems working sufficiently for a long crossing. Luttrell will have the injured transferred over. Shall I send those who belong to Avalon directly to *Carnatic*?"

"You might as well. Now get out of my quarters if you don't want to see your acting commodore as naked as the day she was born."

*

"Admiral Corwin's dead?" Rissard's voice was a hoarse whisper.

She nodded at the Marine lying on a sickbay cot. "He preferred to take the honorable way out. It's been logged as a battle death and his grave has been registered."

"He was a visionary."

Siobhan was shocked to see tears forming the corners of his eyes. Perhaps the Marine had shared Corwin's madness. She stared down at his recumbent form covered by a silver blanket and felt pity.

"Captain Devall tells me you had an altercation with one of the folks in the lock-up."

"Yes. One of the Avalon technicians attempted to escape, and he nearly made it. Knowing we were in a battle, I tried to restrain him so he couldn't wreak havoc. He was a very good fighter."

"But you, apparently, were just a bit better, colonel."

"Yes." He nodded. "I understand that he was probably the one who betrayed the exercise plan to the enemy."

"More than likely. He killed himself when Devall tried to interrogate him."

"Special Security Bureau, then."

"Yes. I daresay they were behind the attack, just as they were behind everything to do with spying on, and taking shots at the Arietis operation."

"Damn their black souls to hell," Rissard replied with deep feeling. "How can we expect to win a war when the SecGen's minions keep playing their power games?"

"Perhaps," Dunmoore mused, "it's intentional. The Admiralty gained much power since the start of hostilities. Maybe the SecGen is deliberately using the SSB to keep the Navy in check."

"That sounds suspiciously treasonous, captain."

"Perhaps. There seems to be a lot of that going around these days. In any case, Doc Luttrell tells me you'll be up in twenty-four hours. We'll have you stay in Devall's quarters. Second officers on frigates get private cabins."

"Thank you, captain. I can't accept that Admiral Corwin had deviated from the path of duty by so much that you had to relieve him of command, but what is done is done. There's no purpose in reopening it if for no other reason than to remember the man he was."

"A wise course of action, colonel." She smiled at him, but the eyes that locked onto his were as hard as granite. "If for no other reason than to not give the SSB the satisfaction of knowing they counted coup on the Navy."

"What happens now?"

"We're picking up the folks that should come back with us. I have all of my and *Fawkes*' shuttles ferrying them up. The Avalon people are on their own. I've released them from their contract. They can figure out how to collect from the Admiralty if they're so inclined." She grimaced tiredly. "Once we're done, my sailing master has promised he would plot the quickest possible transit to Starbase 39. After that, it all depends on Admiral Ryn, my battle group commander."

Rissard nodded. "I suppose that's the best course of action."

"If you'll excuse me," she said, "I need to sort out a few minor issues before we can break orbit."

— Twenty-Six —

"The admiral will see you now."

"Thank you, lieutenant." Dunmoore rose from the comfortable anteroom chair and adjusted her black service dress tunic. His general demeanor toward her had been much more respectful than the last time, and she gave him a tight smile as he held the door open for her.

Stepping into the tastefully decorated office gave her an eerie sense of being disconnected from reality. The long trip back, followed by the matter-of-fact reception by orbital control, had conspired to create enough distance from the events at Arietis to make it seem like they happened to someone else.

Both ships were docked to the station and going through the normal routine, albeit augmented by the work of handing responsibility for the former internees and Fury Station personnel over to the base's garrison.

She walked up to Ryn's desk and came to attention, saluting.

"Commander Dunmoore reporting to the admiral as ordered."

Ryn, who had been staring out the porthole at the planet below, turned and absently acknowledged the salute. She looked tired and tense, the worry lines on her face deeper than Siobhan remembered.

Before either could say anything else, a very brief but delicate yip filled the momentary silence and Dunmoore looked down at a small, furry creature rounding the large desk. It halted a regulation three paces in front of her and sat on its haunches, looking up at her with shiny, intelligent black eyes. Its caramel and cream-colored fur was smooth and silky, and its pointy ears stuck up proudly through the mop on its head, twitching to catch every sound.

Siobhan looked at the admiral in surprise and Ryn smiled, a hint of embarrassment on her worn features.

"Meet Kimi. I rescued her off a raider just before the war. She hasn't had an easy life, but she's given me company and companionship over the years. She usually stays in her basket under my desk when I'm working, but she seems to have decided it was time to meet you."

Without knowing quite why Dunmoore crouched and offered the back of her right hand for the small dog to smell. It took a few sniffs and briefly licked her, before rising and daintily walking back behind the desk.

"She approves of you, Siobhan, as do I."

Unsure what to answer, Dunmoore rose to her full height again and remained silent. Ryn had surprised her a few times since she had taken command of the battle group, but this one spoke volumes about the woman beneath the stars on her shoulders.

She gestured toward the settee group.

"Why don't we sit down here? You have a long tale to tell, and we'll be much more comfortable. I got some of it from Lieutenant Commander Gulsvig. You'll be glad to know he brought your convoy home without encountering any further surprises, but he had no details of your doings after you left Yotai. He sends you his best, by the way, as does Lieutenant Stoyer. Both have since taken up other duties in the far reaches of the sector so I doubt you'll see them again anytime soon."

Dunmoore nodded in acknowledgment but let the admiral continue.

"Other than the order detaching you to Admiral Corwin's command, I was in the dark about your doings until your report came in, though I'm sure that there is much more to tell than what you recorded officially."

The admiral surprised her again by wordlessly pouring two mugs of coffee before settling herself down across the low table from Siobhan.

"You might as well start from the very beginning when you almost saved the *Nikko Maru*."

*

"It's a shame a good officer like Lucius Corwin should lose his marbles," Rear Admiral Ryn said, shaking her head sadly when Dunmoore had finished, almost an hour later. "I should thank you for not including those details in your logs and your written report. He has given too much to the Commonwealth and the Navy over the last thirty-five years to be remembered as a delusional madman with a fixation on overthrowing the established order. I cannot imagine what he might have been thinking; though I'm sure *he* believed he was doing what was necessary."

"So there truly is no such thing as Operation Valkyrie?" Dunmoore kept her face as expressionless as she could. Ryn must believe at all costs that the crew of *Stingray* had chalked it all up to Corwin's madness.

"If there is, Siobhan, I've not heard of it, and I cannot see an upstanding, honorable officer like Admiral Nagira being involved. In fact, I can't imagine any of the good flag officers willing to depart from the path of duty to such an extent." She shook her head. "On the other hand, I wouldn't be surprised if the SSB got a bee in their bonnet about a non-existent plot, so for the good of the Service, neither you nor any of your crew must ever refer to it again. Having the SecGen's spooks tearing through the Fleet, looking for conspirators that never were, will hurt the war effort worse than any real or imagined political transgression have up to now."

"I understand, sir. Have no fear on that account. Only a handful of us were privy to Admiral Corwin's crazy schemes, and none of them are prone to loose lips, especially since we never could believe the plans were for real. My people understand the damage a witch hunt chasing imaginary traitors could cause."

Ryn nodded and stood, signaling the end of the interview.

"Your orders will be sent over in a few hours. I'm afraid that I can't grant you more than a day or so aboard the station as shore leave. No rest for the wicked, as they say. You may shift your prize crew back to your ship. My staff will take care of *Fawkes*. I doubt we'll be able to buy her into the Service, at least not openly, but I equally doubt the SSB will make any loud claims to her. No doubt we'll have to wait for word from Earth for her final disposal. If she is bought into the Service, I'll make sure the prize money comes to you and your spacers."

"Thank you, Admiral."

"I trust you'll be able to sail quickly?" Ryn asked as she guided Siobhan to the door.

"Another convoy?"

Ryn smiled. "Do I look that cruel?"

Dunmoore smiled back. "Do you really expect me to answer that question?"

"Touché." The smile faded. "You'll see when the orders arrive. My flag captain is finalizing some of the details. If there's nothing else?"

"No sir." Siobhan snapped to attention and raised her right hand to her brow in a crisp salute. "With your permission?"

"Fair sailing, Captain Dunmoore."

When she was alone again, Ryn returned to her desk and allowed a deep frown to crease her features. She hoped the mission she was giving Dunmoore and *Stingray* would keep them out of the line of fire. Corwin overreaching had been unfortunate, but perhaps not entirely unexpected.

He always had a touch of the sociopath in him. From there to believing he could carry Operation Valkyrie on the strength of his mostly mercenary strike force was not precisely a stretch. Not after spending almost two years building himself up as a petty tyrant on a planetary scale. But his plan had had its supporters, and they would not be pleased with his demise. Dunmoore would make a good target for their wrath, notwithstanding Nagira's patronage.

She was glad Siobhan had told her the truth. Her tally matched that of Captain Reade's, whose report she had read the previous day. The master of the *Alkris*, working for an obscure and barely known section in naval intelligence, had witnessed the final events around Arietis from a distance, her ship running silently as it crossed the planet's orbit. Counting on Reade to keep track of Corwin's activities had always been too optimistic in her opinion, but she was not part of the inner circle and thus had no say.

It was probably inevitable that things would unfold as they did the moment Corwin decided to add a frigate to his little empire. Another captain might have kept faith with him but in retrospect, it was clear that Dunmoore could not. Maybe Nagira had let him keep *Stingray* as a check on his ambitions. It was something the wily old fox would do without thinking twice.

If Nagira trusted Dunmoore to that extent, he would trust her to keep any mention of Corwin and his supposedly plot silent. That and that alone might be all that would save them.

The alternative was too awful to contemplate but if it meant choosing between *Stingray* and the success of the operation, one aging frigate could not count for much in the balance, certainly not for most of her co-conspirators.

It was a shame about the proto-Shrehari artifacts, though. From the pictures, they were quite stunning, even if finding advanced technology had turned out to be a chimera. Ryn shook herself and reached for the console.

"Russ, please send a congratulatory message on behalf of the 39th to Admiral Nagira on the occasion of his promotion."

"Immediately, sir," her flag lieutenant replied.

She sat back, not exactly satisfied, but calmer than she had been when Dunmoore first walked in. Valkyrie was safe, Nagira was one step closer to the levers of power, and the pre-arranged congratulatory message informed him that the leak was contained. *Stingray* could be allowed to continue serving the Fleet, and even the SSB would have a hard time finding plots hidden in her next mission.

Ryn had never been comfortable with the option Corwin was preparing and perhaps now Nagira would find a better way. Keeping Dunmoore and her folks as a sort of unwitting reserve would not be a bad thing. Her handling of the situation at Arietis spoke of a brilliant tactical mind, even though it needed some tempering, not to mention the courage she displayed in pursuing what she thought was the right path.

Perhaps by removing Corwin, she had done Valkyrie an even greater favor than she could have, had she gone along with the plan to assault the government precinct. At the very least, the more hotheaded among them would have to think again before proposing a solution that involved naked force.

*

Pushkin was waiting for her at the main airlock, anxious to find out how fast he had to turn around the replenishment and repairs before sailing again.

"What news?"

"Orders are to come, but we've been given time for a day's worth of shore leave on the station. You should figure we'll be sailing in three days at most."

He grimaced.

"We'll be doing repairs under way again. It's becoming a bad habit."

"I know," she clapped him on the shoulder as they headed for the heart of the frigate, "but I get the feeling Admiral Ryn wants us far away and out of sight for our own good."

As the door to the ready room closed behind them, ensuring their privacy, Pushkin asked, "She didn't buy that we believe Corwin made Valkyrie up, that we've decided he was a nutter?"

"I don't know, Gregor. But I have the feeling that Ryn is trying to protect us. If she figured out I was lying on that account, I'd have sensed it. She seemed much too relieved at the end of the interview. We'll probably be off on some crappy duty in an even deeper dead-end of the galaxy than the Coalsack, but I don't think *Stingray* will have a fatal accident or encounter. At least not one engineered by the Valkyrie people."

"Shame we couldn't keep *Fawkes* as company." He drew two mugs of coffee and handed one to Dunmoore. "Devall was pretty depressed when he came aboard."

She took a sip and grimaced. "It was naive to think the Navy would let us sail around with an SSB ship pressed into service. Parading her around under our own colors would be counter to all the efforts the Navy's put out to make the Arietis affair vanish. She might still get bought, but I doubt we'll hear about her again."

"I guess." He sat down across from her. "Do you sometimes think that we might be on the wrong side of history in this instance?"

"Every time I close my eyes and see the dead and dying on *Victoria Regina*."

"But?" He had heard the hesitation in her voice.

"But even if I were ready to violate my oath, or at least re-interpret it to suit any notion of toppling the leadership, I'm not convinced we'd end up any better and in that, I prefer to follow the Hippocratic Oath."

"First, do no harm." Pushkin nodded. "I wholeheartedly agree."

"I'll still be wondering, probably for the rest of my life, if I did the right thing." She sat back in her chair with a sigh.

"It's better than wondering why you did the wrong thing when it all goes bad and more people die because of it."

She gave him a sardonic look.

"Bucking for ship's counselor, Gregor?"

"Just being your conscience, like any good first officer."

She suddenly felt a wave of gratitude mingled with affection for her taciturn second in command.

"Never stop trying to save me from myself."

Pushkin's face reddened in embarrassment at the emotion in her tone. "If you'll excuse me, sir," he said draining his coffee as he tried to cover his reaction, "I have a ship to get ready for space."

Siobhan smiled at his discomfiture. "You may proceed Number One. I think getting back to some honest frigate work will do wonders for morale."

"From your lips, captain..." He briefly grinned before leaving Dunmoore to her thoughts.

She swiveled to face the image of the star field on the cabin's main screen,

I hope Nagira knows his business, she thought. *I've always believed him to be above the pettiness of those who hide their hunger for power behind platitudes about duty and honor. If he thinks a change in government is the only thing that can put an end to the senseless dying, then I hope that if and when he calls for my support, I can find the courage to do what is right. Just as long as I protect my ship and my crew.*

About the Author

Eric Thomson is the pen name of a retired Canadian soldier with thirty-one years of service, both in the Regular Army and the Army Reserve. He spent his Regular Army career in the Infantry and his Reserve service in the Armoured Corps. He worked as an information technology specialist for a number of years before retiring to become a full-time author.

Eric has been a voracious reader of science fiction, military fiction, and history all his life. Several years ago, he put fingers to keyboard and started writing his own military sci-fi, with a definite space opera slant, using many of his own experiences as a soldier for inspiration.

When he is not writing fiction, Eric indulges in his other passions: photography, hiking, and scuba diving, all of which he shares with his wife.

Join Eric Thomson at: www.thomsonfiction.ca/

Where you will find news about upcoming books and more information about the universe in which his heroes fight for humanity's survival.

Read his blog at: www.ericthomsonblog.wordpress.com

If you enjoyed this book, please consider leaving a review on Goodreads, or with your favorite online retailer to help others discover it.

Also by Eric Thomson

Siobhan Dunmoore

No Honor in Death (Siobhan Dunmoore Book 1)
The Path of Duty (Siobhan Dunmoore Book 2)
Like Stars in Heaven (Siobhan Dunmoore Book 3)
Victory's Bright Dawn (Siobhan Dunmoore Book 4)
Without Mercy (Siobhan Dunmoore Book 5)

Decker's War

Death Comes But Once (Decker's War Book 1)
Cold Comfort (Decker's War Book 2)
Fatal Blade (Decker's War Book 3)
Howling Stars (Decker's War Book 4)
Black Sword (Decker's War Book 5)
No Remorse (Decker's War Book 6)
Hard Strike (Decker's War Book 7)

Quis Custodiet

The Warrior's Knife (Quis Custodiet No 1)

Ashes of Empire

Imperial Sunset (Ashes of Empire #1)

Printed in Great Britain
by Amazon